2/05

# AN OBITUARY FOR
# MAJOR
# RENO

*Richard S. Wheeler*

A TOM DOHERTY ASSOCIATES BOOK
NEW YORK

AN OBITUARY FOR MAJOR RENO

Copyright © 2004 by Richard S. Wheeler

This book is printed on acid-free paper.

Book design by Nicole de las Heras

A Forge Book
Published by Tom Doherty Associates, LLC
175 Fifth Avenue
New York, NY 10010

www.tor.com

Forge® is a registered trademark of Tom Doherty Associates, LLC.

Library of Congress Cataloging-in-Publication Data

Wheeler, Richard S.
    An obituary for Major Reno / Richard S. Wheeler.—1st ed.
        p. cm.
    "A Tom Doherty Associates book."
    ISBN 0-765-30708-1
    EAN 978-0765-30708-8
    1. Reno, Marcus A. (Marcus Albert), 1835–1889—Fiction. 2. Little Bighorn, Battle of the, Mont.,
1876—Fiction. 3. Terminally ill—Fiction. 4. Journalists—Fiction. I. Title.

PS3573.H4345O23 2004
813.'54—dc22

                                                                                2004050627

First Edition: December 2004

Printed in the United States of America

0  9  8  7  6  5  4  3  2  1

*For my brother, Timothy J. Wheeler*

## THE GIRL I LEFT BEHIND ME*

I'm lonesome since I crossed the hill,
And o'er the moor and valley,
Such heavy thoughts my heart do fill,
Since parting with my Sally.
I'll seek no more the fine and gay,
For each but does remind me,
How swift the hours did pass away,
With the girl I left behind me.

Oh, ne'er shall I forget the night,
The stars were bright above me,
And gently lent their silv'ry light
When first she vowed she loved me.
But now I'm bound for Brighton camp,
Kind Heav'n may favour find me,
And send me safely back again,
To the girl I left behind me.

The bee shall honey taste no more,
The dove becomes a ranger,
The dashing waves shall cease to roar,
Ere she's to me a stranger,
The vows we've registered above,
Shall ever cheer and bind me,
In constancy to her I love,
The girl I left behind me.

—Samuel Lover, 1797–1868

*The tune played at Fort Abraham Lincoln as the
Seventh Cavalry marched toward destiny.

# PART ONE

---

## 1889

*Being an Account
of Major Reno's Request*

# CHAPTER ONE

RICHLER DIDN'T WANT TO INTERVIEW RENO, THE COWARD, REPROBATE, and whiner, but newspaper correspondents don't always have a choice. Bennett had cabled Richler from Paris, which is where the great man ran the *New York Herald* these days, and that was command enough. Do it or turn in his press card and cease scribbling for the greatest paper on earth.

The *Herald*'s ace Washington correspondent Joseph Richler made his way through a bitter March rain to a nondescript redbrick neighborhood north of Capitol Hill, found a sawed-up apartment building priced just about right for a six-hundred-a-year Interior Department pension clerk, climbed two flights of creaking stairs, and located the correct four-panel door, varnished almost black.

He knocked and was admitted to a gloomy two-room flat by a fleshy, dark, and dour man whose gray skin and bagged eyes suggested illness.

"We've met," Reno said. It wasn't exactly a friendly welcome.

"Several times."

Reno motioned Richler to a wooden chair and relit a much-gummed cigar. The flat exuded the rank stink of cigar smoke. Gray light filtered through tobacco-stained lace drapes from the single window.

"It's simple," he said. "You get the last interview of Major Reno."

"Are you planning on dying?"

"Not if I can help it. Tomorrow they're cutting out my tongue. Or most of it, anyway. After that, it's silence and paper and pencil."

"Surgery on your tongue?"

Reno looked annoyed. He sucked on the yellow cigar, bringing its half dead business end to bright life. "Providence Hospital, tomorrow at eight, March fifteen, eighteen eighty-nine. I lose my tongue. Cancer. After that, I'll talk Swahili."

"I'm sorry."

"Good riddance." He smiled at Richler, and the newsman saw life in those agate eyes at last. "The tongue is the second most important member."

Reno was running true to form.

"So you want to talk before the knife silences you. You told Mr. Bennett it would be the last interview, and he cabled me, and here we are, and you get your last shot at Whittaker and Elizabeth Custer and the rest, courtesy of the *Herald*." Richler pulled out a notepad and a couple of soft-lead editing pencils.

"It's honor I want. I want my rank back. I want my record cleared. I want my *good name*. That's all a man has in life, his *good name*. I want the true story of what happened on the record. I want the name of Major Marcus Reno to be sunlit and bright. I want my boy to grow up proud. I want the whole damned nation to know what I gave to it in the wars I fought for it."

There was passion in his voice. And maybe other things as well. Anger, bitterness, desolation, defiance. Richler discovered a malevolent light burning in Reno's eyes, the first opening into the man's sulphurous soul.

"And if that doesn't happen in your lifetime?"

"My ghost will walk the halls of justice until it's done. I'll rattle every flagstaff, and the Seventh will never know peace until I have peace."

Richler thought about the petitions to the president and the army, the private bills introduced in each session of congress to restore Reno's name and rank, and the great wall of pained opposition each of those efforts had encountered. He thought about Reno's rejected writings, the ones no one would publish, his version of the horrendous events of June 25 and June 26, the centennial year of the Republic.

"Good luck," he said wryly.

"I thought your publisher might be interested," Reno said.

"He is. That battle is always good copy."

"Here's the usual newspaper story," Reno said, scorn underlying the word *newspaper*. "I disobeyed orders at the Little Bighorn, turned my tail and ran, was eaten by guilt, turned into a drunk, got court-martialed and convicted twice, the second time for conduct unbecoming to an officer, their way of calling me a Peeping Tom, and I'm responsible for the death of two hundred brave men of the Seventh Cavalry, along with its illustrious leader. And I was cashiered, with a dishonorable discharge."

Richler nodded. The interview was going about the way he supposed it might. His pencil had yet to touch paper.

"You haven't written one damned word. During the big war I fought in twenty-four engagements. I started as a lieutenant, was breveted for gallantry in action, to brevet brigadier general of volunteers. Phil Sheridan and others stuffed my files with warm commendations. No one called me a coward. In those days I was Sheridan's kind of sonofabitch."

Richler waited for something new, something he could print. The whole interview would amount to a six-inch story, the way it was going.

"My speech is slurred. My tongue has a big cauliflower lump on it, and it hurts. But I'm used to slurs."

Richler elected not to smile at Reno's witticism. The major's speech was indeed slurred, oddly inflected by the painful lump on his tongue. He pitied the man.

"I earn six hundred a year in the pension office." Reno waved a hand at his humble gray surroundings. "It fits. I was comfortable once, earning better than three thousand as a major in the regular army. But those were other times."

"You had my publisher send me here because you have something new to tell me?"

Reno ignored him. "I inherited my wife's estate. A farm, city lots, houses, real estate mainly, but cash too. Lawyers have it now. My honor has cost me thirty thousand dollars. My second wife, Isabella, wants the rest. She's suing me for divorce, for 'insults to her person.' You will wonder about those insults. I kissed her with a mouth full of cigar smoke. She took offense at my body and then took offense at my empty purse."

Richler doodled on his notepad. He had scarcely asked a question and doubted that he would have to. He would listen. He could do that much for the man, then walk out and write a few words for a pitiable devil who would slide into perpetual silence in a day or two. He disliked Reno. Hardly anyone liked him. The man put off people, and that seemed ingrained in his very nature.

"It didn't start with the Little Bighorn, you know. It started earlier."

Richler was interested at last. Here would be a confession that Reno and Custer had been at odds for years, that this thing had roots deep into the origins of the Seventh Cavalry.

But that was not it at all.

"In eighteen and seventy-four, Mary Hannah died. It started then."

"What started?"

"The curse, the bad luck."

"You were far away when it happened," Richler said. He knew that story.

"With the boundary commission on the Canadian border. I had some cavalry and infantry under me and we were keeping the Sioux off the backs of the commission while they surveyed the line. Then she died. For years she had taken care of her mother in Harrisburg at the family home, and then her mother died, and then she died of kidney disease, and I was a widower with a boy who needed a mother.

"I couldn't get away. I applied for leave at once, but they were shorthanded, with so many officers away and they wouldn't let me go. Not until a month later. So she was buried in her Ross family plot in the Harrisburg Cemetery, and I wasn't there, and I couldn't go there for several more weeks, and the Rosses held it against me, even though I explained that my orders kept me there on the boundary."

Richler knew that was leading somewhere, at least in Reno's thinking, though he couldn't fathom it. Not yet.

But then Reno stopped talking, as if a water gate had clamped down and the flood ceased. He was lost in his own world, a world he was not sharing with the correspondent. He smiled at last, offered Richler a green-leafed panatella, which the correspondent refused, nodded toward a bottle of Old Orchard bourbon, which the *Herald* man declined also, and settled at last in his battered Morris chair.

"The *Herald*'s been fair to me," Reno said. "Your man O'Kelly reported the Little Bighorn story accurately in the days that followed that fight. I think highly of Bennett and his rag. He's put correspondents all over the globe, and taught them how to cable the news to New York. That's why I went to him, and why you're here now."

"I'm not quite sure why I'm here, major. You have not given me anything new."

"I suppose you want me to talk about the battle. I intend to."

"Actually, I want you to talk about the army's court of inquiry in Chicago in 1879, held at your request, if I remember rightly. They exonerated you. 'Major Reno did nothing that would merit the animadversion of this court,' or something like that."

"It cleared me."

"But it didn't change anything, did it? Your critics still want your scalp. It's as if that court didn't exist. They've never ceased laying the blame for that disaster on you. It was all your fault that Custer and his command perished. What I want to know is, why didn't it change things?"

Reno sucked, lighting up the end of the cigar, and exhaled noxious smoke.

"You don't feel exonerated, not even by an official inquiry. Why is that?"

"I don't know the answer," Reno said.

"You have enemies," Richler said. "Who are they?"

Reno stared sadly into the drifting cigar smoke, and turned at last to Richler.

"Myself," he said.

# CHAPTER TWO

MARCUS RENO STUDIED THE GAUNT AND ILL-FED RICHLER AS UNOB-
trusively as he could. The newspaperman exuded impatience and skepti-
cism, and was ready to bolt. His bright blue eyes swept Reno with a
glance, and noted the obvious signs of dissipation. Reno knew the correspondent was registering all that and everything else about him, including
the dingy flat, the cigar-stained lips, and especially the halt in Reno's voice.
The story, if it appeared at all, would not flatter.

The interview would last a few minutes and Richler would politely fold
his notes into his pocket and retreat into the cold rain.

Reno had wanted to tell the newsman about Mary Hannah, but had
stopped abruptly. The subject was too tender. He didn't even know how
to put such deep feeling into words, as if things felt so profoundly could
somehow be translated into something some other mortal could understand. So he did not tell Richler that something in life had shifted when
Mary Hannah departed from him; things were never the same after 1874,
and now, in 1889, his life and dreams were fading.

It was hard enough to talk to a reporter; hard enough to talk to anyone. He had always been solitary, even among his fellow officers, his real
thoughts veiled from scrutiny. No one on earth knew Marcus Reno except
Mary Hannah. She alone was his friend as well as his wife and lover. And
she was dead. And he could not tell Richler anything about that.

No life had been more lonely, but as long as he had a tongue and words to form, it was not hopeless. Now he faced the horror of silence. He had spent a while trying to speak without moving his tongue, depressing it with a spoon, and knew the cruel truth: he would soon plunge into a world of silence and guttural grunts, a world of penciled notes and signs, a world of mute despair. The thought had been frightening, and he had wildly cabled Bennett, told him he wanted one last interview to make his case while he could still speak.

And the interview was about to fall apart. It was hard enough to talk at this hour, with a swollen tongue that hurt sharply whenever he formed the simplest word but it was much harder to release the flood of words dammed in his heart.

John Hamilton, his doctor, didn't know how much tongue would be removed, but most of it would go. The carcinoma was large; a mass of cauliflower-like flesh with a pulpy crater in the center that kept bleeding. The whole mass hurt and kept words from forming. The surrounding tissue was affected.

So Marcus Reno stared at his interrogator, aching to pour out a justification of his life, desperate to do so because it was his last chance and he was a poor scribbler, inept with words, and he saw nothing but loneliness and despair and dishonor on the dark road ahead.

But then Richler helped him.

"Let's start with the fight, major."

Reno nodded, gratefully, and the officer within him took over and filled his mind.

"I was the ranking officer in the Seventh at Fort Abraham Lincoln when George Custer was here in Washington, testifying against the Grant administration's Indian policy. I should have led that command. If I had . . ." Reno wanted to say that the disaster would not have happened, which is what he fervently believed. And that the Sioux and Cheyenne would have met their match. But he checked himself.

"If you had?"

Reno ignored the prompt. "Colonel Custer pulled strings and got back just in time. I had trained some green troops, mixing them thoroughly with seasoned soldiers to hasten the process. The Seventh Cavalry was full of new men, some of them scarcely able to ride a horse. It was not anything that the lieutenant colonel took into account."

"How do you know that, major?"

"I knew the man, watched him for years."

That was a weak answer, and Reno knew it.

Reno stumbled on, cavalry politics, personalities, Benteen, Weir, Keogh, George Armstrong Custer, Tom Custer, Boston Custer, the task assigned to the Seventh, marching out of Fort Abraham Lincoln to the strains of "Garryowen," the meeting of three corps on the Yellowstone River, Reno's scout, looking for the Indians, in which he violated orders and found them, or at least some recent village sites.

Richler hadn't written a word.

"What are you waiting for?" Reno asked, pointing at the naked paper.

"For you to say something new, major. Everything you've said has been hashed out in the press over and over. The partisans of George Custer blame you; others blame Custer himself. Have you anything to add to that?"

"My record, Mr. Richler. I was cited for gallantry several times in the late war. Isn't that enough to put the lie to my enemies?"

Richler wrote not a word.

Reno saw how it would go, and how the rest of his life would spin out. A man without a tongue was a man without a voice.

"I met Mary Hannah Ross at a dinner in Harrisburg in the fall of sixty-two," he said. "She was the granddaughter of my host, Mrs. Halde-man. I'd been buying horses for the cavalry there, on detached duty, while I healed up from a wound. Established people, the Haldemans and Rosses, banks, farms, all of that. I'll never forget that dinner."

Richler's eyes betrayed little interest.

Talking tormented Reno's tongue. It ached savagely. What he was about to say tormented him even more, but something was knocking down ancient reticence.

"I was taken with her. She was eighteen, slender, bright, and her gaze kept drifting my way. I was older, twenty-eight, you know, and I imagine my blue uniform didn't harm my appearance any."

Reno managed a smile. Richler still had not penned one word.

"We looked a little like each other, you know, except she was slim and I never was. But that wasn't the attraction. Who can say what it was? She only had eyes for me, and I saw no one else or even remember what was spoken that evening, though the people of Harrisburg, so close to the South, were wary of a Confederate thrust their way, the state capital being a prize of war."

"And when the thrust came, you defended, if I recall."

"We were ready. I helped organize the militia. But Jeb Stuart's cavalry never arrived, and Harrisburg was spared. And meanwhile, there were other things on my mind." He sucked hard on the cigar and exhaled a plume of blue smoke. "Mary Hannah. It's a mystery, isn't it? A man and a woman see each other and everything is predestined. Something stirs in the heart, something takes hold. We found ourselves at several dinners, and there was something about her that caught me. She was not a flirt, and met my gaze shyly, but her eyes held my own. She was accomplished socially and schooled too, as so few young women are, and we were soon sending unspoken messages to each other, and those messages were simply, Yes. Yes."

At least Richler was paying attention.

"I had spent my life in the army. Before that, years at West Point . . ." Reno paused, remembering the troubles he had getting through the school. "I was orphaned at a young age, raised by relatives, and always alone. And then, suddenly, Mary Hannah, with her glowing eyes and long curls and slender form was there, and I wasn't alone anymore, and she was smiling at me, and pulling me out of myself at last, and making much of me and my dress blues, and suddenly there wasn't anyone else I cared about, and I knew I loved her and she loved me, and that was all that mattered. It mattered more than my career, more than the cavalry, more than honor."

Reno stared at Richler's blank pad. Reno's last time of conversing would end with a blank page. If he ever saw Richler again, it would be with his own notebook and pencil in hand, to respond to men with tongues.

"I asked permission to court Mary Hannah, and her mother granted it. Her father had died the year before. I was suitable enough, even for a wealthy family. I had no wealth, but I was an officer in command there, given responsibilities, and the family felt protected by men in blue. So I was offered the chance and I took it. Now I could take Mary Hannah by the hand and walk the riverbank.

"I remember her voice, soft but with a bright lilt to it, making melodies in my heart. I am not a talker, but she evoked talk from me, and we laughed, and I held her hand and pined for her, and kept honor bright. She didn't ask about my life as a soldier, but she listened solemnly to talk of war. She listened while I told her about selecting remounts for the cavalry, checking on hooves and pasterns and looking for splints and fistulas and bad teeth and evil temper."

He saw not a word in Richler's notepad, and knew the interview had already failed. He wasn't sure what he had expected; only that he wanted to use this last day that he possessed speech to talk about things that mattered, things that might change the trajectory of his sorry life.

"Mary Hannah said yes. Yes to me! Yes, she would be my own, my bride! But that came later, after another tour of duty with the Army of the Potomac as escort for General Ambrose Burnside's headquarters command. Later I was wounded at Kelly's Ford, and breveted a major for gallantry. I spent several weeks in Harrisburg, recovering from my wound, a hernia from having a horse shot from under me, and sealing my joy with Mary Hannah. I was put on detached duty in Harrisburg but now the Confederates were marching north, Ewell's Second Corps, and we had to

defend. I was made General Baldy Smith's chief of staff. Ewell had cap-
tured Carlisle Barracks and was but a stone's throw from the capital.

"Mary Hannah and her family fled to New York, and after the danger
had passed I was given the briefest of leaves. But it would be long enough
to ride to New York with a minister the night of the thirtieth of June,
marry my beloved the morning of July the first, and go back to war on the
next train.

"It was the best thing I ever did," Reno said. "Captain Marcus Reno,
Mary Hannah Ross. At the Astor House, the Reverend Cattell officiating.
They were waiting for us, the Haldemans and Rosses and a few of her
friends, smiles and flowers and champagne. She greeted me, white lace
and cream silk embracing her slender form, greeted me with warmth and
something flaming in her eyes that I cannot put into words.

"You cannot know how hard it was: we spoke our vows while the clock
ticked, her family congratulated us. Mary Hannah and I clung to each
other for a few moments of fever and joy and yearning, and then we were
torn asunder by necessity; torn from each other's arms by some terrible
force. I had to catch an express and go to war, and we didn't know if
we would ever see each other again, or whether our union . . . would ever
be fulfilled, for that's the soldier's lot."

Richler had not written a word.

# CHAPTER THREE

RICHLER PITIED THE MAN AND LISTENED PATIENTLY. RENO WAS HOURS away from the time he would have no voice to love with, or give thanks with, or rejoice with.

Reno slurred his words more and more as the interview wore on, and Richler knew the major was suffering. That swollen cancerous tongue tormented him. He had to pause and spit now and then into a jar. The spittle was tinged with blood. But the major didn't stop; his last words flooded out, driven by some terrible need.

What did it matter that the major poured out the story of his great love instead of dwelling on the Little Bighorn? Now, in his extremity, his love for Mary Hannah enveloped him, and nothing else mattered. Richler listened, not for the sake of a story, for there was none that he could discern, but for the sake of charity. This was Reno's last will and testament and the *Herald* correspondent could not turn a deaf ear to it.

"Mary Hannah and I finally had some time to ourselves in mid-July, after the Confederate threat was over. I was posted to Carlisle Barracks. The Rosses and Haldemans returned from New York. We stayed with Mary Hannah's mother on Front Street, in Harrisburg.

"We danced. Do you know, Richler, how it is to dance with a woman who is a feather in your arms, her every movement anticipating yours? For two months we danced, and never was I so happy. And never did a woman give so much love, so perfectly and generously offered. Though war raged about us, I cannot remember so blessed and exalted a time, when the touch of her hand upon my cheek sent me into ecstasy. And to make that time all the more sacred to me, it was then that Mary Hannah conceived."

He hawked up some phlegm and spit, a horrible expulsion of vile liquids into the jar he kept at hand. The contents of that jar were unspeakable. He wiped his lips with a grimy gray cloth, and sighed.

"But all things end, and I was posted to the First Cavalry, commanding a squadron, under Merritt and I was back in the war again. Picket duty, skirmishing, reconnaissance, I won't go into all that. We were out in cold and wet, and by Christmas I had gotten lumbago and was sent to a hospital in Washington City. My recovery was slow, and I was given thirty more days."

Richler listened patiently. There were certain charities that only a newsman could perform, and listening was one. He had heard many stories and written some of them. In some cases, he had heard stories and charitably had not written them. Now he listened to an embittered and rejected and friendless man who was remembering those fleeting moments when all of life was aglow. It was good to listen, and Richler didn't mind squandering the time.

Reno doggedly continued, the story of the miracle of the outgoing and ever-cheerful Mary Hannah foremost in his mind. He skipped past battles and horse purchasing duty—he knew horseflesh so the cavalry put his knowledge to good use—and tours of inspection, and focused on the one thing that obsessed him that rainy March day.

"Mary Hannah brought a boy into the world in April, and it had been a hard time for her, her slight build, you know. She was slow to recover, abed and melancholic, and I worried about her. But Robert Ross Reno had come into my life, a son at last, and no man could ask for more."

Reno's face had contorted into a rictus intended to conceal from Richler the torment he was imposing on his tongue. He careened from West Point to New Orleans to Kansas, and always Mary Hannah absorbed him: Mary Hannah charming the dour defeated Rebels of New Orleans; Mary Hannah turning their miserable quarters on the Kansas plains into magical havens of warmth and camaraderie and love. Mary Hannah soldiering through the worst that the cash-starved post-war army could throw at its officers.

Then suddenly he stopped and wiped red spittle from his tormented mouth. "Nothing there for you to write about," he said, eyeing Richler's empty notepad.

"There might be."

"This is my last gasp, and this is how I choose to spend it."

"You've spent it well. I've been listening to a tribute to a woman of rare courage and grace. I know now what a loss it was when she departed."

He nodded, his face crumpled, and Richler thought the major was on the brink of tears.

"I imagine you want some rest," Richler said, preparing to leave.

Reno stood. "Mr. Richler, do something for me," he said. Richler discovered urgency in the man's voice. "Defend my good name. I'll write notes after the surgery. Help you do it. When I have no voice . . . I'll need a voice. More than words on paper, a voice. Be my voice. That's why I got you here."

Richler nodded. By all accounts, Reno deserved his dismissal from the army. Something had gone haywire in the man since the battle of the Little Bighorn in 1876; in less than four years that were marred by fights, drunkenness, indiscretion, insult, obsessive pride, and finally the episode involving Ella Sturgis, Reno had rendered himself a boor, a drunk, and anything but an officer and a gentleman.

It was as if the scathing criticism of his conduct at the Little Bighorn had blistered his soul and driven him to excess. As if those accusations of Frederick Whittaker, Custer's biographer, and Libbie Custer herself, had burrowed into Reno's heart and festered there, eating the soul of a gallant and much commended officer, the way the cancer was eating his tongue.

"I don't know that it's a proper thing for a correspondent to be doing, major."

"Then I will have no one to defend me. I dream of only one thing: getting back my good name."

Richler didn't like it, but he had no way to refuse a man sentenced to silence. "If the opportunity arises, major, and you can write out the things that would help me, I could do something to clear the name of Marcus Reno."

Reno clasped Richler's hand and held it roughly, and for a moment Richler thought the major would topple without the support that Richler gave him. But the moment passed, and Reno saw the reporter to the door.

Richler pulled his black cape about him and plunged into the rain, his mind on the odd interview that sailed so far from what he was sure Reno wanted to say about himself. There was no story; two hours of virtual monologue had yielded not the slightest defense of Reno's conduct at the Little Bighorn, or any rationale for his subsequent barbarous behavior at various military posts in the west, nor a word about the court of inquiry into Reno's conduct, and nothing about Reno's determined, endless efforts, in congress after congress, president after president, to reverse his court-martial conviction and win reinstatement in the United States Army.

Richler would rehash a little history for Bennett's sake and write a few inches of copy, and be done with it. He was a reporter, not a lawyer or advocate. His promise of help would come to nothing, and there would be new stories and scandals and sensations to focus on.

The rain dripped off his plug hat, but he made it to his somber rooms without getting soaked. Nadine was napping. He shook out his cape, hung his water-beaded bowler on the coat tree, and dropped into his creaking swivel chair, staring at the calendar on the wall. He didn't know what he would cable to Bennett; there were no revelations or sensations and nothing had changed. But there was no rush, not on a little ancient history like this: he would cable Bennett that the Reno story would take some checking.

And yet something had changed. Yes, out of the slow afternoon had come something: Richler was certain that Reno believed in his own case, that he was not a wily prevaricator looking for angles, but a man who felt wronged, a man who counted honor and good name higher than all else.

He would grant Reno that much.

The next day, Richler checked at Providence Hospital, run by the Sisters of Charity of Providence, for news about the major.

"Yes," a starchy nun named Sister Monica told him, "Major Reno is resting comfortably. He is heavily sedated with morphia. The operation on his tongue was a success. Doctor Hamilton is quite satisfied."

"May I see him?"

"Are you related?"

"No, I'm a friend."

She seemed surprised that such a man would have a friend, nodded, and led Richler down a dark varnished corridor and into a tan-painted ward where six patients lay on iron cots and a sharp foul odor hung in the air. It was not a rich man's ward. Reno lay in the corner, covered with a wrinkled sheet and a thin brown blanket. He was lost to the world. His face had swollen, his lips distended cruelly, black and blue.

"When will he come out of it?"

"Not today," the sister said. "And when he does, he won't know you. It's a painful surgery, and the doctor will keep him sedated for a few days."

"Will he be able to talk?"

She shook her head, her white wimple twisting this way and that. "Never again."

"How much was taken?"

"Not all. But he'll never again use the Lord's name in vain. We make words with the tip of our tongue and that's gone."

"How will he . . . cope?"

Sister Monica shook her head. "Pray for him," she said.

# CHAPTER FOUR

MARCUS RENO SAW HER THROUGH A MORPHIA HAZE AND THOUGHT she was Mary Hannah. He tried to speak to her, but words wouldn't form.

The woman was wrapped in white, and as his mind cleared he realized it was not his wife, long dead, but a nursing sister gently clasping a hand to his hot forehead. She had black eyes, pale lips, and a long face brimming with tenderness. A dark crucifix rested upon her bosom.

It came to him that he was in Providence Hospital, in Washington, D.C., and that his tongue had been butchered. He tried to move his tongue and found he could not and that it was not there. He tried to form a word to utter, and could not, and his utterance was a hollow groan. He could not say *love,* or *honor* or *courage.*

She smiled at him. "Shhh," she said. "Don't hurt it."

His mouth felt strange. Something scraped about within it, and he realized he was feeling the sutures sewn into what was left of his tongue. A wild despair ripped through him. He could not speak the simplest thought or make the humblest request.

He stared helplessly at her, not knowing how to ask for anything. He wanted paper and pencil so he could make his needs known. And he wanted a hand mirror. He wanted to see what horrors lay in his mouth.

His mind had clarified enough so he could think a little, and finally he reached for her hand with his and tried to imitate writing, pushing his thumb and finger together as if they held a pencil or pen. She watched, puzzled, and then understood.

"You need a paper and pencil," she said.

He nodded and tried to thank her, but only an odd foggy groan rose from within him. He sobbed and turned his face from her.

She took his hand into her own. "I'll fetch something to write with," she said.

He nodded. He tried one more gesture, this time holding his hand up as if he were gripping the handle of a mirror, opening his swollen mouth, and staring intently at the mirror in his hand.

"I know you want something," she said, "but I don't know what."

Marcus Reno felt utterly frustrated.

"Tell me in writing," she said.

He nodded. The young sister left him. He watched her walk away, this woman who had given her whole life to this mission of caring for the sick in the name of her Lord.

He peered about the tan ward, aware of others for the first time. Most of the men lay still. One groaned softly, as if every breath hurt him. One dark-haired patient stared.

Reno could not even speak his own name. He tried again, wanting words to form, wanting the tip of his tongue to perform its accustomed duties, clipping the air, shaping the words, cutting off sound, but he could manage nothing. He fell back upon his pillow, knowing he had entered a new world.

The young sister returned, carrying a notepad and a stubby pencil.

"Here you are, Mr. Reno."

*It's major, Major Reno.*

He took hold of the pencil and forced his tobacco-stained fingers to write. They did not want to write, and he knew the morphia had not left his body.

*Mirror.*

She read the message. "Yes, if you wish. You'll look better soon, you know."

*I want to see inside my mouth.*

"Pretty soon you'll look just like new. No swelling, no bruises."

She patted him on the hand and disappeared once again, and he waited some while. But then she returned bearing a small, ivory-handled mirror.

"I found one in the women's ward," she said. "Men hardly ever want to look at themselves."

He struggled to sit up a little, grasped the handle, and opened his mouth.

"Oh, you shouldn't look in there, not now. Soon it'll be better."

Doctor Hamilton had cut away a tablespoon-sized chunk of tongue, including the entire tip, and most of the left side. Reno stared into the red ruin, studied the coarse black sutures, wondered how he would eat, push the food back into his throat.

The nursing sister sat beside him and held his hand. He returned the mirror to her. He had seen the future, and knew how the rest of his life would spin out. He would return to the pensions office where he was a clerk, and file papers the rest of his days, apply to Congress for the restitution of his rank and honor, and fend off Isabella, who was suing him. She had repeatedly sued him during their separation, wanting maintenance he could not pay. She had forced him into court and now wanted forty a month out of his six hundred a year.

The estate was gone. There was nothing to live on or to pay to her. He was penniless. Still, a man had to go on, somehow, some way.

He remembered that day before the surgery, the eighteenth of March, when he had hosted the *Herald* man, Joseph Richler, and spent his limited energy remembering a great love rather than making his case for honor. Why had he done that? It made no sense. He couldn't imagine it, squandering his last words dwelling on his love of Mary Hannah, and that brief, glowing time in his life.

She had married him before she was twenty, and had died at thirty.

Not much time. Why had he bored Richler with a matter so private, so far removed from the public controversies surrounding him? No wonder Richler hadn't written a word, but had sat there politely, a courtesy to the doomed, lending an ear.

It was too late now. He could not call in Richler and try again, this time dwelling on his memories of the Little Bighorn. Impulse had been the bane of his life; impulse had caught him a peck of trouble from his West Point days onward. Impulse had steered him away from saying anything meaningful to the shrewd Washington correspondent of the most brilliantly managed newspaper on earth.

Even as Reno was thus absorbed, chastening himself for wasting yet another opportunity, the very man who occupied his thoughts arrived, shed a black cape, pulled off his plug hat, unwound his scarf, and clasped the major's hand.

"I wanted to see how you're doing," he said. "Can you talk at all, even a little?"

Reno shook his head.

"I see you have a notepad. Give me a nod or a shake; do you want me here?"

Reno nodded. Give the man one minute. After that he wished to be alone.

"You're hurting, eh?"

Reno nodded.

"Morphia help any?"

A nod.

"I have to think how to phrase things so you can answer. I'll get the hang of it. I'm glad you came through. Soon you'll be back at the pension office. I've been thinking ever since I last saw you that you did something beautiful when I visited you. Instead of dwelling on your . . . the thing that's absorbed you all these years, you talked about Mrs. Reno. You gave her your last utterances, like a bouquet. When I walked away from your flat I was puzzled at first; odd that a man in your position would do that, talk about Mary Hannah, talk so passionately that somehow I came to know what a beloved and special woman she was.

"But it was not what I expected, you know. Before I got there I thought to myself, Reno's going to blister the hides of a few officers. He's going to scorch a few congressmen. He's going to savage a few Custer partisans, like your nemesis, Whittaker, who has wanted you hanged, drawn, and quartered ever since his hero Custer met his reward. But you didn't. You turned to something larger."

Reno could not imagine what to say, even if he had a tongue to say it. So he nodded.

"You're not what I thought. You've awakened my curiosity. You asked me for help; it was one of the last things you said before the operation. I agreed, but frankly, not with any enthusiasm.

"I've been thinking, major. Maybe it's not a correspondent's office to help you, but I am feeling like it. Once you're on your feet, I'm going to consult with you. Oh, it'll be slow, and you'll have to write out your answers, but we'll make progress. You've a story to tell, and I think no one's told it. Maybe there'll be a story for me, for the *Herald*—in fact I'm counting on it."

Reno nodded. *Please do help me.*

"You want to write down some names? Show me where to start? I know some of it, but start from scratch."

Reno nodded again. His mind was too clouded to remember all the names, and he didn't doubt they would be drugging him again soon, because his mouth was tormenting him.

He plucked up the pencil and wrote:

*My army records.*
*Sherman*
*Sen. Cushman Davis*
*Congressman Dan Ermentrout*
*Every surviving man at LBH*

*Every officer Seventh Cav*
*Esp. Benteen*
*Terry*
*Gibbon*

That was enough. He couldn't think of others, though they would number in the hundreds. He tore off the sheet and handed it to Richler, who pocketed it.

"Major, I don't know why you interest me, but you do. I'll report to you soon, and meanwhile, heal up fast."

Reno watched the man don his outerwear and leave, and then he lay abed, alone.

# CHAPTER FIVE

THE PRESS OF NEWS OCCUPIED RICHLER THE NEXT TWO DAYS, AND when he did finally stop in to see Major Reno at Providence Hospital, he was shocked.

Reno stared up at him from feverish eyes set in black sockets. His right hand was swathed with a huge, soft bandage. Reno barely acknowledged the newsman's presence with the slightest nod.

One of the nursing nuns, this one named Sister Carmelita, appeared at once.

"Mr. Reno has a fever and erysipelas, Mr. Richler. It's very contagious, and you should keep your distance."

Richler nodded but did not step back. He knew at a glance that Major Reno would not survive for long. The man could convey nothing now, lacking voice and hand, and yet the correspondent understood clearly what the major desperately sought to convey. It took no words. That burning gaze, that slow searching of Richler's face, that transfixing minute when the failing man conveyed every dream, every hope, every resolve, did not fail to reach Richler. And slowly the newsman nodded.

"Yes, major," he said. "Yes, count on me."

Reno closed his eyes and did not reopen them. Richler tarried a minute longer, and then left the ward, only to run into Doctor Hamilton in the corridor.

"How long?" Richler asked.

"Double pneumonia. His lungs are filling. It often follows erysipelas, you know, textbook case. I don't know how long. Hours now. We all hoped he would have many more years. But unless there's a miracle . . ."

There would be no miracle.

"Have you notified his son?" Richler asked.

The doctor seemed slightly offended. "He's in Tennessee and expected here the first of April."

"Too late, I imagine."

"Who knows? Best you wash up in that basin, Mr. Richler. It's a dangerous disease."

Richler nodded, cleansed his hands, and walked into the March sun.

He had made a commitment to a dying man. A half-hearted commitment, though the major didn't know that. Richler had no great desire to pursue the matter of Major Reno's honor and reputation. Yet he knew that he would do what he could.

Two days later, the morning of Saturday, the thirtieth of March, Major Reno died. No one other than the doctor and the sisters were attending him; no one from his family. No friend, no colleague, no officer, no survivor of the Little Bighorn, who owed his life to the major.

The remains were moved to the John W. Lee Funeral Home where they were embalmed. All this Richler followed in the papers. News was breaking during that period, and he had much to cover. Congress had enacted, in February, enabling legislation to bring four northwestern territories, North and South Dakota, Montana, and Washington, into the Union as states, and now these vast domains were gearing up for statehood.

It struck Richler that Reno's demise coincided with Montana's statehood. Only thirteen years before, most of Montana was utter wilderness, the domain of the Sioux and Crow and Blackfeet and Assiniboine, and there Reno had met his fate on the banks of the Little Bighorn River. Now it would be electing senators and a representative, erecting a capitol building, and running cattle where buffalo had roamed.

There was, at last, the newspaper notice of a visitation on the first of

April, and Richler hastened to attend. He found few names in the guest registry, and none proceeded by a military title. Mostly pension office people, Reno's last contacts. The plain dark coffin was closed, and no flag of the United States lay upon it, nor any military decorations, for this man had been dishonorably separated from the army, and his enemies thought that even that was not enough; he should be forever calumniated and scorned.

A great pity filled Richler; here was the barest of tributes to a gallant soldier who had served his country for almost three decades.

The silence was eerie. The mortician hovered about, keeping candles lit, but no other guests or mourners arrived.

If the visitation was mournful, the funeral was even more so. Now at last Richler got a glimpse of Reno's son, Robert Ross, who appeared to be someone of the flashy sort, dandied up for the occasion. The man had married into a substantial Nashville family that operated a wholesale liquor business, bought a quarter of the business with funds from the trust provided by his mother, and began spending heavily.

Ross, as he was called, and his wife Itty, were there for the brief service at the funeral parlor Tuesday, April 2, 1889. And so was Richler, who came alone and sat at the rear. Reno's roots were French; his name was an anglicized version of Renaud, but he was nominally Protestant, of Huguenot descent, and the brief and toneless service unfolded in that manner.

A graveside service at Washington's Glenwood Cemetery was neither the time nor place to talk to the son, so Richler put it off. But he had been struck by Ross Reno's indifference. It was as though the son had disowned the father and was eager to get these unavoidable matters behind him. There was good Tennessee whiskey to be distilled and sold . . . and drunk. Itty Reno obviously cared much more, and wept at the last. Richler was touched. Itty barely knew her father-in-law, by all accounts, but now her heart went out to the old warrior.

Joseph Richler hurried home to Nadine, depressed by the entire episode. His bride was nursing their sickly son and he did not disturb her, but sat in their ornate parlor at his cluttered desk trying to make sense of a life and death, of glory and dishonor. He could make no sense of it.

He owed an obituary to the *Herald,* but first he would cable Bennett with a request: a factual barebones obituary now; the full story on the controversial major after he had done some legwork. Yes, he would do that. He had already gathered most of the material. The rest he could get easily enough from the army, and he would wire the obituary to New York in a few hours.

He tapped gently on the bedroom door, and at Nadine's soft summons, entered. The little pink boy, Joseph, Jr., lay swaddled in her arms asleep.

"Was it well attended?" she asked.

He shook his head. "He had few friends left in the army; either that or they were reluctant to make their sympathies known."

"I would hate to die like that, without anyone. But his son . . ."

"He came, and his wife too, I'll say that."

"And no one else?"

"I had hoped to see someone, anyone, from the command. There must be things I don't know."

"Major Reno was a lonely man."

Richler thought that was true, and that Reno probably brought his isolation upon himself, with a nature that repelled most people. But he did not say that to his wife.

"I have to write it up," he said.

He headed out into the seductive April day, with life blooming about him, and headed for the *Herald*'s offices off DuPont Circle, which consisted of two cubbyholes for the three Washington correspondents and the telegraph man.

There he spread the material he had gathered and stored in a folder, and studied it. Then he pulled a pen from a rack of them, unstoppered his ink bottle, and began to write.

Saturday last saw the passing of Major Marcus Reno, formerly of the United States Army, of pneumonia. Mr. Reno was born in Carrollton, Illinois, November 15, 1834, entered West Point Military Academy in 1851, graduated in 1857, and devoted the next decades of his life to the service of his country, departing from the army in 1880.

During his period of service, he saw action in the Indian wars, the Civil War, and in the Reconstruction Period. During the Civil War he fought in the First U.S. Cavalry in a number of engagements, including Yorktown, Williamsburg, Mechanicsville, Gaines Mill, Glendale, Malvern Hill, Crampton's Gap, Antietam, Sharpsburg, Kelly's Ford, Hagerstown, Hawes Shop, Cold Harbor, Trevillian Station, Darbytown Road, Winchester, Kearnysville, Smithfield, and Cedar Creek.

For gallant and meritorious service at Kelly's Ford he was appointed brevet major. For gallant and meritorious service at Cedar Creek, he was appointed brevet lieutenant colonel. At that point he mustered into the volunteer service as colonel of the Twelfth Pennsylvania Cavalry, where he engaged Mosby's guerillas, and for gallant and meritorious service was appointed brevet colonel, United States Army, and brevet brigadier general, United States Volunteers.

After the war he returned to duty as captain, and then was promoted to major in the Seventh U.S. Cavalry in 1868. He continued to serve his country in various capacities, including infantry tactics instructor at West Point, Judge Advocate of the Military Commission at New Orleans, service in the Bureau of Refugees, Freedmen and Abandoned Lands in New Orleans, and then as Acting Assistant Inspector General, Department of the Columbia, as well as Board of Survey and court-martial duty. He commanded an army post at Spartanburg, North Carolina, where he suppressed the unlawful activities of the Ku Klux Klan, then commanded the army escort for the northern boundary commission. In 1876 . . .

Richler wasn't sure how to say it, and paused.

Major Reno fought at the Battle of the Little Bighorn, and commanded the regiment from June 26 until September 22. He subsequently commanded at Fort Abercrombie, Dakota Territory, and later commanded at Fort Meade, Dakota Territory.

And now he would leave holes in the obituary, Richler thought. Court-martialed and found guilty May 8, 1877, suspended from rank and pay; defended before a court of inquiry concerning his conduct at the Little Bighorn, Chicago, 1879, court-martialed and found guilty of conduct unbecoming to an officer and a gentleman while at Fort Meade in April, 1880 and suspended from service.

A fine career that fell apart in the years after the Little Bighorn. Almost three decades in the service of his country, and of that time, four years of hell, when all the demons in him were loosed to stir up trouble, and all the world's blamers and scapegoaters heaped calumny on his head.

Richler filled in the rest: survivors, funeral, and burial. It would do until he could write a real obituary. If he ever wrote one. He really wanted to escape the whole damned business. But he had reluctantly made a promise to a dying man, and he would reluctantly keep it.

# PART TWO

## 1876

*Being an Account
of the Battle*

# CHAPTER SIX

MAJOR MARCUS RENO DID NOT WRITE A LETTER. HE HAD NO ONE TO write to, save for Ross, and he scarcely ever wrote to his son. Most of the other officers who did not have their wives with them were writing this evening, telling them that in the morning, May seventeenth, 1876, the Seventh Cavalry would march west and come to grips with the Sioux and Cheyenne hostiles who had not knuckled under to the government's edict to report to their reservations by January thirty-first.

The Officers' Club Room at Fort Abraham Lincoln was barren of men, save for the bartender, Rorty, an enlisted man who was rendered unfit for duty after being wounded in the elbow at Washita, but found a way to stay with the regiment as a civilian. Some officers, like George Custer, had their family here. The post was not without amenities and was not far from Bismarck, either, and several officers' wives graced the post. Those officers wouldn't be writing this evening; there would be sighs and tears in their households this evening, maybe a few small jokes, and a dark unacknowledged fear.

It was very quiet. Major Reno had expected to find at least a few of the old stags present in their old haunt and enjoy some easy camaraderie, but this particular evening only eerie silence reigned. Maybe that was all right. Men going to war behaved strangely, and sometimes sullenly, and the drinking would be moody.

Reno sipped some raw Kentucky bourbon mixed with Missouri River water and pond ice, and felt comfortable in the silence. He was more the solitary man than the convivial one anyway, and he didn't mind the odd, hollow anticipation that hung over the post this taut May evening.

The enlisted men were lounging in their barracks or tents, cleaning weapons, putting their gear in order. The post wasn't large enough to accommodate all twelve companies of the Seventh, so some of the companies, which had gathered from far-flung corners of the nation, were bivouacked in orderly white rows on the flats two miles south. Behind the post, the craggy arid bluffs of the Missouri River topped out on the high plains, and the silent, mysterious prairie stretched westward endless miles, broken only by an occasional slow-moving stream, a rare butte, an occasional gulch filled with willows or cottonwoods. That land, beyond Dakota, in the Territory of Montana, was largely unknown, except to that primeval race that had populated it for generations.

Lieutenant Colonel Custer had just returned from the East, where he had testified before a congressional committee probing into corruption in the War Department, especially the kickbacks post sutlers had paid to War Secretary Belknap. In the process Custer had casually incriminated President Grant's brother, which had offended the president even more.

The testimony had been of no consequence because all of it was hearsay, but Grant had bottled up the boy general in St. Paul and meant to keep him off the field for this last great battle against hostile Indians, on this, the centennial year of the Republic.

Reno had hoped to lead the column, had pleaded with General Terry for the opportunity, but Terry had refused him, saying that if Custer couldn't command, two colonels currently on detached duty were eager to do so. In short, Reno was outranked.

Terry knew the value of George Armstrong Custer, who was far more seasoned at fighting Indians than Reno and a better leader of men as well, so he had helped Custer prepare a good soldier's petition to the adjutant general, asking that he be allowed to *share the danger* with his own command.

The president relented, warned Custer to behave and keep the press away, and on the eve of the campaign, May thirteenth, Custer arrived at Fort Abraham Lincoln, and once again took command from Marcus Reno.

Reno knocked back a whiskey and pushed his tumbler toward the barkeep, who sleepily filled it and set it next to a carafe filled with water. Reno downed that, and another, and stared sourly at the empty club.

"Put it on my tab," he said. "See you."

"Major, would you like to pay your tab?"

"Later."

"Ah, sir, if it was you commandin' I'd be happy to do it, but you're not commandin'."

Reno knew what the man was talking about. Rorty had been in the Washita fight.

"How much, Mr. Rorty?"

"It comes to, ah, thirty-one dollars even, major."

"I didn't know I was so far behind." Reno dug into his purse. He had just been paid; he pushed three tens and a single across the bar, exact change.

"That'll square us." Rorty smiled confidentially. "The paymaster's not going to pay the corps until they're a few miles out." He laughed. "They'll go to war with a pocket full of dollars." The army was not dumb about the temptations lurking near a post when enlisted men had cash in their pockets.

Rorty was a gossip. Reno nodded and pierced into a quiet night. The whole regiment was spread before him, including the sixty or so new recruits he had worked hard to ready for this campaign. Some could barely ride a horse and even fewer could shoot worth a damn. The pinchpenny army had limited training to ten rounds a month. These recruits hardly knew how to aim. He had drilled them, had them dry-fire their carbines, taught them what he could about sitting a horse, but they were mostly dead weight. He had scattered them through the companies, knowing they would learn faster next to veteran soldiers rather than working with instructors.

There was another thing worrying him. Some of those Springfield carbines were faulty. The extraction mechanism sometimes pulled the back of the expended shell off, leaving the copper cylinder jammed in the barrel. It didn't happen often, but in a fight each jammed weapon would be the same as a casualty. He had told his company commanders to make sure the men knew to keep their carbines and shells clean. Maybe that would help.

Well, hell, that was the United States Army.

He bit off the end of a good Baltimore stogy and fired up, sucking and exhaling as he gazed over the post. The place wasn't his anymore, and George Custer had let him know it in a hurry by reorganizing the command, putting Custer cronies, such as Tom Weir, in charge of squadrons.

Well, that was the army, too, and the Seventh was Custer's private domain. Half his family was gathered in the regiment.

The windows of Custer's house radiated light, and there were people on the generous veranda. Libbie was entertaining again, even as the lieutenant colonel gathered his intimates around him for one last huzzah. Tom Custer would be there, and so would Boston, along as a civilian herdsman, as well as Autie Reed, his nephew, and Captain James Calhoun, his brother-in-law, married to Custer's sister Margaret. Calhoun was a good officer, and Reno admired him. There might be others in that bright-lit house: Myles Moylan, George Yates, both capable officers, maybe Myles Keogh, probably Tom Weir, a good man but one Reno disliked, and the feeling was mutual.

Custer had his coterie, and Reno wasn't one of them, though he wasn't openly hostile, the way Captain Frederick Benteen was. Benteen made no bones about his contempt for Custer, and anyone who cared to listen would get Benteen's version of the battle of the Washita in which Custer narrowly escaped disaster and abandoned the hard-pressed Major Joel Elliott and his remnant to their fate.

Reno shared Benteen's perception of that battle. The boy general had conducted a skillful winter campaign up to that point, closing in on the hostile Cheyennes. But once he located their village on the Washita, he abandoned all caution, failed to reconnoiter, and thus failed to learn that there were several more villages camped nearby along the river that winter, and failed to discern that the village he was about to engulf was that of Black Kettle, a peace chief cooperating with the whites. Both the chief and his wife died of soldier bullets in that affray. It was called a victory, but if Custer had lingered moments longer, while the neighboring villages responded to the fight, it would have turned into catastrophe.

Reno was no friend of Benteen, either, and the two had exchanged sharp words in the past. Benteen was a good and competent officer but a carping critic who grated on most every other officer. Mostly, Reno was a loner, keeping his opinions to himself, making few friends but fewer enemies. Once he had had many more friends, when Mary Hannah was with him and entertaining his fellow officers, her outgoing nature and cheer contrasting to his own gloom. Those were good years, when his own house radiated warmth and companionship, and she supplied the graces he lacked.

She was even close to Libbie Custer. Mary Hannah and the officers' wives at the various posts had knit together in complete harmony even when their husbands were rivals or antagonists. Now Mary Hannah was dead at the age of thirty, and Libbie reigned as the grande dame of Fort Abraham Lincoln, perfectly reflecting her husband's every mood and prejudice and opinion, even wearing her own female versions of his cavalry uniforms, in which, Reno confessed to himself, she looked ravishing.

She was beautiful and spirited and Marcus Reno envied Custer his lovely wife. Nothing seemed right anymore with Mary Hannah gone, and only an empty bachelor quarters awaiting him each evening.

Maybe it was time to retire. He had been in the army a long time. He had hoped to make colonel but promotions came slowly in the postwar army; the years had whirled by and he knew he wouldn't even make lieutenant colonel anytime soon. Maybe retire, return to Harrisburg, look to Ross's upbringing. But it would be hard to tear himself from the soldier's world he loved.

He walked through the close evening to his immaculate quarters, and found only emptiness within, like the emptiness within himself. He had long since packed his kit for war; that had taken all of five minutes. He decided to take along his oval miniature of Mary Hannah just for good luck. She peered out at the world, slightly amused, her glossy dark hair hanging down in ringlets, her large eyes wide and questing, and her lips promising a kiss.

He drew on his cigar, felt the old hollowness again, filled his flask to the brim with Kentuck, and tucked it into his tunic. He would take what comfort he could into war.

# CHAPTER SEVEN

GREAT THINGS HUNG IN THE AIR. THE SEVENTH CAVALRY AND ITS scouts and civilians rode out of Fort Abraham Lincoln almost seven hundred strong, its entire complement of twelve companies together for the first time. Custer led the parade, gallantly dressed in a blue flannel shirt, red kerchief, and buckskins. He had shorn his long locks for this occasion.

General Alfred Terry, commander of the Department of Dakota and the top-ranking man present, rode along with a complement of infantry and staff. He was headed for a rendezvous on the Yellowstone with Colonel John Gibbon of Fort Ellis, Montana. And riding up from the south, so far as anyone knew, was General George Crook with another column of twelve hundred cavalry and infantry. Between these pincers, the hostiles would be hunted down and trapped and returned to their reserves.

Libbie Custer rode along beside her husband that first day, dressed pertly in her own blue uniform. She would return with the paymaster the next day. The guidons flapped in the misty air and the soft clop of four thousand hooves in wet clay filled the valley of the Missouri. It had stormed for two days, delaying the march until this hazy dawn.

Major Reno watched the column form by twos, until it stretched two miles in length, nine hundred strong, with a Gatling gun battery included. Behind it came a herd of cattle, the commissary on the hoof, and one of its drovers was Custer's nephew. The long blue line looked impressive, but Reno wondered how effective so many new troopers might be in a fight. In addition to the new recruits, another large contingent had been in the Seventh for less than six months and had seen no warfare. To make matters worse, many of the mounts were green and unruly, and had no experience of battle.

Still, he was content. This was a force to be reckoned with. By the time this long column reached the hostiles, the horses would be subdued, the men would become better horsemen, and they would know more about their carbines and the copper jacketed cartridges they carried.

It was all grand, and the band saw them off with the rowdy regimental air, "Garryowen," which some said Custer swiped from the Irish Brigade that had distinguished itself in the Civil War. But the song that suddenly afflicted the major was of a different sort:

> I'm lonesome since I crossed the hill,
> And o'er the moor and valley,
> Such heavy thoughts my heart do fill,
> Since parting with my Sally.
> I'll seek no more the fine and gay,
> For each but does remind me,
> How swift the hours did pass away,
> With the girl I left behind me.

Some men would have some Sally to come home to. Some wives would light a lamp in their windows. Some men were blessed. Libbie and George Custer would enjoy the privilege of a last night in his tent, a day's ride from the post. Reno tried to put it out of mind. He watched his own command, Keogh's and Yates's battalions, and was content. The two veteran officers had men and mounts moving smartly. Still, Reno could not shake the melancholia that had afflicted him every day of every hour since Mary Hannah died.

At dawn the next day, the paymaster distributed a satchel of greenbacks to the troops, who grinned and stuffed their thirteen dollars into their trousers. They would go to war with a pocket full of cash and no place at all to spend it. While the troops formed up, Custer kissed his lady good-bye, and soon the long blue line was passing in review before the colonel's wife and the paymaster detail that would escort her home.

Custer looked grand aboard his favorite mount, Dandy, but Reno had no use for theatrics. Libbie was smiling and waving, and the troopers smiled back, keeping their thoughts to themselves. After that, all present were male. Reno wondered how that would affect Custer, who kept Libbie with him every possible moment, and had gotten into trouble about it back in Kansas.

Mark Kellogg, a newspaperman from Bismarck, was never far from Custer, and enjoying the trip.

They traveled uneventfully through sultry weather, arriving in Montana Territory the third of June. Custer had been having a high old time in western Dakota, exploring the Little Missouri for some forty-one miles while the column marched west.

One day Reno commanded the column while Custer was off on a scout, and that day he got to know his new adjutant, Lieutenant Hodgson, as they rode together through the quiet afternoon, the guidons fluttering before them in a soft wind, their horses moving comfortably under them at a fast walk, the air neither fierce nor still.

"You know much about the Sioux?" Hodgson asked.

"No. I've been on detached duty for years. Before the war I spent some time in the far northwest dealing with Indians. But nothing like this."

"These are angry people. Won't reconcile, I imagine."

"The army's taking them seriously," Reno said. "Three columns, any one of which could lick them."

"Maybe," said Hodgson. "I keep remembering Captain Fetterman."

"He's a presence among us," Reno said. "He boasted he could ride through the Sioux nation with eighty men, and he got his chance, and he was wrong."

"You see any similarities?"

Reno turned cautious. "Ben, we've all learned a few things, the lieutenant colonel included." He hoped he was right. The fight at the Washita wasn't a ground for much confidence.

The high plains seemed to blot up sound, so that the column progressed in silence, save for the occasional clank of metal or the soft thump of a hoof. The prairie grasses had burst upward but would not grow tall, not in this dry land. The horses were thriving on the fresh grass.

Reno wondered whether this vast land would ever be settled, apart from a few remote ranches running range cattle after the buffalo had been killed. He had no feeling for the country; it wasn't beautiful, nor did it lift his spirits. It was an empty land, but one being fought over by those who had always roamed there, and invaders like himself.

When they struck the Powder River a few days later, things began to change. General Terry, with a body of cavalry and his staff, rode to its confluence with the Yellowstone, and there he made contact with Gibbon's advance guard, waiting for the Dakota Column on the riverboat, *Far West.* Soon Gibbon and Terry were conferring, and when Terry returned to the camp on the Powder, late that night, he knew that the Indians were further west.

On June tenth, Terry summoned Major Reno to his command tent, and welcomed him. Custer was there, looking dour. Terry had a crude map spread out before him, showing the watercourses in a land little known to the army or any white men.

"Major, we have an important task for you," he said. "Some reconnaissance. We wish to make sure that the country between the Powder River and the Tongue is not occupied by the hostiles, and toward that end, we will be sending you out on a scout."

"I'm ready at any time, sir," Reno said.

"We believe the hostiles are south of the Yellowstone. We have no intelligence of their being north of it. They now have a very large village, or several allied villages, and a large herd, and that requires grass and water. Here," he said, tracing the map. "We want you to head up the Powder, examine certain tributaries, here, head west, cross over the divide to the Tongue, and follow it down to the Yellowstone, where we'll await you. You'll look for General Crook, whose column is working toward us. You'll have your scouts and trackers look for the encampments of a large village."

Reno nodded. He liked Terry, a quiet, dispassionate, and thoughtful commander whose Civil War record shone brightly. Terry put on no airs, took no liberties, and won his fights.

"We don't know, but suspect they're on the Rosebud, which is the next stream west, or beyond that, on the Little Bighorn, closer to the mountains. I'll give you a fairly large command for this scout, major, the Seventh Cavalry's Right Wing, plus a hundred pack mules. Not to pick a fight, but to defend yourself. If you can locate the camp without being seen, all the better. Surprise is what we're after. I'm putting the best scouts we have under you, and sending along one Gatling just in case. Now, here are your written orders. Have you any questions?"

Reno studied the document. He would command half the Seventh plus a contingent of crack scouts and guides. It seemed an odd force to engage in a reconnaissance, too large to move swiftly, too small to fight a formidable force of Sioux.

Reno read: he was to make "a reconnaissance of Powder River from the present camp to the mouth of the Little Powder. From there he will cross to the headwaters of Mizpah Creek and descend it to its junction with the Powder. Thence he will cross to Pumpkin Creek and Tongue River and descend the Tongue to its junction with the Yellowstone, where he may expect to meet the remaining companies of the Seventh Cavalry and supplies of subsistence and forage."

There was more, but that was the heart of it. Mitch Bouyer would guide the command. Surgeon Porter would accompany it.

"It's clear, sir. No questions."

"Good. We'll be waiting for you. We'll either have a report of villages on the move, or we'll know we're still too far east. I have every confidence that you will perform these duties admirably, major."

"Reno, faint heart never won fair maiden," Custer said, taunting him, and he did not wish his second-in-command success.

Reno left the tent filled with the pleasantness that comes of being chosen by a general he admired for a delicate and important task, and with other thoughts as well: why had Terry chosen him rather than Custer? To save the experienced Custer for the big fight, or because he thought Custer might act rashly?

Reno knew that Terry was not pleased with Custer's forays and unannounced departures from the column as it wended its way west. And Reno knew that when he returned to the rendezvous at the confluence of the Tongue and Yellowstone, Custer would not be friendly, especially if Reno found the hostiles without Custer's help. But that was the army.

# CHAPTER EIGHT

RENO LED HIS COMMAND UP THE POWDER RIVER AT ABOUT THREE
o'clock that afternoon of June tenth, knowing that Custer was unhappy.
The man had exuded something close to a sulk.

Whatever it was, Major Reno set it aside and concentrated on lining out
his column. He had good company commanders with him, men like James
Calhoun, Algernon Smith, and Henry Harrington, who had worked hard
to turn their troops into effective and close-knit battle-ready units. He had
some good scouts, and the masterful half-breed Mitch Bouyer with him
as a guide and resource.

He had a Gatling, which lumbered along on its limber behind four
condemned cavalry horses. He had the usual mix of men. Some of his
noncoms were Reb officers who had reenlisted as privates in the postwar
Federal army under assumed names, and soon rose in the ranks because
of their skills.

There were no doubt a few criminals in the regiment, but not many on
this trip. The shrewd officers had put those they suspected of dodging the
law in Company A, known jocularly in the regiment as the Forty Thieves,
where they could be closely watched. But Company A was not a part of
Reno's command.

There were immigrants and dreamers, bounders and boys, a few men
who had seen service in Europe with various armies and even the Papal

Guard, but many of those he took with him had never fired a shot in combat and he didn't know how they would respond to trouble.

Reno turned to Calhoun, who was riding beside him. "Have we much of a commissary?"

"Hardtack, side pork, and beans."

"The usual, then."

"An army travels on its stomach, which is about half-starved around here. Put out some hunters?"

"It's beans this time. We won't hunt. Not on a reconnaissance. Tell Bouyer to send the Arikaras out, and wide. I want to know what's on our flank. And tell them not to hunt."

Calhoun trotted off to put Reno's request in motion. The command would be stalking its quarry, and his men would be nibbling hardtack, dry squares of tough biscuit that didn't sustain a man for long, along with some moldy bacon and some beans.

The whole command was close to scurvy. The fort's vegetables had run out, and it was too soon in the growing season to raise more. The army had no practical way to supply greens to its far-flung posts, so it sent seed instead, and the various companies vied with one another to grow the best beans and carrots and peas and corn and squash.

The command traversed southward across broken, silent grassland, the short grasses verdant now in June but they would soon brown. The turbid river flowed slowly north, supporting a thin band of vegetation, pale green willows, lime-tinted cottonwood, and chokecherry along its banks, and sometimes whole mazes of impenetrable silvery sagebrush, which slowed the Gatling limber. About the time the river turned the color of pewter in the late June twilight, Reno called a halt on a grassy flat that offered good fodder for the mounts: they had made eight miles, a good piece after leaving the Yellowstone late in the afternoon. There was nothing around them but aching emptiness.

"Company commanders, set up your guard mount," he ordered. "Double the horse guard. No bugles this entire scout. No shots, no hunting."

His officers would choose men for a horse guard and sentry duty, impose a veil of silence on this large command and hope for an invisible passage through a land the Indians knew far better than themselves.

The cooks busied themselves with the beans while the scouts drifted down from the hills. Troopers on stable duty grained and watered the mounts, brushed them, examined hooves, looked for heat in pasterns and forelegs, and picketed them on good grass. A coyote howled at the rising moon and another replied.

Reno restlessly patrolled the bivouac, paying particular attention to the disposition and care of the horses. He studied the nearby gulches, wondering whether any would permit a raiding party to come close, and decided he had chosen well. A half mile of flat country without cover stretched back from the river.

Bouyer rode in and slid off his spotted Indian pony and led it to Reno's tent. The guide had an odd lumbering gait that matched his heavy features.

"Nothing here," the scout said. "No village recently."

"What about old ones?"

"Few encampments on some creeks, month old, half a dozen lodges."

"Where are they going?"

"Too old to know. Some travois marks westward."

"Can you identify the bands?"

"No. Not yet."

"Are the Ree scouts saying anything?"

"Big damn village around somewheres," Bouyer said.

"In other words, nothing."

Bouyer nodded.

"All right, get them in and feed them. There's beans with some salt pork." He saw black kettles suspended over a dozen cookfires. Each company had its own mess and the packers had theirs and the officers had theirs. Bitter-smelling cottonwood smoke drifted across the flat and hung over the coiling and uncoiling river.

Reno scanned the heavens anxiously, hoping it wouldn't rain, and was rewarded by a sprinkle of stars emerging from the twilight. He enjoyed this lonely place, so far removed from the habitations of civilization. He enjoyed the company of armed men, who together were an armed force that could sting an enemy.

And yet he was restless and distant from his officers and even more so from his enlisted men. He wasn't taciturn, but he had no patience with small talk or gossip, or the run of conversation that made other men companionable, and so he retreated into himself and pushed aside his constant loneliness.

Even before dawn, company commanders were quietly awakening their men. There would be no hot breakfast this day; no fires, no smoke to reveal the whereabouts of his men. By the time the sun had cleared the eastern horizon, his men were riding by twos up the Powder, across an aching alkali-whitened wasteland unfit for habitation. The men yawned, sat passively in their McClellan saddles, let their horses pick their way through the silent morning. Scouts rode ahead; vedettes covered the flanks. Bouyer had vanished forward. The man appeared and disappeared like a conjurer.

No sign, no sign. They may as well have been traversing the Sahara. They walked, trotted, cantered briefly, and settled back again to a walk. Every hour or so Reno dismounted them and had them walk their horses, which was a form of rest for both man and beast.

That day they traversed twenty-six miles and found nothing. Reno again bivouacked on the Powder River, choosing a grassy flat that offered few opportunities to war parties bent on stealing horses. The mounts were holding up well. Reno knew horses better than he knew his men; and his command did not suffer as many lamed or broken-down nags as others did.

He permitted cookfires that night. There was little high ground to hide observers so the fires would not be seen, and his scouts had spread far and wide looking for hostiles. But again they were alone in a sea of grass, hearing only the soughing of the wind as it sucked the moisture out of their skins and chapped and chafed their faces and hands.

The men had individualized their attire. Some wore straw hats, some wore buckskins, a few wore gloves. Reno didn't mind, so long as his men wore their blue blouses and were instantly identifiable as soldiers. He wore a straw panama himself, preferring its cool ventilation and broad brim to the sweatiness of a forage cap. That night he asked his company commanders to inspect arms. The Springfields seemed vulnerable to dirt, so they would by God be kept clean, and every copper cartridge would be kept shiny too.

The next day, the twelfth, the command marched another twenty-four miles through punishing heat. Reno's scouts pushed to the junction of the Powder and Little Powder and found nothing while the command wrestled with long gulches and steep slopes that proved to be too much for the condemned horses pulling the Gatling gun. The troopers had to unlimber the gun and drag it upslope by brute manhandling.

The easy flats had vanished, and the arid land shaped itself into coulees and hills, and required careful scouting by Reno's Arikaras. In the middle of the afternoon the scouts found evidence of a recent village and Reno decided to bivouac then and there, resting his sun-blasted men and heat-exhausted horses.

There were no comforts. No place to hide from the murderous sun or escape the chafing wind. No relief from the monotony of beans and bacon, hardtack and the murky water of the Powder, an aptly named stream carrying a load of brown silt toward the Yellowstone. And no relief from prairie rattlesnakes, which lurked everywhere.

The next day Reno turned west, having explored as directed as far as the confluence of the Powder and Little Powder, and when the command reached the Mizpah, Reno headed downstream while his scouts headed upstream to check on Indian encampments. Somewhere in that vast land, which stretched beyond the horizons, beyond the white haze, beyond the rim of the world, known only to the whispering wind, several thousand irreconcilable Sioux and Cheyenne had hidden themselves from the blue-shirts and were singing songs of war.

Mitch Bouyer made Reno's next decision for him.

"Nothing up the Mizpah," he said, wiping dust-stained sweat off his heavy brown brow. "This drainage is no-how where they're camped. You might head west toward the Little Pumpkin, major. Do some good that way."

Reno consulted his map—and General Terry's orders, which commanded him to descend Mizpah Creek to its junction with the Powder River before turning toward the drainage of the Tongue. It would be more fruitful, he concluded, to cross the prairie divide then and there, and head for Pumpkin Creek. Maybe he would pick up some sign off to the west.

So, on a sun-scorched June thirteenth, he took his command over the parched and treeless slopes toward another river, and another fate. He would have to explain the disobedience to General Terry. But he was out here to find Indians and by God he would do it.

# CHAPTER NINE

RENO SUMMONED HIS STAFF. CALHOUN, HARRINGTON, SMITH, AND the rest collected around a makeshift field table which bore Reno's map and a lantern that cast pale yellow light into bronzed and sun-baked faces.

"Mitch Bouyer's scouts have explored up and down the Mizpah, and there's nothing there. General Terry wants us to descend to the Powder again, completing the loop, here," he said, tracing river systems with his finger. "We're wasting time. I'm proposing that we cross to Pumpkin Creek, here, and start looking in the Tongue River basin. This would depart from . . . instructions."

He waited for a response but no one hazarded any.

"I want results and so does the general."

Calhoun nodded. That was some sort of concession if not agreement, Reno supposed. Commanders in the field had a little leeway to deal with unforeseen circumstances or exigencies. Calhoun was Custer's brother-in-law, and Reno didn't doubt that every detail of this scout would soon reach the lieutenant colonel's ears. Reno not only didn't mind that, he suspected it was a good thing.

"What do our Ree scouts think?" Harrington asked.

"Big village west of here. But not around the Powder, and probably not the Tongue, either. Rosebud, maybe. I want to find the trail."

Reno was met with silence and understood it. His staff agreed with this deviation from orders but didn't want to go on record. That was all right.

"All right, we'll head over the divide," he said.

The next dawn, June fourteenth, the major led his footsore command southwest over the gullied brow of an obscure divide and into the basin of the Tongue, and struck shimmering alkaline Pumpkin Creek a mile below its junction with the Little Pumpkin. Then he directed the command up the intimate valley of the Little Pumpkin for a mile or so and bivouacked there in a good grassy basin that would conceal cookfires. This was hillier country, with high points that could be used for observation, so he chose his site carefully. He was tired of plains. Nothing but empty flats that could drive a man mad.

On the fifteenth, he led his command over jackpine ridges toward the Tongue. The gnarled, long-needled pines made travel difficult, especially for the Gatling gun, and it turned out to be a hard, hot, thirsty day for the troopers. The tongue of the Gatling limber snapped at a gully and the company lost time while a new one was hewn and bolted in.

The Arikaras scouted ahead and reported only empty grass country. One of them, Young Hawk, shot an elk, which annoyed Reno but he let it pass. They reached the Tongue, a substantial river cutting through hill and canyon country that could have hidden a dozen armies. But here was firewood, shade, clear water, and endless grass.

He took them down the Tongue eight miles until Bouyer called a halt. They had reached the site of a vast village, abandoned a month or so earlier, numbering some four hundred lodges. The travois trail led west. The Arikara scouts studied the tepee rings, the kitchen debris, the way the camp had been laid out, and reported through Bouyer that at last they were on the trail.

Reno was on the horns of a dilemma. There was no point in following the Tongue back to the Yellowstone as his orders required. He could return to the rendezvous point and tell General Terry he had found nothing but an old village, or he could follow the clear trail into the Rosebud valley left by hundreds of burdened travois. He could return with no more news for all his traveling than that the Indians were farther west. He would be held blameless. He had executed Terry's orders, with only a minor deviation, and come up with nothing. Or he could try to give the general some intelligence of value.

*Faint heart never won fair maid,* he thought, remembering Custer's taunt. Command seemed oddly heavy that evening. He wanted to test his decision on his officers, but couldn't manage it. He slid into his tent, pulled his silver pint flask from his kit, and took a hard swallow of hundred-proof bourbon. It tore at his throat and quieted his soul.

The men devoured beans and a little elk that night and talked a great deal. Some intangible excitement brewed in the camp. Just how soldiers knew, or sensed portents Reno never knew, but they did, and their spirits were sharp. The horses were in need of shoes and gaunted in spite of good grass and two gallons of grain a day; the troopers were worn with riding, the teamsters footsore from walking, and all had endured alkali dust and blinding June light.

The alkali water had loosened their bowels and their complaints reached Reno's ears. Some were saddle sore, especially the recruits, and a few had boils on their backsides, making every minute in the saddle an ordeal. Some were sun-blinded, and half the command was sore-eyed from squinting through the shadeless glare, day upon day. That was the army: loose stools, boredom, sickness, tedium, dull hours from before dawn to darkness.

His order the next morning was simple: "Follow it," he said.

His officers stared until Reno pointed, and only then did they trot to their companies and tell their sergeants to line them out, again by twos.

The Right Wing of the Seventh Cavalry turned west, trotting silently along an Indian trail. Now they were cutting overland, riding on top of a broad trail that furrowed the prairie, trampled sagebrush, and made each rider alert and cautious and watchful. Reno knew what they were thinking: was this Old Man going to pitch caution to the winds and lead this modest force against the bitterest elements of the entire Sioux nation? Was this Old Man Reno another glory hound who would lay them all in their graves? Was this man another *Custer*?

They called Custer *Hard Ass,* but not when officers were around. They knew his history as an Indian fighter; knew he would shoot deserters without a trial, abandon wounded, neglect to bury the dead, and in the heat of battle leave the besieged to their fate, as he had Major Joel Elliott and nineteen men in the battle of the Washita.

They knew he would break down men and horses when he felt the need, and sometimes that need had nothing to do with military necessity. They knew some of his officers despised him, and that he had collected his relatives around him to strengthen his grip on the Seventh. They knew he had been court-martialed and convicted of being absent without leave from his command, and of conduct to the prejudice of good order and military discipline, and had been suspended without pay for a year.

They knew less about Reno, and he wanted it that way. He was simply distant, evoking no hatreds or enthusiasm in his men. He didn't want their approval, which meant less discipline or hardship, but neither did he ignore their feelings, and kept a sharp eye out for demoralization or discouragement. He had led men through the Civil War with honor and courage by that means, and he would lead them in the same fashion now.

And they knew one thing more about him: he would not needlessly or recklessly risk their lives, especially for vainglorious reasons. He knew he wasn't a favorite among officers of the regiment, but he knew as well that none of them except perhaps Custer and Benteen and Tom Weir found him wanting.

He had struck Benteen once in an altercation, and thought that blowhard of a man deserved worse; he had brought charges against Weir for drunkenness on duty, and from that moment had made Weir an enemy. And Custer's studied disapproval was probably little more than rivalry; Custer distrusted the older Reno.

But if there was serious trouble in the regiment, it lay between Custer and Benteen, not Custer and Reno. After the battle of the Washita, and before Reno had joined the regiment, Benteen had written anonymously to the *St. Louis Democrat* claiming that Custer had failed to go to the rescue of Major Elliott, and had fled the scene after only a minimal search for the missing major and his men.

Custer had gathered his officers in a wrath-charged meeting and told them he would horsewhip the one who wrote that letter. Benteen stepped forward and announced that he had written the letter. Custer had glared at him and walked out.

Reno thought maybe Benteen should have been horsewhipped. The press wasn't the court to try officers of the United States Army, no matter that Custer failed to account for all of his command before ordering a retreat from that perilous field.

Now Reno led this mass of men closer and closer toward the hostile encampment. It was not a force to lead into a fight; he knew it and didn't intend to get sucked into one if he could help it. And Terry didn't want him to give away the army's presence, either.

By two o'clock that hot afternoon of June sixteenth, Reno's command had crossed the pine-covered divide and reached the grassy valley of Rosebud Creek. He dismounted them there. The rank smell of sweat filled the air. Men's shirts had soaked black under the armpits; horses had lathered around the saddles and withers.

It was more than heat that had wrought all that sweat as men peered fearfully at the ridges, down the silent valley, at every crow and magpie and hawk. They had come nineteen miles along the trail of that vast village. Somewhere ahead were hundreds, maybe a thousand, well-armed warriors seething with hatred of the government's edicts and itching to fight.

Reno sent scouts up and down the creek while the men rested, and a few hours later the scouts reported the sites of abandoned villages up the Rosebud, along with a heavy travois trail in that direction. Reno mounted his command and rode up the Rosebud three miles to the abandoned village site, and camped there for the night. There would be some intelligence to gather from examining that place.

He knew now where the hostiles were headed. Follow further, and risk being discovered, or head for the Yellowstone and report what he found.

He decided to explore further, and led his command up the Rosebud another few miles to another Indian campground, riding in deep silence, with all bugles and noise forbidden. It was clear that the hostiles were progressing southwest, and in great numbers, and were not far away.

Through Bouyer, who interpreted, Reno asked the senior Arikara scout, Forked Horn, what he thought of that enormous trail.

"If the Dakotas see us, the sun will not move very far before we are all killed," the scout replied.

Reno knew he had found the right trail. He had discovered what Terry needed to know, the information that would justify Reno's departure from orders. Somewhere not far ahead, in that sullen heat, were the object of three columns of soldiers: Crook's up from the south, Gibbon's from Fort Ellis in the west, and Terry's, out of Dakota Territory.

Satisfied that he had made a valuable reconnaissance, the disobedient Major Reno turned his men north, and headed for the Yellowstone River and a stormy meeting with General Terry.

# CHAPTER TEN

RENO WAS COMING FROM THE WRONG DIRECTION. GIBBON'S MONTANA column was bivouacked on the north shore of the Yellowstone a mile below its confluence with the Rosebud, and there was no way across the river there. Reno's arrival from the west, across the river, stirred some excitement, and eventually a swimmer established some sort of communication. Gibbon dispatched a courier to Terry saying that Reno had appeared at last—from the direction of the Rosebud.

It took another night's bivouac before Reno reached the Tongue River encampment and the irritated officers and men who had waited for days for the absent major. When at last they all came together at Terry's wind-shivered headquarters tent, the mild-mannered General Terry fumed.

"You deliberately violated my orders," he said. "Explain yourself, because your dispatches fail to do so."

"It seemed the best choice, out in the field."

"Why?"

"To identify the big village we were following from the Tongue. To see what direction it was headed. To determine its size. I did so. It's the village we're looking for, and it's drifting southwest. You now know where to go, and you know where the Indians are not."

"And you risked exposing our presence to the enemy. Do you think you weren't seen?"

"We had scouts and vedettes wide and forward, sir, and I doubt that we were seen."

Terry's gaze bored straight through Reno.

"I expressly confined you to the Powder and Tongue Rivers, precisely so you wouldn't give it all away. Do you suppose my orders were a mere slip of paper to read and crumple up? You felt free to do whatever you chose to do?"

Reno had supplied his reasons, and good reasons they were, so he remained silent.

"My entire plan is ruined. I don't know where Crook is or how we can tell him that we'll be doing something else. I don't know how we'll trap that village now."

"You know where the village isn't, sir, and approximately where it is: the Bighorn Valley."

But Terry had had his fill of Reno. "I'll consult with Gibbon. You're dismissed. Report to Colonel Custer. He's paced around this place for four days waiting for you."

Reno saluted. Terry was a lawyer turned into a brigadier general as the result of the Civil War, one of the few civilian volunteers who reached high rank in the regular army. His very nature was courteous, but this interview had been etched with acid, and Reno knew he was facing more trouble than he had bargained for.

His company commanders were seeing to the worn-out horses and footsore men, so Reno headed directly to the field headquarters of the Seventh Cavalry, where guidons flapped lazily in the gusty air. He surmised that if the unemotional Terry had been enraged, Custer would be furious, and one look at the leonine commander affirmed it. Custer was pacing like a caged cat.

He pounced at once. "You deliberately violated orders. Violated written, express orders! You've endangered this entire operation. You were *told* not to go where you went, and now the Sioux know we're here and we've lost any chance of surprise. Worse, having given chase, and itching for some laurels, you failed to attack, and turned tail."

Reno waited.

"Explain yourself."

"I found the village."

"You weren't asked to find the village. You were asked to determine where the village was *not*. I should put you under arrest. I should strip you of command. I would, except we're on the eve of the biggest battle in the history of Indian warfare. Everything's up in the air. General Terry and Colonel Gibbon and I"—Custer emphasized the *general* and the *colonel*—"will be conferring. We'll deal with you later. What is the condition of the horses?"

"They're trail-worn and need shoeing."

"On the eve of a battle you wear out the horses. And the men?"

"They are in good enough shape, sir."

"No, after wandering over half of Montana Territory that long, they are not in good enough shape. They are not rested."

Reno could see how it would go, but he was stubborn and wouldn't quit. "If General Terry had attempted to act on incomplete intelligence, his three-way pincers would have missed the hostiles, sir. They're not on the lower Rosebud as he had thought. It all would have been wasted motion. I took the initiative to confirm what no one knew for certain, and that is the area where the hostiles are hiding, and the size of their encampment."

But Custer had grown weary of the confrontation. His cold bleak gaze raked the major. "Dismissed," he said. "I will decide what to do about you."

"Yes, sir."

It had gone far worse than Reno imagined. Reno's Luck, he called it. Some officers, including Custer himself, could routinely violate or trim or ignore orders and somehow avoid becoming scapegraces. But other men were somehow expected to follow orders to the letter, and not allowed the slightest discretion in the field. Reno wondered how, and why, he had been cast among the latter. And why neither Gibbon nor Terry nor Custer had thanked him, nor even kindly acknowledged, that he had found the goddamn Indians.

It was his turn to be angry. He pulled a stogy out of his kit, bit off the end, and lit it with a lucifer. He had no confidantes and would not whine anyway. He didn't always enjoy being alone; it was simply how his life played out, and what his nature led him to.

That close June night few of the men sheltered themselves. Most preferred to use their shelter half as a ground cloth against the dampness of the rain-saturated soil. But Custer's field tent was up, and a lamp burned within, burnishing the canvas with a mustard glow and limning the boy general's shadow on the cloth wall. Custer was writing again. Reno wondered what he was writing this time, what complaints he was voicing to Libbie, what shortcomings in his staff he was noting, especially Major Reno the order violator.

Reno stalked the bivouac, which was stretched over half a mile. Nine hundred men in all, the whole Dakota column, cavalry and infantry and the Gatling battery reunited. Sentries were posted; the horse herd was secured and guarded. This was the army at its best, turning a riverside flat into a fortress. The lingering twilight of the summer solstice blued the sky to the northwest. Fires blazed at each company mess, and shot sparks into the black sky. The stink of sweat, unwashed bodies, urine, and horse manure crowded the faint breezes. Armies stank, and Reno could sense from the smell whether an army was under duress or at ease. Tonight the odor was ease, even though every man by now knew that Reno had pinned down the hostile village and that a fight was in the offing.

A lamp burned in Terry's tent, and Reno knew the brigadier was revising his plans, based on the information the major had brought to him. But the general did not evoke Reno's anger. Terry was a quiet, reasoning sort of man, and would ultimately come around. Soldiering offered paradox: obey every order, but show initiative and courage.

Reno slid a weather-chafed hand into the bosom of his tunic, extracted his silver-plated flask, unstoppered it, and swilled a fiery charge of Tennessee whiskey, and then another. He stoppered the flask and returned it to his bosom. Whiskey was not something to waste when the supply was so limited. He sucked on his cigar, seeing the end brighten in the darkness. The whiskey washed through his anger, leaching and refining it.

He liked the army. He liked being here in this warrior's camp where disciplined men in blue each looked after the honor and safety of the whole regiment. He didn't like or trust his regimental commander. He balled his left hand into a fist and slammed it into his right hand.

"Nice night," said Lieutenant Hodgson.

Reno whirled, and discovered his friend and adjutant drifting close, faintly lit by the blue band of afterlight lingering in the northwestern sky.

"You could let a man know you're approaching."

Hodgson ignored Reno's testiness, and stood beside him. "I hear you found the village."

"Four hundred lodges."

"That's maybe eight hundred warriors. We can deal with that even if we get no support from the other columns."

"A quarter of our men are recruits," Reno said.

"Were, you mean. They've been hardened these past weeks . . . I hear Custer was unhappy with your scout."

Hodgson wanted to gossip, as lieutenants often did because they were starved for news.

"Don't believe what you hear," Reno said, roughly.

"They should be clapping you on the back. But for you, they would have run their pincers and caught nothing."

"Let it rest, Ben."

"Do you know that the lieutenant colonel was pacing and stewing around here for four days, waiting for you to return? He would have blistered your ear just for being late, even if you had . . ." Hodgson suddenly left the rest of the thought hanging in air.

"Followed orders," Reno said, drawing hard on his cigar.

"I bet he's writing Libbie all about it in that tent," Hodgson said. "It'll go out with the next courier to Fort Lincoln."

"Lieutenant, let's not gossip," Reno said.

Hodgson grinned, unrepentant. "What was his complaint? Why did he chew on you?"

"I risked being discovered. Surprise is everything in a campaign like this. Maybe he was right. I risked it. Maybe I'll end up costing us lives."

Hodgson stared at him. "Touchy tonight, aren't you? It gets heavy to carry. Lives, risks, dangers, getting in harm's way, that's what we're each facing every day in the army, major, you're not alone. We're here with you, and we'll fight beside you."

*And die beside me too,* Reno thought.

# CHAPTER ELEVEN

PLANS CHANGED AND GENERAL TERRY WAS TESTY ABOUT IT. GENERALS don't like shifting realities to get in the way of their operations. Now Gibbon would march his Montana column, primarily infantry, up the Bighorn River, lying to the west. Terry's Dakota column, largely the Seventh Cavalry, would probe the upper Rosebud and move west to the Bighorn if it found nothing. And with any sort of luck, Crook's column off to the south would push the hostiles into the guns of the other columns.

By the twenty-first day of June, the Montana and Dakota columns had gathered at the mouth of the Rosebud. Aboard Captain Marsh's riverboat, *Far West,* the commanders conferred: Terry, Gibbon, Custer, and Major James Brisbin, who commanded four companies of the Second Cavalry in Gibbon's column.

Reno knew he would hear all about it soon enough. He had brought the regiment upriver from the camp at the mouth of the Tongue and had helped whip it into fighting condition as it rested on the north bank of the Yellowstone. Even as the commanders conferred, Gibbon's column started up the Yellowstone to the Bighorn. There would be no more delay: it was time to strike.

On a sultry June twenty-second, the Seventh Cavalry, led by Major Reno, passed in review before Terry, Gibbon, and Custer, the men and horses responding smartly to the bugles shrilling "Boots and Saddles," the silky guidons flapping softly in the summer zephyrs, the men armed and ready. War and glory hung in the air. The Seventh had received the signal honor of finding the village, and that knowledge swelled the bosom of every cavalryman.

Then Custer joined his command. Reno watched the lieutenant colonel, who looked dashing in buckskins, wave to General Terry from his high-stepping well-curried Vic, one of his two mounts, and then wheel his long blue column through thick silvery sagebrush up the Yellowstone to the east bank of the Rosebud. Custer was leaving the regimental band behind, along with the wagons, and relying on a hundred pack mules for provisions. He was provisioned for twelve days.

He plainly wanted speed and mobility. He had declined the Gatling battery as being too slow for his operation, and seemed determined to win laurels for the Seventh Cavalry alone. Custer had over six hundred enlisted men and officers with him, thirteen quartermaster employees, the Bismarck newspaper reporter, Mark Kellogg, and about fifty civilian packers, herders, and scouts including Custer's brother Boston and nephew Autie Reed. Enough to cut through the whole Sioux nation.

"Custer, don't be greedy," said Gibbon.

"No, I will not," Custer replied.

Reno thought that Gibbon's comment was apt and Custer's response was ambiguous. Of Custer's exact orders and plans, Reno knew nothing though he was second in command. Whatever Terry had written by way of orders, it was plain the commander had placed utmost confidence in the lieutenant colonel. Terry himself and his headquarters staff would traverse the Yellowstone by riverboat, accompanying Gibbon's column up the Yellowstone and Bighorn Rivers.

No sooner did the column get under way but the packers were having trouble with their loaded mules. Custer force-marched them twelve miles that afternoon, stopping on the Rosebud at last to permit his teamsters to put their packs in order. It had not been an auspicious start for a commander bent on a lightning thrust against unsuspecting hostiles.

That evening Custer gathered his officers to him. He seemed unusually quiet in the softness of a late June evening, even reflective, with a gentleness in him that none of his officers had ever witnessed before. Reno stood among them, wondering what his own fate would be: Custer could shunt him to some minor command, or embrace him as a part of the attacking force.

The lieutenant colonel began routinely: "I want surprise. That means no trumpet signals. I want speed. That means you'll awaken your men at three each morning and we'll march at five. We'll do short marches at first and then stretch them further. We'll follow the trail of this large village, wherever it leads."

He went on to lay responsibilities on each officer, making it clear who was to do what. And then he paused, ran a hand through his recently shorn yellow hair, and addressed them most earnestly: "We are in this together, and I would welcome the counsel and wisdom of each of you. I will listen to anything you wish to offer me throughout this command. I want you to share in the triumph of the Seventh Cavalry and feel yourselves a part of this, the greatest test ever to come down to us. I honor and esteem you all. In a few days this republic will celebrate its hundredth birthday. Let us give our great nation a gift it will never forget."

Coming from George Custer, that was remarkable, and Reno wondered what had inspired it. Was it something stern that General Terry had said to Custer? Was it something simpler, such as the wish to cohere the regiment as tightly and seamlessly as possible? To heal old wounds and bad blood on the eve of battle? Whatever it was, Reno knew that the gesture, along with those words, were gracious and found their way into the hearts of his staff officers. To a man, they were all startled. It was as if George Custer, the shorn Samson, had transmogrified himself into a new person.

Lieutenant Godfrey caught up with Reno after Custer had dismissed them.

"I'm not sure I believe the evidence of my own ears," he said. "What do you suppose got into him?"

Reno didn't like the discussion of personalities and fended off the question. "Did you double your stable guard, lieutenant?"

"Serves me right," Godfrey said. "But it's a good omen."

The young man rubbed his huge nose and hastened into the twilight. Godfrey was a good man. The camp this night was hushed, partly by design because Custer wanted it so, but also because the men had war on their minds, the whip of bullets, the shriek of the hurt, the hard, exacting thing that was creeping up on them.

It may well have been a good omen, this reaching out to the staff. But it unsettled some of the officers.

The valley of the Rosebud had greened because of ample spring rain, and now the crickets chorused through the night. A mist hung over the creek. Major Reno was long accustomed to the cadences of nature and found nothing amiss.

Some men were writing letters in the semi-dark, letters to sweethearts, or wives, or children, or parents. Those letters might be last words, if that should be their soldier's lot. A few who couldn't write were dictating letters to those who could write for them. The letters would ride safely in the pack train until the engagement had passed, and would wind their way back to Fort Abraham Lincoln, and on down the Missouri.

Reno knew he should write Ross, or Mary Hannah's younger sister Bertie, and brother-in-law, J. Wilson Orth, or his own siblings, but he was not close to them, and scarcely knew what to say. Ross would probably not be interested in hearing from a father he knew so little.

He wished he might be writing Mary Hannah, but now she seemed unfathomably distant, as if her soul had steadily traversed the vast universe, sailing farther and farther toward some destination beyond imagining, while he was caught here in the webs of war and life. He tried to remember her, but even her face had blurred in his mind, as if the hand-tinted photograph had faded and almost vanished.

Then he did remember, not her laughter or her voice, but her pale body, ever unknown to the sun, on just such a June night as this, when the windows of their bedroom in Harrisburg were opened to the soft night breezes that sometimes billowed the gauzy curtains into the room. He remembered her white arms, always timid at first, and then closing tightly about him with a fine sweet madness. "Oh! My captain!" she always said, as some sort of ritual that sealed their union.

Crickets there, and crickets here, and soft summer night winds that dried their sweat after their embrace.

He composed a letter to her in his mind: "My dear Mary Hannah, in a day or two I will once again be caught in war, caught in harm's way, uncertain as always what war may bring to me. Your locket is all I possess of you now, save for the memories. I send my love out upon the stars, out upon the constellations, out upon that road you travel through eternity, and even in the midst of danger the love we bear for each other will sustain me. . . ."

He had seen a bald eagle that day, soaring in circles, its wings motionless, ignoring the column of soldiers.

That seemed an omen too.

The next day, June twenty-third, a Friday, Custer led his silent, sweating column another thirty-three miles up Rosebud Creek, passing several village campsites en route, each one fresher than the one before. The Crow and Arikara scouts, under Lieutenant Varnum, studied manure and dung, kitchen leavings, and pronounced their verdicts.

"Could be just a couple of days away now," Varnum reported.

Bouyer affirmed it. "We'll be on top of them sonsofbitches before they know it," he said.

Custer called an early halt and sent his scouts wide and far ahead while solstice daylight persisted. The pack train had fallen behind and did not show up until dusk, much to Custer's displeasure. No commander going into battle wanted to be separated from his reserve ammunition. But Custer was oddly subdued, and was content merely to urge the mule skinners to resolve their problems.

Reno approached him: "This is as far up the Rosebud as I scouted," he said. "From now on, you'll be penetrating unknown terrain."

Custer nodded curtly. Neither man, apparently, wanted to be reminded of Reno's scout, but the major felt obliged to let his commander know.

Custer's response, given to Varnum, was to throw his scouts out still farther ahead and wider, not only to look for lodge trails breaking away from the main body, but to discover any signs of activity to either side of the creek.

Reno didn't sleep well that night. He kept imagining he heard thunder, but the terrible rumble of war was all in his mind.

# CHAPTER TWELVE

ALL THAT HOT SATURDAY OF JUNE TWENTY-FOURTH, THE SEVENTH
Cavalry rode through thickening silence. Every trooper who had bothered to kick open the brown manure left by Indian ponies discovered
bright green within. The fierce June sun had not completely cooked the
horse apples brown. Some vast Sioux village lay just ahead, maybe over
the brow of the next hill or just across a divide.

Reno heard only the creak of saddle leather, the occasional soft snuffle
of a horse blowing, the rhythmic clop of hooves, and sometimes the
whipsaw of wind. He was unsure what his role would be: Custer had dis-
solved the order of command upon leaving the Yellowstone and now Reno
had no companies in his charge, nor did any other senior officer. Whatever the lieutenant colonel had in mind, he kept locked within himself.

The command rode through a broad grassy valley caught between dark
slopes covered with long-needled jack pine, passing three huge campsites
as the day wore on. Men didn't talk; they rode toward battle caught up in
their own thoughts, sharing nothing with the men who rode beside, or before, or behind. Some studied the slopes, half expecting a flight of arrows
to burst from the dark shadows where the pines crowded close.

The trail was huge now, a full mile wide, trampled grass furrowed by
travois and dotted with horse manure. This was no ordinary village, but a
savage congregation larger than anything ever seen by any officer or enlisted man, a village that bristled with aggrieved warriors itching for a

fight, a village many times larger than the entire Seventh Cavalry. Men stared unbelieving at the trail and its debris.

That afternoon they arrived at a campsite with a brushy lodge at its center where some sort of sacred ceremony had occurred, something the scouts called a Sun Dance, which was holy to the Sioux and Cheyenne. The grass for a mile around had been chewed down by the ponies. The sacred place raised the hackles of many a man, and drove them all even deeper into their private reverie.

Reno was caught in his own silence. Now and then he saw the Crow and Ree scouts trotting out or racing in with information, which was delivered at once to Custer at the head of the command. Reno wasn't privy to what was being conveyed by the scouts, but he surmised they had no news; real news would have resulted in a halt, orders, preparations.

He felt sweat soak his blouse under his armpits, and bead on his brow. Half the men had purchased straw hats from the sutler, and these were cooler than the army-issue forage caps. Their eyes were inflamed by heat, the glare of the blistering June sun, dust, and tiredness, and that worried Reno. His own eyes stung and hurt from squinting.

Custer halted his command at four thirty, in bright daylight, hoping to rest the column. The troopers wearily stepped down to grass, headed for the bushes, splashed water from Rosebud Creek over their faces, and looked to their horses. The place was an Eden: wild rosebushes in full yellow bloom crowded the valley, while an occasional willow dotted the bottomland.

Custer summoned Lieutenant Varnum: "I want the scouts to keep a sharp lookout for lodge trails leaving the main trail. I want the whole village, not a part of it. Don't let them scatter."

Reno watched several details of Crow and Arikara scouts trot off toward the ridges as the late afternoon progressed toward the long June evening, and then came news. The scouts reported that the huge trail turned right abruptly and headed straight over the divide to the valley of the Little Bighorn. The Crows, who called this country home, knew of a high place where one could observe the surrounding country. Custer immediately sent Lieutenant Varnum, chief of scouts, with his Crows and Rees, to see what could be seen.

Custer called his officers together. "The scouts tell me this trail is not even two days old. We're close. We'll move out at midnight," he said. "We'll climb the divide and conceal ourselves and rest. Tomorrow, we'll reconnoiter, and on the twenty-sixth we'll attack at dawn. That's always the best time, when we can cut right through the village. It's a large village, but not difficult work for the Seventh if we catch it at the right moment. Tell the men to look to their mounts, eat field rations, and sleep. We'll pull out at midnight and use the cover of darkness for our purposes."

Custer was still in a strangely gentle mood. The younger officers concluded their meeting with the commander by singing beloved songs: "Annie Laurie," "Little Footsteps Soft and Gentle," and then a surprise to Major Reno's ears: the Doxology. *Praise God from whom all blessings flow, Praise Him all creatures here below* . . . and then, at the last, for their commander, "For He's a Jolly Good Fellow."

There was nothing to do but rest, so saddle-worn men sprawled gratefully in the grass. Reno patrolled the command, checking on the stable guard, the pickets, the company messes, looking for signs of trouble or infractions of the order to keep a strict silence. These were weary men, half starved from poor rations, nothing but coffee and hardtack that gentle evening, their faces blistered and burned, their hands browned to the color of roasted chestnuts. But the noncoms, along with the company commanders, had done their jobs well, and this was a force ready to fight at a moment's notice.

At twelve thirty in the morning, the command, so briefly rested, mounted in deep darkness and rode toward the divide between the Rosebud and Little Bighorn Valleys. It would be slow going, a moonless night march over unfamiliar ground, guided by the Crows who knew the country. One moment trees would rise out of the darkness, the next moment they were climbing a grassy slope. Reno heard a distant owl.

Reno's horse felt weary under him; he didn't doubt that the rest of the mounts were weary as well, deprived of rest and forage. Led now by the scouts and Bouyer, the command pierced the night along the fresh trail, climbing long slopes, the air acrid with the resinous scent of pine and sweated horses. Reins were useless; one could only let one's mount follow the one ahead.

A black sky lorded over them. In many ways night riding was easier than a day's ride; a man didn't have to squint, and the soft breezes kept him cool. And the horses picked their way without guidance. But sheer tiredness was an enemy now. By three thirty, shortly before dawn in that latitude, the men were ready for a rest, and Custer settled them in a hollow just below the divide, telling them to keep their horses saddled but to get some shut-eye if they could.

At dawn of Sunday, June twenty-fifth, Varnum and his scouts returned from the Crow's Nest, as the high place was called. Varnum reported that his scouts swore they could see the Sioux camp, crawling with horses and sending smoke into the dawn heavens, but the lieutenant could see nothing, not even through some field glasses offered to him, and he was skeptical.

"I'll have a look," Custer said. He turned to Reno. "Be ready to move out at eight."

He and Varnum and the scouts trotted off to the Crow's Nest for another look.

A light overcast kept the early morning cool. Scouts patrolled in all directions, soaking up information like the antennae of bugs, making sure there would be no bitter surprises. But there was a surprise, after all.

Captain Keogh came rushing forward with news, which he gave to Tom Custer in the absence of the commander. Earlier, Captain Yates of F Company had sent a sergeant with a detail to go back several miles to recover a lost case of hardtack, found Indians looting it, and shot at them. The Indians had scattered. So the command had been discovered. Custer's intent to surprise the village and strike at dawn a day and a half hence, had shattered in a stroke of bad luck.

Custer learned of it when he returned from the Crow's Nest. He couldn't see the damned village either, but trusted his Indian scouts. If they said the village was there, it probably was.

Then Tom Custer broke the bad news about the skirmish over the hard-tack box to his brother. Custer instantly called his officers together once again, and paced back and forth before them, his mind working feverishly on a plan, the bright gaze from his sun-baked face swinging from man to man, seeking accord at this moment of truth. His voice was taut and tight and high.

"We've been discovered. That changes everything. The sooner we march, the better chance we have," he said. "We're going to attack when we get there, midday if need be. We can't surprise them but we can hit them before they're ready, painted up for war, and armed. Those Indians we surprised won't get to the camp much before we do. All right, gentlemen, let's move, and I want total silence.

"Judging from the lodge trail, we're attacking the largest camp ever seen in North America," he said. "The Seventh Cavalry." For a moment he gazed at horizons, seeing something over the hills, something beyond what the rest of the officers would ever see. "It will be a fight to remember."

The bone-weary and ill-rested column started up again, topped the divide, and followed a rough trail downslope, screened by the terrain and jack pines which quickly gave way to arid grasslands, and still they rode while the morning slipped away and the heat built along with their thirst.

At midday and under a fierce sun, Custer called a halt and organized his command. His long-bearded adjutant, Lieutenant Cooke, told Reno that the major would command Companies A, G, and M, and that the commander desired that six enlisted men and one noncom from each company be posted to Company B to protect the pack train.

"Is that all?" Reno asked.

"That's all," said Cooke, who then dashed off to make other assignments.

Reno could pretty well guess the rest: Captain Benteen would have a battalion, Captains Keogh and Yates would each have a battalion.

The column reorganized itself, with companies gathering behind their commanders while the lieutenant colonel watched impatiently. The men detailed to guard the pack train headed to the rear. Custer, surrounded by his trumpeters, his staff, his guidons, his aides, seemed charged with energy and impatience, and something else: wild joy. He pulled off his fringed buckskin coat and tied it behind his cantle. He wore a light colored slouch hat, Wellington boots, buckskin trousers, and a blue flannel shirt.

Many times had Reno watched men prepare for battle. Those heading toward the pack train found themselves collecting letters and lockets from those who were about to fight. Miniatures of wives, last wills, locks of hair in envelopes, sometimes even greenbacks stuffed into an envelope with a name written upon it, all sent to the safest place by men who thought they might not live to see the sun rise again. This would be no routine skirmish; every man knew that. The awesome lodge trail over those hills told them all they needed to know.

Now Custer sent orders to his commanders: Company B, under Captain McDougall, would guard the pack train and follow twenty minutes behind. Benteen had Companies D, H, and K, about a hundred and thirty men, and would ride an oblique left, scouring the west side of the Little Bighorn Valley for outlying encampments. Reno would have the Arikara scouts and a hundred and twelve troopers and would attack the village head-on, at the center. Custer himself would lead five companies, C, E, F, I, and L, along with Tom Custer, their nephew Autie and the newsman, Mark Kellogg, on the right flank.

"The general says to make haste, attack, and he'll support you," Cooke said. "Understood?"

Reno nodded. "Is that all of it?"

Cooke nodded.

"Will there be any further reconnaissance? Do we know where the village is?"

"Varnum and his scouts have already started ahead. They'll direct us."

Reno watched Benteen's command strike northwest and disappear from sight. It wasn't clear to him what role Custer intended for Benteen to play in the fight unless he was to keep the Sioux from fleeing in all directions, as had happened so often in the past. For days, the commander had been obsessed with keeping the village from flying apart under attack. If Benteen's role was to drive outlying camps toward the center, that would accord with the thing that had been on Custer's mind and which was consuming him, and would account for Benteen's disappearance.

Neither was it clear to Reno just what sort of support Custer planned to offer when things got hot. Would Custer follow? Attack from the right flank? But how could he, when he didn't know the terrain? They were riding into battle with only the sketchiest notion of where that village was, and how the separated forces would support one another.

Reno did not even know what Benteen's explicit orders were, or whether Custer would attempt to attack this village from several quarters, as he had at the Washita. Or where and how the three commands would link up.

Reno bit down hard on the stump of a dead Baltimore cigar and led his column by fours into battle.

For the next two hours Reno and Custer, on opposite sides of the little creek they were following, kept their columns riding by fours at a fast horse-saving trot as they approached the village. They were traversing rough, dry ground with gulches leading down to the creek, some of them choked with sagebrush and an occasional cottonwood. It was dry, and the fast-moving commands stirred dust.

They reached a meadow with a lone tepee in it, and swiftly discovered it was the final resting place of a dead warrior. Custer ordered it burned. Then Custer signaled the major to move forward, and soon Marcus Reno and his soldiers and scouts were alone.

# CHAPTER THIRTEEN

RENO RAISED AN ARM AND SWUNG IT FORWARD. HIS COLUMN, STILL riding by twos, broke into a fast trot that covered ground. He saw nothing that looked like an enemy village, only hilly terrain on the right, mostly grassy, with dense sagebrush in the gulches and copses of cottonwoods dotting a vast valley.

He led the command across the Little Bighorn, which was deeper than expected, three to four feet of cold water, and reformed it by fours on the other side, while water dripped from the legs and bellies of the mounts. Thirsty horses paused in the middle for a drink, and troopers turned their hats into scoops, and drank as well.

The crossing and forming into fours took longer than Reno wanted, but men and horses had slaked their thirst. After the crossing men dismounted and tightened their saddle girths. Girard, a scout Reno distrusted, told him there were plenty of Indians ahead. Reno nodded. He had yet to see one.

The Crow and Arikara scouts worked ahead and on the left. They were to cut off the Sioux horse herd and drive it away from the village. Reno could no longer see Custer's column, which was lost from view somewhere to the right. He felt the sweat build under his arms and soak his blouse, felt beads ooze from his forehead and drip down his cheeks. Reno assuaged his thirst with a good suck from his flask.

*Attack.*

They swung into an open plain and he could see clouds of dust rising ahead, obscuring whatever lay beyond it. The hostiles were raising a screen, which meant this assault was expected, and would be resisted by armed and ready warriors. They seemed a vast distance off. The attack had begun much too far from the village, and the approach had taken so long that his mounts, already worn from days of travel, were slowing. But he refused to worry about that.

Behind him rode a column containing many troopers who had never been in a fight. They carried fifty rounds of .45 caliber ammunition for their carbines, and another twenty-four rounds for their Colt revolvers. They had an additional fifty carbine rounds in their saddlebags. Each weapon had its uses; both were wildly inaccurate when fired from a running horse.

The Ree scouts peeled off to the left, heading for the Sioux horse herd, and ran into scattered shots from defenders. Reno clamped down hard on his dead cigar. His newly appointed adjutant, Lieutenant Hodgson, pulled up beside him.

"Where's Custer?" he asked.

"He said he'd support us."

"We'll need support. That's a lot of Indians. And they're not running from us, either."

It was true. These Indians, still a mile off for the most part, were swiftly raising dust and running in small groups to either side of Reno's column. A hundred. Two hundred. Three hundred. Beyond counting. Knots and groups, dark dots against green grasses. Swarms. Bright red, bright yellow. White and black. Coppery bodies. Some mounted, some on foot. Some dodging and darting, some stolidly running straight into battle. Some carrying lances. Most armed with bows. Some carrying rifles or muskets that glinted dully. More Indians than Reno had ever before seen. Too many. It was time to form a line.

"Tell them to form a line of battle, Ben. Moylan and French up front, McIntosh in reserve."

The adjutant dashed off, while Reno slowed. He called his striker, McIlhargy, to him. "Find General Custer and tell him the Indians are in front of me in strong force," he said. His striker spurred his mount to the right, where Custer was thought to be. The command sweated through most of another mile without coming under fire, but Reno could see, through the haze, large parties of Indians swarming toward his flanks, right and left, while a body of defenders was gathering dead ahead.

He knew he needed men, far more than he had with him.

"Mitchell," he yelled. The cook pushed his mount forward. "Go to General Custer, off on the right or behind those bluffs, and tell him the Indians are before me, in strong force. You have that? Before me, in strong force."

The cook nodded and spurred his mount.

It was the same message he had sent with the striker, but he meant to get through and get help.

Hodgson returned, and Reno told him to bring up Company G from its reserve position, and take the right side of the line. He would put every last man into the line of battle. Hodgson slipped back again, and Reno saw his reserves swing right and spread into an evenly spaced battle line, each mount well separated from the others, all of it done by the book.

His mouth was so dry that he could barely lick his gummy dead cigar, so he clamped it between his stained teeth.

His horse had blackened with sweat. It was a hell of a hot Sunday. Nothing was gained by a hard gallop now, and he kept his column moving at an easy canter, eating up prairie, a thin band of blue. Now he heard the occasional crack of rifles. The Indians had plenty of arms, including Winchester repeaters, but not much ammunition, and they would be cautious about expending it. That was one thing in Reno's favor, but there weren't many others. Five hundred, six hundred, seven hundred Indians. All over, left and right, mixing with the scouts on the left, driving the scouts away from the village herd.

Damn!

Hodgson looked as taut as a fiddle string, and Reno studied him. The young man hadn't seen much action.

"Lieutenant."

"Sir?"

"Think about what's coming at them, not what's coming at you."

Hodgson smiled and nodded.

Where the hell was Custer? Reno craned his head to the right, and to the rear. He heard and saw nothing, no bugles, no signals, no support. And where the hell was Benteen? The captain and his command had vanished, still hunting outlying villages so that Custer could sweep the whole encampment.

A horse sneezed, stumbled behind him, and then recovered. This was not quite tabletop land, and the command dipped into shallow watercourses and up again. There would be such little dips ahead, and each one could swarm with hostiles. Dust, swarming on the flanks, knots of warriors getting behind Reno's line, dark deadly knots of men against the green of the river brush.

"They're not running, major," Hodgson observed.

Reno pulled his cigar out of his teeth and spat, or tried to. "They're supposed to run. That's in Custer's book. Attack in force, and the redskins scatter."

"See that?" Hodgson asked.

On the right, close to the river and half concealed by green river brush and lofty cottonwoods, a large column of warriors was trotting into a flanking position. They sure as hell weren't scattering. Others were flanking on the left, driving back the Arikaras, who were grossly outnumbered.

There were pops and snaps now, nothing finding its mark, but no firing from the flanks. The Indians between the command and the village were backing slowly, shooting now and then but putting up no great resistance, luring the command forward, giving way, scarcely fighting.

"We're about to be flanked, lieutenant. They're sucking us in."

"I was thinking that. There must be five or six hundred in sight, and more coming."

"Where's Custer?"

"Someone's up on the bluffs across the river, major. Too far away, but I'd guess that's Custer or someone from his command."

Far away, indeed. The figure on the bluffs was so small Reno could barely make him out. "At least they see what the hell we're up against," he said.

He heard a pop, and behind him a man screamed. One wounded. A horse screeched and stumbled. Men yelled. Something whipped across his sleeve. Some of the Indians were very nearly behind the command, on the right. Getting ready to fire at Reno's backsides.

He needed firepower now, and you don't get much of that from horseback. "Hodgson, tell them to halt, dismount, form a skirmish line. Time to start shooting."

This was a familiar maneuver. Every fourth man became a horse holder; the other three deployed in battle formation.

"Pick your targets; watch the flanks, and move forward," Reno said. The company commanders and noncoms led their men forward, step by step, a hundred more yards on foot, two hundred . . . and then men began falling. Reno had heard that terrible sound in many battles, a thump, scream, groan, sob.

"Volleys," he yelled, and a ragged blast from eighty or ninety carbines stopped the flow of the Sioux on the right, but only for the moment. As fast as the men ejected the spent copper cartridge and jacked in another, the Sioux flankers were scurrying toward the side.

"Wheel the right line, face them," Reno called, and the noncoms set to work, swinging Company G toward the flankers along the river.

Where was that damned Custer?

Reno clamped teeth over the cigar, kept his men moving forward, and was met by peppering shots that found its mark here and there. Men fell, and there was no way to help them. Horses screeched. Reno smelled the sweat and stink of his own mount.

Where was the goddamned commander? And Benteen? He no longer had time to send messengers. His untrained men were no longer pushing ahead, but standing and firing, half wildly, missing targets, wasting shots. Jamming fresh cartridges into their carbines. This attack was falling apart.

"Shoot low, shoot low!"

Where was Benteen?

He scanned the horizons. "You see any support?" he asked Hodgson.

"Not a damned thing."

Reno sighed. He hated this, hated to do what he had to do, knew he had no choice. He would soon be surrounded. "Company M, Company F, into the timber."

He lifted an arm and pointed at the dense cottonwoods flanking the river. His lieutenants got the message, and pointed their noncoms toward the woods where Lieutenant Hare had already taken the horses for safety. It was an orderly maneuver, with the volleys keeping the Sioux at bay. But another man fell, and no one could help the wounded.

As fast as they reached the woods, they formed a perimeter, with the horses collected in the center, in an open glade. Here was brush and wood and tree trunks, as well as an old riverbed that made an ideal breastwork. Porter, the surgeon, was working on several wounded who had found their way into the woods.

Where was Custer?

Reno thought he heard a distant volley, but who knew?

He saw to the defense, put men behind fallen logs, started some men to cover the bluffs—where some Indians had climbed in order to shoot down upon the soldiers in the trees.

"How are we on ammunition?" he asked Hodgson.

"I'll find out."

The lieutenant, revolver in hand, trotted off to check with noncoms. He soon was back.

"We're alright for the moment."

"What are our casualties?"

"I'll find out."

It was getting hot in the woods. Clipped leaves filtered down. Some arrows hissed through. The hostiles were within bow range, out in the brush. The scouts slipped in, excited, and joined the rest, firing at will. The men were digging in, hunkering down, throwing up anything that would stop lead. Reno thought they could hold . . . for a while. An hour, maybe. Until help came. In the distance, brought coyly on the zephyrs, came the sounds of another hot fight, volleys, rattle, and then the wind shifted.

Reno wasn't even sure of it, but he didn't have time to wonder what it was. But if Custer was in a fight of his own, that meant that Reno could expect no help from that quarter. He was on his own, with around a hundred surviving troopers and some scouts. And out there, in numbers unfathomable, were ten times that.

And where was Benteen?

# CHAPTER FOURTEEN

RED MEN RUNNING. YOU SEE THEM, YOU DON'T. GROUPS OF THEM burst out, vanish, pop up. Warriors rise, loose arrows, disappear. Popping rifles, silence, snapping, odd quiet moments. Slap of bullets into wood. Clipped twigs drop. Now and then a sally, several dusky savages, howling, driven back by ragged volleys. Always closer, closer and closer. Sweat and smoke, stinking air. Crack and scream, men hit, bloodred blouses. Sobs, white bandages blooming red.

More and more and more and more Indians, hundreds, then maybe a thousand, more than Reno had ever seen at once, wraiths dancing, dodging, diving, creeping, ducking, shooting. Indians pressuring that woods, bullets snapping in from all quarters, no barricade safe, Indians at the rear. Closer and closer.

Where was Custer?

Reno paced, revolver in hand, studied the attacking red men, tried to plug holes, yelled at his company commanders, made sure the noncoms were keeping men from bolting. Steady now, steady. His men lined a shallow embankment, once a riverbed, carbines poking over the top.

"We going to hold them off?" Hodgson asked.

"An hour, maybe. We're flanked now, and there's no going back. Got to keep them from our rear. Any word about the pack train?"

"Nothing."

"Benteen?"

"Vanished from the earth."

"How many men down?"

"Eight, nine."

"We're holding, then." Reno chomped his dead yellow cigar. "I sent two dispatches. Maybe we'll see some blue somewhere. You have any idea where Custer is?"

"Across the river. Varnum saw the gray-horse troop on those bluffs. They saw us. Custer has to know we're in the thick of it."

Reno stared. The cottonwoods extended to the Little Bighorn where the river meandered close to the steep bluffs beyond. A half a mile away, perhaps, loomed a grassy high point, several humps, a crown of naked grassland frowning over this field of blood. A place where a few could hold off many. Maybe he could get another message out, around behind that hill, and over to wherever Custer was. But to think it was to reject it. At the foot of those bluffs, and across the river, the Sioux were thick, and those without rifles were pouring arrows into the command.

"We'll stay here."

"I'm guessing it's ten to one," Hodgson said. "Twelve hundred out there."

"That shouldn't slow down the Seventh," Reno replied.

The lieutenant didn't smile.

Moylan was sending every other man back to the saddlebags for reserve ammunition. Reno watched, knowing that if his men were digging into their fifty-cartridge reserves, they could hold the timber for only another half hour. Time was running out unless the pack train showed up.

Some of the hostiles' arrows and balls were striking the horses, which were gathered in a glade as far as possible from the perimeter. Reno heard screeching and snorting as horses were hit.

He watched Lieutenant DeRudio of Company A hustle some troopers into a defensible thicket and organize several volleys that stopped a dozen warriors in their tracks.

Good.

"I want ten men from Company G to ride with me to the river," he said. "I want a look."

Swiftly, a squad mounted and accompanied Reno on a dash through the timber to a spot where he could see deep into the village, with its endless circles of lodges. He could see even more warriors filtering into timber across the river, concealing themselves in the woods as they slipped forward.

"Stay here: keep them pinned across the river," he told these men. "Don't let them get behind us."

The troopers dismounted, hastily set up some defenses, and held the warriors at bay for the moment.

Reno was facing decisions. He could not hold out here. The damned woods were too big. His men were firing slower and more carefully, a sure sign that they were conserving the cartridges they had left. There was no sign of support. His horses were being hit. They screeched, pitiably. His only hope was to find the rest of the regiment and the safety of numbers.

If the command was to survive, it would have to reach those distant bluffs. He spit out his cigar, summoned Moylan and McIntosh, and told them to mount their men and form in fours: they were going to sally across the river, drive the hostiles out of there, and keep on going to high ground. He sent Hodgson to inform French. They would try to mount the ambulatory wounded and take them, but some might be left behind. Those were the hard choices of war. What other choice was there?

He collected his horse, saw Hodgson trot off to find French, and saw the men pull out of their perimeter and head for the herd. No sooner did the men abandon their lines than the hostiles swarmed in, and what started as an orderly troop movement, even an attack, swiftly fell to bits.

Too damned many Indians. He saw commanders yelling at the troopers: line up, load, fire in volleys! But now the troopers were not listening but heading pell-mell for their mounts, not waiting to form in fours but racing straight for the river, which flowed under a steep muddy bank on the far side, meaning the horses had to claw up six or eight feet of mud to reach level land.

And there the blue-bloused men were dying and horses were floundering and red men were darting close, loosing arrows and balls at shooting gallery range, and escaping unscathed to reload. The water turned red. A man floated facedown, and drifted along with the slow current. It was like shooting ducks.

A rout. Horses whinneying, trying to flail up that muddy bank, slow, bullets picking off men, troopers jolted, tumbled slowly into red water, facedown. Pistol shots, troopers firing point blank at red men in their midst, a bang, Indian down, his head red, another down. Blue shirts moving, some riding hard into the gulch beyond, the only way up those looming cliffs, some helping the wounded, some retrieving riderless horses. A rout but not entirely without discipline.

Reno wanted an opinion from a scout, Bloody Knife: what would the Indians do once the command reached the bluffs? He waved the scout to him. Bloody Knife trotted his horse to Reno. They would have to talk in crude signs; no translator was near.

He pointed to the bluff and the troopers heading that way. He pointed to the Sioux. "What next?" Reno asked.

Bloody Knife started to point, and then his face turned into a mass of red and white, and he fell from his horse, dead. The scout's brains soaked Reno's blouse. Shaken, Reno jerked his horse back, stared, fighting back the vomit in his throat.

He kicked his mount into action. Get to the bluffs, organize a command, charge, drive the devils away.

French's company was no longer a rear guard. There was no one facing the rear, no line volleying, no order or discipline, nothing. French was yelling but his orders had no effect. Men kicked their mounts savagely into the river, clawed up those muddy banks, and died there.

"Form a line!" Reno yelled, but no one heard.

He saw Hodgson try to wrestle the troopers into a line, and then Hodgson lifted out of the saddle, a rag doll, tumbling off his horse.

"Oh, Christ," Reno said.

There was no time. Hodgson lay still, his bosom red with his own blood.

Reno felt the air part; the balls were thick now. He spurred into the river, his revolver barking at red men, and then he angled up the bank, easier passage, found the slippery grass, and spurred his horse up the gully. He fired at another stalking red man until his revolver clicked empty.

His good horse clawed the soft soil and he felt its powerful legs pull him upward, almost jerking him out of his saddle. They were, for the moment, free of assailants, but one look behind told him that the Sioux were finishing off the wounded out on that murderous field.

Moylan and French were ahead. DeRudio had vanished. McIntosh was dead, caught at the river crossing. The surgeon, DeWolf, had died near the river. He thought fifty, sixty men had gained the heights, maybe even seventy, and these were spreading out. Moylan was deploying them into a line. It was no longer a rout.

Reno reached the grassy top, dismounted from his heaving horse, swiftly surveyed the perimeter, saw that the whole place was vulnerable to fire from the east, but there was no choice. The last of the command straggled up the bluffs, momentarily not under fire because the howling Sioux had plenty of coup to count below.

He shuddered, swiftly jacked empty shells from his revolver and reloaded. Six shots. Men were flopped on the ground, seeing to their weapons. The horses were driven into a central basin, along with the wounded.

Men were pillaging the saddle packs for spare rounds, distributing bullets to those who had few. Others were throwing up defenses, killing wounded horses and dragging them into the line, clawing away dirt with knives. There wasn't much ammunition left. One man was trying to pull a jammed cartridge out of his carbine.

Where the hell was Custer?

"French, put your company there," he said.

It was a redundant order. French was ahead of him. The company commanders had worked out their own deployment.

Reno counted men. Seventy-some up here in a place that would require two hundred to make use of the high points. But he saw more blueshirts on foot, scaling the bluff. They were still crawling in.

Scarcely a shot reached these breezy crowns of the hills, but he knew that wouldn't last. And in the hazy distances, out of range, hordes of Indians were on the move.

Where was Benteen? Where was the pack train? Where was Custer?

His men needed little direction; they were deploying well. But all Reno could think of was the fate of Major Joel Elliott in the battle of the Washita, not long before. The major and his men had been left to die when things got too hot for Custer.

# CHAPTER FIFTEEN

RENO SAW BENTEEN, HIS COLUMN AT A TROT, OFF TO THE SOUTHWEST. No sign of the pack train. He folded up his spyglass. Benteen had seen the troops on top of this barren knob and was heading this way, cautiously, his men riding by fours. Benteen's column was still south of the hostiles.

Too far to signal. Benteen might head for Custer, wherever Custer was, and bypass Reno's defensive perimeter.

"Moylan!" he yelled.

The captain rushed up. Reno pointed at the tiny figures far away. "Mount your company. We're going to get Benteen. He may not know we're here."

"Yes, sir," Moylan replied, and dashed to his company, which retreated from the perimeter and formed into a column. They trotted south with Reno, along the bluffs until they attracted Benteen's attention. After a hesitation, Benteen turned his command toward the bluffs, and minutes later his fresh troops ascended a gulch and rode into the hilltop perimeter.

"They'll have the pack train behind them," Moylan said. "Cartridges!"

Benteen rode up, and the combined column headed toward Reno's defensive position. "Where's Custer?" Benteen asked.

"Damned if I know," Reno said. "We haven't seen him. Not a message. Some sharp volleys a while ago off to the north. Pretty hot there."

"What's your situation, major?"

"Bad! Driven out of the valley; they threatened to engulf us. We were flanked. Retreated to those woods. Couldn't hold. Lost a quarter of my men and some scouts, mostly crossing the river there beside those cotton-woods. Heavy hostile force north and west and now east of us. Surgeon DeWolf killed. Lost Hodgson and McIntosh. We're low on ammunition, troopers deep into saddle reserves."

"No Custer?" Benteen stared sharply at Reno. "Washita again?"

Reno shook his head.

"My orders are to come quick, help Custer," Benteen said. "Only he didn't say where. 'Village ahead. Come quick. And bring the packs.' I've got the packs a mile or two back."

"Twenty minutes? Damn!"

"You going to strike out for Custer, major?"

"Not yet; not with empty carbines. We can't go find him with a dozen or twenty cartridges to a man. You have spares; please distribute them to my men."

"Of course," Benteen said.

"I'll send Hare back to cut out the ammunition mules from the pack train and drive them ahead. When we're resupplied we can move."

They reached the knobs and swiftly drove the horses into the basin in the middle that protected them from all sides but the east.

Reno found Lieutenant Hare: "You've got a fresh horse. Quick, go back to the pack train, cut out the ammunition mules, and rush them ahead. We're stuck until we can resupply."

"Yes, sir, right on it, sir."

Reno watched the lieutenant dash south toward McDougall's slow-moving pack train, where an additional twenty-four thousand rounds were being carried by the mules.

Benteen swiftly organized his command: K Company facing north toward a higher ridge that would cause trouble; D Company under Captain Weir facing east across a vast grassy flat, next to Wallace's G Company, which joined to Moylan's A Company facing southeast, and Benteen's H Company along the south-stretching ridge.

Tom Weir approached Reno. "Where's Custer?"

"North. We haven't seen him. He promised to support us and didn't."

"Have you tried to reach him?"

"We were rolled back."

Captain Weir, a tough and gallant Civil War veteran, paced. "We need to find out," he said.

"I intend to. We're low on ammunition and can't do much until the packs come. I've sent Hare back to cut out the ammunition mules and drive them ahead."

"We've heard some hot firing. We've got to reach him. My troops are fresh and armed."

"Not yet. We can't support you," Reno said. "I can't send men into a hot fight with fifteen or twenty rounds."

Weir stalked away, burning.

When Hare rode in with the ammunition, the quartermaster men were slow to move and tended to huddle behind their mules.

"Get them out of there and working," Reno snapped. "Get those rounds out, company by company!"

Wallace nodded and blistered the ears of the packers and those who were lounging around.

They brought three shovels and a few axes, and these were instantly distributed and put to work as men threw up works with anything at hand, including knives and mess plates and tin cups. Others dragged crates and saddles and sacks into the line, anything to stop a bullet. Others dug at the hot dry turf with knives and fingers, trying to erect something, anything to lie behind.

But there was only hot wind, fierce sunlight, and a parching fear that took the moisture right off a man's tongue. The fight seemed distant for the moment, with hardly the crack of a rifle to strike fear into hearts. But some men looked longingly at the river, knowing that a man could die as easily from thirst as from a bullet.

Benteen came up. "What are you going to do about Custer?"

"What's Custer going to do about us?" Reno snapped.

"I would like to probe north."

"After men have some ammunition. It's being distributed," Reno said.

"They have it now. The sergeants have seen to it."

"Where's Weir?" Benteen asked.

"I don't know. He wanted to link up with Custer and I told him to wait." Reno peered around. "Don't see him. Don't see D Company, either, damn him. Edgerly's not here either. The whole damned company took off on a scout."

Benteen grunted. Weir, commanding D Company, was one of Custer's coterie.

"Where were you?" Reno asked, tartly.

"The lieutenant colonel ordered me to ride a left oblique and search the valleys leading off the river, looking for runaways."

"He said nothing to me about it," Reno said.

Benteen wiped away the sweat. "He keeps his purposes to himself. I received a message directing me to keep on searching those valleys. His purpose was plain enough: he was remembering Washita where there were Cheyenne villages strung all along that river that he didn't know about, and those villages got him into trouble. He didn't want to make the same mistake twice. That's how he looked at this, I think: find the villages and drive them ahead."

"That doesn't make sense," Reno said. "He was heading into a big fight. I thought you'd attack from the left flank while I took the center and Custer the right flank. That's classic Custer. Hit the village from all sides."

"The next orders told me to hurry up, bring the packs, and join him. So I tried."

"It took you long enough."

Benteen didn't respond, and turned away. Reno didn't like the angry look on the man's face.

"Where are the rest of the packs?" Reno asked.

"Coming in. They were stretched all over hell and gone. Damned skinners couldn't keep together."

"Are they guarded?"

"McDougall's on it, sir."

Indeed, one by one, laden mules were popping over the crest of the ridge along the south, and being hustled into the basin where livestock and the wounded were collecting. Quartermaster men raced to drop each pack and open it.

"Captain, take over here. I'm going after Hodgson."

"Sir?"

"Take over. You're in command up here for a while. That boy's down there, dead or wounded. If he's dead I want to get his class ring and papers."

"Sir?"

"Detail two or three troopers to cover me."

Benteen stared at Reno, his face crawling with unspoken thoughts. "Yes, sir," he said.

"Good. Keep the troops digging in. There's not a rock or a tree up here for cover."

"The noncoms have it well in hand, major."

Reno headed for the herd in the hollow. Behind him, Benteen shouted commands at two or three men, and shortly Reno was joined by two troopers.

"Come with me," Reno said. "Cover me. I'm going after Lieutenant Hodgson."

They nodded.

Moments later he swung easily into his saddle and the troopers followed, leading spare horses, across the lines, out into the fields of fire, in this case the precipitous gulches leading down to the river where Hodgson's body lay.

There were no Indians now. They had abandoned the woods where they could do no good, to fight elsewhere. It was oddly quiet. His horse jolted as it picked its way downslope.

He found Ben Hodgson lying facedown, unmolested, his blouse browned with drying blood. No life flickered in him. Reno stood a moment, hat in hand, grief running hard within him. Then he rolled Hodgson over, pulled stained papers from his pockets, and tugged hard until the West Point class ring slid off. This he dropped gently into his own pocket.

"Sorry, Ben. I'll get those to your family," he said.

He heard scattered shots. The troopers saw no targets but stood at the ready. Reno slowly mounted, grief burdening him, and the three clambered up the slope again, under the guns of his command.

Benteen greeted him: "Weir went on a scout to the north, to a high point for a look. Took D Company with him. There seems to have been a big fight a few miles north. That's all anyone knows."

"Unauthorized scout," Reno snapped, but his own unauthorized scout came to mind. "All right."

"Packs are mostly in, ammunition's being distributed; now how about letting me probe?"

Reno nodded. "Probe, yes. Link up with Weir. Find Custer if you can, find him if he hasn't quit us." A thunderous anger was building in Reno, a white-hot hatred of Custer for betraying the rest of his command. The man was probably halfway to the safety of Gibbon's column now after things got too hot.

Benteen didn't wait. He was off, shouting orders, summoning troopers, calling for mounts. Sniper fire was raining in now, pops here and there, zings, bullets thumping earth. The Indians were rounding the flanks and settling in for some sharpshooting from every ridge surrounding this knob. No longer could officers or men navigate from one place to another. Reno paced from company to company, and then came to a decision: it was time to move the entire column, wounded and all, toward that sonofabitch Custer.

# CHAPTER SIXTEEN

WEIR'S D COMPANY HAD HEADED NORTH ALONG THE RIDGE AND VAN-
ished. Benteen's command followed. Reno called his men to mount up.
Moylan's A Company had charge of the wounded, and these would be
carried in blankets on foot. It was that or abandon the wounded. There
were eight of them who could not ride, and it would take forty-eight
troopers, six to a blanket, the whole of A Company, to carry them. And
there would have to be a rear guard behind the packers, who were hastily
reloading the mules.

The tides of war had swept past him, and now Reno intended to ob-
tain momentum. There had been hot volleys off to the north, but now
only sporadic firing drifted upon the breezes. They would find Custer, or
rather, chase after him on his flight toward Gibbon's column.

"Mount your companies," Reno called.

He watched troopers abandon their shallow defenses and rush to their
horses while noncoms strove to put order into the maneuver.

"Advance by twos," Reno called.

The troopers twisted north, past a knoll and along a sloping ridge dotted with jack pine. The column looked ragged. Moylan's A Company
walked behind, burdened with the blood-soaked and bandaged casualties.
It was late afternoon but the June sun shone high in the heavens, blistering the earth.

Benteen's fresh troops had ridden smartly north, ready for anything, and looking for Weir and D Company, still farther ahead. The disjointed columns rode a precipitous cliffside laced with gulches, while below the Sioux and Cheyenne were swarming south from whatever had taken place on that smoky crest on the northern horizon. Some were reaching the pine-covered lower slopes and were firing up at the column, while troopers answered as best they could at the fleeting glimpses of the enemy.

But before Reno's battered column could reach Benteen, they ran into Benteen's retreating troops, protected by Lieutenant Godfrey's rear guard. It had gotten too hot up there. What seemed like thousands of warriors were swarming through the jack pine, engulfing the column. Weir, too, had pulled D Troop back and was riding with Benteen's column, his face gray with anger and frustration.

Weir glared at Reno as he rode by, accusation in his face. There had been bad blood between them ever since Reno had brought charges against Weir for drunkenness on duty during the boundary survey. But now there was another kind of accusation filling his eyes: *Too late. Too slow.*

Reno wheeled his column and retreated, by fours, back to the hilltop. A bullet from below blew one of Benteen's troopers out of his saddle as the howling warriors dogged the column every inch of the way. It wasn't a rout this time; the troopers made it to their defensive knolls, and settled into their positions along the perimeter. But now the hostiles had arrived in strength; bullets peppered the command, finding their marks now and then. The hilltop was naked, without breastworks, and vulnerable.

Reno swiftly assessed the site; it was the best available, close to water and defensible if men could dig in. Nothing else was. He had been right all along. Weir and Benteen and their fresh troops had now tasted what Reno had been up against, but from the bitterness in Weir's face it hadn't changed the lieutenant's mind any: all this was Reno's fault.

The rest of that afternoon the clifftop was a perfect hell, and there was no safe place in that barren ground, especially for Moylan's A Company, whose line stretched across the open end of the horseshoe, exposed to the eastern ridges. Reno's commanders ducked and dodged to their former positions, saw to defenses, put the quartermaster troops to work.

They all heard the unique crack of shots from the Springfield carbines that had been in Custer's command. The Seventh Cavalry carbines were being used against them now, which boded ill. The carbines had good range, farther than most of the Indians' repeating rifles, and those bullets were hitting everywhere.

It was almighty dry up there.

"Save your water; don't drink. Suck on a pebble," the noncoms were advising.

Reno stepped aside, pulled his flask from his bosom, lifted it, and swallowed a good slug of fiery whiskey and then another. The flask was nearly drained, and there would be no more. He capped it and put it in its nest. A teamster stared at him.

"Get down," Reno snapped.

The worst trouble lay on the eastern side, Moylan and Wallace's perimeter. And that's where the warriors were dealing death, one bullet at a time, fired by superb marksmen.

"Kill wounded horses and drop them there," Reno commanded.

Stable sergeants pulled wounded horses out of the pack, led them to the defensive line, slit their throats, and let them collapse there. No sooner was a horse down than troopers positioned themselves behind it. Reno stared, disgusted at the bloody business. He hated the destruction of good horseflesh.

Troopers were firing back now, taking aim, conserving their ammunition. They all knew they were in for a siege. One of them lifted a canteen, only to have a bullet yank it from his hands. Water gurgled into the earth.

"No water. Save it!" yelled a corporal.

The sun sank lower in the northwest, blinding troopers guarding the bluffs there. The battle had settled into the slow crackle of sharpshooting. Gunsmoke drifted across the hilltop, mixed with the smell of fear and sweat.

The surgeon, Porter, crawled over to Reno. "Wounded need water, fast, or they'll die," he said.

"Benteen, get a canteen to the wounded," Reno yelled.

Benteen shook his head, but finally found half a canteen and gave it to Porter.

"Men losing blood need water and plenty," Porter said. "They seize up and die."

Reno studied the river below, glinting silver and seductive and beckoning in the late light, wondering how the hell anyone could get down there and live long enough to get back up the hill. He pulled his last stogy from his pocket, bit the end off savagely, and stuffed it into his mouth. He didn't have enough saliva to wet it, but it felt good.

The dying day wrought new crisis. Indians creeping up a draw from the river bottoms almost reached the lines, and only a burst of shots turned them back. Benteen crawled over to Reno: "You've got Indians so close on your side they're pumping bullets into the backside of my lines," he said.

"We'll scare them off," Reno said. "All right, men, get ready. We're going after that bunch."

Reno watched his men turn, look to their carbines, gird themselves for the rush.

"Charge!" he yelled.

Reno ran with the charge, right in the thick of it, forty, fifty yards, to the brink and down, driving scores of howling Sioux before them. Benteen watched from the perimeter.

"Now back," Reno yelled. They had accomplished their purpose. No one was hurt. The Sioux were driven a hundred yards down, and Benteen's line was out of their range. The panting men, too dry to sweat anymore, slowly retreated up the bluff, still pumping an occasional shot down the slope, and settled into their shallow trenches.

He was damned thirsty. The sally had done the job. But the afternoon and evening had taken a terrible toll. Seven more men had been killed and twenty-one wounded that evening, and the moaning of the wounded pierced everyone's ears that night.

Reno wondered what the hell was the matter with himself: Weir had acted on his own to find Custer. Benteen had suggested advancing behind Weir, organized a sally on Reno's side of the perimeter, while Reno had watched passively. He wasn't thinking. He could find no reason for it; he just wasn't thinking, acting, or reacting to danger the way he should be. He was being stupid.

But once Benteen had suggested what to do, Reno put himself in the thick of it, leading that sally and keeping the men steady and bringing them back. Not the whiskey; he couldn't even feel the dram he had downed to steady himself. Not anything, just tired. It was around nine. He had been fighting since two o'clock, nonstop; Benteen and Weir and their command didn't even taste lead or fire a single round until they headed out to find Custer. Maybe that was all there was to it.

When it was too dark to see targets, the Sioux sharpshooters quit, but not without firing an occasional round into the hilltop, just to keep the exhausted command sleepless and worried. Far below, out on the flats, huge bonfires lit the sky, shooting up plumes of orange sparks, and soon drumming reached the ears of the troopers. There was a huge scalp dance going on down there, or worse.

Reno sprang into action: build breastworks, see to the defenses, plug gaps, figure out a strategy. He patrolled the lines, looking for weaknesses. The digging in went slowly for the want of shovels, but in time a few shallow rifle pits were completed, the men never ceasing to protect themselves in any way they could, though some didn't seem to care, or supposed Custer would soon rescue the command.

Reno found slackers among the civilian packers, collared them and told them to drag anything, everything, out to the lines, slabs of bacon, chests, boxes, and above all, to put spare ammunition within easy reach of every company.

"Get out there, get to work, or I'll have your hide," he growled.

Then he called a staff meeting, and one by one the officers trailed in and sat close to him in the thickening darkness.

"We need to reach Custer. It's as dangerous as anything gets. Any volunteers?"

No one volunteered.

"I'll talk to the scouts," said Varnum.

"We need to talk about our tactics tomorrow. We could pull out tonight, in the quietest, darkest time of night, head for the Powder. If we can't hook up with Custer, we should look for Gibbon. That column is due here tomorrow."

"And leave the wounded?" Benteen asked.

"We would have to if that's what the choice is. We have no litters and no spare mounts."

"Never," said Benteen.

"Well, that's my sentiment too," Reno said quietly. "But it had to be considered. It comes down to this: we can get out under cover of darkness, or fight tomorrow. There's going to be some Sioux watching us all night. They're not all at that scalp dance. But we can slide past, I think."

"We don't know where Custer is," Wallace said.

"He's north of us and can't get through," Weir said. "I could see something of that fight. The whole village is between us and him."

"He might try to signal us. He knows where we are," French said.

"Tell the pickets to keep a lookout."

"They'll come at us at first light, and we'd better be dug in because we're going to be hit from all sides, and maybe rushed from all sides." That was Moylan speaking. He had lost several men from his A Company, in its exposed position.

"You're exposed. You got a shovel?"

"We've got one and we're digging."

"I see no need for works," Benteen said. "We'll be out of here before my men get dug in."

The meeting came to very little. They were trapped and surrounded and bone dry and running out of time.

Reno sent a trumpeter to the eminence at the north end of the perimeter, and told him to signal Custer. Maybe the quiet night air would carry that call over the fields and hills and bluffs to the other command. The trumpeter took up his call, the mournful brass-bound notes of "Tattoo" echoing over the hills. After that, the trumpeter played "Taps."

# CHAPTER SEVENTEEN

A LITTLE WHISKEY COMFORTED A MAN AND SUBDUED THE ACHES OF his body. Marcus Reno didn't care who knew he nipped at a flask. His officers sipped, and sometimes shared a flask with him. It was one thing to sip; another to drink too much and impair his command. He had never crossed that line while on duty and never intended to.

That June night was balmy, and he lay on a shelter half that was spread over grass on a protected slope. Men moved freely in the stygian deeps, safe from the searching rifles of the hostiles. One could not ask for much more, save for the want of water. No one had any, except that Dr. Porter kept back a pint for the desperately wounded.

The distant throb of war drums and dancing rose darkly into the night, lancing the peace of every trooper and packer in the hilltop camp. Reno could hear men scraping rifle pits with cups and mess plates, or dragging cases of hardtack into place. Anything to turn a bullet.

Benteen commanded the companies facing east and south; Reno the companies facing west, over the river bluffs, and north. Both men had restlessly walked their lines, tightening them, seeing to discipline. Reno had dressed down some packers who were malingering, and ended up kicking one's hindquarters.

The first sergeants had completed a list of casualties and missing, and Reno knew there were big holes now in every company. Some of the dead had been dragged away from the lines, out of sight as much as possible. There were many more bodies below, near the river. Lieutenant DeRudio was missing and presumed dead, left below somewhere.

Now Reno sat on his shelter half, eyeing the bright stars in clear heavens; it would not rain. Benteen settled beside him in the grass.

Reno pulled his flask and handed it to Benteen. There was little whiskey left.

"Keep it," Benteen said.

"Where is he? You have any idea?"

"He got mauled pretty badly up there and skedaddled. He probably did try to reach us, but there's too damned many Indians. He probably thinks we're all right. Could be clear up the Bighorn linking up with Gibbon's column."

"What'll happen tomorrow?"

Benteen didn't reply for so long that Reno wondered whether he would. Then, "Custer's gone. He's quit us. That means the whole village can work on us. It'll be pretty hot for us."

"Water?"

"We can hold a while. A massed charge by a thousand or more hostiles is what worries me."

"You think Custer's circling around to come for us from the south?" Reno asked.

"We'd know it. We'd see Indian movements to counter him. Maybe even a bonfire, a signal. What we saw all evening until full dark was more and more warriors right here."

Danger had drawn them together, these two officers who had barely been on speaking terms. Reno felt comfortable with Benteen, even though he didn't much care for Benteen's intrigues and politics and harsh judgments. He was a first-rate man in the field, and had won the loyalty of every man under him.

"He's probably writing Libbie," Benteen added.

Reno laughed.

"We need to think about tomorrow," the captain said, drawing Reno back to some planning.

"I have no plan. Either we hold out long enough for Custer or Gibbon to reach us, or we don't. Get some sleep. You'll need it." He watched Benteen clamber to his feet. "Frederick, you fought like a lion today," Reno said. "Thank you."

"Tell it to Terry," Benteen said. "Good night, major."

He vanished into the night. Reno pulled out his flask and sucked it dry. There wasn't another drop of spirits in the whole command.

Far away, the drumming continued, the scalp dance shooting fear into the night like embers. But Reno thought he heard wailing too; plenty of red men had died this day.

He lay back, his eyes upon bright stars, but his mind was clouded with doubts. If he could relive this day, would he have done anything different? He visited the crucial moments, the key decisions. He felt worst about the failed attack. Should he have kept on, riding hard into that village, his men armed only with revolvers because carbines were almost useless at short range?

To think it was to know the answer: that was suicide. Had he failed Custer? No, Custer had failed him, failed to find him and help him, as the man had promised. The other bad moment was the flight to the hilltop, which ended up a rout. But could he have prevented it? The company commanders had not been able to slow down the men, organize a rear guard, keep the swarming warriors—who very nearly reached the column as it fought the riverbank—from killing troopers at will.

Could something he had ordered or done saved Ben Hodgson? Reno could not think of a single thing that any commander could have done differently.

Could he have reached Custer from the hilltop? Not until ammunition was available; it would have been madness to gallop into another fight with only a few rounds per man.

Had anyone failed him?

His mind turned again to Benteen, who had arrived an hour too late. But Reno put that out of his head. Custer had sent the man out on a wild goose chase.

Tom Weir? The captain had taken off on his own and came close to being shot to bits, along with his company.

Reno dozed lightly until around two, when something stirred. He hastened to south, along the bluff, and found a dozen troopers crawling up the slope, shouting their presence so they wouldn't get shot.

They were led by a first sergeant.

"Sergeant, please report," Reno said, yawning.

"We hid in deep brush, sir. Indians everywhere. If we'd been found, we wouldn't have lasted but a few moments."

"Any wounded behind?"

"The wounded are not alive, sir. All killed, stripped, and . . . violated. You would not want to see it."

"Lieutenant Hodgson?"

"You would not want to see him, sir."

"What about Lieutenant DeRudio? He's missing."

"We know nothing of him, sir."

"You bring any water?"

"No, sir. We have no canteens."

Thirteen men safe. Reno sighed. The men were fed hardtack, supplied with ammunition, and directed to their companies. They had no water but most had drunk heartily at the river before ascending.

Back from the dead. The news was whispered from company to company, and men rejoiced.

By two thirty the northeastern horizon was turning blue.

Slowly the heavens lightened, turned murky gray, while the veils of darkness drew apart and distant horizons came into view.

Then the Sioux and Cheyenne started in. A shot from very close, and then a scatter of shots, and then the ping and snap and thump of bullets everywhere, long before full light. A man would take his life in his hands walking from one company's line to another. But both Reno and Benteen were up, patrolling the lines even as the northeastern sky bloomed into color.

Almost at once, Benteen's Company H, defending the southernmost ridge, took casualties because its commander had scorned breastworks. Swiftly, its men dragged whatever lay at hand into shelter, and set to work with the shovels, but while they worked, men died, tumbling silently to the ground, or screaming, or sobbing into death.

Reno wished that Benteen, an excellent soldier, hadn't been full of bravado the night before. Benteen's men were paying for it now, and within a short period, the company was decimated.

It boded trouble.

The first sergeants kept the men down and heads low.

"Don't reply. You'll be shot. Let them waste their rounds," they advised.

Another man's rifle had jammed; the extractor had pulled off the head of the copper cartridge leaving a tube stuck in the chamber. The cursing trooper tried to claw it out with a knife.

"Find another carbine for the man," Reno ordered, not sure there were any.

The sharpshooters on the higher ridges to the east commanded the whole hilltop, but at a thousand yards. They were good at it, too. When their rifles barked, men died. One ridge to the northeast was the source of murderous fire as the warriors lying in the grass picked off men, one by one by one as the June sun burned away from the horizon and threw an eerie orange glow over the hilltop.

Now and then groups of Sioux or Cheyenne rushed the line, only to be driven back by disciplined volleys. But usually one or another soldier was hit, and Dr. Porter had another injury to treat in his perilous hollow.

Reno studied the horizons looking for Custer, looking for guidons, listening for bugles, wanting to see the blue column riding by fours, wanting to see the Stars and Stripes, fringed with gold, wanting to see a general's pennant flapping in the bright breeze.

His men had no more moisture in their body to sweat. Porter told him that unless the wounded got water right away, they would die.

And still Major Reno waited through the hot fierce morning of June twenty-sixth.

But he heard no bugles. And no blue-bloused army appeared, not even in mirages riding in ghostly procession across the white sky, as the heat built and men grew desperate for cool, cool water.

# CHAPTER EIGHTEEN

THE WORD FROM DR. PORTER WAS UNAMBIGUOUS: WATER, NOW, OR the wounded will die fast.

The rest of the command was suffering grievously in the hot June sun.

Reno studied that seductive river at the foot of the bluffs, where abundant cool water flowed steadily toward the Bighorn. "We need water right now," he said to Benteen. "See about volunteers."

The captain stared. "That bluff's crawling with Indians. I don't know if we'll get any volunteers."

"See about it!"

Benteen ducked and dodged his way south, toward his own company, spreading the request as he went.

Amazingly, there were volunteers, enough to sally down the closest gulch to water, fill whatever came to hand, and maybe return alive—some of them.

Empty canteens and kettles were swiftly handed down the lines to the spot overlooking the gulch where the volunteers were collecting. Reno admired those men. They would race into the maw of a hundred rifles, collect what water they could, and race back again.

The whole command watched. Their hopes lay with fourteen volunteers and four others who had agreed to stand up, draw fire, and return fire while the water party slid and careened down those arid, hot slopes.

Reno thrust his tongue around his own cottony, dry mouth, so dry he could not even make spit. Men had tried everything, even sucking at the pulpy insides of prickly pear cactus, but nothing helped.

Benteen raised and lowered an arm. Four riflemen from H Company jumped to their feet. Indian fire crackled; the foursome returned fire wherever they saw puffs of smoke. The volunteers, pails and buckets and canteens rattling loudly in the morning heat, leapt into the gulch, skidded, and slid downward.

The hostiles understood and began sniping at the water party; bullets snapped close, then one was wounded and another. The water party wasted no time fighting back, but careened downward, almost faster than the hostiles could shoot, reached the river, scooped water into the kettles, plunged canteens under, and struggled slowly uphill carrying water, their bodies undefended.

One slumped, fell, died, spilling his cooking kettle. Another, saddler Michael Madden, caught a bullet at the ankle and fell. The rest grabbed him and pulled him along, even as the Sioux made it hot. The standing sharpshooters rained bullets against the hostiles, evening the score a little.

The volunteers returned with water, and a cheer erupted along those thin, blue lines. The first canteen went to Dr. Porter, there in the hollow with his suffering wounded.

The top sergeants took over, passing canteens along the lines and growling when anyone took a second swallow. Men took one and passed the precious water along. There wasn't much of it, not for over three hundred men, and nothing for horses and mules. But there was enough to stave off madness.

Porter looked to the wounded volunteers. Six had been hit, none gravely save for Madden. One had died down below. They were all heroes, along with the riflemen who had drawn fire away from the water party.

Reno dodged his way to them.

"You're brave men. The entire command thanks you. You'll be remembered," he said. "You are heroes and every man in the command will never forget."

Then he took his own drink, wanting badly to swallow many more times. He knew now they could get to the river; not cheaply, not without loss, but unless the hostiles congregated there, they could get water. The Sioux and Cheyenne preferred to fight from the eastern grasslands where they could command barren ridges from which they could shoot down upon the soldiers.

All that hot, weary, ominous morning the rifle fire continued, and many of those shots the troops recognized as the familiar deep-throated bang of the Springfield carbine. Whatever had happened to Custer's command, it had left weapons and ammunition behind.

The toll continued to mount; Dr. Porter had a procession of new casualties to treat. And he faced a daunting task: Madden's shattered ankle would go to gangrene in that stinking hot hollow unless his leg below the knee was amputated at once, right there, without so much as a fire with which to cauterize the wound.

Porter administered some medical brandy to dull the pain and set to work. Madden took the surgery quietly, and won himself another slug of brandy from the surgeon when it was over. The news spread through the command, and men cheered.

Then, midmorning, the steady fire from the warriors slackened noticeably, and Reno sensed change in the air, though he did not for a moment suppose the assault was ended. Some of the Indians were observed retreating from the ridges, heading toward the huge village. Indeed, things were stirring in the village, though no one on the hilltop could say what was transpiring.

Not that much had changed. If fewer bullets were coming, that did not mean that sharpshooters had abandoned the ridges. There were hostiles out there trying to pick off the whole command. Reno himself, walking briskly through the command, felt the whisper of a bullet, and ducked.

"Damned if I want to be killed . . . I've been through too many fights," he told Lieutenant Godfrey.

But something was happening down at that village, and Reno didn't know what. Lieutenant Varnum approached the major with an idea: maybe it was time to send out some scouts with a dispatch, assuming he could find some who'd go and try to locate Custer.

"Good. Do it."

"Write what you want to write, sir, and make four copies."

Reno did, at once, addressing them to General Terry. He described his whereabouts and condition and casualties and the fact that he had lost contact with Custer. Varnum talked two Rees and two Crows into making the effort, but they didn't go far beyond the defenses before returning. The country was still thick with Sioux.

The village was on the move. That much Reno knew. Pickets and scouts could see the squaws dropping the lodge covers and loading ponies, and hurrying away, amid a great exodus westward out of the valley and toward the distant mountains. By four that afternoon the sharpshooters on the ridges had vanished, or were silent, and a few men began to stir, after hugging the grassy wastes for two days.

Reno kept the command on the hilltop, but moved it closer to water, and waited. The size of the village awed every man on that cliff top; thousands of ponies, many dragging travois, hauled thousands of households away from the valley of the Little Bighorn. An endless line of women, children, old people, dogs, colts, mules, and mounted warriors paraded across the distant horizons, so many they were beyond counting. This was no ordinary village; this was the larger part of a *nation* abandoning its homeland to the enemy, going who knew where?

"Jaysas, will you look at that," Godfrey said. "Is that what we ran into? We're lucky to be alive."

Reno pulled his battered dead cigar from a blouse pocket and jammed it into his still-parched mouth. He thought better while chewing on the butt of a cigar.

The Sioux leaving for some reason, and that had to be the approach of Gibbon's column. They were heading west, not south; not toward Crook, who was off to the south somewhere. Gibbon was to meet Custer this very day, the twenty-sixth of June, on the Bighorn River, and Gibbon's men were no doubt not far off. And no doubt had Custer and his shattered command with him.

"All right, we'll send water parties down. Take the horses by fours to water and bring them back here," Reno ordered. "Doctor the horses, sort out the injured ones."

Benteen approached. "Are you planning, sir, to stay up here?"

"For the moment, captain. It's a place that can be defended, and I don't know of any other. We have fifty-two litter cases here, and no way to take them down. There's not a litter in the command and no way to fashion any."

Benteen nodded. "They're pulling out. Look at 'em. That line stretches from the village over the brow of those benches miles to the west. Is it possible that we were engaging two or three thousand warriors?"

"That many, yes."

"You're looking for Custer?"

"Varnum's on it. He's been unable to talk the scouts into riding, but I think they'll try now."

"We were luckier than Elliott," Benteen said.

Reno let it pass. Custer's abandonment of Elliott was ever on Benteen's mind and topped his list of grievances against the commander of the Seventh.

"We've got to signal. Build fires. Get a man out to that high ground where Weir had his look at the village."

"I'll see to it."

Now at last the more daring men sat up, and not even the cautioning of the noncoms could keep them lying low. But no bullets sang into the command. Some few even stood, waited for the details to bring water, stretched, visited with each other.

"You look sharp for the enemy," yelled one top sergeant who was not about to let his men wander.

But the fight was over. They would soon hook up with Custer, and there would be a lot of recounting of what happened. Custer's men would pull out pipes and tell about their sharp and bloody fight and friends lost; Reno's men would pull out pipes and tell about the siege of their hilltop.

And Reno knew he would have to justify his retreat to timber and up to the top of the bluffs, and that he would see the disdain in Custer's eyes once again. It irked him. It was Custer who should do the explaining: why hadn't he come to Reno's aid?

# CHAPTER NINETEEN

THAT MELANCHOLY EVENING OF THE TWENTY-SIXTH, RENO SET ABOUT to put his command in order while he waited for Gibbon's column. He sent men down to the river crossing to recover the body of Lieutenant Hodgson and bury the brave officer carefully. He had horses and mules taken by turns to water, grained, and attended to. He ordered that the dead on the hilltop be buried. He moved the defense perimeter south, closer to water but still high. He sent Varnum's scouts out to look not only for Sioux who might be lurking about, but also for the column.

The men rested as the night deepened. The worst was over, but Reno and his officers would not lower their guard.

That night, Lieutenant DeRudio came back from the dead, along with Private O'Neill. They had hidden south of the battle area and had seen the huge village pass them by, only five hundred yards distant from their hiding place. The procession was three miles long and a half mile wide, a great dense mass of horses drawing travois, men, women, and children.

The mystery of Custer's whereabouts deepened, but Major Reno believed that would be resolved when Gibbon's column appeared.

The next morning, June twenty-seventh, he wrote General Terry:

> *I have had a most terrific engagement with the hostile Indians. They left their camp last evening at sundown due south in the direction of the Bighorn Mountains. I am very much crippled and*

*cannot possibly pursue. Lieutenants McIntosh and Hodgson and Dr. DeWolf are among the killed. I have many wounded and many horses and mules shot. I have lost both of my own horses. I have not seen or heard from Custer since he ordered me to charge with my battalion (three companies) promising to support me.*

*I charged about 2 P.M. but meeting no support was forced back to the hills. At this point I was joined by Benteen and three companies and the pack train rear guard (one company). I have fought thousands and can still hold my own but cannot leave here on account of the wounded. Send me medical aid at once and rations.*

> *—M. A. Reno*
> *Seventh Cavalry*
> *As near as I can say I have over one*
> *hundred men killed and wounded.*

RENO SUMMONED TWO OF VARNUM'S REE SCOUTS AND TOLD THEM TO seek out the column, and if they ran into Sioux, to work around the hostiles and reach Terry. But the messengers returned soon thereafter accompanied by one of Terry's scouts, Muggins Taylor, who carried a note from Terry to Custer saying that Crow scouts had reported that Custer had been whipped but that Terry didn't believe it.

So Gibbon's column was near. Reno sent Lieutenants Varnum and Hare with some soldiers to find the column and direct it to the hilltop redoubt. Reno could only wait. Then, in the middle of that morning of the twenty-seventh of June, General Terry, Colonel Gibbon, and their staffs reached Reno's command, riding up the gulch from the river.

"General!" Reno said, welcoming Brigadier Alfred Terry and his command. They looked gray from hard travel.

Reno stared up at faces so solemn, countenances so grave, that he knew the news was very bad.

Terry slowly dismounted and handed his reins to his aide de camp.

"You have no news of Custer?"

"None, sir."

"You would not know, then, that his entire command lies on a ridge three or four miles north."

"Custer? Entire command?"

"To the last man, major."

Reno stared, pulled off his straw hat, and braced his legs to keep his knees from buckling under him.

"It is such a sight that I would never hope to witness, major." Terry's voice coarsened and then broke. He spoke harshly, words spitting from his mouth like lead balls, his gaze fixed on some distant slope. "His men lie naked, scattered over a broad area of slope and ridge, with about fifty gathered around the brave general at the crest of a low hill there. He lies only a few feet from his brother, whose body has been so ruined by those devils that only a certain arm tattoo identifies him."

Reno felt the air in his lungs hang there. The news paralyzed his body.

"We learnt much of your story riding this way, guided by your officers, major. We rode over the debris of a village beyond counting, larger than any ever imagined. And its warriors took our brave Custer from us, and every brave man."

The news rocked Reno and his men. They could hardly fathom news so terrible. Custer *dead*. His entire battalion *dead*. Dead, stripped, mutilated.

Reno sighed, turned toward the peaceful horizons, and felt sorrow and dread and revulsion steal through him.

"We have had a bad time too, sir, but not like that."

"I know you have, major. As we rode up these bluffs from the valley, we saw your dead, all of them stripped and butchered in a most ghastly manner."

"We have over a hundred dead and wounded, sir. Most of the wounded are litter cases, lying yonder. We need medical help."

Terry stared at the distant rows of bloody, bandaged soldiers. "Oh, oh," he said. He turned to an adjutant, nodded, and the young man raced off.

"I shall want your story entire, major. Show us this place, and we will follow along with you."

Reno waited for the commanders to dismount, and then slowly, painfully, led them around the hilltop, pointing to the ridges where Sioux sharpshooters laid down their deadly fire, pointing to the shallow rifle pits scraped out with knives and axes and mess plates.

He pointed down upon the sunlit flats, far below. "I attacked in good order, sir, about there. When it became plain that the hostiles were in strong force, I put my reserve company into the line, and we proceeded forward in a skirmish line right about there, beyond those trees. When it became plain that we were being flanked, right and left, probably five or six hundred by then and more running up, our only chance was those woods there . . ."

Terry and Gibbon listened gravely, following the battle as Reno's voice and pointing hands unfolded it to them.

They came to the hollow where the wounded lay in orderly rows, some lost to consciousness, others weeping, others groaning.

Terry removed his forage cap, and Reno saw the man's tears streaking his graying whiskers.

There was First Sergeant William Heyn, of Company A, his torso wrapped in bloody bandaging. Beyond was Sergeant Weihe, of Company M, staring at nothing but the sky, his legs wrapped in brown-stained bandages. Next was a private, Newell, his head wrapped, his left leg rising and falling. And beyond, the scout, White Swan, his buckskin leggings soaked in caked blood, and over a way, Privates Holmstead, Foster, and Deihle, Company A, their torsos naked save for swathes of filthy bandaging. Henry Black and John Cooper, privates with Company H, lay with eyes closed, mouths open. Near him was the heroic saddler Michael Madden, one leg a bloody stump, his gaze turned away from the burning sun.

"There, sir, is a brave man who lost a leg getting water for us under heavy fire," Reno said.

Terry knelt, clasped the saddler's hand. Madden managed a smile.

They walked among these suffering men, laid in rows, unprotected from the ruthless June sun.

Terry found Dr. Porter changing the dressing of Private Cooney of Company I, unconscious and plainly a man in desperate condition.

"Thank you, doctor," Terry said. "Thank you."

The doctor nodded, but continued to snip away foul bandaging stained by suppurating wounds. "I need supplies and surgeons or mates," he said brusquely.

"It is coming as fast as we can bring up the column."

The surgeon nodded. Reno knew from the man's pallor that Porter himself was near collapse.

"How many spades did you have here?" Terry asked.

"Two. And some axes."

"These rifle pits. It's amazing."

"Men do what they must, with cups, knives, and fingers."

"Was there any alternative defense position?"

Reno beckoned. "We'll ride, and you'll see."

He soon led the commander of the Department of Dakota out the ridge toward that high point where Tom Weir had tried to find and reach Custer. They followed the path Benteen had taken with his command; the path Reno had taken, once he put his shattered command in order and distributed ammunition from the packs.

"Not here, definitely not here," Terry said.

They reached the bluff that fell precipitously to the north and west. "Weir reached this point, sir. And Benteen also. But it got too hot for them. The Sioux were swarming this way, threatening to cut them off. Apparently the Indians had . . . completed their fight with Custer, and now we faced the brunt of it. We made it back to our hill and dug in for a siege."

"There was no way to reach Custer? With seven companies?"

"Benteen's three fresh companies, sir. Mine had been shot up badly, lost a third, and we were low on ammunition until the packs arrived.

Another fourteen or fifteen men were missing. We took our wounded when we came this way, each on a blanket carried by six men on foot.

"That task consumed all of those left in Company A, leaving me with three fresh companies, Benteen's men, two badly shot-up companies from my battalion with many wounded horses, not enough mounts for everyone, and the rear guard with the packs. We had less actual strength than Custer's five fresh companies.

"But Weir and Benteen tried to reach Custer and were nearly engulfed; they turned back and were retreating when I came up with what was left my battalion, the wounded, and packers."

Terry nodded. "So you never got there."

"Sir, we were expecting him to reach us, as he promised. 'Attack and I'll support you,' he said. We had no idea . . ."

"You heard the Custer battle?"

"A little, earlier. We knew he was in a hot fight. We couldn't see him. Weir planted a guidon on that bluff so our position would be known to Custer. But then we heard nothing, and soon we were fighting for our lives."

Terry's intelligent gaze measured distances, calculated strategies, and finally came to rest on Reno. He nodded.

They turned and rode back. Below, carrion birds were feasting on something. The foulness of death hung in the air. The rot and stench of dead horses and mules hung over the hilltop.

They returned to the trenches.

"Major, it's time to bury the dead," Terry said. "We'll bivouac down on the flat, there, about where you charged the village. You'll want to detail men to the hillside where Custer fell. We'll lend you shovels. Call on me and Colonel Gibbon for whatever you need. And do begin a report."

Reno saluted.

His men would bury their friends.

# CHAPTER TWENTY

IT FELL TO THE SEVENTH TO BURY ITS DEAD IN THE HARD YELLOW CLAY of the Little Bighorn. Major Reno threw Varnum's scouts out wide to alert the command against surprises, and detailed each company to look to the fate of one of the lost companies.

The sight that greeted them on that hill, that June twenty-eighth, afflicted the heart of every surviving man. Custer's command lay scattered along the ridge, white bodies in trampled green grasses, each corpse mutilated, smashed, brutalized often beyond recognition. Some would go to their graves unrecognized, beyond identification.

But most they knew. Men they had trained with, talked to, shared mess with, fought beside, brawled against, prayed with at many a Sunday retreat, lay lifeless. Not just lifeless, for the villagers had violated the dead so that they might never rest in peace.

Reno, on a commandeered horse, rode through the killing fields, followed the retreat of Custer's battalion, saw where each company had made its stand, where it had volleyed, retreated, loaded, and volleyed again. A fresh breeze blew the scent of death away, leaving only the tang of sagebrush in the warm air. It was a perfect summer day, for those who lived.

Terry and Gibbon and their staffs continued to ride the battlefield while Reno and his beleaguered Seventh borrowed shovels, chopped shallow trenches in the hard earth, and laid their comrades to rest with barely enough cover to keep the wolves away.

Everywhere officers with pencils and pads of paper were recording names, identifying remains, hunting for missing officers, driving a stake into the ground where each officer fell. They wrote a name on a scrap of paper, stuffed the paper into an empty cartridge, and drove the cartridge into the stake marking the grave.

Mystery hung in the air. What had happened? How had it happened? Who was there to tell the tale? Somewhere, off in the shrouded south, were thousands of men and women and children who knew exactly what had happened and had participated in it all. They would tell their tales to one another and dance to their great triumph, and sing their songs.

But for those white men on the field of battle, aliens in this wilderness, there was only the silence of the dead, and the few clues that scuffed grass, piles of expended cartridges, dead horses, and broken bodies could supply. What had happened was scarcely imaginable; it was so improbable that soldiers stared, unbelieving, refusing to countenance the evidence of their own eyes. This could not happen. The savages had not the means to achieve this.

Men vomited. Others sat down in the grass and sobbed. Others could not be induced to shovel, even when top sergeants yelled at them. But most of the Seventh worked slowly, fearfully, doing what had to be done, ever afraid that the demons would return and kill the rest.

The troopers found several wounded cavalry mounts, heads hanging low, suffering from injuries beyond repair, and these they put down. Yet one remained. Captain Keogh's Comanche, seven times wounded but proud of eye and determined to heal itself.

Lieutenant Varnum gently led Comanche to the major.

"Sir, this horse is different. He was the captain's. We want to take him with us, keep Comanche as our own. He is the spirit of our regiment," Varnum said.

Reno studied the hurting animal and nodded. "He is that. Let him live. He alone survives. He will be taken care of for the rest of his days, and I will so order it. One life has been spared."

So Comanche was led away by the saddlers and his wounds were dressed. Troopers came to him just to see him, to touch him, to wonder what his eyes had seen, to remember the feisty Irish Captain Keogh, who fell with Custer.

Reno watched while his men cut into the clay with spades and laid George and Tom Custer side by side in a deeper grave. The commander had not been brutalized, save for a slash on his thigh. A bullet wound through his chest probably was not fatal, but one through his skull certainly was. Reno pulled off his straw hat when the men finally shoveled clay over the remains. A hasty burial for the commander as well as the rest. Gallant warriors both. There was no time.

Reno's wounded were carried, one by one, down from the hilltop to a field hospital on the flat operated by Dr. Porter and surgeons from the Montana Column. Flies swarmed, plaguing the doctors, maddening the stricken. A similar hospital had been improvised for the wounded horses and mules, and there the saddlers set to work on each trembling animal, cleaning wounds, scaping off hordes of black flies, packing the raw red flesh while the animals laid back their ears, screeched, bit, groaned piteously.

Some troopers were detailed to bury Reno's own men, those lost at the crossing of the Little Bighorn en route to the bluff. Reno rode his bay horse there, watched silently while his troopers laid their tentmates, their company mates, their messmates into the moist bottomland near the river. There was so much death that it numbed hearts and souls. Men shoveled impassively, looking no one in the eye.

Men were silent that day, locked within their own thoughts, aware of the thin thread of fate that had detailed them to survive, rather than die, in the valley of the Little Bighorn River.

There was something else hanging in the air: every man alive wondered by what virtue he had survived, and whether his very breath of life was a mark of dishonor among the gallant, brave dead. Whether the life he yet enjoyed was not a sign of cowardice rather than a sign of honor.

It was not rational; they were fated to live because Custer had chosen the companies he wanted with him, and because Major Reno had sent them to that bluff where they held off thousands of the hostiles.

And yet the feeling that weighed in each living survivor didn't need to be rooted in reason; it flourished in the bosoms of the Seventh because honor had fallen upon the dead; honor and glory and esteem. The dead were magnificent soldiers, fighting to the last breath; the living . . . were only the living.

Reno felt it and angrily pushed it aside. He pulled a fresh cigar out of his blouse, lit it, drew and exhaled a great blue cloud of smoke, the sweet scent of tobacco in his nostrils cleansing the stench of death. But it wasn't just loose emotion floating through him; fellow officers from Gibbon's column, from the Seventh Infantry and Second Cavalry, who had been helping to identify the dead officers of the Seventh, sometimes paused and stared at the living; at Reno, at French and Varnum and Hare and Moylan, at Wallace and DeRudio.

Tom Weir, Custer's close friend, glared, and Reno knew the man's thoughts. He did not like what he saw in the faces of those fellow officers who wandered the fields, who did not congratulate him for saving the remnant of the command, who did not commend him for his tactical retreat to the only place where he could defend, for keeping the entire Seventh from perishing. No, they stared and said nothing, all except Terry, who that day had thrown an arm around Reno's shoulder and walked with him.

But even then, these walks were interrogations: where had Benteen been? Why was Benteen so slow? What were Reno's orders? What were Benteen's orders? What had Custer's plan of attack been? Had Custer scouted the terrain? What did he know? Why hadn't he waited for Gibbon's column? Had he been discovered? When and how did Custer know?

"I would like your permission to talk with your staff officers, major," Terry said, always the soul of courtesy.

"Of course, general. They will all have their reports."

Thus Reno often saw the general conferring with the living: with Benteen, with Varnum, with Weir, with French, with Hare and DeRudio and Wallace. Terry, the former lawyer turned military man, would not quit until he had a thorough knowledge of everything that had transpired those two terrible days.

Surely some of them would tell Terry that because of Reno, men lived to fight another day; because of Reno, they were not drawn into the village, engulfed, and destroyed. Because of Reno, they were not flanked and destroyed from behind.

Terry was sharing everything he learned with John Gibbon, the eagle-eyed commander of the column from Montana, intended only hours earlier to be one of the jaws of Terry's pincers.

By the soft and melancholy evening of the twenty-eighth, the exhausted survivors had buried their dead in shallow graves that would not stay predators for long, but there was no time for more. Men nibbled at miserable field rations, beans and hardtack and bacon, drank coffee, and stared at misted horizons, half expecting the Sioux nation to reappear.

Men longed for a raging storm that would wash this land, wash their bodies, wash away the memories engraved on their souls. Some were mad, some weeping, some in a daze, some delusional, driven beyond sanity by what they saw, and Reno knew that some part of his command would be found unfit for service. Some sang to themselves. But most stared silently. Spoken words were very scarce that long June twilight.

The Second Infantry was improvising litters and guarding the field. Each of the wounded would have to be carried to the *Far West,* Captain Marsh's riverboat that would ascend the Bighorn as far as it would be safe to do so. The world awaited the awful news, which would arrive just in time for the hundredth birthday of the Republic. No time. Terry's task was not done. There was a war on, and the hostiles had to be subdued. The Seventh would continue to fight, and its death toll would not prevent it from more service in the field.

The staff officers of the Second Cavalry and Second Infantry clung to their own commands, and did not visit with the survivors, as if the remaining men of the Seventh might disturb their dreams or contaminate their vision. Reno had moved his base away from the hilltop and to the south—but still up above the valley of death—and as the twilight thickened his command collected there, each lost in a desolation beyond anything they had ever endured.

Reno was edgy. There might be criticism. He knew well that the Seventh had been torn into factions by Custer and those who scorned him, and he knew that division would reappear worse than before, would tear at him. He was the commander of the Seventh now, for a while, while it remained in the field. And he would take the heat when senior officers, and Congress, and the president, inquired into every detail of what had transpired, and he would tell them that he was proud of everything he had done on that field of fire.

Were the men grateful? Undoubtedly. They were alive, drawing breath. Their close friends were gone forever. Perhaps they would support him. Would his officers? What would French and Hare and Wallace and Moylan say? Godfrey? DeRudio?

He lit a panatela, puffed twice, and threw it away. He paced the flat where his battered companies lay about in utter silence, stalked through twilight and then dusk.

A few enlisted men smiled. None dared talk to him because they couldn't without their sergeant's permission. But no rule prevented a smile as they sat there. And some did smile, a greeting filled with thanksgiving and appreciation.

"God bless you, sir," said one.

Heartened, Reno returned to his simple field tent and pulled out a pad of notepaper. It was time to write his report.

# CHAPTER TWENTY-ONE

RENO HEARD ABOUT THE PETITION FROM BENTEEN.

"The sergeants are getting up a petition among the enlisted men. It seems they want the president to raise you to Custer's rank, and me to your rank, and have us command the Seventh."

"I am honored," Reno said.

"Well don't be. It's humbug. Neither Sherman nor Sheridan will go along with it. Half those men can't sign their own names anyway."

The major was touched. Some of the men in the command, especially the sergeants, knew that their lives had been preserved by Reno and Benteen, and that the Seventh might well have been demolished entirely if it had been in other hands. It was plain enough: if Reno had continued his charge he and his battalion would have been wiped out, like Custer. And then the triumphant warriors would have destroyed Benteen for good measure, and made off with the pack train, with all its ammunition. So they were doing what little an enlisted man could do.

They were all busy: usable debris from the village and the hilltop defense was being burned to render it useless. Officers were recording the dead and the injured, or running scouts far and wide, to prevent more trouble. At last Reno attempted a muster to determine his actual casualties. Even then, with all the first sergeants in Custer's command dead, he could not be sure. But he reckoned 260 dead, 52 wounded. The Seventh had been cut in half.

The wounded posed a dilemma. They could not be carried for more than short distances even by six or eight men handling a blanket. But Gibbon's infantry officers were solving the problem, building litters from lodgepoles and horsehide peeled off of dead mounts. These could be hung from packsaddles between mules, and the wounded moved in relative comfort, without exhausting the cavalrymen.

General Terry dispatched couriers to find the *Far West* and report to Captain Marsh that the boat would be carrying many wounded and should be prepared to receive them. Then, without further waiting, he put the battered column into motion late on the afternoon of the twenty-ninth day of June, and it walked and dreamed and stumbled its way north from the fields of blood, leaving behind friends and colleagues.

Tenderly, they led the valiant Comanche, sole survivor of the slaughter, in their midst, with great veneration and a wreath of wildflowers over its mane. Heaped upon the brow of that noble horse was the honor and glory of the Seventh Cavalry.

The low sun glared through a summer haze, and men's minds were lost upon distant shoals. A few turned back to look to the toothed and shadowed hills, and saw only flights of crows, while others discerned ghostly images in the haze, spirits of the dead, beginning their long and lonely walk through the land of ever-midnight.

Reno, now under the command of Colonel Gibbon, rode in solitude. He had not been a sociable man since Mary Hannah's death, and now he surrounded himself with invisible walls. The officers left him alone. He did not feel the hero, but he did hope for the command of the regiment.

All his adult life he had been a soldier; the army was his home and his refuge. The esteem of his colleagues was his food and wine. The soldier's ways were the ways of his heart, second nature now. The record he wrote for himself during the war of secession had been gallant and won him accolades from such men as Generals Sherman and Sheridan. Now, he knew his professional skill had spared the command further disaster. He felt proud. He had been a good and savvy soldier.

The regiment was actually still under the command of Colonel Samuel Sturgis, whose son, that bright light, Lieutenant James G. Sturgis, lay unidentified, somewhere near Custer. But Sam Sturgis was not a field commander, and out in the field the regiment would be in the hands of the next ranking officer, who might be himself if he were promoted for gallantry here. Maybe out of all this grief that would come to him.

At first he avoided thinking such things, but the sergeants certainly were, and the petition they were getting up addressed the issue, and so he too thought about a promotion as the weary column toiled down the Little Bighorn River.

Reno was invited to ride beside General Terry.

"Pull along beside me, major. I've been preparing dispatches about all this sad business. Here's what I plan to convey in confidence to General Sheridan. As far as I can untangle all this, I believe George Custer labored under the idea that the Indians would scatter, and so divided his command to round them up before they did, and attacked before getting his men up. The result was destruction by detail. . . . That's what I'll say for the moment. You're the senior surviving officer and I do not yet have your report, which I trust you are working on. Have you anything to add or subtract?"

"No, sir."

"Do you endorse this view?"

Major Reno picked his words carefully. "Sir, George Custer fought gallantly according to his lights."

Terry smiled. "You are a gentleman as well as an officer."

Reno fell back to his regiment feeling that there was more to the meeting than sharing the contents of a dispatch. And he felt he had successfully negotiated some shoals. The old divisions within the command were common gossip, especially the estrangement of Custer and Benteen.

Gibbon, discovering that the wounded rested comfortably in their litters, pushed north deep into that June evening, wanting to make time. The entire command still faced the summer's business of finding the hostiles and subduing them and bringing them to their reserves, and the disaster at the Little Bighorn did not alter the purpose or intention of the columns.

They reached the *Far West* late in the night, having been guided by scouts who knew how to traverse the stygian darkness. The vessel was emblazoned with light to show the way. The amazing Captain Marsh had pushed the shallow-draft boat to the absolute limit of navigation at the confluence of the Bighorn and Little Bighorn Rivers, and there he waited and prepared for his suffering passengers.

By lamplight, Reno discovered that the rivermen and the infantry guarding the boat had cut bountiful native grasses and laid them tenderly over the deck to receive the wounded, and in short order these suffering men were settled on the deck of the steamer, given better food and medical attention than they had in the field, and were comforted. Somehow the shadowed white boat lying in placid and shimmering waters seemed like a home to them all, an outpost of the world they had come from, with glass in its windows, railings around the decks, unseen flags hanging from masts that probed the night sky.

General Terry would go with them. Reno and the Seventh would remain with Gibbon's column and make their way to the Yellowstone, and a bivouac where they could be refitted for combat.

The next noon, after those troopers had been settled as gently as possible on that deck and Terry's staff was stowed aboard, the general turned to Marsh, and spoke with gravity: "Captain, you're about to start on a trip with fifty-two wounded men aboard. This is a bad river to navigate and accidents are likely to happen. I ask of you that you use all of your skills, all of the caution you possess, to make the journey safely. Captain, you have here the most precious cargo a boat ever carried. Every soldier here who's suffering from wounds is the victim of a terrible blunder."

Major Reno listened quietly. He concurred with Terry in ways he could never give voice to. He shook hands with the general and hastened down the gangway to the grassy shore.

Then they were off. Black smoke billowed from the twin stacks of the riverboat; it shuddered and the great wood and strap-iron paddle splashed deep into the flowing river. The boat would be going with the current, which would speed its passage but make maneuvering more difficult and dangerous.

The remnant of the Seventh quietly watched the riverboat chatter and thump away, round a bend and vanish, until only the smoke from its chimneys announced its distant passage. An odd quiet hung in the air. With the *Far West* out of sight, the wilderness closed in again, and men searched horizons warily for signs of the hostiles.

Gibbon's adjutant arrived: "Sir, Colonel Gibbon desires that you mount your column at once; we will cover all the ground we can for the Yellowstone."

Reno passed word along, and he watched his weary, grubby men mount their horses and line them up.

That evening, after they had bivouacked in a wooded flat on the Bighorn River, Benteen sought Reno in his tent.

"They've entrusted it to me," he said, handing a document to the major.

It was the enlisted men's petition. Reno pulled on his spectacles and studied it. It was addressed to His Excellency the President and the Honorable Representatives of the United States.

Gentlemen:

We the enlisted men the survivors of the battle on the Height of the Little Big Horn River, on the 25th and 26th of June 1876, of the Seventh Regiment of Cavalry who subscribe our names to this petition do most earnestly solicit the President and Representatives of our Country, that the vacancies among the Commissioned Officers of our Regiment, made by the slaughter of our brave, heroic, now lamented Lieutenant Colonel George A. Custer, and the other noble dead Commissioned Officers of our Regiment who fell close by him on the bloody field, daring the savage demons to the last, be filled by the Officers of our Regiment only. That Major M. A. Reno, be our Lieutenant Colonel vice Custer, killed: Captain F.W. Benteen our Major vice Reno, promoted. The other vacancies to be filled by officers of the Regiment by seniority. Your petitioners know this to be contrary to the established rule of promotion, but prayerfully solicit a deviation from the usual rule in this case, as it will be conferring a bravely fought for and justly merited promotion on officers who by their bravery, coolness and decision on the 25th and 26th of June 1876, saved the lives of every man now living in the Seventh Cavalry who participated in the battle, one of the most bloody on record and one that would have ended with the loss of life of every officer and enlisted man on the field only for the position taken by Major Reno, which we held with bitter tenacity against fearful odds to the last . . .

Marcus Reno was never so moved. He peered up at Benteen. "This is one of those things a soldier never forgets, never in all of his days, a remembrance that will be with me when I go to my grave. A gift from the regiment."

"They wanted to send it with Terry, but didn't get it signed until now. There are two hundred thirty-six signatures."

"I am honored to accept it. Tell them I will keep it close upon my person and dispatch it at Fort Pease. And, captain, extend to them my personal, profound gratitude and esteem. They are brave men, every one."

# PART THREE

---

## 1876

*Being an Account
of Reno's Fall from Grace*

# CHAPTER TWENTY-TWO

RENO AND HIS BATTERED SEVENTH CAVALRY WERE CAMPED ON THE
Yellowstone, licking wounds, awaiting reinforcements and provisioning,
along with General Terry's command and the Montana Column under
Colonel Gibbon. The two steamers plying the river, the *Far West* and the
*Josephine,* were shuttling between the bivouac and Fort Abraham Lincoln,
bringing men and supplies.

On July fifth he had completed his report to General Terry, writing at
length about the disaster, and as a courtesy showed it to his staff who read
it by the light of a lantern in his tent. They studied it with ill-concealed
heat.

"Is that it? The whole report?" Benteen asked.

Reno nodded.

There was something malign about all this. The captains and lieutenants passed the pages back and forth, and then passed them to Reno
abruptly.

"Anything wrong with it?"

Benteen responded. "It suits you."

Reno dismissed them, wondering what sort of ill humor they were in.
The dead. There was not a moment they weren't all thinking about the
dead on Custer's hill, and those dead in Reno's retreat and defense. He
put it out of mind. There was no love lost between Reno and Benteen
anyway, and if the captain didn't like the report, too bad.

The report filled page after page with dense handwriting. He had wanted to write a report so definitive and complete that it would settle any issues that might erupt from the fight. He made a copy and sent an adjutant to the general's headquarters tent with the report.

Terry soon summoned him.

"This is a most complete report, and I thank you, major. I have one question: did not your officers display gallantry in the course of this desperate struggle?"

"Most certainly, general. Especially Benteen. I believe I singled him out for gallantry."

"I see," he said. "Thank you."

Reno was dismissed, and he hastened to his own tent, scratched a lucifer, lit his coal oil lamp, and reread his report. He had cited none of his fellow officers for conspicuous gallantry while under fire, though he did say that "during my fight with the Indians I had the heartiest support from officers and men, but the conspicuous services of Bvt. Col. F. W. Benteen I desire to call attention to especially, for if ever a soldier deserved recognition by his government for distinguished services, he certainly does."

Irritably Reno snuffed the wick and settled into his bedroll. He had mentioned no other officer by name, and wasn't persuaded that the others had done anything exceptional, though they no doubt thought they had. As for Weir, he had acted without orders and risked his company and the whole command.

He was damned if he would hand out a lot of malarkey.

That night, lying in his soldier's bed—a piece of carpet on the hard ground—he relived the battle in his own mind: he had relived it every night since the fight, sometimes sipping from his flask, which he had refilled from riverboat stocks. He saw in his mind's eye the advancing line of battle charging the village, the hundreds of enveloping warriors who were flanking him, his retreat to the woods, his envelopment there, and command to retreat to the bluff.

And that's the part he saw in his mind's eye over and over. The command disintegrated. His company commanders wrestled with panicked men. Their sergeants could impose no order. There was no rear guard. No lines formed to volley at the warriors driving into the flanks. He saw it over and over, and argued with himself in the darkness, with the strong smell of hot canvas permeating the air, and the hard earth under him. He asked himself what he might have done, what his company commanders and noncoms might have done, and he could come up with nothing different. The troops were flanked, the ford was in hostile hands, and the only way across that river took them up a steep and muddy bank.

The sipping failed to pluck the thorn from his heart, and he felt doomed to relive that disaster night upon night.

By day, he was busy restoring the command to fighting strength. Horses and men needed healing. He needed new arms, ammunition, field gear of all sorts, and especially horses and tack. By day, he did what he could do to defend the honor of the Seventh, which seemed to wallow in mortal embarrassment.

He nerved himself to write another, more emotional report directly to General Sheridan, dodging the protocol that requires that such things be sent up the chain of command. In it he took Colonel Gibbon to task for failing to pursue the village and crush it when Gibbon's column was but a few miles from the battle field, and Gibbon's own scouts had reported to him that the village was just ahead. If the campaign had failed, Reno wrote the general, it was because of Gibbon's lassitude at a time when the great village was just pulling out, and within the reach of the Second Cavalry.

He hoped Sheridan would get the point: this failure to herd the hostiles into reservations could not be laid to the Seventh Cavalry alone.

Reno chafed under Colonel Gibbon; it showed in his every act, and he wanted it to show. His bloodied Seventh was being pushed about by an infantry commander whose column had not fired a shot in this desperate struggle. Gibbon, still fearing a surprise assault by hostiles, ordered Reno to send his scouts out wide, as vedettes, to protect the encampment on the Yellowstone, but Reno was so opposed to this, and so full of vitriol, that Gibbon finally had him arrested and charged him with insubordination.

General Terry dismissed the charges, but with a long, quiet stare at Major Reno.

"War and honor breed heat in soldiers, major," Terry said. "We must rein ourselves in."

Thus Reno was restored to his command of the Seventh Cavalry, and set about to rebuild his shattered regiment through those furiously hot days of August, when the command was choking on dust and horses constantly needed new pasture to recruit themselves.

The major wrote a report to General Stephen Vincent Benet, chief of ordnance, about the failure of the Springfield carbines. Six that he knew of in his battalion had failed in the heat of battle, in each case because the breech block failed to close, "and when the piece was discharged and the block thrown open, the head of the cartridge was pulled off and the cylinder remained in the chamber."

While he didn't know how many of the carbines failed Custer's men, he did note that an Indian scout who had seen something of the Custer fight had spotted troopers kneeling over their carbines under fire, trying to get them to function; that afterward, burial details had found various instances where broken knife blades lay beside dead soldiers. It was a radical deficiency in the weapon, and one that needed immediate attention.

He sent that letter off with satisfaction: he loved the army, and wanted everything right, and wanted no soldier to be without a reliable piece in combat. He had acted diligently to alert the general command of a serious defect in the arms. Maybe some men would now be living if the defect had been known and corrected before the fight.

On July twenty-sixth, Terry moved the recuperating column to the mouth of the Rosebud where there would be fresh grass and where the command might soon engage the hostiles again. As the month of July slipped by, the command was resupplied, and a hundred and fifty recruits arrived on the *Carroll* to fill the depleted ranks of Reno's Seventh Cavalry. But they were without mounts and green and knew little of riding, and until he could put them on horses, the Seventh would be part infantry. Still, those long lines of blue-bloused troops filled Reno with joy. He set about training them as cavalrymen, putting his top sergeants to work as instructors.

And still he relived that battle every night in his tent, when he was alone, when no one could dispute him. Under the starry skies over that arid prairie, he fought that fight, sometimes angrily, usually washing it away with whiskey.

Word came that the nation was in an uproar. The press, especially the powerful *New York Herald,* had front-paged the story, sent a man named O'Kelly out to the camp on the Rosebud at enormous expense and effort, and was printing frequent dispatches about the battle, the morale of the troops—and more, the fractures and disputes among the officers, which O'Kelly had sniffed out and written up.

Still, that was of no concern to Reno. He was a soldier, and what appeared in newspapers was of little consequence.

It was called the Custer Massacre now, and every officer in the affair had come under national scrutiny. President Grant had called it a tragic blunder, entirely avoidable. General Sheridan had ascribed it to an excess of zeal on Custer's part. Still, there were those who wondered what Marcus Reno and seven-twelfths of the Seventh Cavalry were doing on a hilltop when Custer was meeting his doom.

Reno sure as hell had an answer to that: what they were doing was fighting for their lives against overwhelming odds. What they were doing was trying to reach Custer only to be driven back just before being engulfed.

All of this Reno ignored until one day O'Kelly showed him a letter published in a St. Paul newspaper, and the newspaper's editorial response.

The letter was written by an old friend and West Point classmate of George Armstrong Custer, General Thomas Rosser, who had joined the Rebs and risen high in their army, and then had become a railroad man in the Twin Cities. After the war, Rosser and Custer had renewed the old friendship, refought the engagements, laughed, and slapped backs, no matter that during the conflict they had tried to kill each other.

The letter laid the defeat and the death of Custer's whole command at the feet of Major Marcus Reno and his officers.

# CHAPTER TWENTY-THREE

JAMES O'KELLY OF THE *NEW YORK HERALD* WAITED WOLFISHLY WHILE
Reno scanned the battered page torn from the *St. Paul and Minneapolis
Pioneer Press and Tribune.* The newsman was fitted up for an elephant
hunt, with a tweed hunting coat and canvas trousers and high-top boots
and a huge slouch hat against the prairie sun.

The Confederate major general, Rosser, started civilly enough:

> I am surprised and deeply mortified to see that our neighbor
> the *Pioneer Press and Tribune,* in its morning issue, has seen fit to
> adjudge the true, brave, and heroic Custer so harshly as to at-
> tribute his late terrible disaster with the Sioux Indians to reckless
> indiscretion . . .

But then the tone changed swiftly:

> I feel that Custer would have succeeded had Reno, with all the
> reserve of seven companies, passed through and joined Custer
> after the first repulse. It is not safe at this distance, and in the
> absence of full details, to criticize too closely the conduct of any
> officer of his command, but I think it quite certain that Gen.
> Custer had agreed with Reno upon a place of junction in case of
> the repulse of either or both of the detachments, and instead of

an effort being made by Reno for such a junction, as soon as he
encountered heavy resistance he took refuge in the hills, and abandoned Custer and his gallant comrades to their fate.

Reno fought back his bile. Like most military commanders, he was
used to being judged by armchair generals revising battles from the safety
of their parlors, but Rosser was no armchair general.

"Well, what do you think?" O'Kelly asked.

"I think I will study on what General Rosser writes. I will also put it
aside."

Reno returned to the letter, while the reporter watched hawkishly,
looking for a story.

> It was expected when the expedition was sent out that Custer
> and the Seventh Cavalry were to do all the fighting, and superbly
> did a portion of them do it. As a soldier I would sooner today lie
> in the grave of Gen. Custer and his gallant comrades alone in that
> distant wilderness, that when the "last trumpet" sounds I could
> rise to judgment from my post of duty, than to live in the place of
> the survivors of the siege on the hills.

He read that, and again, and knew he too was a casualty of the battle
of the Little Bighorn, for this was an attack on his honor, and the honor
of his men, who would live in disgrace until the last trumpet, while only
the gallant were lying in their graves. Rosser would rather lie in Custer's
grave than live in Reno's shoes.

Marcus Reno felt the slap across his face.

He could correct the general's facts. But there was no way any man
could respond to the rest. His *honor* had been impugned. A soldier without honor was a walking dead man, a man to be shunned by the corps, by
friends and strangers, by fellow officers.

Major Reno knew he must respond, and must do so with all civility, and with such power that Rosser, and those whom Rosser spoke for, would change their minds. Here was the crisis of his career, here was the cloud upon his life. Honor. Here was the deadly danger to an old soldier.

"Well?" asked O'Kelly.

"I will write General Rosser and supply you with a copy for publication," Reno said. "May I keep this tear sheet?"

"Long as I don't need it," the reporter said. "When'll you have this ready?"

"When I'm ready to release it. Good day, sir."

Something boded ill about all this. The gallant Custer lay in his grave, and fault would be found. How casually Rosser had assumed that Reno could "pass through." Pass through what? And where? And how? Reno half wished the sonofabitch had been in command and had seen for himself.

If Rosser wanted the honor of dying along with the whole regiment, he could have found it. And if he took the whole regiment with him to the lonely grave he thought so highly of, that would only mean that the Sioux and Cheyenne would have gotten another three or four hundred carbines, a few hundred saddled horses and mules, and an entire pack train loaded with ammunition, and would have been in fine shape to take on Gibbon's and Crook's columns.

Reno stuffed a long yellow cigar into his mouth and went back to work. He had 150 recruits to turn into soldiers in a few days, and then he would be off to war again. Each day brought fresh troops, horses, and supplies, along with several infantry companies under Nelson Miles and fresh officers drawn from numerous regiments. It was the busiest of times.

But after retreat that evening, he invited Benteen to his tent, turned up the wick on the coal oil lamp, and showed the Rosser piece to the captain.

"This attacks us both," he said. "If Rosser wants to fight it out in the public prints, I will meet him in that venue. I would welcome your help."

"Major, the dead Custer will have his partisans forever, and you won't change a single mind. But let's get it down for the record and hope sanity prevails."

"I hate like hell to have to explain myself. I'm on the defensive."

Benteen was studying the letter. " 'Pass through,' " he said, and laughed. "Make a junction! Jesus Christ. He had me riding to hell and back looking for stray villages."

"I can handle Rosser," Reno said.

Benteen looked skeptical.

"But I would welcome support from you. An interview with the *Herald* man."

"I will do it."

Reno studied Rosser's accusations for the next few days, and finally settled down to work at his small field desk, writing by the light of his coal oil lamp after the day's drill was done.

The important thing was to confront Rosser's notion that Custer had given orders to Reno to make a junction somewhere; something that Rosser had invented out of thin air.

"The only official orders I had from him were about five miles from the village, when Colonel Cooke, the regimental adjutant, gave me orders in these words: 'Custer says to move at as rapid a gait as you think prudent, and to charge afterward, and you will be supported by the whole outfit.'

"No mention of any plan, no thought of junction, only the usual orders to the advance guard to attack at a charge."

The major patiently described his charge, his retreat when he was about to be overwhelmed and surrounded, the woods fight, the ascent to the bluffs, the arrival of Benteen and McDougall, and the defense of the command on the hilltop.

"As you have the reputation of a soldier, and, if it is not undeserved, there is in you a spirit that will give you no rest until you have righted, as in you lies, the wrong that was perpetrated upon gallant men by your defense of Custer . . ."

He drafted a copy of his long letter, added the Rosser letter published in the St. Paul paper, and addressed a note to General Terry:

> *Sir,*
>
> *I have the honor of submitting to you as a courtesy a public attack upon my conduct at the recent battle, penned by General Rosser, CSA, and my response.*
>
> > *Respectfully,*
> > *Marcus Reno, Major, Seventh Cavalry*

With that, he sent his adjutant off to General Terry's headquarters tent, and turned down the wick of his lamp.

Not until the evening of the next early August day, did the commanding general summon Reno.

"Come in, come in," he said, waving the major to a camp stool. The tent was large but spartan, its furnishings all business. The general had a folding cot. A single lamp, hung from a pole, threw light into the corners.

Alfred Terry had that quality about him of a polished lawyer, for that was what he had been before the Civil War gave him a new calling. Somehow he was at home not only on the field of battle, but in wars of rhetoric, and now he smiled at the major.

"I appreciate being made privy to this correspondence," he said. "We've been so occupied with this campaign I hardly had a moment to study it all day. You know what generals do? We wrestle with quartermaster men. That is our primary occupation."

Reno smiled. It was Terry's way of putting Reno at ease.

"General Rosser is writing from a great distance," Terry said. "He admits it. Your response is certainly appropriate and to the point."

"I hope it changes his mind, sir."

Terry shook his head. "This is the kind of battle I know something about, major, because of my years as an attorney. I'm afraid that you'll discover that this won't change his mind at all. When a man means to hang you, it doesn't much matter what you say in your defense; he'll take your statements and consider them more meat to pluck from your bones, pick them apart into fine slivers and then attack the details. You'd be most fortunate to change his mind one iota, and I thought I would just caution you that this tragedy is charged with high feeling, and men determined to hang you are going to find ways to do it, no matter what defense you raise."

"It is a matter of honor, sir."

"Indeed it is, major, and for the sake of honor, say what you must say, and let the record speak, and we can hope that you can keep the vultures at bay. I just wanted to warn you, as a lawyer, what you may expect. And to wish you every success."

Reno headed into the starlit night feeling no less alone.

# CHAPTER TWENTY-FOUR

MORE RECRUITS AND UNITS POURED INTO GENERAL TERRY'S CAMP ON the Yellowstone in the latter part of July. Marcus Reno found he had another 150 men to integrate into his Seventh Cavalry command, along with three new officers, but no mounts for any of them. Then Colonel Nelson Miles arrived on the *E. H. Durfee* along with six companies of the Fifth Infantry.

Reno now commanded 16 cavalry officers and 543 enlisted men, so the regiment was nearly up to its former strength, save for the fact that most of the newcomers had no mounts and could not do much more than guard duty. He divided his regiment into two battalions, one commanded by Benteen and the other by Weir, the two war-tried captains who were his best men. He made Wallace his Seventh Cavalry adjutant and Edgerly his quartermaster.

For the most part, the Seventh was back in fighting shape. The sun-bronzed veterans, gaunt and ragged, were flanked now with pale newcomers in clean, shelf-creased uniforms, looking exactly as inexperienced as they were.

He kept to his own business, retired early to his tent, and was scarcely aware that he was a solitary figure among the officers who gathered at General Terry's headquarters tent to plan and talk. His flask was his only companion.

James O'Kelly of the *Herald* hovered about, writing dispatches, interviewing officers, getting the gist of the new campaign. The man had gifts, and was able to worm stories out of silent officers and talk enlisted men into opening up. He had a veteran correspondent's way of catching men unguarded and ingratiating himself with some of those who seemed to know what undercurrents were floating through the massive camp on the Yellowstone.

O'Kelly had gotten exhaustive comment from both Reno and Benteen, elucidating and clarifying what had previously been written about the terrible fight on the Little Bighorn, but Reno had not seen the printed version of those statements, nor the publication of his letter to General Rosser.

But what did it matter? He was a soldier, doing a soldier's duty, whipping a regiment into combat-readiness amid the withering August heat, which had a way of enervating men there on the high plains.

Reno didn't much like O'Kelly. The man should have been a big-game hunter in Africa rather than a reporter. And after the first interview, the major tried to steer clear. He wanted as little to do with the press as possible. O'Kelly probably would not come along on the forthcoming campaign, and the regiment would soon be rid of him.

Thus it came as a surprise one evening when O'Kelly stood outside Reno's command tent and asked for a private word.

Reno nodded and stepped out. The prairie twilight caught the world in purple, and the first stars had broken through the veils of dusk.

O'Kelly pumped the major's hand. "The *Herald* is sending me out with the next campaign, major, attached to your regiment. I've covered the story of the Little Bighorn as well as a man can, and now I'll be tagging along on the next push. There's no mount for me except a condemned horse that can't run, and I would just as soon fare better than Mark Kellogg of the Bismarck paper."

"You did me a service, Mr. O'Kelly, alerting me to General Rosser's letter."

The man paused, sniffed the soft cool air, and came to some sort of conclusion. "I'll do you another service, sir, but mind you, none of what

I'll say comes from me. This has nothing to do with the paper, nor my job. It is something you should know, and something a reporter who calls himself a friend can advise you about."

Reno nodded. He didn't like gossip, and in his solitary way avoided the gossipers. And probably he was going to hear something from O'Kelly he wished he hadn't.

"The new officers, major, the ones from the Fifth Infantry, and Otis' Twenty-second Infantry, and those in Gibbon's Seventh Infantry, the new officers in your Seventh . . . well, sir, how shall I put this? They talk, sir. About, you know, the battle. Nothing else fires their minds as that fight. The battle, Custer's death, and all that. And every one of them, without exception, believes the fight was, ah, not Custer's to lose."

"Then it was Reno's to lose. Thank you, Mr. O'Kelly, and I wish you a safe trip with us." Reno turned away.

"Your officers, the survivors, don't agree with that. Not even Weir. There's been some hot debate between the ones who were with you, and the ones who got the story from a distance."

"I've heard enough, Mr. O'Kelly. We'll go into this next campaign united, and not torn by that sort of idle talk. There's always some grousing in the army, and when the time comes to pull together, we do it without question."

The newsman held his ground. "Not idle talk, major. Not idle at all. Heated. I've heard plenty of it around these campfires. It's all the talk when you're not around. There are officers . . . Well, I've offered my little bit here. Probably stepped out of bounds. But I felt the need."

"I've already heard it, Mr. O'Kelly. Nelson Miles is saying that Custer could hardly expect to survive when seven-twelfths of his regiment camped on a hilltop instead of coming to his aid. I've heard it, and responded to it. The sonsofbitches can say whatever they want; I don't care. If any one of them had been with us, he'd sing another tune."

"They weren't there, sir. That's the whole of it."

"Indeed they weren't."

"You're a hero to your men, major. There's not a one who's not grateful he was with your command and not Custer's. Your men admire you, especially the sergeants, who've been in fights and know the tactics, and knew you were smart to back out of there. I just wanted you to know that."

Reno nodded. "Thank you, Mr. O'Kelly. I hope you get some good stories."

"One more thing, sir. Have you seen the other letter in the *Herald*?"

"Other letter?"

"The anonymous one, but plainly from General Custer, written well before his death and dispatched to my paper." He handed Reno a clipping from the July 23rd *Herald*.

Reno studied it. Here was George Custer at work, playing Benteen's game of trying officers in the public press through anonymous letters. The letter focused on Reno's scout before the fight.

Had Reno, after first violating his orders, pursued and overtaken the Indians, his original disobedience of orders would have been overlooked, but his determination forsook him at this point, and instead of continuing the pursuit and at least bringing the Indians to bay, he gave the order to countermarch and faced his command to the rear, from which point he made his way back to the mouth of the Tongue River and reported the details of his gross and inexcusable blunder to General Terry, his commanding officer, who informed Reno in unmistakable language that the latter's conduct amounted to positive disobedience of orders, the sad consequences of which could not be fully determined. The details of this affair will not bear investigation.

That sounded like Custer, all right. But there was more:

A court-martial is strongly hinted at, and if one is not ordered, it will not be because it is not richly deserved.

Reno studied the lengthy letter, which celebrated Custer, in the third person, and denigrated himself. Was this the same Custer who, not long before, had been so enraged by Benteen's anonymous letter to the St. Louis paper criticizing Custer's conduct during the battle of the Washita? The Custer who threatened to horsewhip the author?

"Thank you, Mr. O'Kelly. I should have expected something like this."

"You care to comment, major?"

Reno shook his head, and returned the clipping. He had suspected all along that Custer wanted him out of the Seventh, and now there was proof of it in this trial by newspaper. "You are a thoughtful friend, Mr. O'Kelly, keeping me posted. But now I will beg leave."

"Certainly, major."

The newsman drifted into the soft evening, and Marcus Reno settled down in his tent. He hung his tunic from a post, unbuttoned his blouse, and opened his bedroll. He uncorked his flask and downed a good slug of fiery whiskey, and felt it melt into his belly and steal out into his limbs and quiet his mind. So the battle wasn't Custer's to lose. And every shavetail lieutenant in the army was privately thinking he could have done better.

He grunted, pulled off his boots, rubbed his sore feet, and wrapped himself in his blanket. He was regular army, had been for a lifetime, and by God if push came to shove, he'd show them what an officer was made of. He had saved the command from disaster and they by God would respect that or he'd see to it that they got the lesson.

That night he thought of Ross, and knew he should have written his son long since, and written the Rosses and Haldemans too, and let them know he was all right. They would have only the sensational newspaper reports. But whenever he tried to write, his pen froze in his fingers.

He thought of Mary Hannah, her lithe, frail body beside him in the soft nights, her social charms that opened his own world for him and brought friends into their parlor. In the nights she was always asking questions, and he didn't mind telling her about the cavalry, everything from "Boots and Saddles" to trumpeters to inspections to personalities. She would rest her head in the hollow of his shoulder and absorb it all, and sometimes kiss him.

"My cavalry man," she would say.

It was a long time since he had had a woman. Just then, he would settle for any woman.

He would ask for leave after the summer campaign was over. Travel, take his ease, go to Harrisburg, see his son, see his in-laws, shake the prairies out of his mind, let this cloud hovering over him drift away.

The next day General Terry moved the whole command downriver a mile to new grass; the day after, they rode out to war once again, this time as the Yellowstone Column, and they were by God going to corral those hostiles and march them onto their reservations or see them pay the price. Not that Marcus Reno believed they would find any Indians, except by wild luck.

They headed up the Rosebud, an enormous column slowed by heavy six-mule wagons hauling provisions to keep the ponderous column in the field. In the van was Major Brisbin's Second Cavalry, followed by infantry, then the wagons with more infantry on the flanks, and finally Reno's Seventh Cavalry as rear guard, the green troops all but worthless in war.

Reno had kept his dismounted newcomers back, posting guard duty and building defensive works for "Fort Beans" as Terry's camp at the mouth of the Rosebud had come to be known. But he had eight companies, some of them filled with veterans of the brutal fight; most of them green.

They rode through brutal heat, an occasional downpour, hail, lightning, and howling winds, as well as prairie silences, and fields of yellow daisies, but there were no Indians around, and Reno didn't expect to see any. Such a column, which raised huge clouds of dust, could well be spotted from many miles away, and wherever the hostiles were, they weren't anywhere near and would stay a hundred miles away from this giant caterpillar plowing over their homeland.

Then, after several days up the purling creek, the scouts ranging far ahead discovered a column of dust rising well to the south, a migration so formidable it had to be the hostiles.

"Sioux!" the cried.

Swiftly the two cavalry units formed a line of battle while the wagon masters boxed in the wagons and the infantry guarded its flanks. Major Reno ordered Weir's battalion to form a skirmish line, and Benteen's to move to the front.

On General Terry's orders to start a reconnaissance, Reno sent French's Company M to the task. French's men rode out to meet the oncoming horsemen, who were making the exaggerated signs of friendship, holding rifles above their heads, so the horsemen, Indians, half-breeds, scouts dressed in blue, and frontiersmen in buckskins were allowed to ride in.

They were the advance guard of Crook's column, and Crook's scouts were being led by the actor William F. Cody, all duded up in buckskins with a dashing sombrero keeping the sun off his face.

Reno stared, amazed. Here was a theater man, gotten up in the gaudy dress of the borders, erect and commanding and looking like he was born to the saddle, and riding for Crook! He was a handsome longhaired devil, but how capable he was Reno didn't know. Perhaps this was all an actor's publicity gimmick, but maybe not. Reno vaguely remembered that William Cody had fought for the army, gotten into hand-to-hand combat with Indians, and knew the plains as well as anyone alive.

After the initial excitement, Terry's column continued south, with the scouts from Crook's command, to meet with the Crook column that was heading north down the Rosebud.

Buffalo Bill hand-shook his way through Terry's command, thoroughly enjoying himself. And at last he came to Reno, who stared stiffly at the man.

"Ah! Reno! The hero of the Bighorn!" Cody exclaimed in a piercing voice, offering a hand across the withers of his horse.

Reno nodded.

"I am honored to meet you, sir. Much has been written of you and your gallant Seventh these last weeks. I've gobbled up every dispatch. I must say, I'm impressed. What fine, hard, seasoned men these are, major. How well they bear the burdens of their recent ordeal.

"I've just ridden through your command, and see the marks of hard use on the veterans. Here are men who fought, sir, fought to the death, bullet for bullet. I see scars. I see bandages. I see the pale look of near death in their eyes. You have my boundless admiration, all of you, fighting there against overwhelming odds."

Reno nodded, taking the measure of the gaudy showman riding beside him. "They know as much about Indian warfare as any outfit in the army," Reno said.

"I was so inspired, major, that I closed my act. Yes, canceled twenty-three bookings, cut them off cold, caught the first train west, and volunteered my services. That's what the gallant Seventh did to me: because of you, I am forgoing thousands of admission tickets!"

Reno nodded. He had a command to run, and his gaze swept from company to company, looking for anything amiss. But now the column rushed ahead to join up with Crook's, and men rode toward reunion, not war.

Cody twisted in his shiny saddle, and drew close. "Say, major, I must tell you, when I return to the stage I'm going to do a tableau of the Little Bighorn fight; yes, the American people will soon see the brave Custer and his men surrounded by howling Indians, fighting to the last man. Oh, there will be goose bumps when the last man falls. And that last man will be Custer. I can see it now. A great hush after that howling melee. And then a lone bugle off in the wings playing 'Taps.' Ah! Won't that be grand! Think of the tears in all those eyes! Oh, America will eat it up! It'll pack every theater from San Francisco to New York. Now, I'm so pleased to meet you, sir, so that you can be my technical advisor, help me get it all right, eh?"

"I'm not sure that's something I'd ever want to do, Mr. Cody."

Cody steered his lively dappled horse close up. "Ah! Think on it. What I have in mind is for you to play the noble Custer before the footlights! Think how that would look on the broadsheets. Custer fight, authentic in all detail, with the great Reno playing the gallant Custer!"

"I, ah, think perhaps you had better get an actor to do it, Mr. Cody. I'm regular army and the army is my life. And I could not imagine myself playing the part of a man who threw his command away."

# CHAPTER TWENTY-FIVE

WHEN THE WEARY SEVENTH CAVALRY MARCHED INTO FORT ABRAHAM Lincoln, September 26, 1876, they found a post hung in crepe. The frames of doors and windows had been painted black in mourning. A desolation hung in the air. Major Reno, who had taken a riverboat a few days earlier, met the command, traveling to its home base under Captain Weir, and posted half of it to a camp below the post because there were not quarters for all.

The late-summer campaign had become a farce, and the combined infantry and artillery forces under General Terry had scarcely seen an Indian all summer. Terry's and Crook's and Miles's and Reno's forces had prowled the rivers south of the Yellowstone, closed pincers on nothing, and then Reno's Seventh Cavalry had probed the Missouri River country far to the north, always well behind the fleeing fragments of that huge summer camp. Many hostiles had reached Canada.

At last, as the weather turned, Terry posted all those infantry and cavalry units back to their bases in Montana and North Dakota Territories, and began preparing for a winter campaign, always effective against Indians whose ponies were weakened by a lack of forage.

The Seventh Cavalry returning to Fort Lincoln was not the one that had marched away one fine May day. Recruits had swelled its ranks, and even these had acquired hard field service riding endless miles over empty prairie under a brutal sun. These men were sunburned, skeletal, and worn by hard use. Their eyes burned from dry air and hurt from squinting, their flesh had blistered, their slouch hats were stained, their blouses and britches were sun-faded and grimy.

But the sought-for goal, resolving the Indian War, remained as elusive as ever.

Reno watched his command ride silently home. He received them curtly, not knowing why, for they had distinguished themselves in the field. But there were dark currents flowing here, and perhaps spit and polish, barked commands, protocols, duties, and snapped salutes would veneer something that burdened the soul of each man.

In time, after the horses were cared for and stabled, and the men settled, there would be time for letters, a hearty mess for a change, a real cot above the hard earth, cloth or planks overhead to ward off weather, and news to share.

On General Terry's instructions, he had caught a boat from Fort Buford and assumed command at Lincoln, finding the place steeped in a strange desolation. Awaiting him was a copy of the August 22nd *New York Herald* which contained Rosser's reply to Reno's letter and the statements given the paper by Reno and Benteen. Captain Benteen himself was no longer with the regiment, having been posted to recruiting duty, a transfer that Reno regarded with some suspicion.

But Rosser's letter revealed only the slightest alteration of opinion, though it was all phrased civilly enough. The destruction of Custer's forces were, Rosser concluded, entirely the failure of Major Marcus Reno, who had faltered when he should have attacked, pressed forward to Custer's rescue instead of falling back. It was a failure of nerve, caused by Reno's inexperience as an Indian fighter, and no other reason could be properly ascribed to Custer's demise. And Custer himself lay "sublimely in an honored grave, and all patriots and lovers of heroic deeds, performed in devotion to duty, will join in his requiem."

Reno sighed. Custer had died an honorable death, or so the world believed, while Reno . . . He put the thought aside.

"The Indians appear to have withdrawn from your front as soon as you recrossed the river. Why, then, could you not have gone in pursuit of Custer earlier? When you did go you say that you heard 'chopping shots.' Do you not think that, even then, by a bold dash at the Indians, you might have saved a portion, at least, of Custer's perishing command?"

Reno had wondered the same thing a thousand times, and had always come to the same conclusion: not without adequate ammunition unless he wanted to march a suicide column toward the vast numbers before him, and not without some way of protecting the wounded.

Rosser's jabs, no matter that they were couched in respectful language, opened wounds in Reno's heart.

"I have heard that someone has advanced the theory that Custer was met, at this point where he first struck the river, by overwhelming numbers and so beaten that his line from that point on was one of retreat. This is simply ridiculous."

"Had Custer been repulsed at this point his column would have been driven back upon the line on which he had approached and the proposition is too silly to be discussed. I claim that the part which Custer acted in this engagement was that of a bold earnest man, who believed he had before him a rare opportunity to strike the Indians a blow which, if successful, would end the campaign, and it was worth the bold effort. . . ."

And so the armchair general, poring over maps, didn't budge an inch. And he was dead wrong. Custer had not retreated along the line of his approach. But whether or not Rosser was wrong, this view had spread like black ink through the sinews of Reno's command, stained his record as a soldier, dripped into the counsels of the highest officers of the army. And there was little a major on active duty could do to counter it.

That night saw a great reunion at the Officers' Club Room, and Marcus Reno was present. So were Weir, Varnum, Hare, Robinson, Craycroft, and Eckerson of the Seventh Cavalry; Lieutenants Manley, Ogle, and Finley of the Sixth Infantry, and Post Trader Harmon. By the bright homecoming light of the kerosene lamps, the lieutenants and captains gathered, washed and shaven and primed and powdered in clean blue, and the whiskey flowed swift and gold into tumblers dissolving the hurts of the road. Spirits ran high. Men laughed, and reminisced, and Marcus Reno laughed and reminisced until his ears caught the tenor of a conversation in a corner:

Infantry Lieutenant Manley was agreeing with Rosser.

Reno peeled away from the crowd, braced Manley, and told him he didn't have things right.

"I'll come to my own conclusions, sir," Manley replied.

"If they agree with Rosser, then they're ignorant. You weren't there."

"I agree with Rosser. You could have rescued the lieutenant colonel if you tried. You didn't even try."

"The hell I didn't."

"One good charge, sir, one brave charge, rallying your men, and Custer would be here right now."

"Manley, you're an ignorant sonofabitch."

Manley rose suddenly. Reno grabbed a fistful of tunic and began pushing the lieutenant back. Manley's fist found Reno's shoulder. Reno countered with a fist into Manley's midriff.

"Stop that!" yelled someone, but Reno was too busy pummeling to heed the yell. Reno swung hard now, feeling his fists collide with flesh and bone, feeling Manley's fists smack home, knock air out of him, whack his head aside.

Reno pushed. Manley tumbled to the grimy floor. Reno landed on the younger man, pounding hard, a demon loosed in him, while Manley writhed and bounced and shoved Reno off.

"You sonofabitch, I'll kill you," Reno breathed, hot craziness welling through him. He was filthy; the floor slop staining his uniform. Manley's was even more begrimed.

Varnum stepped in. "Hold up, major. Enough. Get off of him. Manley, back away."

"God damn you, Varnum, if you don't let me finish up here, it'll be personal with me."

Varnum, who had fought beside Reno at the battle, backed off.

Tom Weir shouldered in to the arena and helped both men up. Manley retreated.

"Now shake hands, major," he said. "And you, lieutenant. You'll behave like officers and gentlemen."

Varnum tentatively pushed a begrimed hand forward.

"I won't touch your goddamn hand. We'll settle this, all right, with revolvers. I'm calling you out, Varnum."

Lieutenant Robinson intervened, and said sharply: "You bring revolvers into this club and I'll arrest you both."

"Who the hell are you?"

"Lieutenant Robinson, Seventh Cavalry."

Reno had barely noticed him before.

"Cool off, major," Tom Weir said. "We're stopping this here and now."

By then the rest of the officers, suddenly sobered by the prospect of a duel, drew Reno apart.

"Don't touch me, damn you," Reno snapped.

They let him alone. Furiously he wiped muck off his miserable blues and retreated into a corner, apart from his staff officers, and demanded a bottle and a tumbler. They stared, brushed their own uniforms, and returned quietly to their sipping. But the evening would never be the same, this night the Seventh Cavalry returned to Fort Abraham Lincoln.

Reno drank until he was tired of drinking. Drank until a great weariness crept through his limbs, and then stepped into the chill night, feeling the gazes of a dozen officers and gentlemen on his stained back. He stepped into blackness. Autumn was in the air, the autumn of nature, and the autumn of his career in the army. He did not let the cool air undo the heat within him, the heat he needed to defend his honor.

He would defend his good name, defend it in heaven or hell, defend it in the streets, in officers' clubs, defend it on the parade ground, defend it to Sheridan and Sherman and Terry, defend it to adjutants and courts and second lieutenants, defend it until he could no longer see stars or know the sun was rising.

The anger did not leave him as he wove through the night to his quarters, where a sentry saluted. Reno returned the salute, but growled at it.

His room was dark and cold. He found a lucifer, lit the coal oil lamp, jammed the glass chimney down, adjusted the wick, and saw orange light fill the room. He found a looking glass and peered into it, discovering the ruin of his face and flesh, and he knew he and his image were alone.

# CHAPTER TWENTY-SIX

HARD WORK WAS ALWAYS THE SALVATION. RENO THREW HIMSELF INTO rebuilding the regiment. New men and horses were flooding in, arriving almost daily, and suddenly the Seventh was at full strength. But these five hundred men and five hundred mounts didn't know anything.

He set his company commanders and first sergeants to work, drilling men, turning useless horseflesh into disciplined cavalry mounts. The men were the usual raw material of armies, some off the immigrant boats, some a few steps ahead of sheriffs, and some too dumb to hold a civilian job. But there would always be those few who loved the cavalry, had an aptitude for it, and would rise through the ranks to become first-rate soldiers.

If his manner was brusque, that was exactly what he intended. If he was prickly, it was because he wanted to be a thorn in the side of everyone around him. He would show them what a soldier was made of, and what Marcus Reno was made of, too. There would be a winter campaign shortly, and Reno intended to whip his command into fighting shape.

But he was also walking the edge of an abyss, one he understood perfectly and felt helpless to do anything about. He especially felt the reproach of the youngest officers, those first and second lieutenants fresh out of West Point who secretly thought that they could do better than the major, and who devoutly believed that soldiers, properly trained and mounted, could have swept through that village, knocking over the warriors, women, and children like tenpins, and reached the beleaguered Custer in time to save the command and pull victory out of disaster.

Reno knew the feeling. It had burned brightly in his bosom during the Civil War. He had watched timid generals fail to grasp the chances that opened to them, retreat at the very brink of success, see danger where the enemy was actually falling to pieces. He had then been the lieutenant, the captain, helpless to alter events, seething with that secret scorn that the young and untried reserve for their commanders.

Now he felt himself to be the target of exactly that scorn, unspoken, buried behind geniality, hidden in smiles, scarcely revealed even to wives and sweethearts in letters, hinted at only by the cliques that formed in the Officers' Club Room. It was not visibly present, but it was there, staining his honor and eroding his career. And he hated it.

The only defense against it was a brusqueness that could scarcely be borne by his men. And he was especially brusque with the new officers, the ones who had not been at the Little Bighorn, the ones with inflated notions of what white soldiers could do and what red soldiers could not do.

One of those new officers was Captain James Bell, actually a veteran army man who had a much younger wife, Emily, who was unusually handsome and vivacious as well. And there was something else about her: certain rumors concerning her virtue, her easiness with other officers, had been bruited through the staff of the Seventh Cavalry for years. Whether true or not, they did not escape the attention of Reno, and he eyed Emily Bell with curiosity and interest.

At one of the many social events at the post, she surprised him.

"My dear major, I should very much enjoy having a photograph of you," she said.

He eyed her bountiful beauty, was tempted, and thought better of it.

"Madam, I am afraid I have none. I haven't been near a photographer in years. Press of business, you know. The army's a great taskmaster."

"Ah! A pity! Well, when you have one taken, please make a copy for me."

"I'm flattered, Mrs. Bell," he said.

He had been over two years without a wife, and he felt a rush of hunger as he watched Emily Bell circulate through the party, drawing the long gazes of handsome career army officers. He was forty-one, had a twelve-year-old son being cared for by the boy's aunt and uncle, and lived a solitary life, save for the occasional parties at the post. It would not do to get involved. Especially not then, with an angry cloud poised over him. But he could not help but watch Emily, her rose satins rustling, as she drifted through those ranks of blue and gold, catching attention from men who pretended not to look. He headed out to the veranda, and downed a sharp splash of whiskey, capped the flask, and restored it to its nest.

Colonel Samuel Sturgis, the commander of the Seventh, arrived in October, and swiftly put plans into effect to disarm the Sioux at their agencies. The Seventh would ride to Standing Rock and the Cheyenne Agency, collect weapons and ponies, and make very sure that the reservation Indians would not again furnish guns and ponies to the hostiles.

Reno found himself commanding one column that descended the Missouri River on its west bank, while Sturgis took another column down the east bank, and then they spent a few days at the agency collecting arms and horses. It was harsh business, taking away the means to hunt, and leaving the Sioux dependent on wormy and erratic starvation rations from the government. But he didn't pity them; no one in the Seventh pitied any of them. The Sioux, wrapped in shabby blankets, stared as the troopers systematically ransacked each lodge for firearms, and then made off with the scraggly ponies. Reno saw bitterness in their eyes, but he didn't much care.

The two columns returned with eight hundred confiscated ponies and a few wagonloads of arms. Now the Seventh could settle down to a peaceful winter without worrying about surprises. The regiment was scattered to various winter posts in the area, and began the long wait for spring. It would be a time of musicales, dancing, holiday feasts, charades, balls, and other light games, and gossip. It would also be a time of chafing; officers who didn't get along always did worse in close quarters than out in the field.

Reno received a twenty-day leave and was glad of it. He had been out in Indian country too long, and was ready for the sights of any large city. He chose Chicago. There would not be time enough to reach Harrisburg, see his son, Robert Ross Reno, and the Rosses and Haldemans this time. Nor did he particularly want to. He wanted to don the mufti, live anonymously for a few days, and . . . do whatever he might do. The river took him south; the railroads took him east, the rattle of wheels against rails numbing his mind until the overheated passenger train squeaked and rattled into Union Station and he stepped out into damp, cold Lake Michigan air. He checked into the Palmer House, signing himself as Marcus Renault. He did not lack for money, having banked his major's salary all the while he was out where he could not spend it. And he commanded a substantial income from Mary Hannah's estate as well.

He felt right at home among the potted palms, the high and ornate gray marble lobby, the drummers in brocade vests, black-suited moguls and green-uniformed lackeys; the fashionable ladies in ermine-lined coats, glossy boots, and furry muffs; the comfortable dark saloons glowing under gas lamps that spilled buttery light into corners, redolent of good Kentucky whiskey and Havana cigars . . . and sometimes lilac perfume.

He wore his black worsted suit with a dove gray vest, a monogrammed kerchief in his vest pocket, along with a paisley cravat, gray spats, and a good silk bowler. He was not the handsomest of men, but he was a natty one, and with soft brown eyes he surveyed the hubbub, especially the ladies, and remembered nothing of the hard days beyond the western horizon, when a mouthful of bad whiskey hastily swallowed was the only luxury, and an extra blanket the only warmth.

He began with a steaming bath in the enormous Palmer House clawfoot tub he found in his suite, then summoned a barber to shave him and trim his moustache and cut his black hair and leave the scent of witch hazel upon him. The barber, an obvious gossip, tried to make conversation, but Reno gave him no opportunity. He did give the man a dime tip. He summoned a boy to black his boots, and a laundress to press his white shirts.

He examined himself: medium sized, paunchy, sun-stained about the face and neck and hands; far from pale elsewhere, sad-eyed, knowing, and permanently tired. But still not an unattractive package, he thought, not even in civilian clothes. He sent his uniforms out for a cleaning, and would have them back in a day or so.

But for now, just for now, he was Mr. Renault, not Major Reno, not the man who had commanded at the Battle of the Little Bighorn. Mr. Renault would look for entertainments and business opportunities. The country was beginning to blossom again after the Crash of 1873. Mr. Renault was unknown, had never appeared in the public prints, and could go about his business at will.

He sipped three good bourbons at the Palmer House saloon that evening, content to be alone, listening to the chatter around him. Two gents were debating whether to invest in traction stocks. Traction companies were the coming thing; streetcars, interurban trolleys promised to weld great cities together. Reno listened attentively. He might invest in one, especially one located in a great metropolis.

He dined alone at the famous Palmer House restaurant, enjoying the white linens, the cut glass carafes, the waiters in livery. He ordered a porterhouse steak, with pearl onions, twice-baked potatoes, California asparagus topped with hollandaise, and baked squash. He ate quietly, far from howling savages, sipping a good French red table wine, and watching the women.

One, in the booth across, wore a splendid pearl necklace, three strands in graduated sizes. She was brown-haired and ethereal, and wasn't paying the slightest attention to the middle-aged gent squiring her through a glittering evening. They talked about theater, and Edwin Booth, and Shakespeare.

Reno declined dessert, paid his tab from a wad of greenbacks stuffed in his trousers, gathered his black wool cape, and headed for the portico on State Street. There, while the Chicago winds gusted about him and swirled his cape tight, he engaged a hansom cab drawn by a tired dray in blinders.

"Nine-twelve North LaSalle Street," he said.

The driver turned and smiled. "Yasser, just a few minutes," he said. "I'll move right smart."

It was a famous address, well known to any bon vivant: it was the handsome three-story brick parlor house of Madam Porphyrie DuPont, whose select clientele had included Major Reno for many years. And for a fortnight, he would not think of Armstrong Custer and the dead.

# CHAPTER TWENTY-SEVEN

SLATE SKIES SHROUDED FORT ABERCROMBIE, WHICH LAY ON A FEA-
tureless plain, open to the blasts of winter. Subzero air sliced through the
frame buildings of the dismal post, driving men to the wood stoves or
under their blankets. The little fort, lying on the Red River of the North
at the boundary of Dakota and Minnesota, had long since ceased to be
important in the defense of settlers in the lush river valley, and now was
occupied merely as precaution. Until the last of the Sioux were collected
on reservations, the little army posts dotting the northern plains would
have their complements of troops.

Reno arrived in mid-December, after detraining at Breckenridge, twelve
miles south. He would command here, on orders issuing from the Department of Dakota. His post housed Company A, Seventeenth Infantry, under Captain William Van Horne, and Company F, Seventh Cavalry,
under Captain James Bell. Five officers in all: Lieutenant Troxel, quartermaster for the infantry company, Lieutenant Robinson, post adjutant,
and Lieutenant Slocum, Seventh Cavalry. All but Slocum had their wives
with them.

Reno surveyed the bleak post, studied the open plains which did nothing to allay the Canadian winds, and knew it would be a slow, grim winter.
No sooner did he arrive than Bell departed, on leave to attend to his dying
father. There was not even a nearby town to solace the men: Breckenridge
was little more than a Northern Pacific whistle stop with a telegraph line.

There wasn't a brick building on the place to stay the wind or turn the terrible cold.

So he plunged into a sea of nothingness, little relieved by the society of his fellow officers. It was all he could do to keep the post in firewood, because the only source of fuel on the treeless plain was the streambank timber along the Red River. These men and officers were cast adrift, in snowy wastes, under a brooding sky, to ponder their lives and find entertainments. They were over two hundred miles from Fort Abraham Lincoln, two hundred miles from that heartbeat of the regiment.

There was one solace. The young, vivacious, and utterly seductive Emily Bell was on hand to liven officers' lives with her brightness. The other solace, if it could be called that, was that this place was far away, in miles and temperament, from that Montana battlefield that had stamped itself forever on the Seventh Cavalry. Maybe the officers could amuse themselves through a long bitter winter without those subterranean currents that Reno had discovered wherever he was among commissioned men.

The other solace was a good stock of whiskey to numb the slow evenings and settle him for bed. If he nipped a little, what did it matter? Most of the officers got through the slow times with a little whiskey to ease the way.

Emily intrigued him. Bell was away, en route to Altoona, Pennsylvania. She was plainly interested in him; hadn't she asked for his photograph? He was alone. Not just alone, but solitary, although even this tiny outpost had an Officers' Club Room where he might find companionship. Each bleak and gray day seemed an eternity, and nothing but Emily brought warmth to the post. It was hell not having a wife.

He had meant to send a postcard to Ross from Chicago, but somehow never got to it. He knew he should be more attentive to his son, and intended that they would travel together whenever he could arrange a long leave. And yet, he was no regular correspondent, and the boy was growing to manhood barely knowing his own father, barely hearing from him even at Christmas.

It was something to remedy, and Reno planned to do so. Spend time, get to know the boy, see to it that his inheritance from Mary Hannah's estate was being spent wisely to educate Ross, get him ready for life.

It took him no time to settle into his new quarters as the commanding officer. And then he had nothing to do.

Emily.

She and her captain lived in one side of a duplex, with the Van Hornes occupying the other side. A common enclosed porch connected the two officers' quarters. Reno visited her at her quarters the day after he arrived, along with other officers and their wives, but stayed only briefly.

The next day he offered to take her for a drive; she declined. He returned later in the day to find Lieutenant Slocum present, reading to her. Slocum swiftly closed the book and retreated into the cold, leaving Emily to entertain the post's commanding officer, which she did for two hours that evening.

Reno sensed, and enjoyed, her discomfort. They talked of little things, army life, food, weather. None of it mattered. All that mattered was that she was there alone, and he was sitting in her parlor, by the light of a single coal oil lamp. The evening wore on, and the lines of her face grew grave. He enjoyed the tension that filled the air, and the increasing difficulty she was having making conversation. She surely wanted to be released from this visit from the post's senior officer, and he was deliberate about it.

But at last he rose, and she did too.

He took both her hands in his.

"Good evening, Mrs. Bell," he said, and slid his hands up her arms, tugging her toward him.

"Colonel Reno, is that the Masonic grip?" she asked, brightly.

"Yes, Emily, that's it. I have a book that tells all about it." He laughed. "Would you like to read it?"

"Why, yes, I suppose."

"I'll get it over to you, then. Good night."

He pulled his cape around him and plunged into the darkness, entertained by the evening. It was a start. He had barely arrived, yet he might make something out of a long cold winter.

The major busied himself with his new command the next day, but he kept Emily in mind. There would be another gathering that evening: Lieutenant Robinson's sister would be leaving the following day, and the officers would gather at the lieutenant's quarters to bid her adieu. Reno had an escort in mind, and called on Emily Bell.

"Ah, you're still here, Emily. I should be most pleased to escort you to the Robinsons," he said.

"Well . . . I imagine that would be most gallant of you."

He offered her his arm, and they walked the few paces to the Robinsons, where they congregated with the other officers and their wives for a little while, making a pleasant visit of it, and then he offered his arm to Emily to take her back again. She felt light and supple on his arm. He took her into the enclosed porch, saw her to her door, paused a moment, said good night, and then left her there. The door closed, and he turned away.

But the door opened, and he saw her release her skirt, which had been trapped in it, and totter momentarily.

"Why, Emily, let me help," he said, catching her.

He clasped her waist and steadied her, but she twisted away and reached the Van Hornes' front door.

"Don't you do that again!" she said.

Reno laughed. "No harm intended," he said.

"Don't you ever do that again."

He nodded, bowed, and abandoned the enclosed porch, making his way through the December darkness. He felt cold. It was not yet Christmas, and he wondered whether there would be much of a Christmas at Fort Abercrombie in 1876.

And so things stood. When Christmas approached, he invited her to be his escort at the enlisted men's Christmas party, but she said only that she would consider it. He took it for acceptance, but found that she wasn't present when he knocked at her door. She was being escorted that evening by Lieutenant Slocum, which irked the commanding officer.

Then he discovered that he alone had been excluded from a Christmas gathering at Emily Bell's house; all the other officers and their wives, plus the post trader, attended. It was de rigueur to include the post's commander, so the snub was deliberate. He repaired to the Officers' Club Room and drank his way through Christmas, his thoughts dark and mean.

A few days later the Episcopal minister from Fargo arrived to hold services at the post. The Reverend Richard Wainwright always stayed with the Bells during these excursions, and had a standing invitation to do so. But this time, the twenty-ninth of December, Reno interceded.

"Reverend, the captain's away, and you would not want to stay there," he said.

"But major, that's not a matter to be concerned about."

"You're welcome to stay at my house, sir."

"Why, I'll see if Mrs. Bell's expecting me."

Reno heard no more of it for the moment, and Wainwright seemed to be ensconced at the Bells' quarters. The situation produced some ribald comment in the Officers' Club Room, and Reno didn't like it. This had gone far enough.

He summoned the minister.

"I hear you've chosen to stay with Mrs. Bell. It is causing some unfortunate remarks here."

"If you're worried about her reputation, don't be."

"Her reputation won't stand much scrutiny, reverend. For the sake of your own reputation, and the good of the church, I would advise you to billet yourself elsewhere. She's a notorious character, and various staff officers . . . well, she's not welcome here."

Wainwright looked angry. "I'll think about it," he said, and turned on his heel.

Reno soon received a note: "After advising, I have decided not to change, as I cannot remove without offering a slight to Captain Bell in the person of his wife."

So, he had lost. For the moment. He paced hotly, and decided on a new tack. He summoned Lieutenant Robinson, his adjutant, and instructed him to tell Mrs. Bell she could not play the organ at the New Year's Day service; he would stop the service if she did.

Robinson frowned, looked like he was about to speak, saluted, and retreated from sight.

There was no music. And the Van Hornes persuaded the reverend to move to their quarters.

After the service, Wainwright found Reno and passed along the news.

"I'm staying with Lieutenant and Mrs. Van Horne, major."

"I'm glad you are. If you hadn't moved, I would've asked you to leave the post."

The clergyman rocked back, as if slapped. Then he nodded and was soon out the door.

Reno watched him hurry off, satisfied at last. Emily would soon know what it was to tamper with Marcus Reno's affections. Fort Abercrombie would be better off if she were a thousand miles away, and with any luck, he'd force her out. He pulled a cigar from out of his humidor, lit it, and exhaled a vast blue cloud of smoke. He would just as soon get rid of both: the coffee-cooler officer who wasn't around when blood was being shed, and his troublemaking wife. He drew hard, blew hard, and stared at the icy plains beyond his frosted window.

Bell returned on January fifth, and soon heard the whole story, as Reno hoped he would. There was plenty of gossip, and Reno didn't need to hear it to know that it was buzzing through the small post. There are no secrets in a command of two companies, with five officers, and that's how Reno wanted it. Whenever he walked into the Officers' Club Room, he met walls of silence. He didn't much care. These were not men who had been beside him at the Little Bighorn. Let them stew.

But it didn't shake out like that. The veteran captain and old-line soldier approached him angrily, along with Van Horne and the Reverend Mr. Wainwright, and accused him of defaming Bell's wife and embarrassing the command.

"I deny it!" Reno exclaimed. "Don't believe him! I deny everything this holy Christian man, this meddler, accuses me of. I've never said anything derogatory about Mrs. Bell to anyone."

"You've quoted others, and apparently with relish," Bell said, his gaze steady. "Mr. Wainwright says you quoted Benteen, Wallace, and who knows who else?"

"That's your problem, not mine," Reno snapped.

"Honor will be defended," Bell said. "Hear me well. I most assuredly will defend the honor of my wife and myself, and you, sir, will answer."

Reno blew cigar smoke. "Go right ahead. I welcome it," he said.

Captain Bell was not mollified, and soon left for St. Paul to see General Terry about bringing charges against Reno. The major thought it would come to nothing; everyone knew about Emily Bell, and it would all be shoved under the carpet.

But he soon found himself summoned to St. Paul, where General Terry attempted to reconcile them all, but to no avail.

"Major, I'm disappointed that all this has boiled up at your post," he said. "I would like you to consider the gentlemanly thing, an apology."

"Maybe it's the other way around," Reno said.

Terry subsided into quietness, but his gaze fell heavily on Reno, who stood stiffly before his commander, not budging an inch.

The affair was blooming like nightshade, not disappearing. Reno left for Fort Lincoln, to consult with Benteen and Wallace, who had also made or heard comments about Emily Bell, but that came to nothing, and Bell decided to press charges, and told Reno he would.

Reno wrote Bell a stiff note, hotly denying that he had impugned Emily's character. He knew what all this was about. The coffee coolers and Custer partisans were going to take over the Seventh Cavalry.

On February 20, 1877, the headquarters of the Department of Dakota issued General Order 20, convening a court-martial against Major Marcus Reno, to be held March 20, on two charges of "conduct unbecoming to an officer and a gentleman."

And Reno was placed under house arrest at Fort Abercrombie and relieved of command.

## CHAPTER TWENTY-EIGHT

AN ILL WIND WAS BLOWING, AND NOT JUST OUT OF THE NORTH. RENO paced the post to which he was confined and found no friends anywhere. On February twenty-eighth he had been relieved of command, and now lived cold and alone. When he approached other officers, they turned away. When he entered the Officers' Club Room, conversation ceased, and if he stayed on, the others drifted off. When he encountered Captain Bell, the man wheeled away. When he met the officers' wives, they hurried past, looking elsewhere.

A few enlisted men smiled; some loyal old first sergeants saluted him smartly. But he was alone, never so alone in all his life, never so isolated from his own regiment. He could not even go to St. Paul to prepare his case with the attorneys he had hired, Cushman K. Davis and Stanford Newell. They would cost him plenty, but he had some reserves, and there was always the money accumulated in Pennsylvania from Mary Hannah's estate; money divided between himself and his son.

All that was bad, and it irked him. But something worse was afflicting him. A copy of the December twenty-third *Army and Navy Journal* had wended its way to Fort Abercrombie, and in it was a scathing review of a new biography by a certain Captain Frederick Whittaker, entitled *A Complete Life of General George A. Custer,* in which, apparently, the author had gone to great lengths to pin the death of Custer and his command on Reno and Benteen.

Reno fumed. This thing would never go away. But at least the review did him honor. It lashed out at Whittaker: "With reckless pen he thrusts right and left, careless of reputations, regardless of facts, darkening the lives of other men in the vain hope that one name may shine more brightly on the pages of history."

And then the reviewer got down to the heart of it:

". . . This rash writer furiously arraigns, tries, convicts, and sentences the president, Major Reno, and Captain Benteen for indirectly causing the death of General Custer. Since the book appeared in print Gen. Sherman and Lieutenant General Sheridan—to whose regard for the gallant Custer his biographer bears frequent testimony—have, in their report to the War Department, after months of careful consideration of all the facts and much of the evidence, not made public, unequivocally commend Reno as a brave and discreet man, who has performed his whole duty and plainly ascribed the disastrous termination of Custer's fight to the unfortunate division of the command."

Reno read it gratefully, and yet with a certain morbid knowledge that this was only the beginning. He would not see Whittaker's book for some while, unless perchance a copy drifted into this obscure frontier post. But at least he could brace himself. He knew there would be a storm and it would land full upon him, and that Custer's partisans, no doubt including his widow, would make good use of the biography. But all he could do was wait. Maybe things would come out well enough.

Somehow, he knew they wouldn't.

He was ordered at last to St. Paul to answer to the charges laid against him. This court-martial would be no small thing, given his notoriety. Not nine months had elapsed since the battle that clouded his name and career, and here he was, before a board of superior officers, colonels, lieutenant colonels, and one major, all Civil War veterans, most of them West Point.

His career in the United States Army hinged on the result. Everyone knew it. The room at Fort Snelling had become a solemn place, a sea of blue uniforms and whiskered faces and humorless stares.

The charges were read: there were seven articles, all spelled out in stiff legal fashion, each ending with the phrase, "This to the scandal and disgrace of the military service at Fort Abercrombie, Dakota," on such and such a date.

Reno listened angrily, stiff at attention before the court.

"Take insulting liberties with the wife of said Captain Bell by taking both her hands in his own . . ."

"Take improper and insulting liberties with her by placing his arm around her waist . . ."

Upon not receiving an invitation, said to the post trader, "This means war! Mrs. Bell has thrown down the gauntlet and I will take it up!" and said further, "I will make it hot for her; I will drive her out of the regiment," thereby dishonorably using his power as commanding officer to revenge himself.

Used an obscene and licentious expression in the clubroom, namely, "That Mr. Wainwright would have his goose as well as another man, and he could have it with Mrs. Bell."

That he has told Wainwright, "Mrs. Bell's reputation is like a spoiled egg—you can't hurt it." And this was done for the dishonorable purpose of ruining Mrs. Bell's reputation.

That Reno had told Lieutenant Robinson, "Mrs. Bell ought to know better than to make a fight with me; her character is too vulnerable."

That Reno maliciously attempted to dishonor Mrs. Bell by prohibiting her from playing the organ at services.

Marcus Reno pleaded not guilty, firmly and with conviction. He had dressed himself perfectly, boots glowing, uniform fresh, everything as spit and polish as he could manage. This was his life on the line.

He sat down, wondering who were his friends and who weren't. Benteen was there. Most of the staff at Fort Abercrombie were there. The Reverend Wainwright. Mrs. Bell, Captain Bell, the post trader, John Hazelhurst. The faces were not friendly. He stared at the row of judges: Colonel William Hazen, Sixth Infantry, was its president and sat at the center of that row.

Colonel Sykes, Lieutenant Colonel Buell, Lieutenant Colonel Lugenbeel, Lieutenant Colonel Hunt, Lieutenant Colonel Huston, Lieutenant Colonel Carlin, Major Crofton, Major Bartlett. The prosecutor was Major Thomas Barr, judge advocate of the Department of Dakota.

Reno requested an adjournment: he scarcely had time to go through the charges with his attorneys. That was granted. They consulted all that day. He liked these lawyers but wondered if they grasped what he was up against. This wasn't just a trial about his conduct as an officer and a gentleman. This was much more, and everyone present knew it.

The next day, March 9, the trial got underway with Mrs. Bell as the first witness. His attorneys had sense enough not to land on her testimony. She stepped down, avoiding so much as a glance at Reno. Then Wainwright. Reno's attorneys questioned the reverend closely, especially as to why he did not move from the Bell residence when asked to do so to avoid scandal. The man simply said it was not necessary.

Hazelhurst was next, and then Robinson, and then two men who were not at Abercrombie: Wallace and Benteen. Both denied saying to Reno that Mrs. Bell should be expelled from the regiment. Then Slocum, and Troxel, and Van Horne, one by one.

Together, they made the prosecution's case, all laid out neatly, the specifics in each article backed by testimony, most of it by men present at Abercrombie.

The only testimony that rankled, as far as Marcus Reno was concerned, was that of Benteen and Wallace, both of them brother survivors from the Little Bighorn.

"Question them closely," he said to his attorneys.

And his attorneys did, making some headway at last. Benteen allowed that Marcus Reno's character was first rate. Wallace agreed that Reno's character had been very good. Benteen acknowledged talking to Reno about Mrs. Bell's questionable character.

It was time for a defense. Reno's attorneys presented a statement to the court, in which Reno asserted that he had never pulled Mrs. Bell toward him, but had only taken her hand gently to bid her good night. And in the episode at the doorstep, she had simply stumbled when she missed a step and fallen into his arms. She had not asked for an apology for these supposed offenses, neither when they happened nor later.

Reno thought his attorney, Davis, had made a good case. If Mrs. Bell had been outraged, she certainly would have shown it.

He had scarcely arrived at Fort Abercrombie when all this supposedly transpired; barely gotten his own bags unpacked, had not even taken over the command. He had arrived the afternoon of Sunday, the seventeenth of December; the first of his supposed outrages had occurred the evening of the eighteenth, before he had even assumed command; the second of these alleged outrages occurred on the twenty-first, a day after he assumed command.

Would the court believe that from the moment he arrived at Abercrombie, he was busy outraging Mrs. Bell? That, upon discovering that Captain Bell had just departed, he laid plans to seduce Mrs. Bell and put them into effect before he unpacked his kit? That he expected to have his way at once with a woman he didn't know except for a brief encounter at Fort Abraham Lincoln? That all of this alleged seduction had transpired in the space of seventy-two hours, from Monday to Thursday?

That all this could have occurred in the hours after he arrived, and on the eve of Christmas, defied credulity. Marcus Reno was certain the court would see a young harpy's machinations in all this and toss out the whole business and free him. He worried more about the rest of it; that he had assailed her reputation. No doubt he had, but if the court pitched out the absurd allegations of seduction, the court would probably pitch out the rest. The real Emily Bell was there, for all to see, and any experienced man could see it.

There was a second charge, that Reno had attempted to bribe Mrs. Bell's colored servant to conceal evidence, but it was as if the charge didn't exist. Everyone knew it was just another item to throw at Reno, concocted by officers with an agenda. And so it was barely discussed.

But the prosecution was intent on proving that he had spotted a vulnerable woman, tried at once to seduce her, had been twice rebuffed, and had found his revenge by blackening her reputation, using his powers as the commanding officer to do so. As if she had a reputation that could suffer any more blackening than it already had. She had irritated him; he would grant her that. She was a peculiar case, all right. Snubbing the post commander at her little party. So self-absorbed and vain that she interpreted everything that happened as seduction.

He sat heavily through all this, aware of the stares directed his way. There was anger in the room, undercurrents of cold hostility, something savage burning in the breast of Captain Bell and others: piety, righteous outrage, holier-than-thou scorn. He studied the judges one by one, their faces masks, their minds masked as well. They were veteran officers, skeptics, aware of the foibles of human nature, but would they waltz with Mrs. Bell? Of course not. Not unless they believed that the new commander had set down his bags and assaulted her, that ministers were unconcerned about their reputations, that Mrs. Bell's motives were snowy.

And so it went, day upon day, in St. Paul, Minnesota that March.

The trial wound up on the twentieth of March, and the room was emptied so that the judges could deliberate. Reno thanked his costly attorneys, and waited, feeling hopeful about it.

When at last the court brought Reno before it, he stood stiffly while the president, Colonel Hazen, read the verdict: guilty of the first charge in almost all particulars; not guilty of the second.

"And the court does therefore sentence him, Major Marcus A. Reno, Seventh Regiment of Cavalry, to be dismissed from the service."

# CHAPTER TWENTY-NINE

IT WASN'T OVER. AT LEAST THAT IS WHAT MARCUS RENO TOLD HIMSELF, as he puffed a fine Havana at a St. Paul chop house. He was alone. He was too much alone, and yet he rejected company.

General Terry had to review the proceedings and could pitch them out if he felt there was anything irregular about them. Then the case would be reviewed by the judge advocate general, and then it would go to General of the Army Sherman, and eventually to the president, Rutherford B. Hayes.

Surely, one of these discerning men would pitch out a case based on the proposition that within three days of arriving at a new post Major Reno assaulted a lady and impugned her honor.

His army career would be over if the charges were upheld. For nearly twenty years he had served honorably, often in harm's way, advancing in rank, winning commendation for gallantry. And now this.

He could only wait and fret and bide his time in St. Paul, where he was still under orders, until all that should be settled.

Things did not go well. Terry passed along the court-martial without comment. The judge advocate general, Brigadier General William Dunn, found largely against Reno:

"His course I cannot thus but regard as having been highly discreditable to himself, and as having most seriously compromised the respectability and honor of the military service."

Sherman confirmed the sentence, but with a certain tenderness for Reno, "who has borne the reputation of a brave officer."

Next was President Hayes, who approved the sentence but commuted it to suspension from rank and pay for two years from May 1, 1877.

Then the matter went to the secretary of war, George McCrary, who called Reno's conduct despicable, but "it is thought that his offenses, grave as they are, do not warrant the sentence of dismissal, and all its consequences, upon one who for twenty years has borne the reputation of a brave and honorable officer, and had maintained that reputation upon the battlefields of the Rebellion and in combat with Indians. The president has therefore modified the sentence, and it is hoped that Major Reno will appreciate the clemency thus shown him . . ."

And so it was settled in early May. Terry sent his adjutant to Reno with the papers. Reno might return to service after two years. He trembled upon reading the news. Hayes had spared him ignominy, and yet what was left? And how would he support himself? There was something of Mary Hannah's estate remaining, even after paying off the two lawyers, but now he would need to subsist himself for two long years without his three hundred a month salary.

But there was more: a great sorrow. He headed for his favorite chophouse alone that evening. There was no one to share this with, not even his lawyers. Especially not his lawyers. He ordered up two doubles of good rye, and had the barkeep bring him a dozen cigars. And there, in the shadowy corner of the saloon, under a hissing gas lamp, he puffed and sipped and finally quit the place, not hungry. He drifted through unknown alleys, had an uneasy time negotiating his way back to Fort Snelling, and several times lost his way. When he ascended the steep bluff to the post, he felt his heart hammer.

He waited for orders, for dismissal, for anything, but days slipped by without word. Would he serve his entire suspension within the confines of the Department of Dakota? He finally obtained a thirty-day leave. Then he petitioned to remove himself from the department, and set out for Pennsylvania, letting the department know how to reach him there.

He would visit his son in Pittsburgh, where he was being sheltered by Mary Hannah's sister and brother-in-law, Bertie and Wilson Orth, and then what? Reno didn't know. It wouldn't be a happy meeting. The Orths had never forgiven him for not coming home for Mary Hannah's funeral, and it did no good to explain that he was under orders and could not get away until the summer's work for the boundary commission was completed. He scarcely knew Ross; the boy was a stranger, and maybe much of that was Marcus's own failing. But now he would visit.

He boarded a steam train, and another and another, wending his way east in rocking coaches, smoking cigars whenever he could, sliding whiskey down his throat now and then from the flask at his bosom, his friend and companion in a time when he had no other.

Ross was an odd boy, pale and unsure, shy and sly around his father, who by then was merely a phantom to him; his real father and mother were the Orths. Reno took the boy to dinner, and on several outings around Pittsburgh. They walked out to the famous old point, where the Allegheny and Monongahela Rivers joined in a turbid flood, and the ruins of old Fort Pitt stood, but he could make no headway with the young stranger.

Ross rarely spoke, and only when spoken to, and seemed as distant and shrouded as the Allegheny hills lost beyond the steel city's perpetual haze.

"You doing all right, Ross?"

"Yes, sir."

"Maybe you'll join the army some day."

"Maybe, sir."

"The Orths, they taking good care of you?"

"Yes, sir."

"Are you wanting anything?"

"No, sir."

"You keeping up your grades?"

The boy paused. "I guess."

"Someday you'll inherit your mother's wealth; held in trust now, but yours on your majority. Enough to go to college. Become a professional man."

"Yes, sir."

"Miss your mother?"

"Yes, sir."

"I didn't get to see her very much. Always stationed somewhere, and she was sick."

"Yes, sir."

"We had some good times, Ross, you and she and I, running around the prairies out in Kansas."

"Yes, sir."

Reno pulled a cigar from his pocket, cut off the end with his cigar cutter, and fired up. "Good cigar is the best thing a man can have sometimes." That and a good wife and some good whiskey.

"I'm going to be in Harrisburg for a while. I'll look after you more."

"Yes, sir."

"Maybe have you come stay with me when school's out."

The boy nodded.

They walked back to the Orths, and Marcus knew he was not soon going to make headway getting to know his son.

He left for Harrisburg, on the Susquehanna River, the only place he could call home, the only place he had known love and hearth and family. They remembered him in gracious Harrisburg. He had helped organize the defense of the state capital, had been brevet brigadier general of the Pennsylvania volunteers during the war, and was related by marriage to the leading families. In Harrisburg, honor still resided in his name.

He engaged a room at the dark, comfortable Lochiel Hotel. He would await orders there. And soon the orders arrived, curtly addressed to "Sir" and not "Major Reno": he was free to leave the Department of Dakota, but not to leave the United States.

He accepted the limitation peacefully, stocked up on Havanas, and wondered how he would spend two years without pay. The Lochiel was expensive, but he chose to live there because it offered social contact. There would be money from Mary Hannah's real estate, willed half to him and half to Ross, whose portion was held in trust. He wasn't far from Washington, and didn't doubt that some personal contact with people in the War Department would turn things around for him.

He had his possessions expressed, and soon his entire worldly goods arrived via Railway Express in a steamer trunk. It amazed him sometimes that he was well advanced in years but without material possessions. He had no home or real estate, no furnishings, no considerable wardrobe, no library, no jewelry, no farms or timber lands or mines, no portion of any business. He had given his whole life to the United States Army, and had only his honor to show for it, and now his honor had been lost to him because of one transient moment he had been tempted by an unstable woman.

In those personnel files in the War Department rested his most cherished possessions: commendations from his commanders. Thrice raised in rank for "gallant meritorious services." There, nestled in his folder, was one he cherished particularly: his commander in the First Division, General Alfred T. A. Torbert, had thought so highly of Reno's conduct at Cold Harbor that he wrote Secretary of War Stanton:

"Sir, I take pleasure in recommending 'to your favorable consideration' Captain Marcus A. Reno, First U.S. Cavalry, for promotion to the rank of Brig. Gen'l . . ." Torbert went on to say that Reno had "distinguished himself at the battles of Coal Harbor and Trevillian Station for coolness, bravery, and good judgment. I know him to be fully competent to fill the position."

And Sheridan approved:

"The recommendation of Brig. Gen'l Torbert is highly approved. The cavalry service has no better officer than Capt. Reno. He is full of energy and ability, has been in all the cavalry engagements of present campaign. He is one of the most promising young cavalry officers of this army . . ."

Nothing came of it, but those glowing recommendations rested in Reno's file.

Later, when Torbert encouraged Reno to apply to Pennsylvania governor Andrew Curtin to give Reno the colonelcy of the Twelfth Pennsylvania Cavalry Regiment, Sheridan weighed in once again:

"I think so much of Captain Reno that I heretofore recommended him for appointment as Brig. General . . . Your Excellency will make no mistake in making this appointment."

And General William Emory concurred: "I consider him one of the best and most faithful cavalry officers . . ."

These were his sole wealth, and all that he really cared to own. These were his gold, his silver, his castles, and his heaven. Let him possess honor and his soul asked for little more.

There in Harrisburg he set out to renew old acquaintances, but fate swiftly intervened.

One day, he picked up his mail at the hotel desk, and found himself facing a new set of charges, these endorsed by most of the officers of the Seventh Cavalry, and dating back to his first hours at Fort Abraham Lincoln after the regiment returned from the Little Bighorn, the very night the worn and weary command had returned to its base.

By the light of the purring gas lamp, alone in his room, he read the accusation.

Three charges in all:

First, drunkenness on duty. It accused him of being drunk on September 26, at Fort Abraham Lincoln, at a time when the post was endangered by Sioux; and second, that Reno had become drunk while on duty, commanding at Fort Abercrombie, December 31, 1876.

The second, conduct unbecoming to an officer and a gentleman. It accused Reno of making insulting and malicious remarks to a brother officer and engaging in fisticuffs with Lieutenant Manley to the disgrace of the service, September 26, at Fort Abraham Lincoln.

And third, conduct prejudicial to good order and military discipline:

Reno did provoke an encounter with Manley and attempted to expel Manley from the Officers' Club Room at Fort Abraham Lincoln, and provoked a personal encounter with Lieutenant Varnum, challenging Varnum to a duel. And in addition, sent for pistols for the purpose of engaging in a duel.

Reno read it and sighed.

"We, the undersigned officers of the Seventh U.S. Cavalry earnestly desire . . . that Major Marcus A. Reno be brought to trial on the foregoing charges and specifications."

Reno studied the signatures, and found among them some of the officers who had been with him on the hilltop at Little Bighorn, in addition to the Fort Abercrombie contingent that had brought the earlier charges. Here were McDougall and Moylan and DeRudio, men who had fought beside him during those darkest hours.

He remembered bitterly that he had failed in his report on the battle to commend any of them, citing only Benteen for brave and meritorious service. The other officers had, by and large, fought bravely, and should have been commended. But Reno had not cited them for gallantry or courage or coolness under fire, and now he was paying the price.

They wanted him out, along with half a dozen other officers who weren't there: Bell, Robinson, Eckerson, Slocum, Fuller, Gresham, McCormick, Russell. And the complaint was also signed by Dr. Williams, who had been in the Club Room. Reno scarcely knew some of them; they had joined the Seventh after he had removed to Fort Abercrombie. Yet they had been persuaded to join in the lynch party against a man they didn't know solely on hearsay.

Reno sat heavily on his bed, digesting all this. Benteen had not signed it. Others who had been his friends or at least comrades under fire, had not signed it. Not Wallace, not Godfrey, not Edgerly, not Hare. So it wasn't all of them, but just a cabal, led by the implacable Captain Bell whose sole purpose was to eject Major Reno from the army. But the news afflicted him to his very core. The cabal was not content with his suspension for two years, and wanted him out, out forever, out in disgrace.

He shifted the dead cigar jammed between his teeth. He could only wait and see. But he would fight it, fight it hard, spend more on lawyers, fight to the finish.

It took over a month before he got word. Colonel Sturgis, commander of the Seventh, had disapproved the charges, citing their obvious bad grace; so had other reviewers up the chain of command, and ultimately the adjutant general's office concurred in mid-July. Reno was on the mat, but not yet thrown out of the army.

# CHAPTER THIRTY

THAT FIERCE SUMMER, MARCUS RENO HAD, AT LAST, A CHANCE TO study the furious reports and wild accusations that had fired up the national press in the months following the Little Bighorn battle. He had seen some of it, even at remote Fort Abercrombie, sent him by his brother or sister, or the Rosses in Harrisburg. But now he had the chance to review it all, and he set about it with vigor and rage, because so little of it had anything to do with reality.

There was, first of all, the incredible array of material published in the *New York Herald,* that most remarkable paper that managed to cover everything important in the whole world. When the *Far West* had reached Bismarck, after the battle, some fifty thousand words had been wired to the *Herald* over twenty-four hours, at an awesome cost of three thousand dollars, or so it was said.

Eighteen seventy-six was an election year, and partisan papers were quick to blame Republican President Grant, and the corrupt Indian Bureau, for the disaster, or Democrat George Armstrong Custer, for recklessly attacking a village that was far too large for his command to handle.

Reno gratefully collected the clippings assiduously gathered by his in-laws, headed for the newspapers to read dispatches and exchange papers, got what he could from libraries, caught up with every issue of the *Army and Navy Journal* where furious rhetorical wars about the battle were being waged in issue after issue. But the *Herald* was the greatest source. Its reporter, O'Kelly, had assiduously interviewed everyone who would sit still.

Reno pulled off his soaked shirt in the furnace heat of the hotel room, lit up a green-leafed Baltimore cigar, laid out the clippings, and set to work. The scope of coverage and controversy flabbergasted him; out in Dakota, isolated from the passion of the nation, he had little idea of the furor that gripped the nation on its hundredth birthday. The blamers were busy from the start: someone had to take the blame, and at first it was General Terry.

Terry's confidential report to Generals Sherman and Sheridan, stolen by an adept reporter and promptly published, reached the public before the official report did, and caused an uproar. While the discreet general had publicly and officially avoided blaming Custer, his private report to his superiors concluded that Custer had violated orders and acted rashly.

But for those who saw the lieutenant colonel as a victim, there were other villains, namely President Ulysses Grant, Marcus Reno, and Frederick Benteen. There was no shortage of those who enjoyed parceling out blame, and officers of every stripe, even former Confederates, were quick to come to conclusions.

Some unnamed officers at the headquarters of the Military Division of the Missouri thought that the disaster was "brought on by that foolish pride which so often results in the defeat of men." And that Custer, with a blind desire to win the glory for himself, had rushed forward, and that Custer was violating orders and even if he had won, he might well have been court-martialed.

The reporters did not neglect Grant, Sherman, and Sheridan, either. The *Herald* quoted President Grant as saying, "I regard Custer's massacre as a sacrifice of troops, brought on by Custer himself that was wholly unnecessary—wholly unnecessary."

The *New York Times* reported that Sherman and Sheridan believed that Custer had been "rashly imprudent to attack such a large number of Indians."

Much to Reno's surprise, he found sharp criticism of Custer issuing from Colonel Sturgis, commander of the Seventh, who had been on detached duty. There had been some friction between Custer and Sturgis, largely because Custer wanted to run the regiment as his own. But now Sturgis's son lay among the dead, and Sturgis opined publicly that Custer was a brave man but also a very selfish one, insanely ambitious of glory. He was, moreover, tyrannical and had no regard for the soldiers under him; that he had made his attack recklessly, much earlier than he had been supposed to, and with men and horses exhausted from forced marches.

Reb General McCausland, on the other hand, who had fought against Custer in the Shenandoah Valley, rushed to Custer's defense, saying he would have attacked exactly as Custer had, and that's what cavalry is for—the charge.

Reno chomped on dead cigars, relit them from the gas lamp, twisted them out in dirty ashtrays, and blotted up the violent opinion seething through the press nonstop.

He grunted. Men who weren't there shouldn't be second-guessing. Those armchair generals had no idea how many Indians there were, how determined they were, and how Custer had divided his command in a way that allowed it to be destroyed in pieces.

There were reasons aplenty for the disaster. The *Herald* thundered that the death of Custer could be laid to Grant's peace policy, "which feeds, clothes and takes care of their noncombatant force while men are killing our troops—that is what killed Custer." And what is more, "that nest of thieves, the Indian Bureau, with its thieving agents and favorites as Indian traders, and its mock humanity and pretense of piety—that is what killed Custer."

That amused Reno.

After devouring the clippings, the magazine articles, and the letters crowding the columns of the *Army and Navy Journal,* Reno turned to the book he knew would excoriate him.

It was hot in Harrisburg, and not much air cleansed heat from his room. Smoke from his cigars had penetrated the draperies and coverlet, but he didn't mind. He could not think or read or relax without a cigar between his lips, dead or alive.

Frederick Whittaker, of Mount Vernon, New York, was a novelist, itself the most dubious of bastard professions, given to lies and fantasies, made-up worlds disconnected from reality. He had regularly pumped out florid romances, the dime-novel variety, but something about the Custer massacre had shot passion through him, and he had hastily penned a paean to his hero, with the help of Custer's widow. Much of it was merely Custer's own journalism reprinted in haste so that Whittaker might rush into print ahead of the rest and thus capitalize on the disaster.

Reno was curious about the man who had criticized him so sharply, and through old Pennsylvania militia connections he soon had Whittaker's military record. The man who called himself a captain had in fact aspired to a law career, but had enlisted when the war broke out as a private in the Sixth New York Cavalry. He rose to become a second lieutenant of Company A, New York Provisional Cavalry. He had not been breveted captain, though he called himself one in the sensational press.

He had, apparently, once met Custer in the editorial offices of *Galaxy,* a magazine for which both men wrote, and formed a friendship then and there. From then on, Custer could do no wrong in Whittaker's view; he possessed no fault, no failing, no weakness of character. And that is what Major Reno found when he lay abed in his drawers, puffing on Havanas, sweat collecting in his armpits, reading idolatry.

Whittaker's book, *A Complete Life of Gen. George A. Custer,* was published in New York just about the time Reno was arriving at Fort Abercrombie and unwittingly getting himself into grave trouble with Emily in the space of four days.

Whittaker's depiction of the battle relied on dubious and contradictory newspaper reports, not official records, and at times Reno scarcely recognized the fight he was in. It was noteworthy that none of the surviving officers had offered any comment, not even Reno's adversary Tom Weir, who had befriended Whittaker and had thought Reno's conduct in the fight was timid. Where were Wallace, Benteen, French, Hare, Godfrey, McDougall? Entirely absent. *Not even Weir.*

Reno grunted, arose, poured some Pennsylvania rye into a tumbler, added a splash, and shot it down his parched throat.

Had Custer disobeyed General Terry's orders? Of course not. The orders were entirely permissive, granting Custer the liberty to conduct his campaign as he saw fit. Reno had seen those orders. They did give Custer latitude, enabling him to use his judgment as circumstances arose. But they also contemplated a coordinated pincer assault on the village, with Custer closing on one side and Gibbon on the other.

It was too hot in his hotel room to read, but Reno wanted to see what the son of a bitch was saying, so he sipped rye, lipped his cigar, sweated, and read.

It all boiled down to a few accusations: Reno had failed to comply with his orders to attack, and Benteen had deliberately disobeyed his orders to rush to help; they had languished on the hilltop instead of relieving Custer, and between them, they permitted Custer and his command to perish. It was the simpleminded explanation of an amateur strategist who had an agenda, the canonization of his hero, Custer.

Reno was tired of being the scapegoat, but thought there was no reason to respond to a dime novelist with a sensational account of the battle. Benteen already had, in a caustic letter published in the *Army and Navy Journal.* In any case, it was plain that the novelist was simply stirring up trouble in order to sell books. That was an old game, and Reno dismissed it. Best to keep his counsel and let the Whittaker controversy die down.

There were more important things to do. He was now close to Washington, D.C., close to the War Department, and he intended to wield whatever influence he could in person. Some interviews, some private luncheons, a little time spent sipping with some of those in the seat of power, and maybe he would find his suspension reversed. All he wanted was to resume his command and career, salvage his honor, and get on with life.

He would spend the next months making contacts in Washington, and maybe it would all bear fruit. But that was not to be: Frederick Whittaker, incensed that Marcus Reno had not been summarily drummed out of the service for cowardice, was making new plans.

# CHAPTER THIRTY-ONE

THE MONTHS OF HIS SUSPENSION DRIFTED SLOWLY BY. HE FELT EVEN more melancholic than he usually did. He saw little of his Ross and Haldeman relatives. His brother-in-law Andrew Ross lived in York township, while Bertie Orth, Mary Hannah's younger sister, lived in Pittsburgh. And none of the Rosses and Haldemans were inclined to invite the disgraced major to their hearths or share his society. But Harrisburg was the only place he could call home, and there was his acquaintance Lyman Gilbert, who handled the estate.

So he camped in his hotel room, solitary, lonely, and moody. It wasn't a home but another bivouac; not a hearth or a haven or a place filled with relatives, for he was a bird of passage, alighting there only to fly again soon.

Sometimes he ventured to the Harrisburg Cemetery and the Ross family plot, where a freshly cut stone marked the grave of Mary Hannah, and there he came alive in his pain, the tearing sensation of loss awakening slumbering feeling. How short had been his sojourn with her, but how sweet. She had been so lively, bright of eye; her unusual education had polished her, made her glow at dinner tables and in all sorts of company.

He remembered her touch and her kiss, and her playfulness. He remembered her sighs, and the tears that rose whenever he went off to war. He remembered the humor with which she tackled dreary billets in miserable frontier posts; the magical way she gathered officers wives to her and made their frontier life a cotillion. It took only a vase of freshly gathered prairie wildflowers for her to turn the billet into a home.

Now he stared at the sunken earth, hollowed over her, as if her small frame could not support the soil above, and the loss that stole through him was keener and deeper than ever before.

He had no one to talk to in Harrisburg, so he talked to her.

"I'm here because of Captain Bell's wife," he said. "You would have been amused by Emily Bell. She thinks all men are bent upon ruining her. I was blind to her mean little ways and what they could do to me. I confess I was lonely; she drew me, until she stung. I'm sorry, Mary Hannah. I'm so sorry. Here I am, in exile, waiting out a two-year imprisonment in this place."

He entrained for Washington frequently, and looked up old Civil War comrades, men who had fought and bled and struggled at his side, but his presence put them in an awkward position; they were the honorable officers; he was the dishonored and suspended major. He did, at least, lunch a time or two with editors of the *Army and Navy Journal* and gave them a true account of the struggle out in distant Montana Territory.

The controversy never ceased.

When a year of his sentence had elapsed in the spring of 1878, he wrote President Hayes seeking clemency. He had not meant to insult the reputation Mrs. Bell, he explained; what he had said was private, for one person, and he had never imagined it would slip into public circulation. The suspension of his pay was a heavy burden; he was responsible for the upbringing of his son, and needed his salary. He would like to return to duty.

The president responded swiftly, and sent word through Secretary of War George McCrary:

"Sir, I am directed by the president to inform you that the question of a further modification of your sentence has been considered by him and he feels constrained to decline to reopen the case or change his order therein. I am obliged to inform you that the president's decision in this matter is final."

Reno settled back to whiling away his suspension, living a life marked by restless prowling of bistros. What could a man without honor do? What hearths and salons and drawing rooms would be open to such a man?

He saw little of his son; the Orths seemed almost to shield Robert Ross Reno from his father, and the boy was a stranger, or rather, Reno was a stranger to his boy. Here was a lad in his teens, and the whole time Marcus Reno had spent with his son could well be numbered in months, and most of those when the boy was but a child. Maybe someday, someday, Marcus Reno and Robert Ross Reno would discover the bond that joined them.

Often he relived his times of war. Sometimes the War of the Rebellion preoccupied him, especially those months when he was General Torbert's chief of staff, riding everywhere, always in harm's way, seeing the blood and scream of battle in his mind's eye, hearing the whisper of shot, the muted roar of distant cannon, and the rattle of a cavalry charge.

But most often when his mind wandered from the confines of his cloistered hotel room, it was to the wilderness of the far west, where the Seventh Regiment of Cavalry rode into the largest Indian village ever known on the continent. He remembered it all so clearly: the sluggish horse under him, the weary horses of his brave hundred and twelve, horses that had been punished by long marches for days, and could scarcely carry men to war.

He remembered that swift chaotic flow of red men around his two flanks, their bodies barely visible through the dust raised by Indian ponies, ghostly multitudes running, dodging, sliding through river brush, even as his weary horses cantered forward. He remembered the occasional snap of their rifles not from ahead, but from the flank. He remembered the way the scouts, who had been detailed to drive off the village horse herd, had fallen back on the left, retreating before the fury of the Sioux.

He lived it all again, as he smoked his panatelas and sipped his Monongahela rye, and he always came to the same conclusion: he would do exactly what he did; he had chosen the only course; had he not re-treated to the woods, his command would have been engulfed; had he not broken out and crossed the river and headed for the bluffs, his command would have been slaughtered.

He daydreamed of refighting it all, in some fantasy world in which he could permit his harshest critics to ride beside him, see what he saw, draw their own conclusions. He wanted the ones who weren't there—the ones whose views were shaped in drawing rooms and parlors—to see, to know, to feel, to experience, every shred of the violence that swept through that command. He wanted to grin at them when they beseeched him to retreat to the bluffs. He wanted to smile when they headed out to find Custer's command, and were driven back. He wanted to put Whittaker on a cavalry mount and let him command the battalion, lead it into that swarm of Indians, and let him see.

But it was idle to dream, to relive the past. He scolded himself for it, as if he had been doing something embarrassing and unmanly.

The entire controversy concerning the Battle of the Little Bighorn had simmered down and vanished from public consciousness. The press had other stories to pursue. Whittaker's idolatrous book about Custer at last flagged and died in the bookstalls. And maybe Reno should have taken that as a warning.

As spring surrendered to summer in 1878, things suddenly changed. There in the Harrisburg papers were dispatches from Washington about . . . himself. Whittaker, it seemed, had been busy all the while, scheming to throw Marcus Reno out of the service, or to "purge" it, in his words, of a coward. Whittaker had penned an impassioned letter to the Wyoming Territorial delegate to congress, one W. W. Corlett, asking that Congress itself investigate the battle of the Little Bighorn, and especially the conduct of Major Reno and Captain Benteen, with a view to cleansing the service of miscreants.

There, indeed, in the Harrisburg press, was the letter, a lengthy accusation aimed at himself, Major Marcus Reno, United States Army. He knew what the contents would be even before he settled down to read this amazing story. But first he relit a dead stogy he had stubbed out, and pumped blue smoke into the hotel room until a perfect aromatic haze surrounded him. Then he fired the gas lamp, settled into the sticky chair in that humid room, and read:

"Having been called upon to prepare the biography of the late brevet Major General George A. Custer, U.S.A., a great amount of evidence, oral and written, came into my hands tending to prove that the sacrifice of his life and the lives of his immediate command at the Battle of the Little Bighorn was useless, and owing to the cowardice of his subordinates. I desire, therefore, to call your attention, and that of Congress, through you, to the necessity of ordering an official investigation by a committee of your honorable body into the conduct of United States troops engaged in the Battle of the Little Bighorn . . ."

Whittaker claimed to have information that "gross cowardice was displayed therein by Major Marcus Reno," and because of that cowardice, "the orders of Lieutenant Colonel Custer, commanding officer, to said Reno, to execute a certain attack, were not made," and that this failure and disobedience resulted in defeat of U.S. forces instead of victory. And "after Major Reno's cowardly flight he was joined by Captain F. W. Benteen," and the force was kept idle while Custer was fighting to the death against the whole force of the Indians, and that battle was within Reno's knowledge, the firing being audible, and "the consequences of this second exhibition of cowardice and incompetency was the massacre of Lieutenant Colonel Custer and five companies of the Seventh United States Cavalry."

Reno had heard it all before, but this time the gloves were off, and the attack was proceeding bare-knuckled.

There were other charges. One was that Reno's battle report "is, in the main, false and libelous to the memory of the late Lieutenant Colonel Custer, in that it represents the defeat of the United States forces on that occasion as owing to the division by Custer of his forces, and to ignorance of the enemy's force, all serious charges against the capacity of said Custer as an officer; whereas the defeat was really owing to the cowardice and disobedience of said Reno and to the willful neglect of said

Reno and Captain Benteen to join battle with the Indians in support of their commanding officer . . ."

Whittaker went on to say that Congress enjoys the power to compel the testimony of everyone, and ought to act to get to the bottom of it.

Reno studied the lengthy letter, now percolating through the nation's press, and knew this would never go away, not for as long as he drew breath, and that his troubles had only begun. But maybe there was opportunity in it.

In the selfsame story he discovered that the House Committee on Military Affairs had reported a resolution to the House directing an investigation of the Custer massacre, after members had read Whittaker's letter.

Maybe something good would come of it.

# CHAPTER THIRTY-TWO

RENO PACKED HIS VALISE, STUFFED HIS BREAST POCKET WITH HAVANAS, purchased railroad fare to Washington, and set forth. Upon arriving he headed immediately for the editorial offices of the *Army and Navy Journal,* not far from the War Department.

Within that bleak gray editorial sanctum, decorated with regimental flags, sepia photographs of officers, Latin mottos, and a huge American flag, he encountered an avuncular and fat clerk, and pulled an envelope from his suit coat.

"I'm Reno. Want this run," he said. "It's a letter."

"Major Reno? *The* Major Reno. Ah, indeed."

The clerk took the letter and read it respectfully, then smiled. "Very good; I'd do the same thing, in your boots. We're printing Friday. I'll have it set and put right in."

"Thank you."

"Frankly, major, we're friends of yours here. You'll see some of our own editorial comment on this affair in the next issue. Scoundrels, the whole lot."

"I'm glad to have support here. Sometimes I wonder who's left."

"We are, major, we are indeed."

The clerk extended a soft hand and Reno shook it.

His letter, actually addressed to the chairman of the House Military Committee, H. H. Banning, asked for an investigation.

"During the last two years I have been compelled to suffer the circulation of various malignant reports concerning this affair about myself, emanating, it is presumed, from the same irresponsible source. This being the first time that the author, perhaps emboldened by my silence, has ventured to give them definite shape. I respectfully demand that I may have this opportunity to vindicate my character and record which have thus been widely assailed."

Reno checked in at Willard's hotel and waited. But Congress adjourned without taking action. He was disappointed, but perhaps this was the way to proceed. From his commodious hotel room, where he could gaze across rooftops to the White House, he penned a letter to President Rutherford Hayes:

"The Congress adjourned without taking any action and I now respectfully appeal to the Executive for a 'court of inquiry' to investigate the affair, that the many rumors started by camp gossip may be set at rest and the truth be fully known."

A court of inquiry was simply an elaborate and formal investigation, conducted for the purpose of adducing facts. For him, it would be something of a trial: he would either walk away with the sun shining on his good name, or he would find himself ruined. But he didn't hesitate. He could not imagine the court would come to any conclusion other than to exonerate him. And when his name once again shone like newly polished brass, then would he find his lost life.

This time, Reno didn't have long to wait. General Sherman approved. The Secretary of War approved. And the Department of Dakota, in the person of General Terry, was ordered to convene the court and order Reno's attendance. He had gotten what he wanted this time, in the space of a few days. He packed his black valise, boarded a train for Harrisburg, and awaited orders.

For some considerable while that summer and fall, Reno heard nothing. But a court of inquiry was no easy matter to put together. The witnesses, in particular, had to be gathered. In the case of the Department of Dakota, the summer's campaign against roving hostile tribes had to be completed. Survivors of the Little Bighorn had scattered to various posts, and all must be notified to report at the trial. Reno felt jubilant: now he would clear his name, once and for all.

But there were difficulties ahead. For most of two years he had been without pay. He would be forced to stay in some strange city during the entire proceeding, at his own expense. He would be compelled to pay a first-rate attorney. He had subsisted on the rental income from the farm he had inherited from Mary Hannah, and from the rental on their Front Street home, but that would not begin to pay a lawyer.

He needed cash, and one way to get it would be reinstatement in the service. And that meant asking President Hayes, once again, to reinstate him. He began with a declaration of innocence, added that the punishment in the form of financial deprivation was much too severe, having already reached four thousand and six hundred dollars, and then he went on to point out that he had no income to sustain him during the forthcoming court of inquiry in a distant city, and would like to be restored to active duty. He posted the letter with hope, and thought surely this time the president would see the merit of his case.

But no answer ever drifted his way. The last response from War Secretary McCrary had indicated that the president's decision was final, and so it proved to be.

He set out to find a lawyer in Harrisburg. The inquiry would not be a criminal trial, with a verdict of guilty or innocent, but it could lead to a court-martial if he were found to have violated the army's battle standards. Here was the chance he had pined for; the chance to show the world what he was made of; the chance to trump all the newspaper speculation and misinformation with the careful deliberations of a court. That meant not just a lawyer, but a lawyer so fine that the best case would be made in his favor.

Harrisburg did not lack excellent lawyers, and the man Marcus Reno chose to defend him was widely regarded as top flight. Lyman Gilbert was still a young man, but had served as deputy attorney general for the state.

What's more, Gilbert was a friend of the Ross family and his son's court-appointed financial guardian.

Reno visited Gilbert in his office, and shook hands with the slight, cheerful, blue-eyed man.

"I'm here, Lyman, to ask you to defend me in a forthcoming court of inquiry, I know not where. It will be in some distant city."

Swiftly Reno described the nature of a military court of inquiry, and its purposes.

Gilbert nodded. "I'll do it, Marcus, but I should caution you I've not had experience before such a tribunal."

"It's not a criminal trial. They'll ask about the battle and my conduct in it. About that, sir, I am adamant. I gave a good account of myself and have nothing to be ashamed of."

Gilbert nodded.

"Lyman, I am presently suspended from the army, and have a year to go before reinstatement. You must know about it. The press has made much of it. A woman was involved. A most dubious woman, whose reputation was universally understood to be too fragile to withstand much scrutiny. I played the fool, though not as you might imagine, and she bit me, like the black widow spider, and no appeal on my part has altered events since then."

Gilbert laughed softly. "We shall exclude all that. What's before the tribunal is a matter of honor, and I believe your record bears scrutiny."

"It does, sir! Here, look at these." Reno undid his portfolio and extracted the commendations that had accumulated over twenty years of life in the service. "I ended up a brevet brigadier general of Pennsylvania volunteers, and a brevet lieutenant colonel in the regular army, and Lyman, one doesn't arrive at that estate by acts of cowardice."

Gilbert donned wire-rimmed spectacles and studied the material. "I shall want to examine this closely, but now, major, we must discuss things more immediate."

"You mean, the battle?"

"No, not yet. We'll go over that in such detail that I'll have everything you did, everything you thought, everything you observed in your fellow officers, and everything you said to your superiors, such as General Terry, following. I'll break your battle down into hours and minutes and account for it all. But that's for the future. No, sir, what I want now is how you fetched yourself to this mess. It was that novelist, wasn't it? Isn't that what I read?"

"Whittaker, yes."

"That's the name. God spare the world from novelists. I followed the account in the press with some interest, of course. This battle attracts attention even now, two years later. Whittaker, the finger-pointer. Start with him, and tell me how it led to walking through my door, there, and expending your dwindling resources on a man who charges a considerable fee."

Gilbert's face wrinkled into humor. But everything he was saying was to a purpose, and his object now was to see whether he would be paid.

"Sir, you know more about me than I know of you, but I'll refresh you. I was widowed in eighteen and seventy-four, inherited a modest estate here. My son Robert Ross received half the estate, which is held in trust for him, and that makes selling such properties somewhat complex but still possible so long as you, his court-appointed financial guardian, are satisfied. But as for your services, sir, I will sell my inheritance if necessary."

"That's an expression of your commitment, major. Some might value honor as something less than so much real property."

"Mr. Gilbert, if I valued honor less, I would not have asked for this court of inquiry to clear my name. The army went right along with my request, probably because there's such a controversy about the whole affair, or maybe to thwart a congressional investigation by preempting it. I could just as well slide through, wait out my suspension, and return to the command without spending a dime."

"I like a man who will spend his last, if necessary. It tells me much about him, and assures me of some degree of success."

"I will spend my last, Mr. Gilbert. And if the estate does not suffice to pay you, I'll devote my major's salary to it until it is paid off to the last cent."

# CHAPTER THIRTY-THREE

---

MARCUS RENO CHECKED INTO THE STATELY PALMER HOUSE IN CHICAGO, where the Reno court of inquiry was convening.

There, in the marbled rooms of a grand hotel, would unfold an inquiry into his conduct in the battle, and in particular, his *cowardice*. How does a man defend himself against such an accusation? How does he prove to veteran officer-judges that he conducted himself gallantly in the heat of battle? And even if he were cleared by this court of examiners, would he still be the victim of mean gossip and scorn?

It seemed a trap from which he could hardly escape, no matter what the verdict. And yet, a clean record was the place to start. Let them scrutinize everything, let nothing be overlooked, let these men put themselves in his shoes during that fight, and he felt fairly sure they would conclude that he did what he had to do, and acted incisively.

So, this thirteenth day of January, 1879, the Palmer House housed a number of senior army officers and their aides, as well as a body of witnesses mostly but not entirely military, and a clamorous press, busy rehashing every facet of the disastrous battle and buttonholing officers of every description for quotable material.

This would be not just a dress occasion, but a spit-and-polish occasion, where the forms of military usage meant everything. Reno himself was smartly attired in a fresh blue uniform, complete with immaculate white gloves. He looked grand.

The conference room filled swiftly; witnesses, reporters, scrambling for seats. Reno watched the tribunal that would decide upon his honor assemble: its president was Colonel John King, Ninth Infantry, the senior officer present. Another was Colonel Wesley Merritt, Fifth Cavalry, a bold soldier if ever there was one. And the third was Lieutenant Colonel W. B. Royall, Third Cavalry. The recorder—this was not a trial, and did not utilize a prosecutor—was First Lieutenant Jesse M. Lee, young and inexperienced, and an odd choice indeed if a serious case were to be made against Reno.

All this was costing him more than he could afford. He had borrowed eight hundred dollars from his son's trust fund, pledging his life insurance policy as collateral. Since Lyman Gilbert was his son's financial guardian as well as Reno's counsel, he approved, and the major had for the moment some expense money.

Gilbert himself could not be present that first day, but everyone else had assembled. All but three of the officers who had survived the battle were present. Tom Weir had drunk himself to death and had been buried only a few days before. And Captain French was himself being disciplined and thus was unable to testify. Lieutenant Gibson was not present either.

But there they were, sitting in a row, waiting to testify: Benteen, Godfrey, Mathey, McDougall, Moylan, DeRudio, Edgerly, Hare, Varnum, and Wallace. Porter, the surgeon, was present also, along with some of the civilian packers and scouts, and a few enlisted men.

And there was Reno's bête noire, gaunt, wolfish Frederick Whittaker, scribbling notes to young and earnest Lieutenant Lee, making himself an éminence grise in the courtroom. Reno studied the man, noting his averted gaze, his downturned mouth, his sour presence. This was the hanging judge whose accusations had started it all, and who was now present to shepherd—if a civilian could—this affair to the conclusion he had in mind, ousting Marcus Reno from the service.

Because Lyman Gilbert could not be present, that first day passed without event. But the next day the court admitted into evidence the letter written by Whittaker to Wyoming's congressional delegate W. W. Corlett.

So Marcus Reno was now branded a *coward* and an incompetent in a military tribunal; suddenly this was no longer merely a newspaper affair.

Lieutenant Wallace was the first survivor to testify for Recorder Lee. He noted that Reno had received the fewest troops and was ordered to charge the village with these and Custer would support him. He recollected that both men and horses were exhausted after a long forced march. Wallace described the skirmish line, the retreat to the woods where the horses and fresh ammunition were, the disorderly flight to the hilltop.

Wallace was straight and true.

Was Major Reno's decision to abandon the timber a sound one? Gilbert wished to know.

If they had stayed in the timber, "Major Reno and every man with him would have been killed," Wallace replied.

And what about Reno's coolness under fire, and judgment?

"All that you could expect from anyone."

The next day, Wallace's testimony continued. Gilbert asked whether there was any point when Reno displayed a lack of courage.

"None that I can recall or find fault with."

Gilbert asked whether there was any point at which Reno showed a lack of military skill.

"No, I do not recall any."

That was a start. But Whittaker, off to the rear, was furiously scribbling notes, and Reno knew his ordeal had barely begun.

Frederic Girard was next. There was no love lost between the civilian interpreter and Reno, because Reno had fired him once for helping himself to government property. The lean old border man, weathered to the color of a chestnut, hadn't much to say, other than he believed that the major's command could have held out in the woods indefinitely. Considering the source, Reno didn't think the testimony was damaging.

Next was Lieutenant Varnum, who was chief of scouts during the fight, and who claimed he had seen Custer's Gray Horse Company up on the bluffs, which was a remarkable feat of vision, given the distances. But again, Varnum saw no cowardice in Reno's conduct.

"Certainly there was no sign of cowardice or anything of that sort in his conduct and nothing specially the other way."

Varnum added that Reno didn't have enough men to hold the timber.

Dr. Porter took the stand, and said he saw nothing heroic nor anything cowardly in Reno's conduct, but he seemed somewhat flustered.

"The bullets were coming pretty fast, and I think he did not know whether to stay there or leave."

Captain Moylan followed, and Gilbert elicited from him the belief that the command had exhausted two-thirds of its ammunition in the valley fight; he himself had sent several men during the valley fight to retrieve ammunition from saddlebags.

Lieutenant Lee asked Moylan about Reno's courage, and Moylan replied that Reno rode at the head of the column and his orders "were given as coolly as a man under such circumstances can give them, and I saw nothing that indicated cowardice about him." And in the timber, "there was a certain amount of excitement, I suppose, visible on his face, as well as that of anybody else, but any traces of cowardice I failed to discover." As for leaving the timber, Moylan concurred. "In my judgment, the command, without assistance, would have been annihilated in the timber."

George Herendeen, civilian scout, testified and added nothing new.

Each evening, after the court adjourned, Reno found himself alone. None of the officers wished to fraternize with him, not only because of the inquiry, but because he was a man on suspension from duty, and a man once convicted. While that suited Lyman Gilbert fine, Reno ofttimes peered across the smoky hotel saloon at knots of men in blue, yearning to rejoin them, wanting their esteem, wanting to slap them on the back, see a smile in their faces. But for the moment he was a pariah.

He downed a rye whiskey and fired up a cigar, breathing pungent blue smoke into the air, which drifted under the gas lamps on the wall.

Gilbert, the quiet and urbane Yale College man, ignored them, and focused entirely on the day's testimony and what might come next, while barely touching the glass before him.

"Lyman, there's something those judges should know. They mostly are not Indian fighters. They're men who fought bravely in the War of the Rebellion. But Indian fighting's not like that."

"What's different, major?"

"There's no surrender. In a war between white men, you can run up a white flag, lay down your arms, put your hands high. You can't do that fighting the Indians, Lyman. You surrender, and you're dead. You put up a white flag, you put down your arms, you raise your hands, and you die. That affects command, sir. There are no prisoners of war. The Indians won't take you off to a camp, feed you and then release you when the war's over. No. In the Indian wars, you fight, flee, or die. Those are the choices."

"How did that affect your command, Marcus?"

"When the warriors weren't running, the way Custer said they always did, when they kept coming and coming and surrounding me and turning my flank, Lyman, I was exactly in the position Custer got himself into. But he still believed they would run, so he kept on, kept on, kept on going until he was engulfed. He couldn't retreat in my direction because they'd already cut him off. They all fought to the death because they had to.

"In the valley I saw the handwriting on the wall, and I knew there was no prison camp waiting for us, no prison camp, only the end of everything, and it was my duty to save my command from annihilation.

"I think I saved not only my command, but Benteen's. If I had charged onward, the way Whittaker wants, I would not be here, nor any of those who are testifying. And then, with Custer finished off, and Reno finished off, and Benteen on exhausted mounts, those two or three thousand warriors would have finished the rest, without one prisoner.

"So I think what I'm saying is, when you know there's no way to surrender to an Indian, your tactics are a little different. I saved over three hundred troopers from certain death."

"I'll make note of it. You look drawn. What's worrying you the most, Marcus?"

"That I'm here alone, and after we win this, I'll still be here alone."

"That the court won't matter?"

"It matters. But something is let loose in all this, something I see in Whittaker's conduct. He's in a rage, and he's going to vindicate his hero, Custer, and no court of inquiry will satisfy him unless I get thrown out of the service."

Gilbert reached across the dim-lit table and caught Reno's arm. "One thing at a time, Marcus. First, your honor, your record in the War Department. Then your reputation. And little by little, you'll win your friends back. Those men are not your enemies. They don't want to destroy you. Not a one of those officers has torn into your conduct. Not a one has called you a coward. Those men at the other end of the saloon can't come here or talk to you because propriety prevents it; you wouldn't come here, if you were in their shoes. Give it time."

# CHAPTER THIRTY-FOUR

THE NEXT DAYS WENT WELL ENOUGH. WHITTAKER APPLIED TO THE court to assist Lee in the prosecution, but the judges declined. This was a military inquiry, not a civil court. Lieutenant Lee did, however, recall the scout, Herendeen, and asked him some questions submitted by Whittaker about Reno's courage. What was Reno's reaction when Bloody Knife was killed a few feet from him? Was Reno under the influence of fear? The scout hedged his responses to Lee, but when Gilbert examined him, Herendeen said, "I am not saying he is a coward at all."

That, coming from a civilian who despised Reno, was satisfying to the major. He was starting to feel that he would emerge from this ordeal in good shape. Gilbert was quick to bore into any negative or hostile statement, and as often as not the witness backed off.

Lieutenant Hare, in the main, supported Reno, saw no evidence of cowardice, and expressed the belief that if the troops had remained in the timber they would have been annihilated.

Lieutenant DeRudio said he saw no evidence of cowardice in Reno, and had admired Reno's conduct. He said the command would have been butchered if it had ridden five hundred yards further instead of dismounting and forming a skirmish line.

An enlisted man followed, Reno's orderly, Sergeant Davern, and then Sergeant Culbertson, who served under Moylan. Asked about Reno's cowardice, both men said they saw nothing of the sort.

Asked if Reno could have held his position in timber, Culbertson said no; only for a few more minutes.

Then it was Benteen's turn. He testified emphatically that he saw no cowardice on Reno's part; indeed, he had cautioned Reno not to expose himself to fire on the hilltop.

Lieutenant Edgerly described Reno as cool and collected on the hilltop, and saw no evidence of cowardice there.

So far, so good. But on the twentieth day of the inquiry, things suddenly changed.

One of the civilian packers, B. F. Churchill, testified that when he and another civilian named Frett had gone to the pack train area to get food the evening of the twenty-fifth, Reno found them there, demanded to know why they were there and not on the line.

Churchill said that when Reno tried to strike Frett he spilled whiskey, and that Reno was under the influence of liquor.

That was serious business, and Gilbert bored into it, as he always did. At lunch he raised the issue.

"Marcus, did you have whiskey?"

"A pint flask, Lyman. I always carry it."

"You're a drinker?"

"Yes, but I never impair myself. I didn't have enough whiskey with me to get drunk."

"Were you drinking when you went after the packers?"

"I don't recollect it. I was angry. Those men were skulking, hiding among the mules and supplies instead of defending the perimeter like the rest, and I tore into them."

"You made enemies."

"In the heat of battle, you don't make friends, Lyman. I was damned if I'd let them skulk in safety."

"Is this liquor testimony going to crop up again?"

"I doubt it. The officers know I have a flask. Benteen knew it. He takes a nip too, when he can."

"Were you impaired?"

"Absolutely not. I didn't even finish that flask until a day after the battle. You know when I really drank? When we saw all those naked, mutilated corpses of friends, of people we know, our brothers, the life gone from them, lying all over that hill. Yes, that's when I really downed a swallow or two, and when every man in the command wished he could have."

"All right. I'm going to pursue this. I'm going to put my bulldog canines into it. I hope your officers agree with you, because this is damaging to you, and needs to be dealt with."

Reno paid the restaurant bill, stubbed his cigar butt, and the two returned to the courtroom, which stank of sweat and wet wool.

Edgerly: He was perfectly sober.

Gilbert: Did any officer or men suspect Reno was not sober?

Edgerly: Not the faintest, I never heard of it until I came to Chicago at this time.

Gilbert to Benteen: Was Reno sober the night of the twenty-fifth?

Benteen: He was as sober as he is now . . . I think he's entirely sober now and he was then.

Gilbert: Could he have been staggering and stammering at this time?

Benteen: Not without my knowing it.

That seemed to settle that, at least for the moment. But Lieutenant Godfrey was next, and Godfrey thought little of the major. He said he wasn't impressed by Reno's conduct, and thought the real command was being exercised by Benteen. He thought Reno displayed "nervous timidity."

The second civilian mule packer, John Frett, testified that Reno had slapped him, and had a bottle of whiskey in hand, which flew over Frett, and that Reno staggered. "If any other man was in the condition he was, I should call him drunk," Frett said, and added that Reno had to brace himself against a pack horse because he was incapable of walking.

Gilbert let it go, for the time being, but Reno knew this was not the end of the question of drunkenness.

Captain Mathey, who had been in charge of the pack train, testified that Reno seemed somewhat excited when the pack train arrived, but thought that was natural, given the fight Reno had just been through. He added that he saw no evidence of cowardice.

Gilbert: Was Reno drunk?

Mathey: I saw no evidence of it, and never heard of it until the spring of 1878, when Girard mentioned it.

Captain McDougall followed. He said that when he arrived at the hilltop, after guarding the pack train and commanding the rear guard, he had found Reno perfectly cool and "as brave as any man there in my opinion."

As for Reno's conduct, "I thought after he came to me the next afternoon and asked me to take a walk with him, he had plenty of nerve. The balls were flying around and the men in their entrenchments firing away."

Gilbert: Was Reno drunk?

McDougall: There was no whiskey in the command that I knew of, and if Reno had been staggering and stammering, someone would have found out.

Gilbert to Lieutenant Wallace, back on the stand: Was Reno drunk?

Wallace: I never heard of it till the second day of this month. . . .

Gilbert: Did you observe Reno, at any time, failing to do his expected and required duty as a commanding officer?

Wallace: No, sir, I did not.

The inquiry was winding down, and Reno wanted to testify. He thought the court should receive his own account of the battle, and he was willing to be cross-examined as a witness. Gilbert set about achieving this and found it was no easy task. He could not simply call Reno to the stand. But finally the court agreed, and Reno, at last, offered his account of the struggle, slowly reading from a prepared statement.

This was his moment. This was his chance to correct misimpressions, explain himself, and maybe even put that ravening wolf Whittaker out of his life. The testimony had fallen strongly on his side, save for the civilians. His fellow officers had, except for Godfrey, found little wrong in his conduct, and had even discovered some gallantry.

And yet the cloud seemed to hover about him, and only he could dispel it once and for all.

He had worked a long time on his prepared testimony, and Gilbert, playing devil's advocate, had poked holes in it, and he had gradually evolved what he wanted to say into a strong and coherent whole.

Now he read, taking his audience through the preliminaries, the order to charge, the promise of support, the engulfing flood of warriors on his flanks, the realization that he was in peril of annihilation, his retreat to the woods, his stand there as the woods were surrounded, the chaotic breakout—which happened in spite of the best efforts of his staff to break for the hilltop in an orderly way.

Quietly he read the story of the hilltop fight, the attempt to reach Custer, the utter ignorance of the fate of Custer's command, and the struggle that lasted through the next day.

It was a good account of the fight.

There remained only Lee's summation of the case against Reno, and Gilbert's summation of the evidence in Reno's favor.

Recorder Lee quietly probed everything that put Reno in an unfavorable light. But there wasn't a whole lot, perhaps because the young man had not probed deeply into the conduct of the battle. The judges listened carefully. There was not a word that was not being registered in their minds.

Gilbert, as usual, did a masterful job, probing into each area, especially the testimony of civilian packers who had grudges against Reno. The court sat transfixed when Gilbert went straight to the heart of hostile testimony, pulled it out for all to see and showed it to be motivated by malice. He didn't dwell long on the support Reno had received from most of his fellow officers.

When at last it was over, the reporters dashed for the exits, writing their stories in their minds even before they set pen to paper, while the courtroom slowly emptied. Reno noted that some of the reporters had corralled Whittaker, who was talking in animated whispers. Reno knew what the novelist was saying: that some of the officers had changed their tunes, and it was all a whitewash, and Reno would still be guilty of gross cowardice no matter what all those colonels, protecting the officer corps, would say to the public.

"Well, Marcus, what do you think?" Gilbert asked.

Reno shook his head. He wished he could know for sure, but a dread haunted him. "I think you did a fine job, Lyman," he said at last.

It was as fine a job as any lawyer could do. If there was trouble ahead, it wouldn't be the failing of his lawyer, he thought. And meanwhile, all one could do was wait for the inquiry to reconvene, and listen to the conclusions.

# CHAPTER THIRTY-FIVE

RENO WAS SURE THIS COURT OF INQUIRY WAS THE STRANGEST EVENT in military history. He was put before a body of judges to determine his *courage or cowardice*. He was the subject of an investigation into his *state of mind*. Did he cringe when under fire, expose himself to the enemy, issue orders based on the alleged flaws in his character? Witness after witness had been sworn in to testify to the nature of Reno's emotions during a pitched and desperate battle. There was something so bizarre in all this that it defied reason.

And yet, that afternoon of February 10, 1879, when the court reconvened, he found himself listening to the conclusions of three senior army officers empowered to probe his soul and decide whether he should remain in the service or be subject to court-martial for any of the various charges they might concoct. It struck him as the oddest moment of his life, but a man who had faced bullets and shot and shell and the cries of howling savages could, indeed, weather the judgment of his superiors.

They exonerated him, after a fashion.

The wind gusted against the windows, eddying cold air through the room now and then, as the court's conclusions about the nature of the battle were read to the reassembled tribunal.

"The conduct of the officers throughout was excellent and while subordinates in some instances did more for the safety of the command by brilliant displays of courage than did Major Reno, there was nothing in his conduct which requires the animadversion of this court.

"It is the conclusion of this court in view of all the facts in evidence, that no further proceedings are necessary in this case, and it expresses this opinion in compliance with the concluding clause of the order convening the court."

And so it ended.

The reporters leapt away, hot to write their story. They would want to talk to him, he supposed. He didn't know what he would say to them. Smile, lift a glass, light a cigar, tell the world he had won. Even if he hadn't. He had hoped for more.

Frederick Whittaker whipped his scarf around his neck, jammed his hat down, buttoned his overcoat, and stormed away. Reno knew that with the novelist, it would never be over.

Lyman Gilbert shook his hand and patted him on his arm.

The judges vanished from sight. The clerks and recorders folded up their ledgers. Benteen paused to shake his hand; the rest of the old command had slipped into the hallway, and out of sight.

"We won," Gilbert said. "And I'm deeply pleased that you're exonerated, Marcus. You'll be able to start over in a few weeks. That's when the suspension ends, doesn't it?"

Reno nodded.

"Good, you'll be glad to be earning your salary again," he said. "Your honor is returned to you. Your life may begin again. You're a man with a fresh slate, and I'm grateful to have played some small part in it all."

Reno nodded again. Gilbert would be getting some of his salary for many months to come. Reno didn't have the bill, but he knew he was going to be in hock for years. That sort of lawyer didn't come cheap.

"Well, back to the humdrum in Harrisburg," Gilbert said. "I'll continue to reach you at the Lochiel Hotel."

"It'll be a few weeks. I'm going to visit my sister."

"Yes, of course. We'll wait and see how this all turns out," Gilbert said.

The lawyer had boned up on procedure. The findings of the court would have to be approved by the General of the Army William Sherman, and finally by the Secretary of War, George W. McCrary. So nothing was final. But Reno sensed that none of these men would overturn what the judges had ordained.

He found himself alone again. The clerks had supplied him with a fair copy of the findings, and this he tucked into his portmanteau. Male aromas lingered in the room, mixing with the hot air off the clanging radiators.

Reno saw the empty hard-bottomed chairs where the judges had sat, saw where the clerks and scribes had taken it all down, saw where the witnesses sat, where Lyman Gilbert and Lieutenant Lee had sat or stood, and it all seemed unreal, an inquiry into something so intangible that none of the witnesses could pluck it up and make it real. The only one who came close was Lieutenant Godfrey, who said Reno was full of nervous timidity, his euphemism for cowardice.

They hadn't called him courageous. They hadn't remarked on his gallantry. They had opined that subordinates did more for the safety of the command with brilliant displays of courage. He was hurt. All he had done was keep the command from annihilation. All he had done was to foresee that further attack would have left every one of them quite as dead as Custer. But that apparently counted for nothing. They said nothing about the deep field experience he possessed that grasped, in time, the peril his command was in, the field experience that wisely chose to retreat to the woods.

After that battle, he had walked that meadow where he and his hundred twelve troopers had charged, walked its trampled grasses, found that only three hundred yards farther a shallow trench ran across the flat, deep enough to conceal many hundreds of warriors. And it was plain from its condition that they had indeed gathered there, waited for him, and would have emptied every saddle when his command galloped in.

But he had made the most difficult of command decisions, the one that required the most courage of all, in response to every instinct he had acquired over the long years of battle during the War of the Rebellion. He called a halt. Dismounted his men so they could use their carbines effectively, started forward again, and wheeled toward the woods when he could no longer move ahead.

That was a retreat, and retreats win no admiration for gallantry, and he who saves commands from certain doom are less the hero than the sort who takes every man with him to death. Had he taken his command to its death, he would have been another dead hero.

So they damned him with faint praise, and he saw no victory in it, but he knew that he would act the part of victor when the press converged, as it would, over the next days. He would be at the Palmer House for a day or two more, putting things in order, and they would clamor for a comment, and he would light up a Havana and tell them that he was delighted, and the conclusions were just, and the army had officially wiped the slate clean.

He ate alone that night. The witnesses, fellow officers from his command, had scattered, heading for the train stations, reporting back to duty. He wore mufti again because the trial was over and he could wear the honored blues only during that trial. So no one knew him, the slightly paunchy, bag-eyed, slick-haired moustached man in a rumpled brown suit who had been the focus of a month-long probe. Not even the waiters in the hotel restaurant, who had hailed the man in smart blues and white gloves, knew the man.

He found a dozen written messages awaiting him at the hotel desk: Marshal from the *Sun,* Josephson from the *New York Herald,* Cobb from the *Chicago Times.* The *Army and Navy Journal.* He was in no hurry to speak to any reporter. And when it came time, he would guard his language.

Yes, he was pleased and grateful. Yes, he considered the findings an official justification of the report he had written after the battle. Yes, he planned to return to the service and serve with honor. Yes, he mourned the brave Custer, whose courage no one ever doubted. Yes, he was honored by the findings, and felt they justified all that he had achieved. Yes, yes, yes . . .

And smile. He was good at smiling. He was good at slapping backs. He was good at the friendly arm on the shoulder.

They would all go back to their battle-scarred desks in grimy newsrooms and scribble about Reno's happiness, and his bright future.

He scanned each of the papers, looking for Whittaker, but didn't find his adversary. Not now. But the novelist would not be silent for long. Rumors were afoot. It was being said that the surviving officers of the Seventh Cavalry were saying one thing in court, quite another among themselves. That their testimony was skewed, bordered on perjury, because the high command didn't want to dig too deeply into defeat, or besmirch far more than one disgraced major. They were saying that the officer corps had gathered together, agreed on what would be said and not said, that the young recorder, Lee, had been chosen for his inexperience . . .

It was true that Lee hadn't dug very deeply into the battle. In fact, Reno wished the man had asked harder questions, questions that would have laid to rest the rumors he was hearing from the press. Yes, he would hear from Whittaker. The press had already heard from Libbie Custer, who was scornful of the whole proceedings.

The word "whitewash" was floating in the air. Reno wondered whose whitewash: his or George Custer's? The less the court had dug into details, the less scrutiny was thrown upon the lieutenant colonel and his private ambitions and recklessness. There was a whitewash, all right, and the whitewash was to preserve the memory of a gallant and dead officer and mollify his widow.

Reno tucked all that deep within himself, checked out, headed south for a few days with family, and prepared for the future. He was nearly broke. He might have to sell the Front Street house, sell some city lots, pay Gilbert, find means to stay in the Lochiel Hotel for a couple more months.

These things were Mary Hannah's parting gifts, and now they would fall away from him. She had bailed him out from the grave. He felt a strange and poignant sorrow. It had not been a true victory at all, and the wolves still circled.

# CHAPTER THIRTY-SIX

THE MAJOR RODE THE HUFFING TRAINS BACK TO HARRISBURG WEARING a chip on each shoulder. The court of inquiry, triggered by Frederick Whittaker's accusations, had devastated him financially, and had done little for his reputation even though the outcome was favorable.

But he was a fighting man, and he intended to show some fight to Whittaker. After he resumed life at the Lochiel Hotel, where he would remain a few more weeks before his two-year suspension ended, he made haste to contact Lyman Gilbert.

"Ah, Marcus, the soldier has returned," Gilbert said, affably, waving him into an office lined with law tomes.

"I have more business for you, Lyman."

The attorney arched an eyebrow.

"I want to sue Whittaker for libel; and his publisher, Galaxy Books. He called me a coward; the court said it could find no reason for animadversion against me. I want to sue and wring him out."

Gilbert settled back in his swivel chair, stared into the brightly lit window, and smiled.

"I suppose you could do that," he said. "And I certainly understand your feelings. And there does seem to be a case. He's accused you of cowardice and gross incompetence; the army's inquiry has cleared you. But have you thought this through entirely?"

"I have. I want to wring every cent out of him. I've just put myself in debt to defend against his accusations."

"Libel suits cost money. Not just my time. Witnesses, preparation, all of it."

"I'll win it back."

"Is he rich?"

"I don't know."

"My impression of novelists is that they're rather, shall we say, judgment proof."

"I'll still have a victory in my pocket."

Lyman Gilbert's gentle gaze settled on Reno again. "A civil suit is quite a different matter and might produce a different outcome, Marcus."

"What do you mean?"

"A strong defense could be mounted against your suit by delving into areas not really explored by the army's inquiry."

"Such as?"

Gilbert hesitated. "An army court weighs the evidence offered by officers as being more reliable than that of civilians. All those packers and scouts and guides who had hard things to say about you would be back in civil court, and their testimony would not be, shall we say, less credible than anyone else's."

"I'll meet it with officers' testimony."

"That might change, too. They'll be asked many questions that they weren't asked by Lieutenant Lee during the inquiry. He wasn't exactly a bulldog, was he?"

"No, and that's because the command didn't want him to probe too much," Reno said.

"Because it was sensitive about officers' reputations?"

"Not my reputation. Custer's. It didn't really want to dig too deeply into Custer's past, including his court-martial conviction. The man's dead. He was a national hero. Lyman, just think what would have happened if

Lee had started questioning Benteen about Custer. Benteen on the stand, talking freely about Washita, about Custer's abuse of soldiers, about the man's recklessness, about the way he collected favorites in the Seventh Cavalry, about a dozen other matters.

"But Lee didn't open that door, and for damned good reason. Sure, Lee didn't probe very deeply, but that wasn't to protect me. It was to protect Custer. And maybe Terry, too. Some of the blaming was washing in Terry's direction."

Gilbert nodded. "Perhaps you make my case for me, Marcus. There would be no closed doors in a civil libel trial. A civil court wouldn't be under the slightest constraint. There would be subjects introduced that might embarrass you. Including your own suspension. And imbibing. And no guarantee that the officers who survived, and enlisted men who survived, would testify in the same way. Why don't you think on it? If you're certain of the results, come back, and we'll discuss costs."

Reno left the offices of his attorney feeling unfulfilled. He wanted to punch a fist at Whittaker, and now he was not at all sure he could. He itched for a scrap; itched to haul that skinny novelist right through the legal mill and spill every dime from his pockets. He itched to tell his own story in a public venue, a court of law. In his mind's eye, he saw Gilbert honing in, boring deep, until Whittaker recanted or made a fool of himself.

But it would not happen. Reno felt he had scores to settle, and no one to settle against.

The weeks went slowly. No orders came from the War Department. His suspension began May 1, 1877, and ended May 1, 1879, but they had not posted him. He decided, in April, to catch a train to Washington and visit the War Department.

He felt irritable: the damned cloud seemed still to hover over him. He reported to the War Department, where a clerk told him to report his whereabouts to the adjutant general, and he would be issued orders.

He returned to Harrisburg and wrote General Townsend on April 29 that he was at the Lochiel Hotel, awaiting orders.

A telegram swiftly arrived from the War Department, informing him that he should have reported for duty with his regiment on May 1.

That wasn't very clear: he had no inkling of where to report. Fort Abercrombie, his last post, had been shut down in 1878 and stood empty.

He had begun this process with his April 9th trip to Washington, and now the boneheaded War Department was holding him responsible for not reporting. So he wrote again, explaining his conduct. But still no answer came.

He tried again, this time by wire: "Was informed by you I should report by letter. Did so. Where is my station? Will start at once."

In two days he received orders to report to Fort Meade, Dakota Territory. His bags were packed and he was ready to go. A new post, a new start.

Fort Meade, named after the Civil War general George Gordon Meade, was not quite complete. The army had been building it through the harsh winter, and it was well along. It stood close to Bear Butte, the sacred mountain of the Sioux and other tribes, north of the Black Hills, and was a frank expression of power in the heart of the country the Sioux had always called their own. It was there to protect the miners in the Black Hills.

Once again Reno headed west, transferring from one line to another, from crack eastern trains, rich with comforts, to rude western ones where coach passengers sat on wooden benches and suffered from excesses of heat, cold, smoke, draft, and noise. But he was wearing the blue again, his record newborn and clean, his bearing entirely army and his mood mostly cheerful, except when he remembered he was heading into a regiment that harbored some vipers.

He drifted to the smoking lounge, bit off the end of a stogy, and fired up. He sure as hell would deal with that any way he had to. He was forty-four, had years of service left, had a chance to advance, was out on the front lines again, and maybe life would be good at last. He plucked the flask from his bosom and swallowed enough whiskey to keep him in an affable state of mind. He had a long trip before him, but there were always pretty girls aboard to fire up his imagination.

When he arrived at Fort Meade he found raw buildings perched on a broad plain fourteen miles from booming Deadwood. Looming over the place was the blue bulk of Bear Butte, mysterious and strange, a sacred place for many tribes. He arrived on May 21, and the next day took command from Major Lazelle, who was overseeing construction. Shortly afterward, the Seventh Cavalry was transferred there from Fort Abraham Lincoln, and Reno welcomed the regimental staff, the band, and four companies.

And he welcomed one last newcomer, Captain Keogh's Comanche, the sole survivor of the Little Bighorn, which by Reno's own order would be used only for ceremonial purposes. He looked the grand old cavalry horse over, brimming with vast affection, and ran a hand down its neck. It was all good. He was back with his regiment. Major Marcus Reno was home, a veteran soldier among soldiers, in command for the moment, putting a new post in order, and renewing old friendships.

By God, he was back in the army! Almost with the passing of hours, the bad times receded, the good times lay ahead. His salary was flowing to him again. His regiment had congregated, looking sharp and clean and lean.

Many of the officers were new to him, but he had old friends here too, Benteen and Varnum among them. There was a handsome new Officers' Club Room, complete with a billiard table and bar, where a man could light up a Havana and buy a rye or bourbon and fraternize with the staff officers once again. Good times! And there was always wild and rambunctious Deadwood to relieve the monotony of a Western post. He sent his regimental band there on July fourth to help the folks celebrate Independence Day, and the miners cheered.

His command did not last long. In July, the Seventh Cavalry's commander, Colonel Samuel Sturgis, transferred himself and his family from Fort Abraham Lincoln to the bright new post and assumed command.

Sturgis had been a fair-minded superior through the time of trouble, and Reno felt comfortable with him.

Sturgis had, also, been fully aware of Custer's failings and had had a few run-ins with the late lieutenant colonel. All of which led Reno to believe that things were good now, and would stay good.

The regiment's lieutenant colonel and two senior majors were all on detached duty, leaving Reno the regiment's second in command for the time being, the very position held by George A. Custer. And if there was fighting to do, Reno would likely do it because Sturgis rarely took to the field. All in all, it seemed to be a most promising new start on life.

What's more, Sturgis had brought with him not only his wife, but his utterly enchanting, slender, dark, gray-eyed twenty-one-year-old daughter Ella. Reno took one look at her and his world was transformed.

# CHAPTER THIRTY-SEVEN

GOOD TIMES. FORT MEADE TURNED OUT TO BE THE BEST OF BILLETS. Reno drifted through the summer, finding plenty of time to visit rowdy Deadwood, playing billiards in the Officers' Club Room, and keeping an eye on Ella Sturgis, whose dark beauty captivated him.

He liked a little sip several times each day, and was never without his flask, which he took care to fill with the finest bourbon whiskey imported by Deadwood saloons from the States. A residual pain lingered in him, the remembrance of bad times and indignities that needed numbing with a swift sure sip. Sometimes he overdid, but he had the good sense to retreat to his quarters. He was walking the lip of the abyss, and did not intend to fall again.

Something bristling about his manner steered the conversation of fellow officers away from the topic of the Little Bighorn. His insignia of rank these days was a chip sewn to each shoulder. The post's lieutenants and captains knew better than to bring up that sore and still-bleeding topic around the major who had taken so much blame but had been, after a fashion, exonerated. What they said among themselves Reno didn't know and affected not to care; he was affable with them all just so long as nothing about the fight burned his ears.

As second in command, he found himself routinely invited to all the post's social functions. He took to calling on the family of Colonel Sturgis, often spending some considerable while with Mrs. Sturgis and Ella, a lady still grieving for a rejected fiancé, Second Lieutenant Charles Carrow, who had killed himself over the broken romance. Nor had the family forgotten the son they lost in the Little Bighorn fight. Whether Sturgis blamed Custer or Reno or no one at all, Reno could not ascertain, but the commander was cool toward Reno, and growing more so, and making it plain.

But it was Ella he was protecting.

"Major," he said one day. "My daughter is fragile, grieving, and but twenty-one, and I'm afraid, rather unsuitable for you, a man of forty-four. I think, under the circumstances, you ought not to call except in my presence. I'm sure you'll understand."

"If you say so, colonel," Reno said, suddenly disheartened. Ella's soft and melodic voice, her sweet melancholy, her wide and sensuous eyes and lush lips had drawn Reno to her as he had not been drawn to anyone since Mary Hannah. Indeed, there was much in Ella Sturgis that seemed a fair copy of his long-dead wife. So Sturgis's dictum hit him deeply, and from that moment life in Fort Meade was not so sweet.

He retreated to his room after that admonition, downed two shots neat, letting the fire burn its way into his belly, and then downed a third after the heat had radiated through him.

He knew he had become a love-crazed swain. She conjured up visions of sweetness and lust in him, visions of warmth that had ceased when Mary Hannah died. Every time he saw her, walking the parade under a parasol, or in the post trader's store fondling an apple or fingering gingham, or on the arm of her father taking the air, something stirred within, and the moment was painful.

Maybe the colonel was right: Ella was too young. He was forty-four, feeling abraded, worn down by army life, adversity, sheer bad luck, and maybe his dissolute ways now and then, though he could not fault himself very much for that. This was the army, not a Sunday school.

On August 3rd the post trader's store burned while the trader was off in Rapid City. The whole command rushed to put out the fire, man buckets, salvage what could be salvaged, but much was lost. The trader's wife stood by distraught, wringing her hands, and Reno wished to console her.

"Mrs. Fanshawe, I propose that we get a buggy and go toward Rapid City and meet your husband. I think it'd do you good to take the air, after all you've been through."

"Why, Major, I'm not sure . . ."

"Hush now, we'll go find him."

"But I think . . ."

"It'll do you good. Take the air."

He would not take no for an answer and soon brought the horse and buggy to her door, and they set off through the long August evening toward Rapid City, driving through quiet, empty reaches of grassland. But they did not see him.

After a couple of hours she stopped him.

"Major, we've come far enough. I wish to go home now."

He nodded, wheeled the buggy around, and they rode slowly back to Fort Meade.

The conversation went badly. She sat as far from him as she could, wrung her hands, and plainly felt distressed. But he was affable, making talk about the buffalo and army life and the mining in the Black Hills. He dropped her off but suggested he would sit at her porch to guard her until her husband, William Fanshawe, should arrive.

She joined him there, along with Lieutenant Nicholson, Dr. Bell, and another civilian, Edward Johnson, who had a part interest in the ruined trading post.

Fanshaw didn't return until late at night and was greatly troubled by the bad news, which Reno broke to him on the porch, along with the other men who had vigiled into the night.

"Why, gentlemen, thank you for keeping a watch over my house and home. Why don't we have a supper? It's late but it would be a most fitting thing to do."

"Yes, I can put some things on quite quickly," Mrs. Fanshawe added.

Reno saw the lamps bloom in the kitchen as she stirred about back there. "Gentlemen, come over to my quarters for a drink, and we'll leave the Fanshawes to themselves for a while," he said, and the others acquiesced at once. At his quarters he struck a lucifer, lit a lamp, quickly poured Tennessee whiskey neat for them all, and they downed it and had another.

"Time for dinner, I imagine," Nicholson said.

"I'll join you in a moment," Reno said, and saw them to the door. Then he wheeled back to his kitchen and poured himself a double and downed it. He was tense and needed something to quiet his nerves. Then he, too, returned to the Fanshawes for a midnight dinner.

The meal was quiet and decorous, but Reno was half asleep, having been numbed by the sudden charge of spirits in his veins. More spirits were served, and he had his fill, and sunk into ever deeper quietness. The conversation flowed around him, and he nodded amiably, said little, and then it was time to leave.

"Here, major, let me help you down this porch step," Johnson said.

"I'm able to care for myself, thank you," he said, and meandered home, aware that they were watching.

It didn't mean a thing. He had not been on duty.

The dog days of August stretched long and hot and wearisome, but at least he could repair to the Officers' Club Room for a drink and some billiards. On the seventh he did, engaging in a four-handed game of billiards with Captain Benteen and Doctors Bell and Brechemin. Reno bought himself some rye whiskey and another and another, and settled into the game, playing a little clumsily as the spirits thickened his tongue and slowed his fingers. Then he popped off an easy shot but the ball careened away from the pocket.

Peeved, Reno lifted a chair, smacked it down, and then threw it into a window, shattering a pane. Men stared.

He handed Lieutenant Scott a bill and told him to pay the bartender, Smythe, for both the booze and the windowpane. The lieutenant hastened to the barkeep, who totted up the damages, made change, and handed it to Scott.

But Reno wasn't happy.

"Why are you bringing the change to him? It's my bill."

The barkeep retrieved the coins and handed them to Reno, but Reno dashed them to the floor. Smythe picked up the change and handed it to Reno, and again Reno smacked the change down. So Smythe left the coins on the top of the wainscoting and walked away.

There were plenty of officers staring, but Reno didn't give a damn. He was steaming, and he didn't care who knew it.

The summer slid away, and Reno filled his lonely evenings at the Officers' Club Room, playing billiards, betting on games, and losing heavily at times. What else was there to do?

Then, in October, everything blew up.

A billiards debt triggered it. Reno owed Lieutenant Nicholson $380, a lot of money. When he apologized for not paying, Nicholson said it was all right.

That night of October 25 at the Officers' Club Room, Reno bet Nicholson a hundred dollars on a pool game, and Nicholson agreed.

Reno won, and Nicholson said, "That leaves two hundred eighty dollars on pool."

"But you told me the pool debt was square."

"No, I just said it was all right. You still owe it."

"I don't owe any such damned thing."

"Look, let's get Smythe over here to settle this, major."

"No, I don't want him to settle it. He's not the proper person to settle it."

Nicholson flew into a rage. "I could lick you in two minutes any way you want."

That was too much the insult for Reno, but he remained at the end of the table, punching balls into pockets with his cue.

Nicholson threatened him again, hammering the pool table.

That did it. Reno walked straight in to Nicholson, and whacked him with the cue. It struck Nicholson's left arm and broke. Nicholson jumped Reno, dragged him to the floor, and pounded him.

The rest of the officers in the club leapt in to pull the pair apart.

Captain Peale and Lieutenant Pettit warned that the brawlers would be arrested if they didn't quit, and both men quieted down. Reno sat up, brushed himself off, saw the way things were going, pulled his coat over him, and vanished into the night. It was a cold, bleak walk to his quarters.

Three days later he was put under arrest by Colonel Sturgis, and again faced court-martial charges.

# CHAPTER THIRTY-EIGHT

CONDUCT UNBECOMING TO AN OFFICER AND A GENTLEMAN.

There were three specifications:

Reno "did create and engage in a disreputable disturbance or brawl in a public billiard saloon, and did violently assault and strike Second Lieutenant Wm. J. Nicholson, Seventh Cavalry, with a billiard cue, with the manifest intent of inflicting severe bodily injury . . . and did persist in continuing said disturbance until threatened with arrest . . ."

Reno "was drunk and disorderly in a public billiard saloon, and did several times wantonly and in riotous manner, knock money out of the hands of the saloon keeper (or tender) Mr. Joseph Smythe, scattering said money over the floor, and did in a wanton and riotous manner, smash in with chairs the glass of one or more windows of said billiard saloon . . ."

Reno "was in a disgusting condition of intoxication at the residence of Mr. W. D. Fanshawe, post trader . . . on or about the third of August, 1879."

So they had been lying in wait after all, he thought. Watching, watching, watching.

General Terry set the court-martial for November 28, to be convened at Fort Meade, with Colonel W. C. Wood, Eleventh Infantry, presiding.

So they were going to try him for getting mad and busting some window glass. And being drowsy at the Fanshawes. As for the fight, Nicholson had started it, and there were witnesses enough, and he could beat that one, too. He felt fairly optimistic but still something bleak and mean was lurking below the surface. Many of the officers of the Seventh Cavalry Regiment wanted him out and were determined to achieve it.

He was confined to the post, which wasn't so bad. He had become something of a pariah, but he had a few friends, and he could beat this rap too. Sturgis had become hostile, though; danger loomed there. Reno had long since been unwelcome at the commander's home and Sturgis had made it plain that his family was to be left entirely alone.

At least Reno could solace himself with a drink or two or three at the Officers' Club Room, and that is how the next days ticked by.

But then, one quiet evening while he was taking the air after a few nips, he passed the Sturgis residence, which was well lit, and noticed Ella sitting in the parlor. His long-suppressed affection bloomed. She sat reading, the glow of the coal oil lamp turning her face golden, her dark hair sweetly framing her lovely oval face. He could not visit her. He could not even step onto the grounds of the commander's home. He was under arrest and facing new charges.

And yet, he yearned to let her know of his fondness.

He saw no sign of the colonel. Maybe it would be a small amusement to rap on her window. Someone passed him in the darkness, and he continued on, but when he was alone, he returned. There she was, dressed primly, passing a pleasant evening in her parlor, reading a book.

He drifted across the yard, smitten. How lovely she looked, how much he yearned for someone just like her sitting in his own parlor. And yes, there was her mother, too, invisible from the front window, but plain now; both reading.

He would let her know his admiration. He approached the window, having to stand as high as he could, and tapped cheerfully on the glass. She gazed at him. He tapped and waved his hand.

The look on her face was one of horror, as if he were committing some heinous crime, as if this weren't a downstairs parlor window, but a bedroom. He waved cheerfully, and seeing her start, and her mother rise, he smiled, waved, and wandered on to his quarters. It had been a pleasant eve, and he began to prepare himself for bed.

But there was a knock at his door and Reno admitted Lieutenant Garlington, who stood stiffly and ill at ease.

"Colonel Sturgis sent me to get some explanation of your conduct," Garlington said.

"Conduct?"

"Did you invade the colonel's yard and tap at the colonel's window?"

"Oh, it was nothing."

"They don't think so. Ella is distraught. She nearly fainted away. She could barely speak. They feared she might succumb to Saint Vitus Dance. The colonel searched his yard with cane in hand, ready to thrash you. You'll explain now, and I will convey your explanation to the commander."

"But there's nothing to explain."

"You admit tapping on the Sturgis family's window?"

"It was just a whim, that's all."

"I'm afraid that won't do, major. The colonel is, shall we simply say, in a rage."

"Well, no offense was intended, lieutenant. I'll write her a note of apology."

"I'll tell the colonel you have no explanation, then. I am authorized to tell you that you're confined to your quarters by his command."

Garlington wheeled about and vanished into the night.

Reno knew he faced the gravest charge of all.

He could not explain to himself why he did it. Impulse, whimsy. One thing he knew: he had meant no offense to her, especially her, and this was not something foul or unspeakable.

He bit off a cigar, lit it, and smoked and paced half the night, wondering what to do. An apology was in order, not only to Ella but to Mrs. Sturgis, so he sat down and penned one. He explained himself as best he could; he had been for a walk, and saw her, and was drawn to her.

"It would be a matter of deep regret to my dying day should you and she think me capable of an untruth of being a spy or doing anything with a mean motive. This is the truth as I expect to answer for it before my God and I sincerely ask your pardon for all that does not seem to you as innocent, for I do assure you if not guiltless the fault was in the judgment and not the heart."

But there was only frosty silence in response.

The charge, added to the rest, was:

That Reno "did in the darkness and at a late hour in the evening surreptitiously enter the side grounds adjoining the private residence or quarters of his commanding officer . . . and did peer into a side (and retired) widow of the family sitting room of said private residence or quarters, approaching so near and so stealthily as to very seriously affright and alarm that portion of the family . . ."

His brief interlude in sunlight was over and for the saddest of all reasons. From the moment he had set eyes on Ella, he had loved her. He could not explain it; he just did, and each day at Fort Meade that he was separated from her by her father's rejection of him as a suitor, he pined. Not since Mary Hannah, his great love, had a woman affected him the way Ella Sturgis did. He had never known what he might do about it, if anything; only that she was there, he pined for her, and could not ever have her.

The court-martial began November 24, 1879, at ten o'clock.

The Department of Dakota had lined up a fancy row of judges, including Colonel W. C. Wood, Colonel William R. Shafter, First Infantry; Colonel John W. Davidson, Second Cavalry; Lieutenant Colonel Elmer Otis, Seventh Cavalry; Lieutenant Colonel A. J. Alexander, Second Cavalry; Lieutenant Colonel Edwin Townsend, Eleventh Infantry; Major Bernard D. Irwin, Medical Department; Major Orlando Moore, Sixth Infantry; and Major Joseph S. Conrad, Seventeenth Infantry. Captain W. W. Sanders, Sixth Infantry, would prosecute.

But not enough judges were on hand, and the proceeding was delayed until the twenty-eighth. Reno pleaded not guilty to all but one charge, and pleaded bar of trial—that the charge was beyond the purview of the military—to the accusation that he had been drunk at dinner at Fanshawes. The court did not agree with him.

For the next several days, various officers, along with the Fanshawes, Dr. Bell, Colonel Sturgis, and Ella Sturgis, all testified. Reno acted as his own counsel and when the prosecution was done, swore himself in and gave the court his version of events. He thought he was making good progress: the charges were, at bottom, frivolous, and even if one stuck, it might be worth a brief suspension, or half pay or something of that sort. But he saw nothing in any of it that could result in being suspended for long, or any worse punishment. What did he do? Got into a fight he didn't start. Got mad and broke a window. Got sleepy at the post trader's house. And . . . went rapping on a window where he should not have been.

The last worried him the most. Ella Sturgis testified about the fright that had visited her. The colonel testified about the disarray of his wife and daughter when he was summoned from bed.

Benteen testified as to whether Reno's motives toward Ella Sturgis had been honorable and said that he thought that Reno's letter of apology did not fully express what Reno felt. It was a hint to the court of something that Reno's old friend and occasional adversary Benteen well understood: that Marcus Reno was in love.

Not one to pass by any opportunity, Reno labored hard at night to produce a closing statement, and this he read to the court on its final day, December 8. He took pains to point out that "it has been my misfortune to have attained a widespread notoriety through the country by means of the press . . ." He pointed to his twenty-two years given to the service of his country, and tried to cast his offenses as indiscretions rather than the serious matters that could result in being expelled from the army.

The court deliberated, and when it reconvened, with the major standing stiffly before it on a cold December day at Fort Meade, it found Reno guilty on the first specification, the brawl with Nicholson, though it moderated the language a bit; on the second, the occasion when he pitched a chair at a window, they found him guilty, but toned down the language; on the third, being drunk at the Fanshawe residence, they found him guilty but not to the extent of disgracing the military service; and on the fourth, invading the grounds of the Sturgis home, Reno was convicted as well, of conduct unbecoming to an officer and a gentleman.

That was the torpedo that could sink him. He felt himself slump as the court adjourned, and then he was all alone.

# CHAPTER THIRTY-NINE

THE VARIABLE DAKOTA WINTER RAN COLD AND WARM, MATCHING THE major's moods. He remained under close quarters at Fort Meade while his case wound its way up the chain of reviewers. It would end on the president's desk.

He was often solitary, but not alone. People addressed him. And yet a veil had fallen between himself and most of those on the post, intangible, maddening, but always present. Most doors were closed to him. Most officers avoided him, or had little to say beyond a pleasantry.

Christmas arrived, and he found himself in painful solitude, broken only by a visit from a few old, enduring friends, such as Captain Benteen, who cared little what others thought and brought Reno a bottle of good brandy to tide him over the sacred feast.

Some days the winds blew cold through Dakota, racing south out of Canada, and those days reminded him of what lay ahead. Other times the high plains basked in an odd warmth, a pleasant winter of a sort unknown in the East, when the low sun shone sweetly and the breezes were mild.

The case had a long way to go before anything was final. It would be reviewed by the judge advocate for the Department of Dakota, and by General Terry, and then it would go on to Washington.

Reno heard a rumor or two, mostly gotten from Benteen, who had a way of picking up gossip not intended for Reno's ear. Five of the seven judges who sat for the case had recommended leniency; they felt that they had to convict Reno in order to comply with military codes of justice, but that the punishment was too severe for such offenses, which did little harm to anyone.

In the end, he had no way of knowing. The walls of military official-dom rose high and impervious. The day after his melancholy Christmas, he wired the Secretary of War, Alexander Ramsey: "Do not let me be dis-missed. Rather resign if such conclusion be reached."

He heard nothing. He knew nothing. He wondered what General Terry would do. Terry had always treated him fairly enough, and was in fact a lawyer. That struck him as hopeful.

But the winds of January and February blew cold and carried stinging snow upon them, and Marcus Reno scarcely knew what to think. The case would go from Terry to the Bureau of Military Justice in Washing-ton, where it would again be reviewed and passed to the general of the army, the secretary of war, and the president.

In that bureau, the case would come under the scrutiny of Judge Ad-vocate General W. M. Dunn and Major Henry Goodfellow. In his mind's eye, sometimes, Reno saw both officers reviewing the material kindly, an eye upon Reno's long military career, which now spanned almost twenty-eight years from his arrival at West Point, and recommending something mod-est, like a year at half pay and a brief suspension.

As the days of winter ticked by at Fort Meade, Reno grew more and more confident. Spring was just around the corner. Nothing terrible had be-fallen him and nothing would. Sherman himself had always admired Reno and thought well of him as a cavalry officer. Surely it would all smooth over.

He heard rumors that all would be well and that was all he needed; on March 16, with winter ebbing and the sun burning holes in the snow, he wired the secretary of war rescinding his request to resign if he should face dismissal.

On March 17, 1880, the adjutant general's office issued the verdict: "By direction of the Secretary of War, the sentence in the case of Marcus A.

Reno, Seventh Cavalry, will take effect April 1, 1880, from which date he will cease to be an officer of the army."

Reno learned of it on March 18, through a wire delivered by the adjutant.

Out of the army.

It hit him in the stomach. He read the flimsy, not believing it. Out of the army after twenty-eight years. It was the only life he had ever had.

He stared out of the window upon the greening sward of the unfinished post, the rows of austere white buildings surrounding the parade. Mysterious, bleak Bear Butte loomed not far away, the holy place of the Sioux. The fort was the intruder in an alien land.

He pulled a bottle off a shelf and poured himself a good dollop of bourbon in a tumbler, and downed it neat. It scolded its way into his belly and spread heat through him. Anger at first, fear, desolation, and ultimately loneliness. If he were separated from the only society he had ever known, the company of his fellow officers, he would be rudderless. He had always been solitary but still a part of a band of brothers, and now the brothers were abandoning him.

He wondered whether there was any hope of reversing the decision, and knew he wouldn't know until he saw the review papers. There would be assents or dissents all the way up the chain of command, agreeing or disagreeing with the court-martial judges. He would examine each. He would, if there was any hope at all, fight to reinstate himself. He was a cavalry major in the army and intended to stay a major in the army.

He stepped into a fine spring morning, the air mild, the earth moist and soft and pungent in the coy sun. He could hardly remember so fine a morning. A few rotting snowbanks clung to the north sides of buildings. A mist of green faintly covered the brown turf. A breeze lifted the United States flag on its staff, and fluttered the regimental colors.

He saw details at work, men in blue fatigues heading for the horse barns, policing the grounds, distributing firewood, forming into columns under the lash of gravel-voiced sergeants. He felt the pulse and rhythm of the fort ripple through him, the familiar chores, the drills, the hastening men, the indolent men, the bachelor men. No woman met his eyes and none would be visible until later, when the post store opened. He studied Fort Meade's guard house, a small, neat building, one of the first erected, and he wondered who was within, and why, and for how long.

He stood on his veranda, while fellow officers hastened by with averted eyes. The news must have careened through the post at once, maybe ahead of the moment Lieutenant Garlington, Sturgis' adjutant, handed him the wire. He waved casually; no man waved back.

He had been a pariah before, during his close quarters arrest; now he was an outcast. Colonel Sturgis managed never to encounter Reno at all. He had the freedom of the Officers' Club, and found the atmosphere so oppressive and hostile that he did not go there for a drink or billiards or talk. Only Benteen had ignored the invisible wall and had visited with the major on occasion. But no man stopped at Reno's quarters to say hello. There were no additional orders or requirements. He was there until April 1, and then he would leave. He had no duties and no liberties.

The rest of March dragged by. Through Garlington Reno requested copies of the judgments of those who had affirmed the sentence of the court.

"It will take some while, major. Maybe you should tell us where to send them," Garlington replied.

Reno didn't know. Harrisburg, probably. The Lochiel once again, for all he knew. The farm and the house on Front Street were still yielding rents; he might barely manage to live in the hotel.

Then the first day of April arrived, and Marcus Reno was no longer a major in the United States Army. That day he would surrender his quarters, again to the adjutant, and depart. He pulled his three uniforms out of the armoire and packed them in a steamer trunk, along with the rest of his clothing, save for what he would carry in a black pigskin valise. He could no longer wear the clothing of a United States Army officer. He owned two suits, one gray, one black, and chose the gray. It fit tightly; he had put girth on his waist during his tour at Fort Meade. It would have to do. He stood before a looking glass, finding not a different man but an invisible one. As a major he was visible; now he looked no different from tens of thousands of other somewhat corpulent men who wore anonymous wrinkled suits and black derbies and went about their private business.

He intended to hire Fanshawe's rig to take him to Deadwood, and from there a stagecoach to the rails, and from there a long, rocking, tiring trip east. Beyond that the future was a blank. He had only one profession, and was trained in no other. But things weren't entirely bad: Mary Hannah's estate still sustained him to some degree. Cash wasn't the immediate problem.

He tugged at his collar, filled his flask, and slipped it into the bosom of his gray suit coat, stuffed a handful of panatelas into a breast pocket, and closed the brass-chased steamer trunk. Nothing of himself or his effects remained. He traveled light. A veteran army officer usually traveled light.

He headed through the door and toward the post sutler's store, where he could purchase a ride, but Frederick Benteen intercepted him.

"Marcus, I've had a carriage harnessed. I'll take you to Deadwood."

"That would be good, Fred. Are you sure . . . ?"

"I don't give a damn."

Moments later, Benteen pulled up before Reno's quarters, and the pair loaded the steamer trunk and valise into the boot of the carriage.

"You got anything else to do?" Benteen asked.

"Tell Garlington," Reno said.

He knocked on Garlington's door, and Garlington opened.

"I'm out," he said. "Here's the key."

"Thank you, Mr. Reno."

The door closed.

Reno stepped into the swaying black buggy, and Benteen flapped the reins over the croup of the dray.

A stab of anguish, terrible and knife-edged, shot through him, feeling so shocking that he could not bear to let his old friend see his face, so he turned aside, watched the troops at drill, watched the details at work, watched them grow smaller and smaller until they were invisible, and there was only the anonymous road.

"It's a hell of a fine day," Reno said, and fired up a stogy.

# PART FOUR

## 1889

*Being an Account
of the Correspondent's Quest*

# CHAPTER FORTY

THE SHEER MASS OF OFFICIAL MATERIAL JOSEPH RICHLER GATHERED amazed him. For weeks he had dug into congressional files, pestered the Office of Military Justice, badgered congressmen, and bothered Reno's last attorney, Scott Lord.

Marcus Reno had not quit trying to return to the army after he was ejected. Before it was over, he had exhausted his inheritance, borrowed from that of his son, and died in penury, all because he wanted what he believed to be justice.

Richler, dogged reporter that he was, had dug deep, and now he had the story of a life, but in the form of starchy correspondence, private memos, terse marginal notes, and carefully censored documents with portions redacted.

He asked himself why he did it, apart from a promise he had made weeks before to a dying man. He had no answer. He didn't even like the man. But there were reasons. Some of it was his curiosity. Did Reno deserve his fate? Some of it was the contradiction: how could a man like Reno be so despised, have so many friends, be a loner, be sociable, conduct himself crudely, win the love of more than one woman, act recklessly, be accused of excessive prudence, scorn the opinion of others, yet curry every favorable notice he could? It was not enough to say Marcus Reno was a man of contradiction. He was plainly an enigma, a mystery, perhaps unfathomable.

So the reporter found himself, with so many others, liking and disliking Reno, wanting him to win his honor back, guessing he wouldn't, wishing Reno would have repented just a little along the way, thinking his critics were right, thinking his critics were scandalous and scurrilous.

It was too much to comprehend.

Richler knew he would write that obituary one way or another, write the most penetrating study he could manage, and he knew the *Herald* would feature it prominently. Even now, 1889, the year of the major's death, anything new about Reno, or Custer, or the Little Bighorn, would excite public fascination.

It wasn't a task the newspaper had assigned him. He continued his day-to-day coverage of Washington and its politics, and he did it routinely. This was something else, an unscratched itch, a mass of questions without answers.

He hardly knew where to begin, but at least this was not ancient history. Many of the survivors of the Little Bighorn lived. Many of the officers who knew Reno well still lived. But they were falling away fast, and Richler knew he could not delay long. If he wanted to redeem the honor of Major Marcus Reno, and he half-hoped he might, he would need to interview scores of men before their clocks reached midnight.

Frederick Whittaker would not be among them. The novelist and accuser of Marcus Reno had died by his own hand in a bizarre manner. He had, over the years, gone half mad, embracing Spiritualism, becoming eccentric and starkly suspicious of everyone and everything. He had taken to carrying a revolver at all times, to defend himself against the ghostly legions of enemies stalking him.

Then one May day, a few weeks after Reno's death, Nadine spotted a story, clipped it, and handed it to Richler: Whittaker had stumbled on his stairway, caught his cane in the bannister, tumbled, and accidentally shot himself in the head. And so ended the career of the self-proclaimed "prosecutor of Major Reno."

"It fits," he told her over supper.

"How so, Joseph?"

"The novelist, in his wild imaginings, thought Custer had been betrayed. By the end of Whittaker's life, he thought everyone was betraying himself."

She smiled. Joe had an analytical mind, the sort that found connections in events. Baby dozed, so they could have a rare repast by themselves in their modest flat.

"When are you going to write it?" she asked, toying with a napkin.

"Not yet. I can't fathom Reno. I don't want to write until I do. Nothing about him makes sense."

"But the longer you wait . . ."

"I've written the notice of his death, Nadine. The real summing up can wait. When it's done, the *Herald* will publish something important, something worth a few columns, and not just a quick pass at a complex man."

"Did you like him, the time you saw him?"

"How could anyone like Reno?"

"I don't think I would like him."

"I think I might have liked him some moments, but not others."

The baby squalled. She rose slowly, not wanting to be drawn away from the table and the husband she saw all too little of. Richler watched her go, his thin and unwell wife wrapped in gray, to see about an unwell infant. The doctors argued about what was wrong with her, and one diagnosis was as useless as the others.

She lived through him; he brought her the only respite she had from humdrum domesticity in a cheap flat. He brought her the news, the gossip about famous men, the prestige and romance of being a correspondent for a great paper. He tried to share his days, his worries, his pursuits, with her.

Sometimes she didn't grasp the importance of a story or a man or a woman, and then he let it drop, let her do the dishes, stir a soup, change a diaper.

Maybe someday she would want to join him; there were so many things he covered, from banquets to receptions to theater events, where she would be welcome. But she never had the wish, and that somehow disappointed him. She whiled away her life living vicariously through him. He sighed.

The rolltop desk beckoned. He headed for his sanctuary in a corner of the parlor, a place she had learned to leave quite alone no matter how messy she thought it was. Here were his manila folders, jammed with papers and clippings and fair copies laboriously wrought from originals. He rolled up the oaken cover, settled into his creaking swivel chair, lit a kerosene lamp because the gaslight stretched too dim here for scholarly purposes, and set to work.

This night he intended to string together, once and for all, the events that followed Reno's dismissal from the cavalry.

It seemed Reno had scarcely paused in Harrisburg before heading to Washington and the War Office to try to put his case in order. He had friends in Washington, better friends indeed than those within the Seventh, where the service rivalries and abrasions of lonely outposts had isolated Reno and finally turned him into an outcast.

In Washington, apparently, he had begun the business of obtaining the entire body of court-martial records, including the opinions of the reviewers. He had, as well, presented himself as a native son of Illinois, and asked two of its congressional delegation to sponsor a bill restoring him as a cavalry major. Indeed, Representative James Singleton and Senator David Davis did place the private bill into consideration, and the committee chairmen swiftly requested records from the Department of War.

Richler had copies of the court-martial material, and saw at once why Reno was brimming with optimism. General Terry and his judge advocate, a certain Major Barr, had recommended leniency, arguing that the punishment scarcely fitted the triviality of Reno's offenses. General Sherman had agreed. But the top men in the Department of Military Justice had overruled the rest, and President Hayes had firmly sustained the dismissal.

Reno's initial efforts in Congress came to nothing; no bill was reported favorably out of committee in 1880, and there the case seemed to die.

What was hurting Reno was not just this final collection of charges, but a string of them running back several years. And hurting him more, plainly, was that no congressman wished to be known as a supporter of a man who had dishonored womanhood with his unwanted attentions. That was the prickly, unspoken thing. Richler made a note of it.

Reno was not a man to rest on his oars, so he had peppered the War Department for documents, commendations, citations, anything that might help his cause, and the department reluctantly supplied him with some, told him to consult congressional committees in possession of other documents.

He had rented a flat on Indiana Avenue in Washington, from which entrenchment he could conduct his campaign. He wrote the new Secretary of War, Robert Todd Lincoln, explaining that he had been done in by "prejudice entertained against me" emanating from the judge advocate general.

That struck Richler as a reckless thing to say, and a mark against Reno. It was also a clue to the former major's state of mind. He was seeing enemies and betrayals, just as the crazed novelist Whittaker was discovering enemies under every rosebush. But there was something dogged in Reno's attack. This was a full assault, employing every person he could enroll in his cause, every scrap of paper, every argument he could muster.

Plainly, it was costly. Reno had hired a fancy New York lawyer, Scott Lord, to shepherd his private bill through Congress and perhaps deal with the administration. He had done this, apparently, on the advice of Lyman Gilbert, who had declined to handle the matter. Richler wondered whether Reno's old friend, and his son Ross's legal guardian, was dancing a slow two-step away from the notorious former major.

So Reno had ventured to New York and found the welcome mat out at Lord, VanDyke and Lord—for a price, no doubt. Scott Lord was well situated to handle the case, being at once the brother-in-law of President

Hayes, and at the same time a Democrat, able to deal with Hayes' successor if the Democrats should win the election. They didn't: Garfield won narrowly, only to succumb to an assassin's bullets, and Reno found himself dealing with Chester Arthur, who had no military background. And also with Robert Todd Lincoln, son of another slain president, and a man not easy to persuade, judging from the correspondence in Richler's files.

Richler again studied the whole case, the repeated efforts to put Reno back into the cavalry, the bills offered in each session of Congress, the diligent and genuinely heartfelt efforts by Scott Lord, for a price, always a price, and saw how it all came to nothing.

And how Reno began selling off large pieces of the estate, lots mostly, and borrowing money. What a remarkable thing, Richler thought: the man cared so much about honor that he was willing to impoverish himself. And did so.

# CHAPTER FORTY-ONE

ALL THOSE EFFORTS TO REVERSE THE COURSE OF MILITARY JUSTICE came to nothing. All those efforts to have Congress enact a private bill, reinstating Marcus Reno, also came to nothing.

And in the background, Libbie Custer, engaged and bitter, watched hawkishly over the reputation of her husband, quietly fought any effort to rehabilitate Reno, and wrote elegiac tributes to her dead warrior.

Richler pored through packets of letters, studied official documents, examined Scott Lord's very able pleadings—which were largely based on technicalities—and knew that he was examining a lost cause. Reno's reputation had been buried long before his body, and nothing short of divine intervention could resuscitate it. Richler felt a certain pity for the man. Reno had been stable enough before the Little Bighorn; indeed, far more stable than most officers, including Custer.

Yet the aftermath of the battle, in which the major had found himself called a coward and an incompetent in the national press, had scarred his soul, and the wounds had altered and coarsened Reno's very nature. Gradually he became combative, reckless, hard-edged, trouble-prone, and a sot on occasion, though not ever a serious drunkard.

Richler knew that Reno had been hurt far more than the cigar-chomping major would ever admit; hurt less by Whittaker than by high-ranked officers such as Nelson Miles, whose open scorn cut deep. It was Miles' flippant view that when seven of twelve companies of the Seventh

Cavalry were halted on a hilltop by a timid officer, Custer didn't have a chance.

It was scarcely a measured opinion, didn't weigh the difficulties, and yet Richler knew it must have cut deeply to the heart of the cavalry major. Reno could endure the press but he had a bad time enduring the condemnations of his peers, the whispered criticism, even contempt, that sometimes burst into his awareness, often from the correspondence published by the *Army and Navy Journal*. There, in that undaunted magazine, he had found few friends. And with every sting, he lifted his flask, and with every nip of spirits, he courted trouble.

He had tried to resume his life and career, command the bases to which he had been assigned, but nothing was ever the same after that. He was listening for insult, listening for disdain, and he who listens hard enough will surely find it.

And yet . . . Joe Richler was not a man to sympathize too deeply. Reno could have weathered the storm if he had governed his appetites better. He could have had an illustrious career. He might have ended up as a general officer. The Little Bighorn was not so devastating as to ruin his military life. That was the paradox of the man. Just when you began to empathize with him, you were suddenly aware that he was not made of stern stuff.

Richler could find nothing unexceptional in Reno's later life. He moved to New York and lived there for a while, working closely with Scott Lord to forward his case. The attorney aggressively pursued every possible avenue, and Reno did not lack for a superb advocate. But the bright lights of New York were a far cry from the crude life of a Western fort, and Reno did not spare the expense of good food, good cigars, and good wine.

That was when he met Isabella McGunnegle, widow of a naval lieutenant commander. She was a little older than Reno, had four adult children, and was struggling to survive on a small government pension of thirty dollars a month and a clerking position. They took to each other, and eventually married.

The marriage began to deteriorate soon afterward, and Richler could only guess at the reasons. Perhaps it was money: Marcus Reno was living high in New York and Isabella may have thought he had more of an inheritance than he actually had. Whatever the case, Richler knew the reasons lay buried along with Marcus Reno. She was estranged from him at the time of his death and had filed for divorce, citing intolerable, but unspecified, insults to her person. And later she sued him for nonsupport. There was no way of knowing what that was all about.

Richler wondered what sort of man Reno really was. The odd thing was that he didn't have the faintest idea. He had known only the dying man, and everything else was hearsay, or gossip, or correspondence. What's more, everything about him was contradictory. But that sort of puzzle was the usual lot of reporters, and if he was worthy of his craft he would penetrate to the bottom, read between the lines, and come up with a true bill. The more he tried to grasp Reno, the more elusive the major became.

Reno had eventually moved to Washington, rented a small flat, and had gone to work as a clerk for the Pension Bureau of the Department of the Interior for sixty dollars a month. It was no living at all, not after a comfortable major's salary and emoluments. There, in perfect anonymity, he toiled away, shuffling file cards, making notations, recording deaths and address changes. It was a long way down a terrible slope from his days in the army.

He had trouble with his son, who developed spendthrift ways, and Reno found it necessary to go to court for permission to pay Ross' debts from the trust set up for him. Richler thought that was natural; Reno had hardly set any good examples for the boy. And yet . . . there was the major, toiling honorably day by day at a nondescript job, setting a good example, faithfully and without complaint making something of a living during hard times, and that should have been example enough for Ross. Eventually the boy reached his majority, acquired control of his estate, and headed toward Kentucky where he married and bought into a liquor wholesaling company operated by his wife's family.

The financial records revealed what Reno was falling into: he sold numerous lots and properties to his brother-in-law for a token hundred dollars. What of that? Did it conceal a loan? Or repayment of a debt? In 1887 Reno was compelled to sell the larger properties, the excellent farm, his rented house in Harrisburg. It all slowly vanished, some into the hands of his lawyers, some to his son, the rest into making ends meet.

And there was the striking thing, the amazing thing. Richler marveled at it. The man refused to give up or settle into a new life. To his dying day he sought to return to the cavalry, to repossess his rank, to engage in service to his country. With every new session of Congress there would be bills introduced to reinstate him into the ranks of officers.

The details were no longer important. What he said was no longer important. What Scott Lord did by way of lobbying or filing briefs was not important. But one thing flabbergasted Joseph Richler as he reviewed those last declining years of Reno's life: the man spent a substantial inheritance trying to reinstate himself, cleanse his name and honor, and died broke. There was not enough to pay for a funeral or a gravestone. What other man, given the circumstances, would spend his very substance on all of that?

Why had he done it? What had he believed about it? What led him, year after year, to assault the military establishment? When he began putting the last of his properties on the block, had he come to any understanding that his long struggle would not avail? Was this dogged effort, this bulldog tenacity, the true nature of a man who had been pilloried as a coward?

Richler marveled. In all of his years of reporting the affairs of great men and small, he had never come across anyone else with so fierce a mission, so obsessive a need, so rigid a goal.

Yes, Marcus Reno was different.

Richler turned down the wick until the lamp blued out, and he sat at the rolltop in the dim light of a gas lamp across the room. Fog lay thick over the capital city, and he could see nothing from his dew-streaked window. He would go to bed in a moment, the evening having yielded few additional clues about the late Marcus Reno.

There were things to think about: the major's deathbed wish was to have his name and honor restored. But there were really two issues here. Did Reno want only to triumph over accusations of cowardice at the Little Bighorn? Or was it the indiscretions and unsettled conduct that followed the battle that Reno wanted expelled from the record of his life? Or both?

The dying man had asked for his good name and honor.

Why bother?

For a moment, Richler thought he might simply scuttle the whole project. Yes, he had promised the man on his deathbed that he would defend his honor. But what did that come to? He was only trying to comfort a man who had unfinished business and no time left. That was all it was; a quick, kind way of letting Reno die in peace.

And yet . . . Richler was not a man to discard his promises. Some sure swift voice in him told him that he had made his commitment, and he must do all that was required, or he himself would be a man whose words were as loose as sand.

"All right, then, I will," he said into the near gloom, with only the faint light of the city probing into the parlor.

He had some leeway. He could not defend the indefensible, and some of Reno's conduct after the battle fell into that category. But he would do what he could, if only out of that charity that all human beings hope covers their worst failings and forgives them their trespasses.

# CHAPTER FORTY-TWO

JOSEPH RICHLER EYED HIS LUNCHEON COMPANION, CAPTAIN EDWARD Godfrey, wondering how much the man would say. The captain was well known as one of Marcus Reno's detractors, and during the court of inquiry had come closer than anyone else to calling the major a coward.

Godfrey exuded an impatient, patronizing air, as if nothing in the world quite suited him, especially lunch with a newsman. He peered down his formidable nose, which so dominated his face that Richler found himself staring at the long lumpy proboscis, which terminated in thick shrubbery. Somewhere in that foliage a mouth opened periodically to receive dessert.

The interview that Richler had in mind was forbidden in the hallowed chambers of the Washington Cosmopolitan Club, but Richler thought he could get away with it. The imperial and imperious club had admitted him only reluctantly; it didn't want reporters and other lowlifes mucking about among those who ran the country. On the other hand, James Gordon Bennett's *New York Herald* was the nation's preeminent newspaper, and the club had finally opened its doors to Richler, with the gentle admonition that its quiet chambers were not to be employed for business. Whatever was spoken in the Cosmopolitan Club was to be treated as private and sacrosanct. If there should be the slightest complaint, his name would be brought before the membership committee.

Richler had nodded, avoided reply, paid his dues, which he passed along to Bennett because they were ten times what any working newspaper correspondent could afford, and regularly patrolled the precincts where cabinet secretaries, generals of the army, admirals of the navy, and powerful legislators gathered to forge friendships, say unguarded things, and generate policies. He always got his best stories there, but was so adroit about it that none of the nabobs noticed.

This was business. But as far as Richler was concerned it was more. The Reno case had an odd hold on him, bordering on obsession, and he itched to dig deeper than anyone had so far into the Little Bighorn. And hovering always in the background was a promise made to a desperate and dying man. He hated that promise, which now imprisoned him and kept him occupied.

Maybe the potted palms and Sevres china would open the captain up.

"Captain, the Little Bighorn still fascinates me, and I thought I would pick your mind a little," Richler said, after a vanilla ice cream and tangerine dessert. "It's an obsession of mine."

"Richler, I've said what needs to be said. It's all in the court of inquiry."

Richler ignored him, and stirred sugar into his coffee.

"You commanded Company K, under Benteen, I take it. And lived to tell about it."

"It was a hot fight, all right."

"You came up with Benteen, found Reno up on the hill, right?"

"I did. We were at the rear. There was a fight ahead, plenty of shooting, and Reno was scrambling up there, and we couldn't see Custer at all. None of us imagined what had happened or what was about to happen. Damned if I can't see it all again, before my eyes."

"I've studied the transcript of the court of inquiry. It's plain you didn't think that Major Reno conducted himself gallantly."

Godfrey stared. "You know, I'd rather refer to the man as Mr. Reno."

The correspondent smiled. "I guess that says it."

"Yes, it does."

"You are no admirer of Reno."

"Let us speak no ill of the dead."

"But you didn't like him."

"Oh, in the army, one gets along with all sorts."

"You didn't like him."

"Let us change the subject—ah, it's well known. He was an ass."

"How so?"

Godfrey paused, plainly wondering whether he should plunge into such a topic, and obviously decided that he would. His thick finger started wagging, like a hammer pounding a nail.

"The cavalry is not a place for cowards."

Now at last Godfrey was showing signs of candidness.

"From the beginning of that fight until it was over, Reno showed himself for what he was. The cavalry, Richler, is an attack force. It's not much good for defense. You attack; you drive forward, you don't count enemy but you do count objectives. You head into a village and send it scattering like tenpins, and you don't quit just because you're outnumbered."

"You were there?" Richler asked, knowing that Godfrey had not been on hand in the valley fight.

"In a way, yes. I walked that terrain afterward. Every foot of it. I saw every tepee ring. I walked through those woods. I saw no reason why a cavalry charge should be aborted, or men should dismount and form a skirmish line or hide in the woods. At close range in the village, their revolvers would have been effective. They would have met Custer, two pincers with the village in its jaws, and the result would have been very different."

"You're a firm Custer partisan, then."

"It was a sound plan, sir."

"Then how did it go awry?"

"Reno. I'll say it now, I'll say it until I die." He wagged that blunt finger again. "Custer did not receive the support he counted on."

"Reno fought well during the War of the Rebellion."

"Bah! He was supposed to control Mosby's guerrillas in Pennsylvania, and played the fool. The man was not only craven but incompetent."

"He received glowing reports from his superiors after several fights."

"Battlefield talk. You didn't see him being elevated one brevet after another, the way Armstrong Custer was."

"Reno was a brevet brigadier of volunteers by war's end, I believe."

"Politics."

"General Sheridan called him one of the best."

"Bah! Nothing."

Richler was delighted. He had opened the reluctant captain up entirely. "Why didn't you like him, captain?"

The finger started wagging again. "I'll tell you why. I wasn't there, but I heard all about it. The night of June twenty-fifth, when the command was surrounded on the hilltop, Reno and Benteen had a little private powwow about what to do. Reno put it to Benteen: we've been deserted by Custer. We could sneak out, try to hook up with the command, wherever it is. If we did, we would have to mount the wounded who could ride, abandon the rest. Benteen told Reno that he wouldn't have any part of abandoning the wounded to those fiends. That, Mr. Richler, is reason enough to despise the man. Leaving wounded behind to save his fat carcass."

"I've heard the story, captain, and most people interpret it differently. It was simply a look at an option. He and Benteen were discussing options, the pros and cons of any tactic at a time when the command was isolated, in danger of being overwhelmed, and out of touch.

"No one, including Benteen, has ever suggested that Reno actually advocated the plan. He could have ordered it, you know. He was commanding. In fact, by all accounts, Reno attempted to contact Custer; the scouts wouldn't go. By the same token, no scout from Custer had gotten through to Reno. I'd be looking at all options myself, if I were commanding."

Godfrey reddened. "That porker just wanted to sneak out to save himself from the Sioux butchers, and that's all there was to it."

"You're sure of that? You knew his mind that well?"

"I'm as sure of it as I'm sure I'm sitting in the Cosmopolitan Club."

"Then you feel that Reno's entire conduct was not honorable."

"The word should not even be applied to the man."

"Well, you make yourself plain. But what about competence? Was Reno a competent officer, do you believe?"

Godfrey snorted, wiped crumbs from his thick moustache, and eyed Richler. "The man was West Point, but barely made it, you know. I suppose even the class dunce is competent to a degree, or else the academy is failing to do its duty."

A nice evasion. Godfrey always started gently, but a little prodding would open him up, Richler thought. "That retreat from the woods at the Little Bighorn. What do you think of it?"

"I'm glad you called it what it was. Reno called it a charge. I admit there's some controversy among officers as to whether Reno should have tried to hold there. The testimony at the court of inquiry varied widely." Godfrey leaned forward and waggled that finger. "It was a rout, cost Reno a third of his force. They didn't even cross that stream at a ford. High banks, horses clawing up, and the Indians shooting them like ducks."

"Is that a commander's failing?"

"Who else's?"

"What if the troopers bolt? Panic? What if sergeants and company commanders can't hold them? What if nothing any officer says can stop them?"

"Then the officers are . . . less then competent, shall we say."

"Who? French? DeRudio? Moylan?"

"You're not going to trap me into something like that, Richler. They're all good men, led on that occasion by an incompetent who panicked and ran."

"Did anyone see Reno running?"

"He ran across that river with the rest. He should have stayed behind, restored order, been the last man to reach that summit."

Richler suppressed a smile. "You saw none of this, though. You weren't there. You arrived later, under Benteen?"

"Richler, officers talk. I listen."

Richler nodded, sipped some cold coffee, and eyed the dining room, which had largely emptied. Several of the new Harrison administration's fat-bottomed undersecretaries were huddled in a corner.

"Put yourself in Reno's boots, captain. What would you have done at that point?"

"Richler, I don't appreciate this grilling," Godfrey said, pushing back his chair. "I thought we'd just talk a little about the fight because it's your hobby."

"I plan to write something. How about it? What would you have done?"

"I don't have enough facts to tell you anything like that."

"But you're certain Reno panicked."

"I have never said so."

"Reno sounds like a man you disliked as a person; you would have disliked him even if the Little Bighorn had never happened."

"I have no need to hide my private feelings, and have been most forthright with you about them."

Richler pulled out his pocket Waltham, and saw the hour was late. "One last question, if I may, sir. What do other officers in the Seventh Cavalry say about the late major?"

"I don't think . . ."

"Was he admired?"

Godfrey sat upright. "There never was more of a misfit, and on that note I think I'll head back to the War Office. I'm wrestling with their record bureau, you know."

Richler nodded, summoned a waiter, signed the tab, and followed the captain into the steaming Washington summer.

Godfrey had made himself finger-wagging clear.

# CHAPTER FORTY-THREE

BENNETT SAID NO, HE WOULDN'T PAY, DAMNED NONSENSE, SO RICHLER stewed. There was no thwarting the Great Man when he said no. Correspondents never knew how James Gordon Bennett would come down on an issue. The man would spend thousands of dollars for stories cabled to New York on one occasion, and forbid the payment of a streetcar token on another.

But Richler had to go to Atlanta, and one way or another he would go. At least Bennett had agreed to a serious assessment of Major Marcus Reno; anything to do with the Little Bighorn caught the man's attention and the public's interest. And Reno's death had started it all going once again.

"I'm going," he told his able assistant Basil Vanderhyde. "Cover for me. Gone four days. I'll send Bennett the bill and see if he relents. I've nothing to lose but a week's pay."

"What do I say if New York wires you?"

"Tell them I'm in Atlanta on a story, back Wednesday."

And so it was arranged. Richler packed his battered pigskin portmanteau, bought a forty-six-dollar round-trip coach ticket to Atlanta, and set off, passing through somnolent Virginia countryside at first, obscured by summer's haze.

The heat built all the way, and Richler sweated in spite of the wide open coach windows that admitted a little air and a ton of soot which blackened his face and turned his clothing gritty.

The South was no place to travel in the heat of summer and not much of a place to travel in the winter, either, Richler thought. It had fallen into lassitude since the War of the Rebellion, outwardly little changed.

Atlanta was a new city; the old was ash. Richler wondered why Frederick Benteen had chosen to retire there, deep in the heart of Dixie, where ancient hatreds of Yankees in blue simmered just below the surface. Colonel Benteen. They had breveted him when he retired. And there was talk that he would be breveted again, become a brigadier general, for gallantry during the war and at the Little Bighorn. The man had friends and used them, Richler thought.

Benteen was a Southerner who had chosen to fight for the Union. It was a brave decision, running violently contrary to the passions of his Missouri family, and especially his father, who cursed him and wished his own son a fatal bullet at the hands of the Confederacy. The curse never was fulfilled. Benteen survived the war, and his gallantry was beyond question.

The man was good at hating, though, and maybe that was what would make a good interview. In retirement Benteen would probably unloose the bridles on his tongue even more than before, and Richler would end up with some valuable and quotable material.

But that was speculative. In reality, Richler didn't know whether this odyssey to the retirement home of the man who knew Reno best, and watched him in action at the Little Bighorn, would reveal anything new. At least Benteen had agreed to see him; indeed, there was genuine hospitality afoot. Benteen and his wife Kate were enjoying retirement. Their only surviving child, Freddie, was heading for a military career himself.

Richler knew he would have to dodge the last year of the man's service, the court-martial conviction for drunkenness that had cost the then-major a year's suspension at half pay. When that was over in 1888, Benteen had swiftly resigned, suffering rheumatism and heart disease, and settled into comfortable retirement.

Benteen had been assigned to build a new post in Utah, Fort Duquesne, to control the Utes, and had run into trouble with suppliers and the post sutler, and his acerbic ways soon won him bitter enemies who brought charges of drunken conduct against the old veteran. These poorly substantiated accusations had been enough, and Benteen was very nearly pitched out the way Reno had been.

Oddly, Richler sympathized. The army had a way of brutalizing some of its best men, and by all accounts, Benteen was a fine officer and bold man in combat.

He listened to the mournful whistle of the engine ahead as it dragged the grimy coaches into Atlanta. He listened to the click-clack of wheels over rail-joints, was affronted by the acrid smell of coal smoke, felt the train slow, heard the hiss of steam, and saw the ramshackle depot crawl into view. He stood, retrieved his battered portmanteau from the overhead rack, felt sweaty cloth cling to his thin frame, and slowly wended his way down the aisle, then the metal steps, and into the burning sun of Georgia in June. He saw more black faces than white.

He checked his bag, and received a sweaty brass token with a number on it. He would deal with hotels and meals later; newsman that he was, he would go straight to Benteen's house and see what awaited him. If he could complete his interview before the day was done, he could catch an express north, and save some money. But he did pause at a lavatory to freshen himself, not for Benteen's sake but so that he would give no offense to Kate Benteen, the colonel's lively and opinionated wife. He stopped at a tonsorial parlor in the basement of the station for a shave and an application of witch hazel, and then found a hansom cab.

They were expecting him.

Benteen stood on the verandah, which circled and shaded the white frame house. The man had that odd cherubic look that had struck the *Herald* man; a look of anyone other than an army officer.

"Mr. Richler," Benteen said, "do come in. I'm looking forward to this." He steered the correspondent into a surprisingly cool parlor, with a high ceiling and deep shade. The verandah kept the sun out of the room. Here were morris chairs, a brown horsehair sofa, and all the comforts. Oval photographs of small children cluttered a small desk. An officer's memorabilia filled the room. A silk regimental flag, sepia photos of men in uniform, a sheathed sword.

"Would you like to refresh yourself, sir?" Benteen asked.

"I spent a little time at the station, colonel. It wasn't such a bad trip, save for losing some sleep."

"Ah! Colonel. I don't get called that much, except by Kate. I call her the general. We both know who's commanding around here. You'll meet her in a bit. She's fixing us some tea and tarts. Now then, tell me again what we're after here. The fight, yes? Always the fight. I'll talk about it, you bet I will."

Richler pulled a notepad from his breast pocket. "About Marcus Reno, in particular, colonel. I'll tell you exactly what this is. On his deathbed he asked a favor of me. He couldn't talk, you know. He wanted his name cleared. He wanted his honor back. He didn't want to lie in his grave in dishonor. I . . . agreed. Maybe foolishly. I wrote up a simple death notice for the *Herald,* but I'm working on a real obituary, and I hope I can give the man his dying wish."

Benteen studied Richler from bulging, gray, and unblinking eyes that gave him a startled look. "You can award the man his honor," he said so flatly that it seemed as final as a Supreme Court opinion.

"I know you were close, so I thought I'd ask a few questions."

"Close? Reno and I tangled all of our lives. Not close. No man could ever get close to Reno. He wouldn't allow it."

"But you were thrown together in a moment that still excites talk. That's what I hope to talk about."

"Fire away, then. I can't get into any worse trouble than I've been in all my life."

"You've had a gallant career, sir."

Benteen's ruddy face lit up. "Bull-headed is what it was. And it didn't end well. I'm going to bring that up so it doesn't sit here like some stone between us. They tried to cashier me. A long story. They pick on old majors who like a sip now and then, as our Major Reno did. But it was civilians that got me into a jam. I'm well out of it now, and we're happy."

"Why did you come here?"

"Family. Investments. A most pleasant society. I'm a Southerner, a Virginian by birth, only I chose the Union."

"And it's not held against you, the blue uniform?"

"Sure it is. That makes life entertaining."

Kate appeared, bearing a tray with a steaming teapot and scones, cups and saucers.

Richler was struck by her bright beauty, and also by her Southern way of wearing layers of gauzy white cotton that seemed to give Georgia women an ethereal grace. Richler couldn't imagine Nadine in such a costume.

"Ah, Mr. Richler, you've arrived at just the right moment. The colonel is itching for another scrap, having gotten bored in retirement," she said, pouring tea. "Unless you would prefer that I retire, I'll sit in on it and add my dime's worth. He'll give you the meat, and I'll add some salt and pepper."

"I'm sure you'll have plenty to add to the colonel's reminiscences," Richler said, wondering if it really might be so. He knew that Benteen shared everything with Kate, including the last scrap of officers' gossip. She had lived apart, finding frontier duty stations too taxing, and Benteen had kept her informed by regular correspondence.

She smiled cheerfully and settled in a morris chair, wanting to hear every word. Richler wondered whether it might inhibit Benteen, but the robust old man simply settled back, pulled out a meerschaum, tapped pungent dark leaf into it, and lit up.

"Where do you want to start?" Benteen asked.

"Custer."

"My feelings about Custer are well known, sir."

"Yes, and some say they lie at the core of what happened at the Little Bighorn."

Benteen puffed a moment, and Richler watched smoke curl up from the pipe and dissipate.

"It behooves me not to speak ill of the dead. George Custer was a man of great courage and gallantry, a soldier to the core. The army lost a fine officer."

Richler wondered whether Benteen, for all his cheerful bravado and announced intention to speak his mind, was going to clam up after all. It had been a long train ride, and maybe for nothing.

"He was also a sonofabitch," Benteen added.

# CHAPTER FORTY-FOUR

BENTEEN PUFFED SLOWLY, PLAINLY RELISHING THE MOMENT. HE WAS out of the army. This interview was the first since his retirement. It would be gloves off.

"Whittaker and his cabal accused me of mass murder," Benteen said. "Mass murder because they said I didn't like Custer. They said that I deliberately kept my forces out of the battle after Custer had told me to hurry. That my slow arrival resulted, by my *design,* in Custer's destruction. That's the gist of it, eh?"

"Something like that," Richler said, "but usually put less harshly."

"No, that's exactly it. Tear a veneer of civility off those charges and that's it: I'm a mass murderer, letting Custer have his just desserts. I did it by design."

The *Herald* man listened intently. This was getting very good.

"Do you believe it?" Benteen asked, leaning forward. "That I wanted Custer and his entire command to perish? Or at least, that I wanted to embarrass him, let him get into hot water?"

"I've heard it," Richler said.

"Do you own a horse? Have you ever?"

"No."

"Ah, then I have the chance to explain something. Horses tire out just as any animal does. We had been under a forced march, day and night, and our mounts were exhausted. Any good cavalryman knows what he can get out of his horse. And he knows what the horse will give him when asked. Any cavalry officer worth his salt knows not to go into a pitched fight on exhausted mounts, if at all possible.

"I received orders from the adjutant, Cooke, to steer off to the left and look for outlying villages in the hills. Custer wanted the whole bunch herded in. He didn't want any flight this time. So off I went, with my three companies, looking for outlying Indians, miles and miles, on tired mounts, not finding even one, and then I received word to return, 'big village ahead, come quick.' In cavalry terms, I did come quick. But I had just been on a *ten-mile detour.*

"We started at a trot and maintained that pace mile after mile. That's how you make time and preserve the horses for a fight. A horse can hold a trot without tiring. He cannot gallop over long stretches without wearing out. Our whole command had worn-out mounts. Custer's own companies were riding worn-out mounts, but ours were in worse shape because of my long detour.

"We heard firing ahead, a fight starting up, and Tom Weir wanted to run, and I held us to a trot, because what is worse than heading into a hard fight on worn-out mounts? Some mounts even quit. I would have imperiled my command if I had led it into that fight on fagged-out mounts. Does that make any sense to you?"

"Would it have helped if you had arrived earlier?"

Benteen was animated. Plainly, he was relishing this. "Now, hindsight is a wonderful thing, isn't it, sir? We all expected the Indians to scatter under cavalry attack. I did, Custer did, Reno did. So we all went into that fight blind. How the hell was I to know, or Reno to know, that this time the Indians were ready to fight to the death?

"Would you mind telling me why I should believe that Custer was in any kind of grave trouble, just because we heard some shots as we approached? Can you point to any reconnaissance that would have alarmed me? The commander attacked without knowing the terrain or the numbers. Neither Reno nor I had the faintest idea what we were getting into and Custer didn't tell us because he didn't know either!"

Richler shook his head.

Benteen's ruddy face had turned even redder. "Hindsight is wonderful, isn't it? Looking back on a disaster, everything leading into it looks sinister. Let's get to the heart of this. Do you really suppose, just because I didn't like the sonofabitch, that I would deliberately let my own Seventh Cavalry men perish?

"If you believe that, sir, you must believe that every man's hand is turned against every other man's hand. You must believe in a world without loyalties, without honor, without decency. There are those who believe in conspiracies and back-stabs. Once in a while that happens. Mostly, it's nonsense.

"You followed the Whittaker business? The paper's been full of it. Whittaker believed in just such a world, and he died a few weeks ago because he stumbled on a staircase and shot himself with the revolver he always had in hand to kill the shadowy intruders who lurked around him in his mind's eye.

"He believed that there were people out to get him, he had to defend himself, and he carried his revolver against these phantoms who were lurking in the shadows. *That* was the inner world of the man who accused Reno and me. Someday someone will give a name to that sort of mentality, that dour suspiciousness and distrust of everyone."

"I don't think Whittaker ever made much of a case, colonel."

"Among some people he made quite a case. Funny thing is, some defeated Reb officers bought it, believed it. Those who think the world is full of back-stabbers and conspirators believed it. There are people who actually think Marcus and I plotted to disobey orders and let Custer get himself into a jam or kill himself."

"Whittaker didn't really accuse Reno of that, colonel. Just cowardice and blundering."

Benteen grunted, tapped the ash from his meerschaum, and settled it in a pipe rack on a polished table.

"Reno didn't think much of Custer, either; wasn't part of Custer's little coterie, but he kept his views to himself. Not like me. I made no bones about my feelings. The sonofabitching glory hound would get his regiment in trouble sometime, and that time came. But Reno kept his mouth shut. He was a loner."

Richler nodded. Benteen was pouring forth his views without being prompted, and the newsman had only to nod and listen.

"Do you think, Richler, that I felt *guilty* after that fight? That I walked among the dead on that awful grassy slope, men I knew and treasured, feeling some sort of morbid shame, feeling some unbearable self-loathing because it was all my fault?

"Do you think I was filled with revulsion against myself? That I supposed I was a betrayer, a Judas? That I had let them all perish? No, sir, I most certainly did not. I wept, along with the rest. Those were my friends there, Keogh, Sturgis, Cooke, all those good and dear friends. Men whose hands I had clasped, men I grieved to tears."

Kate spoke up. "Whittaker's accusations have burdened my dear Frederick far more than Marcus, you know. Whittaker didn't accuse Marcus of being the Judas. Merely a coward."

She smiled suddenly. "But Freddy's too thick-skinned to let it get to him. Marcus was thin-skinned though he would never admit it. That accusation cut to his core, and changed him, made him hunt for insults. He couldn't bear it. After that, he found offense everywhere, even when none was intended, I'm afraid."

She reached across to Benteen's hand, and patted it. Richler discovered in Kate a true mate and a friend too. Whatever one might say about Benteen, he seemed happily married.

"May I turn to the valley fight, colonel? You weren't there, but you know as much as anyone about it. Should Reno have kept on, ignoring the reality that he was being engulfed and flanked by the Indians?"

Benteen brightened. "One of the little mental exercises I engage in, or used to long ago, was this: what if Custer had sent Reno around to the right flank, and had led the charge on the village, straight up the valley, himself? Driven right in with his five companies? Would the result have been different? Custer would have kept going regardless, and even with more men than Reno had he would have been surrounded and defeated right there in the village or close to it. And Reno, caught in that high bluff country, couldn't have come to Custer's rescue. And I would not have returned in time."

"What does that suggest, colonel?"

"When an attack fails, and the entire command is imperiled, a commander ought to retreat and regroup. Reno saw the peril, organized a retreat to the woods, and bought time. I can't fault the man for good tactical decisions."

"But retreats don't excite admiration," Richler said.

Benteen laughed, an odd harshness in his amusement. "No newspaper ever celebrated a retreat, and no generals do either, not even a necessary retreat. That's a great peculiarity. There went Custer, right into the middle of it all and got himself killed and everyone reported how gallant he was, what a hero. And there's poor Reno, doing the only possible thing to do under the circumstances, and everybody whispers what a coward he was."

"One hears stories that Reno was disoriented . . ."

Benteen shook his head irritably. "In the middle of a desperate battle, sir, you rarely have the chance to examine the conduct of others. That's what amused me about the court of inquiry. The witnesses all swore that Reno was this, or that, or something else. As if they could form judgments under such circumstances. He did, apparently, hesitate or reverse himself a time or two, but under that sort of pressure who wouldn't?"

"You wouldn't," Kate said. "You're a bulldog."

Richler bored in. "He ordered a retreat to the hilltop, and it turned into a rout. The troops were fleeing for their lives. Was that his failing?"

"I wasn't there. But I'll say this. When your men panic and won't heed commands, and the sergeants aren't in control, and the company commanders are shouting at air, it's not likely that the commander of the unit is at fault. Reno was a veteran of the War of the Rebellion. I don't think he panicked himself. I don't know that he could have done more than he did. His decision to get to the hilltop was certainly sound. You've seen the testimony. Nearly every officer under him said he couldn't have survived long in that woods. They were too few to defend such a big patch."

"Did the officers say one thing to the court of inquiry and believe another?"

"Hell, yes."

That startled Richler. "You included?"

"What I didn't tell the court, sir, could fill a book."

"I'm all ears."

"Here's what I might have said: Custer launched the most ill-planned and poorly reconnoitered assault in American military history.

"No one really wanted to speak ill of the dead, so the recorder, Lee, never approached the issue of whether Custer's plan of attack was competent. It wasn't. I should have received far more instruction from Cooke than he delivered to me. I didn't know, for instance, what Reno's orders were, or what to do if I found no Indians on the left. There was no scheme to it, not one word. If Custer had a plan in his head, he didn't reveal it to the battalion commanders. Little of that came out in the inquiry. It needed to come out. Reno was left to his own devices and he did as well as he could."

"How would you rank Reno as a cavalry officer?"

"Not first rate. Never inspired the men, never fired them up. But I've served under worse, far worse."

"Competent?"

"Entirely competent, sir, and the survival of half of the Seventh attests to his competence."

"But on the hilltop?"

Benteen paused. "That's a good question," he replied, slowly. "And the answer isn't simple."

# CHAPTER FORTY-FIVE

RICHLER HADN'T BEEN PREPARED TO LIKE BENTEEN, BUT THE MORE he talked with the retired cavalry officer, the more taken he was. Benteen was candid, never concealing his beliefs, and plainly enjoying his talk with the *Herald* reporter. Maybe the man was a little cynical toward his fellow officers, maybe even abrasive, but there was no hypocrisy in anything he did or said.

It was a good interview, and Richler thought it would help him fashion that obituary, which was steadily shaping in his mind. He had gambled, coming all the way to Atlanta, and now the gamble was paying off.

"Let's go to the hilltop fight, colonel," he said. "There's a lot of conflicting testimony about Reno's conduct there. I've gone through the court of inquiry and ended up with sharply contradictory impressions. On the one hand, the testimony suggests that Reno seemed dazed and passive and left the defense to you. On the other hand, testimony suggests that Reno was aggressive, patrolled the lines, upbraided skulkers hiding among the pack mules, exposed himself to fire so much that others warned him to take cover. What was it?"

"Both," Benteen replied. "Both are accurate."

"Explain that, if you will."

"As I look back upon that period, a time most perilous I assure you, I believe there were two Renos. We were under fire, a small exposed command facing many times our numbers, without water, and abandoned by

Custer—or so we thought. He ordered me to array my men on one side, and his would take the other, but after that he left the defenses to his company commanders. He stared out into the surrounding hills almost as if he expected to find an answer there.

"And then, suddenly, he left the command to me and headed down-slope to recover what he could from Lieutenant Hodgson's body. He picked up a ring and a few personal items and made it back safely. That could be seen as gallant, or as foolhardy. In a different setting, such as a great victory, that would have been an act of utmost gallantry."

Richler nodded.

"Then there was the question of whether to try to find Custer. Tom Weir was probing north on his own, along the bluffs, and his company riding after him, and we resolved to follow as soon as the pack horses with ammunition were in. Reno's ammunition had largely been expended. I've heard reports that his men had around thirty rounds, and he was dead right not to mount an all-out attack with so little ammunition. He had no choice but to wait, though Tom Weir couldn't see it. Weir was well supplied; his company hadn't yet been in a fight. He just didn't grasp that you just don't attack with empty guns.

"Through all this, Reno commanded intelligently, yet in odd bursts of energy and periods of inert watchfulness. That's why I say there were two of Marcus Reno up there."

"How so?"

"Sometimes he seemed to neglect duty and I found myself commanding. Other times he was in a perfect frenzy, rallying the troops, organizing the movement that would follow Weir, once the ammunition was distributed."

"Torn between decision and indecision?"

"Now, there's an odd thing. He was able, and I can't tell you he was anything else. But I've wondered if he was in some sort of shock, kept pulling himself out of it and commanding, only to slip back into a passive mood. I have no word for it. Other moments he was fierce, aggressive, scornful of danger.

"Now what would you call all that? I have no word for it. Maybe some-day someone will supply a word. We're talking about some quality in his nature, his character, that seesawed back and forth. That's why I keep re-turning to the idea that there were two of him on that hilltop."

"That doesn't sound very good to me, a commander sliding in and out of command."

Benteen didn't reply, for a change. Richler could see that the man was reliving those moments in his mind's eye. Finally he spoke: "My memory is playing tricks. During the whole time, I saw nothing in his command that troubled me and that includes any drinking. I'll tell you flatly the man was not drunk. Reno was a sipper, he always had to nip a little, but I never saw him intoxicated or incapable of commanding, and no other of-ficer did either. And by God, I'd have sipped myself if I had the chance."

"At the inquiry, some civilian packers claimed he was roaring drunk."

"That's the old civilian game, sir. Let an officer rebuke a civilian and that civilian knows how to get even, knows exactly where every officer in the army is vulnerable. Believe me, I've just been through it. Reno slapped one of those men for skulking out of harm's way instead of helping to de-fend, and next thing you know, the man is at the court of inquiry testify-ing that Reno was drunk. He wasn't. As I myself said, the officers there wouldn't have let him command if he'd been drunk. And as I also said, I could have used a nip myself, but there wasn't enough whiskey in the whole command to get anyone drunk."

Benteen nodded toward Kate, who rose at once and began pulling bot-tles out of a kitchen cupboard.

"You can't talk man to man without something to sip," he said.

Richler smiled. "If you were in my shoes, wanting to write a candid obituary of the man, what would you say, colonel?"

Benteen peered at Richler wryly. "Reno was my kind of sonofabitch."

"When did you lose track of him?" Richler asked.

"When he was suspended. I saw him briefly at the court of inquiry."

"Had he gone downhill in some fashion?"

"Certainly. Something was eating him, and I'd guess it was those accusations. Worse, he knew the court of inquiry didn't resolve a thing. There were still officers who felt they could have done better on that battlefield, officers who thought Reno tucked his tail between his legs and fled, officers who found fault. They weren't happy with the result.

"And all the inquiry did was isolate Marcus even more. He was cleared, sort of, and half of them didn't want him cleared because they all privately thought they could do better. Even the armchair generals, like that old Reb, Rosser, thought they could do better. Running from Indians! Everybody knows all about the Indians. They don't fight.

"So there's old Marcus, cleared of cowardice, and a lot of smug rivals thinking it had been a whitewash. I wish some of those sonsofbitches could have been there. It was a big thing, you know, worst defeat the army had experienced with Indians, and the high command wasn't happy with Custer, with Reno, with me, and even with Terry. Only I have thick skin, so it all bounced off. Marcus . . . that's another case entirely."

Kate slipped a shot glass of amber fluid and a tumbler of water, to the table. Richler poured the shot into the water and sipped.

Benteen downed his shot neat, wheezed, and smiled. "Damned good stuff," he said. "What are you going to write about him?"

"I don't know yet. I plan to interview General Terry and maybe some others, before I start scribbling."

"You write on one of those typing machines?"

"Longhand."

"I've been writing my memoirs."

"May I have a look?"

"Someday, after I'm gone."

"What do you suppose happened to Reno after that fight? He went from being a soldier who kept out of trouble to getting into serious trouble. Why did he disintegrate after the battle?"

Benteen sipped, and frowned. "I've wondered about that. Sometimes I think he never should have been an officer. Other times I think that's nonsense. He got into trouble at West Point, barely scraped through, mostly because his rambling spirit wouldn't submit to army discipline.

"But, Richler, that wasn't it. There was something contradictory in him, some part of himself he was always wrestling against, trying to contain. Maybe he should have been a poet. He held together until Whittaker, the surrogate of Mrs. Custer, began denouncing him as a coward. He never thought of himself as a coward after the battle; he was proud as punch that he has saved the command from annihilation.

"And then the knifing began, the little stabs, big stabs, and he fell apart. Don't ask me to diagnose a problem within the man; he just couldn't stand up to the criticism, though he put on a good front, that's for sure."

"An aberration of the mind, a divided heart?"

"Something like that."

Richler thought that the whiskey was swiftly expanding Benteen's hospitality and camaraderie.

"Do you think he should have been reinstated? He spent the rest of his life trying."

"Let me put it this way," Benteen said. "I wish he had just settled into a comfortable civilian life. He should have been listed as a casualty, not for wounds to the flesh, but wounds to his soul."

"The corps was his life, colonel. It was all he wanted."

"Yes, and that's why Marcus Reno is a tragic figure."

# CHAPTER FORTY-SIX

THE NEXT INTERVIEW WOULD BE THE MOST IMPORTANT, AND MAYBE the hardest. Joseph Richler sat in his swaying wicker seat in a grimy maroon steam coach examining every possible approach, and knowing that he might well fail utterly.

Major General Alfred Howe Terry had been Reno's departmental commander for much of Reno's later career, and was involved in everything that happened to the major from well before the Little Bighorn to Reno's sudden eviction from the army.

Richler had written Terry a few days earlier, asking to interview him about the troubled major, and suggesting that they meet at the forthcoming encampment of the Grand Army of the Republic in Boston. But the general had pleaded ill health, and said he was largely confined to his home in New Haven. But he would indeed be willing to discuss at length the Little Bighorn and its aftermath with Richler in New Haven.

That was promising. But Richler reminded himself that Terry had been a smooth, successful lawyer before the Civil War, and much of what he did in the army was involved with military law. The chances of getting a candid interview from a man steeped in discretion would be a challenge. But Joe Richler was a veteran *New York Herald* correspondent, and James Gordon Bennett didn't hire amateurs or the faint-hearted. And besides, Joe Richler loved a challenge. The worse the odds, the better he liked it.

Terry had raised and commanded a regiment of Connecticut volunteers during the War of the Rebellion, fought at First Bull Run, and then in Virginia, the Carolinas, and Georgia, applying his remarkable grasp of military tactics to the battlefields. He soon rose to brigadier of volunteers, and after the war was signally honored to receive the same rank in the regular army.

When the Seventh Cavalry was moved to Dakota in 1873, it fell under the command of General Terry, and that was when Marcus Reno found himself under the Connecticut general. It was Terry who detailed him to the boundary survey. Terry who had sent the Seventh Cavalry, led by Custer, off to scout out the hostile Sioux. Terry who was on hand a day after the Little Bighorn. Terry who had approved Reno's various courts-martial. Terry who had approved or modified the verdicts of those trials. Terry who had set in motion the court of inquiry into Reno's conduct. Terry who had dismissed Major Reno from further service, after receiving orders from Washington to do so.

It was Terry whose word would, in the end, shape what Joseph Richler would write about Reno . . . if Terry talked, and that was the question looming large and urgent all the way north.

He transferred stations in New York City, and caught a New England express out to Long Island Sound, detraining at last in the splendid old city where a central green still existed, surrounded by the old churches, where Yale University flourished, where many of the small arms used by the army were manufactured. No wonder the general lived there; Richler had rarely seen such a vibrant and gracious old city.

At the ornate station he rang up Terry on a telephone, enjoying the novelty, and was assured by a servant that the general was awaiting him. He caught a hansom cab and soon stepped out before a substantial brick home.

A maid answered and led him to a parlor where the general was seated, a small lap robe over him even in the summer's warmth.

"Forgive me for not getting up, Mr. Richler," he said, extending a frail white hand. Richler shook it gently, shocked to find the general, who had retired only the previous year, so ravaged by age. His hair, bushy eyebrows, moustache, and soup-strainer beard were shot with gray. "My constitution is not what it was, but I hope the rest of me will prove worthy of the occasion."

"It is good of you to see me, sir, especially because it concerns a subject both delicate and controversial."

"I am not afraid of controversy, nor am I the servant of delicacy, Mr. Richler. I have my own purposes here, among them to clarify things while I am still able to do so."

That was plain enough, and hopeful.

"Please be seated, and speak up, because I have heard too many cannon in my day and I suffer a loss of hearing. Now, shall we have some tea, or something stronger?"

"Tea, sir."

"Iced? We have a good supply of pond ice, which I relish for just such occasions."

"That would be a great treat, sir."

Terry rang a silver bell and swiftly conveyed his request to the Irish maid.

"Now then?" Terry stared gravely at Richler, awaiting the first question. The general radiated an innate confidence. He seemed to be a man who knew who he was in the scheme of things, a man who could handle any question, especially those he cared not to answer.

"I am preparing a *Herald* story about Major Reno, sir. You might call it an obituary. It's the result of the major's own deathbed wish. He could not speak, you know, having lost his tongue to the surgeon's knife, but he expressed that wish when he was fevered and failing.

"He wanted his honor back. He had failed over his life to do that. I said I would attempt it. I have had great doubts, and thought I might escape a swiftly offered promise given a dying man, but I can't do that, sir. I will make the best case I can, without violating any truths or fact. If you can help me, I would welcome it. If not, I would frankly still welcome your view."

Terry smiled gently. "Well, let's see," he said, and in that phrase, so simple in its externals, lay the promise of a most thorough examination. "I presume this shall be a public interview, and whatever is said here might be quoted."

"I had that in mind, sir."

"I shall conduct myself accordingly."

The maid set a sweating glass of iced tea before Richler, and he tasted the novelty with great pleasure.

"I suppose we might start with Custer, sir. Did he violate your orders?"

Terry peered at Richler so long he wondered whether he had affronted him, and whether the interview would cease before it began.

"I reported that he did," Terry said, "After the fight, as I listened not only to Reno but the rest of the officers, I concluded that indeed he had. But of course that's been contested. I gave the lieutenant colonel some discretionary power to act as he saw fit. Still, the plan was to catch the village between his forces and Colonel Gibbon's infantry on the twenty-sixth of June. The Seventh Cavalry jumped the gun."

"Custer's partisans all say he did so because he had been discovered, sir. Surprise was crucial."

"Some surprise," Terry said. "I admire George Armstrong Custer and revere his memory, and have only the most tender regard for his widow . . ."

Richler sat, pencil poised, writing nothing. The general's gaze focused on that pencil and smiled. "My feelings about Armstrong Custer are not window dressing, Mr. Richler. I have had all these years, before and after the Little Bighorn, a deep esteem for his gallantry, his courage, and his way of winning. But what I was saying was prelude to the rest of my observation, which is that he attacked recklessly, without reconnoitering properly, unaware of terrain or the true size of the village, and utterly uninformed about the mood or ferocity of its warriors.

"So, yes, you may express General Terry's opinion that Lieutenant

Colonel Custer fatally abandoned sound military doctrine, and the result was tragic and fatal.

"You may add that while I granted him discretion, it was to be exercised within the framework of my strategy, which was to catch the village between our forces. You may say, as I have many times, that he took my permissiveness as to discretion and reduced it to meaning he was under no restraint from me at all; that at bottom, the long march of Gibbon's column toward the planned rendezvous on the twenty-sixth of June was apparently not even in his mind when he chose to attack."

That was as firm a statement as General Terry had ever made, and Richler took pains to get it down exactly. Terry watched approvingly. Richler sensed there would be hell to pay if he put the wrong words in the major general's mouth.

"Custer divided his forces, sir. In retrospect, given the disaster, it seems foolish. But if you were commanding at that juncture, would you have done the same?"

"A good question, Mr. Richler. It tells me that you understand the odd effect of hindsight; we see the bad result and so question the tactic. But a commander on the spot is considering only the future, and gauges everything on what he thinks will happen.

"I myself might have divided the command in that approach south of the village, but not into so many parts, and not in the same fashion. "With the bluffs and river forming obstacles to the east, I would have employed them to hem in the Indians, and instead sent half my forces straight up the valley, and the other half around to the left, where there are low hills, and where the tribal horse herd had gathered.

"Had half the Seventh attacked from the west side, driving a wedge between the warriors and their horses, scattering the horses, while the other half drove north, the warriors would not have had an easy time, and might well have been deprived of their mounts . . . which is a long way around to my point. I don't think that Custer chose a very intelligent tactic, trying for surprise through those towering bluffs he had not reconnoitered, and he paid for it."

That was as plain as Richler could hope for, and he again took pains to get it right in his notepad.

"General, there's been a lot of talk, especially in the press, about orders, and whether Captain Benteen and Major Reno followed them. The implication is that, because neither man liked or respected Custer, they chose not to follow the orders, and to let Custer get himself into trouble. Do you put any credence in it? Did the captain and the major betray Custer and all of his command by disobeying him?"

Terry's gaze fell so intensely on Richler that for a moment he thought the general would say nothing. Indeed, Richler grew conscious of the clack of a grandfather clock ticking away somewhere. He watched the sun catch motes of dust.

"Well, now," said the general. "Let's examine it together, and then you can draw your own conclusions and put them in your obituary."

# CHAPTER FORTY-SEVEN

GENERAL TERRY SEEMED LOST IN REVERIE, AND TOOK SO MUCH TIME that Joseph Richler wondered whether he was dozing. But at last Terry focused again.

"What, do you understand, were Custer's orders to Reno and Benteen?" Terry asked.

"I believe they were oral, sir, and all the reports and the testimony at the Reno court of inquiry, without exception, indicate that he told Reno to charge up the valley, and Reno would be supported by Custer. And he told Benteen to head on a left oblique and scout for outlying villages. Those were the initial orders, by all accounts."

"Delivered by Adjutant Cooke?"

"According to all accounts, yes."

"And what evidence is there that the orders were otherwise?"

"None that I know of, general. Those who accuse Reno and Benteen of disobedience think that Custer gave different orders."

"On what ground?"

"That Custer would not have sent Benteen so far away, but would have ordered Benteen to attack from the left flank, in much the manner that Custer had attacked the Cheyennes at the Washita."

"And how can they prove this?"

"They simply argue that Custer would have done it because that was how he did things in the past. At Washita."

Some ancient fires were rekindled in the old general's eyes, and he wagged a bony finger.

"Ah! I see. So their argument has no factual basis at all. They *don't know* what Custer ordered in *this* case because the orders weren't written. And they don't know whether Cooke repeated the orders accurately. Adjutants don't always convey a commander's intent precisely, sad to say. They don't always *listen*."

"I hadn't thought of that, general."

"Few people think of that. Somehow, it's always presumed that Cooke got it all straight. Maybe he didn't. Maybe those unclear or incomplete orders were all Cooke's failure. The point is, we *don't know*." The old man rubbed his pale forehead, lost in thought. "What they're doing is a bit of necromancy, Mr. Richler. They have miraculously divined what Custer's *real* orders were, and having plucked up the truth from out in the ether somewhere, beyond the grave, maybe after a seance with Custer's ghost, they have no trouble demonstrating that Reno and Benteen were disobedient. I think General Rosser started it with that letter to the Minneapolis paper a few days after the battle. I remember it keenly, having been caught in the events. The very sentence startled me at the time."

Terry closed his eyes, summoning up something that had caught in his memory. Then his placid gaze focused again on the correspondent.

"Yes, I have it now. Rosser, that old West Point friend and Confederate enemy of Custer, lost no time divining what those *real* orders were: 'I think it quite certain that General Custer had agreed with Reno upon a place of junction in case of the repulse of either or both of the detachments . . .' Well, sir, that still sits in my mind, that bit of necromancy, putting orders in Custer's mouth when there is *not the slightest evidence* that Custer ever gave them. That shabby ploy has been at the heart of every effort to disgrace Benteen and Reno, and it deserves to be treated as the tomfoolery that it is."

There was a fine, lawyerly scorn in the old man's voice.

"It is a great sport, isn't it? If you want to blame Reno and Benteen for the disaster, why, just assert that Custer's orders were very different from what Reno and Benteen said they were. Do you want to condemn Reno? Then invent an order, put it in the dead man's mouth, and tell the world that Reno disobeyed it, or lied, or covered up the truth. And not only Reno, but all the other officers who received the order at that time and remember it well."

Richler encouraged the old man to continue: "If I recollect properly, Reno and Benteen weren't the only two who heard those orders. Lieutenant Wallace heard them given to Reno. His testimony at the inquiry supported that of Reno."

"He did, sir. I obtained a copy of all that and studied it closely. Lieutenant Wallace testified that he heard Cooke tell Reno to attack up the valley, and Custer would support him. That was the understanding of all the officers in Reno's command. Custer would support Reno's attack in some unspecified way. No one has ever disputed that."

"No, no one has, general."

"Well, Mr. Richler, if someone supposes that Custer really gave Reno some other order, then he makes a perjurer, a liar, out of Lieutenant Wallace too, does he not?"

"It would seem so."

"So, Reno's testimony is supported by a witness."

"Yes, sir. And Wallace also testified that Cooke gave no indication of where or how Custer intended that Benteen and Reno should hook up."

General Terry nodded. "I think the matter settles itself without further comment, Mr. Richler, except for those who'll conclude Wallace was part of this alleged conspiracy to do in Custer and hide the truth. If anyone supposes that Custer gave orders other than what the records indicate, let him prove it. And not with speculation. Let him bring real evidence to the table. And if he can't, he has no business making scurrilous charges of disobedience against two officers. May I refresh your tea?"

"I'm doing fine, thank you. I recently interviewed Colonel Benteen, sir. He explains his delay on several grounds. The first is that his horses were worn out, not only from the forced march of the whole command, night and day, but also from the ten-mile scout to the left that Custer sent him on.

"He said the horses were barely fit to take into battle, where they would be put to the test; and that the fast trot he chose upon receiving orders to hurry into the fight was the best way of conserving what little strength was left in the mounts, while still covering ground very quickly.

"He pointed out that horses that won't move in the middle of a fight are a menace to the troops. He added, sir, that no one imagined that Custer was in mortal peril."

Terry pondered it. "I have no objection to that, Mr. Richler. At the time, I'm sure Benteen thought he was hurrying to the greatest degree that he could, given the condition of his mounts. It's only by hindsight that things become different, only by hindsight that his actions look malevolent, and one wonders whether Benteen could have done more.

"Hindsight is a tricky knowledge, sir. When you are commanding and facing an unknown future, things look very different. He might have gained a few minutes, maybe five minutes, galloping into the fight. But then what? A cavalry charge on worn-out mounts. Hand-to-hand combat against warriors on fresh, eager, and rested Indian ponies. No, Mr. Richler, no reasonable man can quarrel with Benteen's decision to move at a fast trot."

"Captain Weir thought otherwise, sir."

Terry suddenly smiled broadly, but said nothing.

Richler continued. "Colonel Benteen told me he feels no guilt, has no regrets about how he comported himself in those hard moments, and felt a great sorrow and helplessness when he discovered the tragedy."

"Major Reno expressed the same horror, Mr. Richler. We all wept."

"You walked the battlefield, general."

"I walked it, I rode over it, every yard of it, I studied the land, followed Custer's route, examined hundreds and hundreds of tepee rings, walked among the naked and mutilated dead, picked up their empty copper cartridges, talked to many of the survivors, soaking up all that they could tell me. I read Major Reno's report, and wrote two of my own."

"You've been blamed, too."

He smiled. "A losing commander is always blamed."

"Has time altered any of your impressions?"

"You know, the battle stirs controversy to this day, and always will. The *Army and Navy Journal* is still publishing charges and rebuttals. There is a regular divide now, between the Custer partisans and Custer antagonists, the former blaming Major Reno and Captain Benteen, and sometimes myself, the latter blaming Custer's own reckless conduct. But the simple and overwhelming fact is that the village was far too large for Custer's force to handle alone."

"Have you drawn up on one side or the other?"

"Custer was a gallant and courageous officer, Mr. Richler, who exceeded his authority in that instance. And in that moment of derring-do abandoned most of the things he learned over the years."

Richler thought the interview was going well, and pressed on. "Could Reno and Benteen have done better, sir? I am getting at the question of Major Reno's competence. Frederick Whittaker's accusations against the major boiled down to two things, cowardice and incompetence. I'm wondering whether Major Reno, in your opinion, conducted himself in the field the way an officer should."

"Every officer in the army, I suppose, asks himself how he could have done better. I imagine both men have asked themselves the same question. I have not heard mea culpas from either one. Then there is a sort of unspoken and unacknowledged rivalry among officers, Mr. Richler, in which many an officer spots the alleged mistakes of other officers, and thinks he could have done better, and should have been in command. It's hindsight again, the miraculous vision we acquire looking into the past, not the future.

"That's a long way around your question, but it explains the odd scrutiny that was focused on Major Reno. I think, by and large, the major was quite competent, especially in the valley fight. He had the field experience to see he was being flanked and engulfed by much larger forces, and that his entire battalion would be surrounded and doomed unless he found safe ground. That is competence of the highest order, sir, and the hardest of decisions to make in the field. It is precisely the sort of decision that George Armstrong Custer failed to make."

Richler thought the old general was tiring, but there still was much ground to cover, and he hoped Terry would be up to it.

"What about the hilltop fight? There are sharply contradictory reports about his conduct there. For instance, when Reno turned things over to Benteen and headed downslope, beyond his lines, to recover what he could from the body of Lieutenant Hodgson."

An odd lift of the eyebrow and faint ironic smile lit the old man's face. "Let me put it this way, Mr. Richler. If Custer had been commanding up there instead of Reno, and if our dashing lieutenant colonel had chosen to slip down that slope to Lieutenant Hodgson's body, the act would have been regarded as the utmost gallantry, the sort of bravado that adds to a man's legend.

"You would not hear one whisper of doubt about the act, had Custer done it. No, sir. It would have inspired awe, sir; young officers would be talking about it to this very hour, the golden moment that gallant Custer braved the hostiles to get Hodgson's West Point class ring."

He laughed suddenly, and Richler laughed too. The irony of condemning Reno's gallantry while lauding Custer's gallantry had not been lost on the old general.

"What did you think of the man, sir?"

"Ah, now you get to the delicate part, where I must make careful distinctions. Are you up to making fine distinctions in print, Mr. Richler?"

"Try me," the correspondent said.

"I believe I will," Major General Terry replied.

# CHAPTER FORTY-EIGHT

JOE RICHLER WAITED PATIENTLY. THE OLD MAN WAS CHOOSY ABOUT what he said, which perhaps is one reason he had risen to one of the highest ranks of the United States Army.

"I am going to rephrase your question, Mr. Richler. I am going to tell you what good I found in the man. You know, that old adage, don't speak ill of the dead, is something I've always kept in mind. I've had occasions to speak ill of the dead in this long life, and I've resisted them. The dead can't defend themselves. But more than that, their long fight is over, their race has been run, and it's simple charity to discover the best in them. We can never know what demons a man wrestled with; and if we knew we might admire him—or her—all the more."

Richler nodded. Bland praise didn't make good newspaper copy and might conceal the truth about Marcus Reno. And yet he understood the old man's sensitivity and even admired it. But he knew he would not get much more out of General Terry.

"Was he a good soldier, sir?"

"He fought admirably during the War of the Rebellion."

"And after that?"

"At times he was excellent."

That was leaving much unsaid, and Richler sensed he should not push, not just then. Maybe Terry would give him an opening.

"I think Reno had a difficult and contrary nature, general, and governing himself was sometimes quite beyond him. One moment he could be passive, but in another moment, such as when he dressed down the skulkers in the hilltop fight and slapped one, he could be abrasive. And one or another of these natures was always cropping up when least expected."

"Two natures, eh? I had not considered it," Terry said. "I thought, in fact, that Reno had acquired bitter adversaries in the Seventh Cavalry, and the fellow should have been transferred to another regiment. I think his conduct would have improved in other circumstances. He might even have rounded out his career with years of quiet and admirable service. It's my regret that I didn't pursue that course at the first sign of trouble. The army doesn't suffer problem officers gladly."

"This whole business of rapping on Colonel Sturgis' window to catch the eye of the colonel's daughter is a strange thing," Richler said.

"Abominable conduct. In one sense, Reno's conduct was not scandalous. He wasn't acting as some sort of Peeping Tom. He approached the window and rapped on it and waved, boldly announcing his presence. But in another sense, he surely violated that household, and violated Ella Sturgis. Colonel Sturgis had denied Reno a welcome at that house, wisely I must say, and had expressly forbidden Major Reno from courting his daughter.

"I've heard, Benteen said it I believe, that the major was greatly smitten by young Ella. But that, Mr. Richler, is the very point. He let his feelings override all sense of appropriate conduct. I have no idea whether he was in his cups, probably was. But he affrighted the young woman and her mother, and said as much in his apology, and I haven't the slightest doubt that it was, in military justice, conduct unbecoming to an officer and a gentleman."

Richler absorbed that, impressed by the old man's sudden energy and unequivocal condemnation of Reno's conduct, the final outrage against the code of military conduct, the act that resulted in Reno's expulsion from the army.

"General, had Reno not engaged in that last affront, might he have survived the other charges?"

"The other charges were trivial. So he got into a fight or two. A slap on the wrist would have sufficed."

"I have the feeling that Reno had deteriorated by then. Whether from alcohol, or the abuse heaped on him after the Little Bighorn, or something else, maybe an abrasive nature. Do you have that sense, general?"

Terry retreated into himself again, summoning memories. "You know, Mr. Richler, right after that battle, Major Reno hadn't the slightest inkling that he would be criticized for his conduct in it. I remember how he was then, throwing his energies into restoring his command, identifying and burying the dead, reporting to me at length about what happened. I admired him. He'd been through a nightmare and survived.

"Historians read dry reports and dusty papers, but the whole truth isn't there in those papers. From the military reports they would learn nothing of the long private talks we had after it was over. They would learn nothing of the grief he felt for the fallen. I watched his anger at Custer turn into shock and sorrow. You know he and Benteen thought that Custer had abandoned them, and were spoiling for a tussle with the lieutenant colonel—until they found out what actually happened. And you won't find any of that in the official reports.

"I saw all of that, Mr. Richler. Yes, I saw it. When Marcus Reno realized he had saved his command from disaster, I saw the pride in him. Neither he, nor I, had any inkling of what was to come, the blame and accusations.

"I myself thought that Custer must bear the blame for the tragedy. But that was not to be. No sooner did the world learn of it than Reno found himself in trouble. The man was suddenly the focus of half the world's newspapers, most of the country's politicians, and every superior officer up the chain of command. Not the least of that attention came from your paper, the *Herald*. And that's just when that odd character of his began to falter. Not on the field of battle, not when bullets where whizzing by, but when stony stares landed on his heart and bruised it. I look back on all that followed not harshly, but with pity, Mr. Richler. Pity."

The old man turned silent again, lost in reverie, and Richler knew it was time to call it quits.

He drained his iced tea. "Would you care to make a summation? Say what's most important to you about all this?"

"Marcus Reno was a gallant soldier who unfairly bore the blame for a military disaster not of his making. It is my deepest wish that his memory be respected and honored."

Richler penned exactly that in his notebook.

"Anything else, general?"

"Yes, Mr. Richler. I would say much the same thing of General Custer."

Richler carefully added that to his notes, folded up the notebook he always carried, and dropped it into his vest pocket.

"Thank you, sir. This is most helpful."

"You'll forgive me for not seeing you to the door, I hope," the general said, offering a cold and feeble hand.

Out on the streets of New Haven, Joe Richler knew he had gotten a key idea from Terry. In terms of the military's strict code, Marcus Reno might not be a gentleman of honor, but in terms that ordinary mortals could live with and by, Major Reno had lived a life of duty and courage. And that was enough.

He had one more interview still to do and then he would write.

# CHAPTER FORTY-NINE

ROSS WAS VERY LATE. JOE RICHLER PULLED HIS TURNIP WATCH AND discovered it was almost one, and the lunch hour was fast vanishing. Just his luck, he thought.

He settled into the lobby divan in the Lochiel Hotel and waited some more. The place was dark and cramped, not at all a grand hotel compared to New York's best, and that fit Richler's mood.

Andrew Ross, Mary Hannah's brother, had been reluctant to be interviewed, saying he had nothing to add. But he did, finally, agree to a lunch with the *Herald* correspondent.

Richler knew why Ross tried to beg off: Reno had become an embarrassment to the Rosses, an officer several times court-martialed and found guilty of scandalous conduct. An albatross hung over the neck of a prominent and impeccable family.

It would take all of Richler's skill to take this interview where he wanted to go with it.

Ross sailed in at ten after one, and Richler recognized him at once from family photographs. The man had thickened but had the same facial lines as Mary Hannah.

The man offered no apology, so Richler led him into the hotel's dark restaurant, so dimly lit that they could hardly see the menu.

"Some spirits?" the correspondent asked.

"Never. I'm in a bit of a hurry, Richler, and hope you'll forgive me if I stay only a minute."

They ordered sauerkraut and corned beef from an acned young man, and Richler turned gently to the topic at hand.

"I'm doing a . . . summation of your late brother-in-law for the *Herald,* and hope you might offer me your impressions of the major."

"That's what I was afraid of. I'm not prepared to talk about that."

"I can understand your reluctance. Tell me about Mary Hannah. She must have been a most gracious woman."

"Yes."

He waited for more, but nothing was forthcoming.

"I've talked with various officers about Mary Hannah. She somehow made herself at home at the various frontier posts, endured hardships out there, welcomed other officers' wives into her home, and all in all, was greatly loved and admired."

"She was all of that, sir," Ross said. "She had a way of warming everyone in a room, you know. You would see her at dinner, the gaze of every unattached man in the room on her. She was superbly educated, you know, Pennsylvania Female College. I always thought she would have her pick of men, and I hoped she would pick the right one."

That was better, Richler thought. Andrew Ross might not wish to talk about Reno, but he loved his sister.

"She was eighteen when she met Marcus Reno. The war was close and menacing, and there he was, a Union officer at your family's table."

"Yes, and he had been in the middle of it. And out West, too."

"She had suitors?"

"Not so many. Maybe that's why she . . . found him attractive."

"By all accounts, it was a good match," Richler said. "And that surprises me. She was open, warm, forthright; he was reserved, private, serious, dour, maybe even shy. I've been wondering ever since whether maybe they found something in each other that completed themselves."

"I wouldn't know about that, sir."

The correspondent supposed it was time to try a gambit. "Major Reno's reputation must weigh heavily on you and your family."

"Richler, I'd rather not . . ."

"Yes, of course. You know, Mr. Ross, the years that Reno, Captain Reno then, was married to Mary Hannah were the best years of his life. He was at ease, his military career was splendid, his home was warmed by friends and fellow officers. It wasn't until after, until her early death, that he fell back into, let us say, bachelor habits."

Ross grinned slightly and nodded. At least he was listening, Richler thought.

"I think she fulfilled something in him; I think he was the sort of man who was incomplete without someone just like Mary Hannah at his side, with a child to care for, responsibilities to leaven his conduct. She was good for him."

"Yes, I'll agree."

"But maybe he was less good for her." Richler let it hang there, between them.

"The army was hard on her. Those outposts were especially hard on a girl born to comfort."

"I've become fascinated by Reno, and the more I probe, the more I discover several Renos, and the one most admirable was the one during those brief years of marriage to your sister. So I have come to think she had some magical effect on him, and that when she died, something died inside of him."

"The family was bitter that he didn't come for her funeral," Ross said.

"He had no choice; he was in the field, and was denied permission."

"He could have wangled it one way or another."

"He tried, Mr. Ross. I've read his correspondence. He actually started to come to Harrisburg, but was stayed by the Department of Dakota. They needed him to complete his duties on the boundary commission."

Andrew Ross was frankly skeptical. "I think maybe he didn't try very hard," he repeated. "He barely contacted us; barely made arrangements for his son."

Ross had won his point, whether it was true or not, and that seemed to satisfy him as he slowly masticated the corned beef.

"It was kidney disease that took her, I understand."

"She was frail, Mr. Richler. Fragile. I think that hard living on the frontier greatly shortened her days, and I confess I hold that against Major Reno. When she finally brought Robert back and raised him here, she rallied a while."

"No doubt you're wondering why I'm interested in all this. You see, Mr. Ross, I'm viewing this as a very great and little-understood love affair. Mary Hannah was so fine and sublime that Marcus Reno's nature found a solace and a home upon her bosom."

Ross laughed. "You have an odd way of looking at things, Mr. Richler."

"Major Reno's dying wish, which he conveyed to me, was that I restore his honor. I promised I'd try. Doubted I could, I might add. I've been probing ever since, and what fascinates me is that there are several Marcus Renos, and the finest one of all is the one married to Mary Hannah Ross during the War of the Rebellion. The Reno beforehand was barely disciplined; the one afterward even less so, though it didn't show up until after the Little Bighorn. So I guess what I'm saying, Mr. Ross, is that your sister had a profound and good effect on him, she was the angel in the life of Marcus Reno, and had she lived, he would not have fallen into disgrace. It suggests to me a love so sweet and true that it was the stuff of ballads and dreams."

For a long while Andrew Ross didn't respond, and then it came, slowly at first, and finally in a rush.

"They loved each other. They weren't alike; I couldn't imagine what they saw in each other. I thought it was his captain's insignia and blue uniform, but I was wrong. I thought it was his adventuresome stories, and derring-do, but I was wrong there, too. She adored him, sat beside him, caught his hand, touched his cheek, smiled as she peered into his eyes, and he was just as smitten.

"I didn't like it, I didn't much like him, I thought he was a bounder, but that was maybe just a brother's suspicions. Our mother gave the blessing; she was quite satisfied and rejoiced in Mary Hannah's happiness and fortune. I guess you're right, sir; for as long as Mary Hannah Ross was there, beside her husband, Marcus Reno was a worthy man."

That left a few things unsaid about the widower, but Joe Richler didn't push it. "That's what I hoped to hear, Mr. Ross. That's what gives me heart to write Marcus Reno's obituary as kindly as I can."

"Well, don't think the Rosses are pleased by how things came out," Ross added, sharply. "Dishonorable conduct. Peeping Tom. You can't imagine what those charges and the exposure in the press has done to my family."

"He never was a Peeping Tom, sir. A man who, probably in his cups, raps on the parlor window to draw the attention of a young angel he cares for is not a man . . . lurking in the dark for his private purposes."

"You can't put any sort of justification on it, and that's final," Andrew retorted. "There's no excuse."

Richler didn't debate the issue.

That afternoon Ross took him to the family plot, where Mary Hannah lay amidst the rest of the family. The Ross plot was full, and there had been no room for Marcus there, nor would Andrew permit young Robert Ross Reno and his wife, Itty, to move Mary Hannah's bones from the Ross plot.

Richler stood, quietly, looking at the solemn gravestone over the remains of the most beautiful thing in Major Marcus Reno's life. It said, "Mary Ross Reno, wife of Colonel M. A. Reno, U. S. Army, and daughter of Robert J. & Mary E. Ross. Born Nov. 16, 1843. Died July 10, 1874."

Andrew Ross had affirmed the very thing that Richler had been reaching for all these weeks. Marcus Reno was somehow completed by Mary Hannah, and after she died, nothing inside of him was ever the same.

# CHAPTER FIFTY

JOE RICHLER CAUGHT A TROLLEY OUT TO GLENWOOD CEMETERY, ON Lincoln Road NE, on the edge of Washington, and found Major Marcus Reno's unmarked grave easily enough. He had watched while Reno's casket was lowered there. Reno's son had bought no stone and now the place was both forlorn and anonymous, as if whoever lay there did not matter. Or whoever lay there was despised.

Young locust trees were beginning to spread their leaves over the burial grounds, casting welcome shade and comforting those who walked tenderly through this place.

Richler had come here immediately upon detraining at Union Station; he regretted not rushing into Nadine's arms, but this would only take a few moments, and would be a fitting end for his trip. It was something he had to do, and wanted to do.

The grave was not tended well, and had sunk slightly, leaving a hollow where there had been a slight mound.

He took off his derby and held it in hand, trying to gather his thoughts. He wanted to speak to the dead, or to whatever restless spirit might hover there, if any. Or maybe he just wanted to put everything in perspective, so he could write his obituary sensibly when he got home.

"Major, I've been tracking you down," he said, tentatively. "I talked to people who knew you or commanded you or disliked you or admired you. I've read the official record. I've read your correspondence. I've looked at the files of the congressional committee that governs military matters. I've talked to your brother-in-law. I've paid my respects to Mary Hannah. I was very fortunate to win an interview from General Terry, especially since he's in fragile condition. He was kind, and even affectionate toward you.

"They were mostly kind. Your friend Colonel Benteen was blunt, as always. Captain Godfrey helped me understand what they have against you. I didn't talk to Captain Bell or any of those in the Seventh who tried to throw you out; they weren't available and weren't worth talking to.

"I'm going to defend your honor. I can't change the army's view. I can't restore your rank to you posthumously. But I'm going to tell the readers of the *Herald* that you fought honorably and gallantly in the War of the Rebellion and the Little Bighorn. I'm going to tell them how much Mary Hannah meant to you, and how good your years with her were. And I'm going to leave the rest to history. I think maybe someday the world will understand how circumstances change us, and how we're shaped by the tragedies that befall us. And I'm going to say something about how some people have trouble governing their impulses, as you did.

"And major, I'm going to tell them that Marcus Reno was a gallant soldier and honorable and worthy of a better fate."

He stood, hat in hand, listening to the silence, and then walked slowly home, composing the first sentence of the obituary in his mind.